IMAGINE

by

LESLEY-ANN JONES

Published in this format 2015 by Mulcahy Books

First Edition

ISBN: 978-1519274649

What the industry is saying about

Imagine

by Lesley-Ann Jones:

'Real, surreal, and uniquely chilling!' DR BRIAN MAY CBE – rock star & astrophysicist

'ROCK STARS! Check. MURDER! Check. SEX! Check. What's not to like? Lesley-Ann brings the rock 'n' roll lifestyle alive in this page-turner.' NODDY HOLDER MBE – rock star, actor, producer, presenter

'Rock hard, rock soft, and everything in between. It's all here between the "sheets" … Enjoy!!!' SUZI QUATRO – rock legend

'What a read! This book is funny, frightening, and terrifyingly accurate. It feels like I know everyone in it.' ED BICKNELL – former manager of Dire Straits, Mark Knopfler, Bryan Ferry, Gerry Rafferty, and head of William Morris Endeavor Europe

'A brilliant read that captures the infamous rock star psyche beautifully.' DR JULIA JONES – musicologist

'Do you remember where you were the day John Lennon died? LESLEY-ANN JONES WAS RIGHT BLOODY NEXT TO HIM. An amazing story told in an amazing way. Unputdownable.' SIMON NAPIER-BELL – fabled manager of The Yardbirds, Marc Bolan, Japan, Wham!, George Michael & Sinéad O'Connor

'A superb mixture of truth and nothing-like-the-truth. *Imagine* is the best possible combination you can have in any read.' RICK WAKEMAN – musician and Grumpy Old Man

'An irresistible rock 'n' roll cocktail of fact and fiction, expertly mixed. Take one sip and prepare yourself for a "lock-in" …' KIM WILDE, pop star & 80s icon

'Lesley-Ann Jones has written a first-time classic. She extricates the glam out of every piece of grunge in this rock 'n' roll myth-fest. *Imagine* broke my heart, and rebuilt it again, until it became like a favourite song: repeating over and over in a dreamlike paradise.' LEO SAYER, singer-songwriter

For

Mum, Dad, Mia, Henry and Bridie

Also for Frank Allen, Clare Bramley, Andy Hill,

Andy Peebles, David Stark, Jane Wroe Wright & Stuart White

In loving memory of Jim Diamond and Rob Lee

Dedicated to the memory of John Lennon

Imagine if everything were fiction:
our experiences and our memories;
the conversations in our heads and with others;
the places we go, the place we call home;
the few whom we know – lovers, children, colleagues, friends;
the many with whom we cross paths, but rarely meet;
what we see, read, hear, smell, eat, drink, feel, think;
what we tell each other;
the things we never share;
the way we take care of ourselves, and of others;
the things we neglect;
the little we remember;
the much we forget.
All made-up.

Imagine memories from the inside,
that are more than what happened,
more than what we want them to be,
embellished, enhanced, eradicated, re-invented,
safer than truth, more menacing than falsehood,
more compelling in the telling …
less mundane.

Imagine fiction as just another word for perspective.

Imagine perspective as nothing more than a point of view.

This is a story about people who really lived, and about people who really should have.

Fearless, charmed but ultimately cursed people.

Some of us survived.

PROLOGUE

NINA

December 8th, 1980

New York

'He shot John Lennon!'

I'm standing only feet away; I am deafened by the shots. *ONE-one-one-TWO-two-two-THREE-three-three-FOUR-fo-fo-FIVE-fi -fi* ... The first shots I've ever heard, nothing like the way they sound in movies. Shots don't 'ring out'; they crack like bones – like legs crunched under boots – and echo upwards. It's a sound I hope I never hear again.

John keeps walking. My ears pick up the creak of his leather jacket, my eyes the pills on his sweater cables. I have a split second to decide whether the peep of the shirt he's wearing underneath is red or dark pink. There's a smell of meat, and the sound of a baby crying from a window way above us, a wail that makes me want to huddle John. His neck is turtling; the shoulders are up, like he's just been punched in the head. Does he know he's been shot? He gives no sign. His legs don't buckle, he keeps walking, his expression rigid. It looks glued. Keeps walking, straight towards me, he's heading in, under the arch, like he's making for the porter's vestibule. His thick-lensed specs fall from his face, and he stops. The glasses are shattered, blood-splattered. He squints at me, straight in the eye.

'*La guerra è finita*,' he gurgles, as if talking underwater.

'What?' I say with a gasp. '*What*?!'

'*Finita*.' He's right in front of me, almost on top of me.

His mouth makes the shapes but the sound is detached, someone else must be throwing their voice.

I glance about, trying to make out who's doing the talking, but then John speaks again.

This time, I know it's him.

'*Alma, Mater*.'

'Who?!'

'*Alma*.'

I can't take it in; I can't believe what I'm seeing. It's a sick stunt, it's staged, it isn't him, this guy isn't John. He must be an actor – a joker; they're probably up there somewhere, some film crew, taping all this.

I crane my neck to scan the thick yellow-brick walls and dark masonry for cameras and lights. As I do so, he staggers, lurching, toppling, creaking like a falling tree, as if he's been chopped above the ankles with an axe.

I fling my arms out, maybe to try and help him or something … to do *what*, exactly? But my hands seem to go right through him.

I shrink, horrified. John's not there. The shape of him is, but it's only that. A silhouette. I hear my saliva crack, like dried varnish. The body that was John is stumbling. My hands have gone numb.

'John's been *shot*!'

This is Yoko. This is when I know that what I'm seeing is real. Not that I *see* her as such; I can only hear her: shrill, nasal, screeching like a child, from the lining of a polar-bear-sized mink coat.

Is there even a face in there, amongst the fur and the matted black hair?

And then she starts lashing about like a – *yes* – like a cornered mink. Frantic, aimless, she's gone ahead of John, under the huge stone arch. She's all the way up to the glass and wood enclosure screening the staircase that leads to the building's reception. She's scuttling away from there, trying to hide. She's running *away* from John, not *to* him. It's what anyone would do, isn't it? The survival instinct kicking in? Wouldn't *I* do that? I'm deafened by piercing shrieks and hisses, yelling and snarling. It feels like hell's opened up right under our feet. The iron Neptunes and sea dragons wrought into the black railings must have gnashed to life. There'll be ghouls and demons rising out of the moat next, I think. Blood slashes inside my skull like waves in a tempest. People shrink into the shadows. Why can't I?

I glance at my watch. *Why*? Ten to eleven. It's still Monday. As dark as it can get in New York.

The wind is up, but it's mild for December – into the fifties, maybe more. I'm overdressed in boots and muffler, and I'm sweating now. My jacket's tied around my waist. I look down at the knotted sleeves, and they're smattered with blood.

John has gone in, up the steps. He's out of sight.

Now Yoko tears back around and flies through the little porter's door on the right-hand side with the sign that reads 'ALL VISITORS MUST BE ANNOUNCED', and she vanishes. She must be up there, cradling his body.

Please tell me that she's got him in her arms.

My heart is pummelling. I'm being boxed for the count from the inside; it takes every shred of guts to stay on my feet.

Suddenly the planet stops.

Silence.

An unbearable pause.

Ripped apart by Yoko's agonizing screams.

Other people, complete strangers out here, most of them fans waiting around on the off-chance they might see John, get a photo with him, an autograph or something, and got more than they bargained for, join in the chorus of screaming. Hideous faces loom, faces crumpled like bath sponges in dripping fists, switchblade fingers stabbing at nothing in the night. I can't run; I can't hide. There is nowhere to go.

'He shot John Lennon. He shot *John Lennon*! He shot *JOHN LENNON*!'

'That guy! *Him!* That man *there*!'

'Who the hell *is* he?!'

'Somebody *stop* him!'

No need. I stare. I can feel my shock radiating out at him, my lips melting, my face opening and closing like an oven door. I try to take him in. Pudgy, twenties, toddler-faced. Leaning against the beast-entangled railing. He's wearing a long overcoat and scarf, and huge glasses. He's not going anywhere.

'José, *nooo*! *Don't*, José! Stay back!'

Someone's yawping at him not to, but the sobbing uniformed doorman rushes right at him, grabs him, joggles him, and shakes and shakes his arm until he lets go of the gun.

'I never used this thing before, honestly,' I hear the man say, although *do* I? His lips never part.

'My name is Mark. I'm from Hawaii.'

Am I imagining this?

I watch the weapon flutter from his right hand. It floats – although it can't possibly – in a zigzag slow motion, as if dangling from a tiny parachute: a single ply of tissue on the ripple of a late-night breeze. It plunks to the path, and the guy they're calling José kicks it right across the pavement.

It's not there when I turn around a split second later. Did I imagine this too, or did someone pick it up?

Calm – so still that he might be waiting on the opening chords of a Eucharist service in St. Patrick's – the gunman reaches inside his coat and pulls out a paperback.

I can hardly believe this. What is he *thinking*? He's going to hang around reading a book now, until the cops come for him?

He paces a little.

José, the doorman, is inside the porter's lobby now; he must be getting help.

No one else tries to restrain the gunman, yet at no point does he try to run away. He just stands there, knowing what's coming, flicking slowly through the pages of his book. He doesn't make eye contact with anyone. Makes no attempt to speak. He stares intently at the text, seeking maybe a telephone number, a hymn, a solution.

I peer through the darkness to see. I'm quite close to him, close enough to see the cover. The book is *The Catcher in The Rye*. He drops it at one point, and it falls open at the title page. Before the rest of the pages flutter and it closes whole, before he stoops to snatch it up, I can see what someone's scribbled there.

'To Holden Caulfield from Holden Caulfield. This is my statement.'

He must have scrawled the words himself. This is when I realise the guy's a loop.

Finally, after what seems like hours, but which is probably only a couple of minutes, a cop tears in, effing and blinding, throws the gunman against the wall.

Pandemonium. I stand rooted, fighting to breathe. The air's been sucked right out of the scene.

Two more cops who must have torn into the porter's lodge while I wasn't looking lurch back out, doddering under the slump of John. *Maybe* it's John. They've got him face up, and blood is leaking from his mouth, running sideways into his ears. I feel like I'm choking on barbed wire. I have to hold myself back from rushing in.

'Wipe his face ... for God's sake somebody wipe John's face!'

Sirens, blaring, deafening. An ambulance? No ambulance. They just fold him into the back seat of a patrol car, and take off. Yoko hurls herself at the cop car behind.

'No! *Nooooo*!'

I vomit silent, pointless monosyllables into my sucked-out lungs.

'Go *with* him!'

I rupture myself yelling at her, no sound coming out. 'Why didn't you just get in the fucking police car *with* John!'

She should have had a chance to say goodbye.

~

Now what? I wasn't even supposed to be here. I just wandered over the Upper West Side with time to kill, waiting on an interview appointment. Just happened to be standing there minding my own business, when *this* happened.

Despite my many excursions to New York for work over the past couple of years, I'd never been up here to look at the Dakota – not that there's much to see, only the outside – just to get a sense of the place. It's not as if you can go in. There's always a gaggle of fans and sightseers, whatever the time of day or night.

I'd never seen *Rosemary's Baby*, the Polanski horror flick, which I heard was filmed here.

Nor did I know much about the 'right people' who live or once lived here: the Bacalls, the Karloffs, the Nuryevs … all the other kooks. It only started getting a rep as New York's most legendary apartment building, to people my age at least, after John and Yoko moved in.

Once 'so far west and so far north', the remotest outreach of Manhattan, an unsmiling Dakota Indian is carved high above its main entrance with the numbers 1-8-8-1, the year it was built. It's like those schlosses you see in the Rhine valley, the sort of place where Cinderella might go a crystal two-step or Rapunzel might fling down her plaits. Gloomy and grim, like the brothers, though people say the interior's like Versailles. Its massive arch, the half-turreted windows, the cast-iron lamps with fake-real flames, pedestalled plant urns, a bronze, coffin-like sentry box: all so evocative in pictures that they fall way short in the flesh.

I replay the scene in my mind, over and over. 22.49: the Lennons' big white limo pulls up at the kerb. Why the hell doesn't it drive through to the courtyard? Why does it stop and make them get out and walk?

It's not like there's a delivery truck or anything obstructing the gate. There's a notice on a post there: 'AUTHORIZED PERSONS ONLY BEYOND THIS POINT'. The doorman would have walked across and moved it aside for them. Why didn't he?

Yoko gets out of the car first, and scutters into the tunnel-like entrance. I presume it's Yoko; I can't see her face.

Then John gets out. He's carrying a tape recorder and some cassettes. It looks as though they've come straight from a studio. He follows his wife towards the entrance.

Someone calls to him – *'Mr Lennon? Mr Lennon, sir?'* – and John looks up and hesitates, as if he recognises the guy, but he doesn't say anything. Walks on by.

Then the guy – the man who turns out to be the gunman – takes half a dozen steps away from the building towards the road, and he turns, pulls out a gun, and fires five shots.

And I see what everyone else sees. What Yoko does, how the doorman reacts, the gunman reaching for his copy of *The Catcher in the Rye*. I see the cops, and I swallow time.

I watch them take the legend away.

~

The cops are appealing frantically for eyewitnesses to go with them down to 20th Precinct.

'It's not far,' they're telling us. 'Come *on*, folks. Help us out here, will ya?'

They can't *make* me go. Land of the free, right? They can't arrest me for just standing here – it's not as if it's a police state – and, besides, I'm not an American citizen.

I'm having none of it. I've got to get away. I can't be sure about what I've seen. Until I am, no way can I talk about it. I don't even want to think about it. I don't want it to be true. But there's no getting anywhere in a hurry tonight.

Word really does spread like wildfire. Quite a crowd has gathered; within minutes we are ten-deep on the pavement. Ten, then twenty, now thirty or more, spilling off the kerb into the road, pressing in from both sides of West 72nd Street and across Central Park West, swelling like an incoming tide.

Unexpectedly there are a lot of older people: Sixties-types in shabby clothes, enough of them smoking pungent cigarettes to make a fug that hangs above us, like an omen. Are any of them the widows, the winos, the rent-a-crowd silent, the old blots who sit around New York, waiting for bad things to happen? There are plenty of faces of the kind you think you recognise. I'm stuck here for a while, I can see that much. Shocked and weeping, we sway to and fro, singing John's words.

'*All we are saying ... is give peace a chance ...*'

Caught up in a choke of more folk than I've ever seen in my life, I feel truly alone.

The good, the glad, the night-before-Christmas part of me feels gone.

I didn't see who poked the first flaming candle into the railings, but I wish I had one to light.

Mourners are flying in now, filings to a magnet, the candle-less wedging cardboard or paper signs scrawled with hastily lipsticked or fibre-tipped words.

'I Love You, John.'

'RIP, John.'

'War Is Over.'

Flowers. White and red roses: the petals of death. Even worse: yellow carnations. Not the kind of blooms I can imagine John liking or ever wanting inside his home.

'*No possessions*,' I think, remembering John's lyrics.

'*Imagine no possessions*.'

What the hell am I doing here? I've got to leave, right this second; this is making me ill.

I wade against the throng, agonise my way back to West 56th, fall into the lift and let myself into my room, take a couple of doll-shots of Smirnoff out of the minibar and topple myself onto the bed, which stinks of menthol and feet. Not my feet. The walls are so thin, I can hear the people in the next room changing their minds.

~

Number 9 dream. Walls. Bridges. Strings. Cellos. Whatever gets you through the night. Harry Nilsson, that doomed, breezy face. I haven't seen it in so long. Has anyone? John once said Harry was his favourite group, a one-man Beatles, trembling, warbling, wistful Harry, many rivers to cross, pussy cats, 44th St Fairies, May Pang, oh God, May Pang. *Ah! böwakawa poussé, poussé.*

There is magic in the air. I'm weightless, floating high above the Christmas tree at the Rockefeller Plaza rink, fixing a star on top that I've plucked straight out of the sky. The moment it touches the tip of the spruce, it glitters to life, dazzling my eyes. Way below, the huddled crowds are cheering, clapping and whooping, but not at me. No one sees me; they have no idea I'm even up here, running the show. How good is this?! I swoop in and out of the wires holding the tree in place.

I'm blissfully invisible; I can float wherever I want. I get bored of it soon enough, though, and I blow a kiss to the birds amongst the branches, and I fly, and land right among the Fifth Avenue revellers. So long ago and yet only last night. Was it in a dream? Was it only in a dream?

~

The next thing I know, it's around five in the morning. The office must be open by now.

I take a breath and another drink, and dial the number. Rhett picks up on the second ring.

'*Roccain* magazine, editor speaking.' Pretentious git.

'It's me. Before you give me a hard time – don't lie, I know you were going to – I saw that guy shoot John Lennon.'

'You *what*?'

I hear, or at least visualise, Rhett gagging on a throatful of Jack Daniels, his preferred breakfast drag. He's snotting into the knuckles of his left hand. Licking it. I can smell his hair from here.

'Not that we knew that he was actually dead, you know, at the time, but you could sort of tell he must be. Guy shot him five times in the back.'

'You're gabbing. *Four* bullets got him. One missed, hit a window.'

'You've seen it then. John carried on walking.'

'What were you doing there?'

'Where?'

'The Dakota. What were you doing up there?'

'Oh, you know. Just wanted to check it out,' I mumble, self-conscious, glad he can't see my face.

I burp like a baby. He chuckles.

'I'd never been there before, ya know? I had time on my hands. Andy Peebles was here a couple of days ago, doing an interview with John and Yoko at the Hit Factory for Radio 1. I bumped into him, we talked; John was kind of on my mind. I don't know. It's like wandering over Abbey Road and hanging around just to see who comes out, I guess.'

Pause.

'Fuck *me*, you've got to *write* this stuff!'

'Write what? What is there to write?'

'You were outside the Dakota the night the music died, for fuck's sake!' screams Rhett.

I could see his rotting Chelsea boots up on the desk either side of his typewriter, knees wide, fingers grabbing at his crotch.

'The forensic pathologist should go over you … you've probably got his blood on your clothes. They might even be worth something.'

'You're hideous. It'll be old news by the time we go to press.'

'It's still eyewitness. *You saw a Beatle die!* I'd bet good money there weren't any other hacks on the spot.'

'It's against everything we say we stand for.'

'Nina, he's a *Beatle*. Was. You're there, you saw it; we can't *not* cover it. We're a *music* rag. Do this right and trust me, it'll make your name. Fleet Street will be gagging for you.'

'It doesn't seem right. Cashing in on a tragedy.'

'And? For fuck's *sake*! You go on and on about it all the time, how you're aiming for big-name columnist on a national one day: what do you think they do up there all day but cash in on tragedy? Every *day*, Nina! Get real. You think *I'm* an amoral fucker. B-b-b-baby you just ain't seen nothing yet. They've got editors up there who'd bugger their own gran for an exclusive. No-brainer, kid, I'm telling you.'

'Is that an order?'

'It is now.'

Pause.

'There's something else, Rhett.'

'What?'

'He spoke to me.'

'*Who* did?'

'John.'

'*John!* John Lennon *spoke* to you! No, don't, this is too good, even for you, just let me savour this a second, I need to piss myself with mirth here. He's standing there shot to buggery, leaking like a kitchen sieve, he's giving up the ghost before your very corneas, and he *speaks* to you! *Course* he does! Come *on*, Nina, gimme a break. What do you take me for! What did he say? "Cool earrings!"? "Nice weather we're having!"? "*Happiness is a warm gun*"?'

'You're sick.'

'*Why*? It's a tune, isn't it? A *Beatles* tune. What could be more appropriate? Wait. What if ... I can hear what you're *not* saying. I know you. I'm sorry, maybe I'm wrong! He really *did* speak to you, didn't he? You're not having me on. Fucking dynamite, this is. Why didn't you *say*?!'

'I did.'

'So what the fuck did *he* say?!'

'Not sure. Think it was Spanish or Italian. "*La guerra è finita*", something like that.

Maybe I got that wrong. '"*Finita*" ...'

'Italian! "*War is over*"! Jesus Christ, Neen, you know what he meant, don't you? This is about his *personal* war being over, like he's saying he's done now, all the heartache and pain and suffering's at an end, that's it, *kaput*, finished, thanks a bunch, folks, and goodnight. Mr Lennon has left the building, peace at last. It's fucking obvious! Led him a mutt's life, didn't she, the old sushi-bag, if everything I've heard can be believed.

We are going fucking global with this. What kind of car do you want, I'll upgrade your ticket home, ring up and see if they've got any suites at the Plaza, you'd better get yourself some backup, too, I'll get on to –'

'There's more.'

'*What*?'

'He said something else. I don't know what it meant.'

'I bet we can figure it out between us. What *was* it?!'

'"*Alma, Mater*".'

'Bloody long time since they kicked me out of school – why are you not surprised? – but isn't that Latin? Something to do with what college you went to, your so-called spiritual home?'

'What college *did* he go to?'

'I don't think he went to … no, wait. Liverpool College of Art rings a bell. Wasn't that it?'

'How would I know? I wasn't even born.'

'All right, no need to –'

'Not exactly Oxbridge, is it, art school? What's that got to do with …'

'Doesn't matter.'

'I think it does, Rhett. There's more. I'm sure there's more to it.'

'How d'you know?'

'I just feel it. The way he said it. The look in his eyes. Not "*Alma Mater*", as in a stock phrase, a saying. There was a comma in there; he was communicating something. "*Alma, Mater*" …'

'Neen. He *said* it. We'll find out, OK? I'll get the girls on it.'

'I bet you will.'

'I'm ignoring that. You've gotta call some of your muso mates, pick their brains, guys who knew John back in the fifties and sixties.

Johnnie Hamp, Frank Allen, Simon Napier-Bell, all those guys. Someone'll know. Meanwhile, *you*, prettiest petal ever to peel off a springtime bud, I've got the headline already. Ready? "THE LAST WOMAN LENNON EVER SPOKE TO". Like it? Start spreading the news, Liza Minnelli, you've hit the jackpot. Hold on tight.'

~

And it hasn't even started yet. Do I want it to? How can I stop it, now that I've told him? I can't, can I? I shouldn't have told him, should I? What I wouldn't give to take it back.

I slide off the bed and crawl back to the minibar, avoiding my reflection in the brightly lit mirror above the desk.

More vodka. I've sold my soul, and it's too late, baby. Do something like this and you know there's no hope. If I'm looking at eternal damnation, I might as well start now. I obliterate myself on whatever it is that's left in the minibar, and sit waiting for the devil to call.

I must have dozed off again. When I come to, the television's on, inexplicably. Did I reach for the remote in my sleep? There's an evil taste in my mouth. Stale garlic from the guacamole in the burrito I wolfed down earlier, befouled by booze and sleep. My hair is noosing me; I have to untangle myself to watch.

Footage in and out of focus, heaving crowds outside the Dakota. I think I spot Jane Fonda, but it's probably only some hip chick who looks a bit like her. I quit at the right time, clearly. Everyone they're attempting to interview is bawling, no one's making sense.

There's this one photographer – they keep showing him – reckons he got to the Dakota earlier that day, got chatting to a guy holding a copy of John and Yoko's new album *Double Fantasy.* Told the other fans waiting around that he was from Hawaii.

When John emerged, the guy asked him to sign the album for him, and John just said 'sure'. He signed it with the guy's own pen, a black Bic. John pushed the button on the pen a couple of times and started to scrawl, it was hard to get the thing to write at first. He wrote his name, 'John Lennon', and '1980' underneath. Then he looked at the guy and asked, 'Is that all? Do you want anything else?' As if he knew. As if he was aware that he was looking into the eyes of the person who would steal his life. The guy said nothing. He just smiled.

John got in the limo.

The gunman must have hung around all day. Where did he go? Didn't anybody see him, think 'that chump's acting suspicious, better call the cops?'

Evidently not.

What nobody can fathom – they're all tearing their hair out over this – is why the Lennons' limo didn't just drive in through the gates into the courtyard. Why the hell did it pull up at the kerb? Exactly what I thought. John often said how safe he felt, living in New York.

'*Mr Lennon*?' the fan called to him.

'*Mr Lennon, sir*?'

It was all it took. John stopped and looked around. Did he recognise the guy from lunchtime?

They said the gunman then dropped into a 'combat stance' before shooting. I didn't see him do that. The weapon was a Charter Arms .38 Special revolver. I didn't know that, either. What do I know about guns? Was I even there?

~

The news channels are in overdrive. I'm addicted, I'm surfing, I'm glued. They're all churning out the same stuff. Boosting their initial reports with as much filler as they can dredge to plug the gaps.

It's getting hysterical. I can picture them in headless-chicken mode at stations across America. The soundtrack needs no introduction, it's Fabs all the way. 'She Loves You', 'Yesterday', 'I Wanna Hold Your Hand', *we*'ve had everything from 'The Ballad of John and Yoko' to 'Rocky Raccoon', cue eerie reference to the black mountain hills of Dakota ...

And I get it. The enormity of what I've seen tonight is no longer lost on me. I got to the Beatles late, just too young to have been a fan first time round.

This is on a par with the death of the President. John Fitzgerald Kennedy, John Winston Ono Lennon. It's like they've morphed into the same guy.

Hadn't the former just been assassinated when the latter first landed in New York? November 1963, February 1964. Not much in it. Some people reckon Beatlemania took hold in America *because* the President was murdered. They say folk needed hope, that the Beatles rocked up just at the right time to give it to them. Timing being everything. It's one theory. Who knows?

I don't. Whatever else, one thing's for sure, whether you're talking JFK or John Lennon, people all over the world will always remember where they were.

~

And it's the morning after.

Too soon. Let me be wrong; let me have imagined it. It's too much to ask. John's still dead. Floods of mourners, an ocean of fans, everywhere. The Upper West Side has crammed to a standstill. The *Daily News* splash says it all.

'100,000 JOIN LENNON VIGIL'.

Join Lennon. Nice. People are clambering over car roofs to get a look at … *what*? The Central Park lawns are a mudbath. A 'wave of grief', I saw headlined somewhere. A tsunami that's engulfing the world, more like.

Only later, confirmation of cause of death: hypovolemic shock, from the loss of more than eighty per cent of his blood.

Only later, Yoko's statement: 'There is no funeral for John. John loved and prayed for the human race. Please do the same for him.'

Only later – an interminable week – on December 14th, a ten-minute silence held in his name, millions forming a ring around the world. Thirty thousand in Liverpool, a quarter of a million in Central Park, every radio station in New York off-air for the duration.

Only later – compounding the fracture – the many tragic, pointless suicides, of fans unable to cope with the loss.

So this is Christmas.

~

I can't get my head round it. I was right here, and yet nowhere near. I drift off again, to voices.

'*Never take a day for granted, life can change on a dime.*'

'*I'm locked in me fuckin' room, darlin'.*'

'*Daren't even go for a piss.*'

'*I miss me kids.*'

'*I'm finished.*'

'*What's gonna happen to me*?'

~

I wake at around nine, from a sweat-soaked nightmare.

I couldn't have seen this, but I *did*, I know I saw it: I saw John up there, huddled amongst the ceiling lights, gazing down on his body in the hospital, staring at the doctor holding his heart in his bare hands. Kneading it, massaging it, praying it back to life.

I saw Yoko in a half-lit waiting room, screaming and beating her tiny head against the floor.

I heard the song – *that song* – pounding out across the hospital sound system, the moment they realised John could not be saved. 'All My Loving'. How could this be? It's as if they knew too. I swear that I heard it.

Only when they give Yoko her husband's wedding ring does it sink in that John is dead. How come I know this already? I can't know this. But I saw it. I saw Sean, God help him, their five-year-old son, tucked up in front of the television with his nanny in their apartment in the Dakota, and I was pleading with God or God knows who, 'please make her switch that damned thing off, please don't let that little boy see the news ...'

My head is a bomb about to go off. I'm still dressed, still wearing my boots. The wires in my bra are digging into my flesh, what there is of it. My glasses are bent underneath me. I lie there.

Within you, without you ... Disjointed phrases expand and contract inside my head, echoes of a lull in a voice I know too well, in a language I no longer recognise.

A couple of fat black-leathered heavies on Triumph Bonnies are revving behind my eyeballs. I grab my skull with both hands, pressing the scalp, willing them to get the fuck out of my head and for the ache to subside.

I drag myself to the bathroom, unzip, sit down, and try to drain the pain out of my body. As if that's gonna work. I stand, stagger, crouch, kneel, straining to retch into the bowl. Not a drop in me but syrup bile. I'm dehydrated to the core. No painkillers in my washbag. No energy to go down to reception and get any. No strength even to brush the stomach acid off my tongue and teeth. I squeeze a glob of toothpaste into my mouth and swill it from side to side, swallowing the foam.

'*Don't wanna be another fuckin' John Lennon*,' says the voice in my head.

'*It'll be me next.*'

'*They'll get me.*'

'*You've gotta help me, Nina.*'

'*I've got more whacko fans than Jesus.*'

That's when the calls start.

THIRTY-THREE YEARS LATER

CHAPTER ONE

NINA

I'm not who they think I am. They reckon they get what they see, but she's not really me.

Take away the hair, the nails, the implants, the lower facelift (which, of course, I deny), the make-up, the wardrobe, the Hermès scarves, the Louboutins – especially the Louboutins – and you'd be looking at a porridge-faced quinquagenarian, maybe a housewife with twenty-something teenagers, a withered spinster or some bunchy little widow in charity-shop frocks, well aware that she has failed to squander her life.

'You look amazing for your age,' people are always telling me. I'm never quite sure they're not taking the piss. Thank you very much, I think. Keep nipping and tucking and trowelling the slap, baby. Keep gumming the avocados and necking the gin. I also ingest gag-worthy doses of bio-identical hormones prescribed by a kook on Harley Street, and never stop sucking. The energy I must have spent over the years, holding my muffin in.

I am a figment of imagination. Mine and theirs. I project a prize-winning image greatly at odds with the real me. Women just like the me I am on the inside – millions of them – read me weekly. They hang on my every syllable, never suspecting (maybe a few do) that I believe barely a word I ever write.

I know how much they love 'me'. They tell me so. Emails by the thousand, in place of the old-fashioned postbag, which has dwindled with the tidal wave of technology. Only lavender ladies write letters to me now. Rose-embellished notelets, robin-infested Christmas cards. In the 21st century, people are even emailing those. I'm not sure I altogether approve, but 'The Worst Lady of Fleet Street' does.

There's no great secret to what I do. I invented a character, years ago, who has achieved fame and relative fortune shooting from the lip. Candy from a baby, what can I say.

My gobby, dolled-up alter ego, 'Bitchiest and Best-Loathed!', has an opinion about pretty much everything, no subject taboo. From Her Majesty's taste in foundation garments to the peccadilloes of politicians. From thieving mobile phone networks to Pippa Middleton's periods – she has them, you know. From stultifying TV soaps to scar-faced celebrity chefs. One minute drug-trafficking, the next think-yourself-to-orgasm. All human life, and every other kind. No habit, no circumstance, no slip of the tongue escapes scrutiny.

She's interviewed the best of them, from Liz Taylor to Osama bin Laden (OK, I made that one up), and every Michael Jackson in between. She once cornered Margaret Thatcher at Number Ten and produced a Rampant Rabbit from her handbag, and snogged Boris Johnson at a *Mail on Sunday* Christmas swill. It made a short column item, at least. Nothing ventured. Get it where you can.

The Worst Lady performs a vital public service for which she is far too well paid. People read her to find out what they think. Some call her a dinosaur, an anachronism. They sneer that she has no place on the 'modern media stage'. Whatever that is. If I knew, I might have to agree.

We – who lushed it all over London in the 80s on vitriol and vitamins, blitzed to the nines, who were rarely if ever sober, who slept our way around the world on unthinkable expenses, who stitched up lovers and brothers and mothers (sometimes our own), who begged, stole and borrowed, cheated, perjured ourselves, put words into people's mouths, got arrested, kipped four-to-a-cell and risked our very lives on a regular basis in the name of a splash headline, confounding the Press Council and killing the competition as we went, who made our names during Fleet Street's lavish heyday and who *still* think that's worth more than the paper it's printed on – know too well that we are living on borrowed time.

Everybody knows that circulations are not a patch on what they once were. Newspapers chase the news now; we rarely break it. The *Telegraph*, the *Mail*, *The Times*, and us, of course, might last another decade at the outside if we play our cards right. But the focus now is well and truly online, and that tide is never going to turn again.

Don't tell me you haven't noticed. Papers are run by accountants nowadays. As more and more of us face the final curtain, they seem to have forgotten, to their detriment, that brilliant journalists are what make newspapers. Always did.

It's the writers who give a paper its personality: flamboyant, irresponsible, irresistible, larger-than-life. We are the ultimate cliché: we are what we write, and have a duty to our readers to remain so. We came from ordinary, most of us; we had to sell our souls to get a look-in. Not that employer-loyalty has ever counted for much.

What was it that the legendary columnist Jean Rook used to say? 'Always cross The Street for more money.' Done it a couple of times myself, I don't mind telling you. But I have a feeling that where I am, I am. If the title survives, that is. This whole Leveson circus hasn't helped, has it. I know it; Hugh Grant knows it.

We're going down.

I make it into the paper's offices overlooking the Thames two or three times a week when I'm in the UK.

The rest of the time I'm on a train here, a plane there, TVs and radios, chat shows, panels, interviewing for features. Anything in a day's work. I've turned down the jungle and *Big Brother* more than once, but never say never, as they say. I'm not made of money. Once or twice a month I'm in New York, occasionally LA.

I'm here today. My PA Allegra always meets me at the lift with coffee in a white china cup, *not* mug. I text her as I hand over my car keys to the guy who parks the Jag, and by the time I've zapped through security and been elevated to the fifth floor, the little angel's right there with it.

I actually gave up coffee a year ago after an excruciating week in rehab, but the last thing I want to do is hurt her feelings. She means well. Everyone else at that mouldy Fawlty Towers-esque retreat was kicking the serious stuff. Amphetamines. Coke. Married lovers – not that I am any kind of stranger to those. But I'd been shaking round the clock for months, a yukka in a force ten gale. It was time to quit. I drink only green tea at this time of day, but I haven't got the heart to keep reminding her.

'Coffee, Mrs V. How you like it.'

She always calls me 'Mrs V', though I'm actually Mrs Kendal. Details.

'You're an angel.'

'You too!' She giggles lightly, a sound like sprinkling talc.

'Keep telling me. And while you're at it, remind me, and then tell me 'til you're blue in the face, how much of a cunt is Bill Hollins again?'

Allegra blushes. 'What hasn't Sir done now?'

'Clever girl. I agree with every word you're not thinking: that I was a dripping dishrag of an idiot to get involved with the tosser in the first place. He has treated me like dog shit yet again, and he's going to have to pay big-time this time.'

'What's happened?'

She pulls out my chair and guides me round the desk into it as if steering a blind person, taking my bag from my shoulder and the cup from my hand without noticing that it hasn't been sipped. No lipstick rim. Classic giveaway. She sets it down on a red cardboard 'PRS For Music' coaster, then flops into the chair opposite. She's wearing grey leggings with a reindeer print, and smells of White Company 'Winter' room spray. In September.

'*Happened?* I just can't get my head round him. He calls me every day, texts several times a day, leaves me simpering voice messages … but I've not seen so much as a hair on his head for six *weeks*. His *son et lumière* rock-fucking-bore-fest is the most important thing in his life. He cancels me because he has to go and see the yet another last-ever Rolling Stones' gig, a private do in some palace in Munich. He couldn't take me with him?'

'Didn't have another invite?'

'No invite, my *arse*. These people can do what the fuck they like. Then, cancels me an hour before the starters to have dinner with Robert Stigwood. What am I: ugly? A hunchback? A dunce of a conversationalist? Can I not speak Bee Gee? Did I not get my hair cut for ten years by John fucking Frieda? Scrap that last one; you're way too young to make the connection. I digress.'

'No one could accuse you of that, Mrs V.'

'*I* think so. *Then*, cancels me yet again to take some dipstick to a preview of the show and then dinner. I can't go too? Finally, last night, the first night of his pissy show. Not that I haven't seen it, I yawned through a preview a couple of weeks back. Not that he was there. But he actually refused to take me to the opening night.'

'Why?'

'Exactly. So Lady fucking Litsy, the fake wife, was going with him. So was Gwynnie, the mother of his bastard. His adult kids and their spouses were going.'

'That's not on.'

'It's really *not* on. What am I, an embarrassment? Can't mind my Ps and Qs when the occasion calls? I've been in the same room as my lovers' partners more times than you've had school dinners. Who hasn't? "Oh, you don't want to come to *that*!" he said. "The press'll be all over us!" "Darling," I said, "I *am* the fucking press!" It went right over his head.'

'There's always Tony, Mrs V.'

'Dear Tony. That reminds me, he must be back from Philadelphia by now.'

Note to self.

'Charlie, Allegra. I need to speak to Charlie before Phil's ready for me; he's off again tomorrow.

I keep trying his number but he's not picking up, and I'm worried …'

'He's twenty-*four*!'

'I do know this, I did give birth to him. But you know what they say, twenty-four going on twelve. Besides, he's Charlie. Oh, and Neal Goddard, if you would, please.'

'The lawyer?'

'Him. Can you get hold of his secretary and book a call?'

'How's that all going?' Allegra leans her head back round the door frame, her sweetheart face crumpled.

'The divorce? Ya know. As you'd expect. Not exactly amicable. Then again, I've always thought that's an oxymoron.'

'What is?'

'"Amicable divorce". I mean, if you're getting on OK, why the hell call it a day? Grass ain't greener.'

Allegra frowns. 'Why go through with it then? You don't exactly *hate* James …'

'I don't like him enough to hate him, you mean.'

'They all stray …' she starts.

'Your point being?'

'My mum says men are all the same.' She shrugs, with a goldfish sigh. 'And at this stage in the game …'

'I'm not gonna find another husband at my time of life, you mean? At *my age?* Why on earth would I *want* another husband?'

'It's not about age, Mrs V.'

'Wise, Allegra. Very wise. *None* of it's about age, not at *any* age. Nothing ever *is*.'

~

'Don't ask *me*, ask Car-sick Peg: *she's* the ditz with the hotline to the stars around here. Now go and play with your balls before I rip over there and sort you out with a one-wood.'

Slam! goes the receiver. *Smash!* goes the capped toe of his double-laced brogue into the side of his desk. *Schlock!* goes the golf ball into the horizontal wastepaper basket. Hole in one. Phil roars.

'Someone having a good day?' I venture. On a scale of candyfloss to peanut brittle, my smile is coconut ice.

'Didn't anyone ever tell you to knock before entering a private office?'

Bark, bark. 'Editor in bad mood' alert.

'Lovely to see you too,' I want to say. My smile feels fake. I rearrange.

'Have you got time to go over this week's column or shall I just fuck off now?'

'The column can wait.' Phil flops into his chair as if onto a bouncy castle. He coughs like a small dog, gobs into a rumple of cotton handkerchief and stuffs it back in his trouser pocket. I imagine flakes of dried green mucus emerging when he undresses.

'Seen this?' He nods at his screen.

I slip behind his desk, lean over my boss's round shoulder, and see a face I haven't thought about in years.

'Eddie Laine, as I live and breathe,' I say.

'Don't tell me.'

'He had me from goodbye.'

'You too? The guy gets around.'

'Bust his last six-string?'

'Rocked up at the great soundcheck in the sky, you mean? Not quite. Seems to be hanging in, by the skin of his tonsils. New album out, coupla days ago. Zero fanfare, negligible promo, in at Number One today.'

'What? You're shitting me. He hasn't had a hit since I lost my virginity.'

'Not that long. Thirty-five years. Some kind of a record, mustn't it be?'

'Understatement of the year.'

'You know him, then?'

'I used to,' I say. Choosing my words.

'What is he, sixty-six? Sixty-seven? One of the last of the great rock frontmen. Who's left? There can't be many.'

'The usual suspects. McCartney. Jagger. Rod. Elton. Daltrey. Gabriel. No Pretenders, either. Not the group, I don't mean. To the throne, as it were. Once this last wave snuff it, it'll be the end of an era. Farewell rock 'n' roll. None of the next generation has got what it takes.'

'No X-factor?'

'Not an ounce. That's it. It dies with these guys.'

'Prince?'

'American.'

'Fleetwood Mac?'

'Septic-Brit. Anyway, it's not the same. Stevie Nicks is still a goddess at sixty-seven, but she's no frontman in the classic sense.'

'I guess not. Being a woman and all.'

'You know what I mean. You can hardly call Mick Fleetwood a frontman, and nobody cares about Lindsey Buckingham.'

'Who?'

'Precisely.'

'There's a piece in this,' says Phil to my colourless reflection in his window. The river below is the colour of Russian fudge. A barge sweeps across my eyebrows, and I brush it away. I actually do this. Phil chews the wrong end of a black lacquer Mont Blanc pen, then scribbles on the pad on his desk with it, puzzled as to why it won't write.

'Brief?'

'"The Death of the Rock Superstar". Who better to write it than our resident ageing rock chick? Give me a couple of thou for Friday, we'll talk column when I get back from lunch.'

'Where you going?'

'House of Lords.'

'Boss?'

'You still here?'

~

Note to Allegra: download Eddie Laine's new album. Maybe I'll listen to it on my way home. Maybe I won't. Fancy him being back, after all these years. Last I heard, a bunch of dodgy venture capitalists were after him for his share in a nightclub that went belly. It must be a couple of decades since we last crossed paths. The BASCA Gold Badge Awards at the Savoy. I was presenting; he was receiving. Different awards, thank God. The irony of the give and take wasn't lost. I passed his table on my way back from the stage. He looked at me, but he didn't flinch.

Had I changed that much in the intervening years? Or was I invisible?

~

Sometimes I leave the Worst Lady in the office and nip out the back way like the delivery boys, on days when it's all been a bit much. Or I'll accompany her to some glitzy do, get her nice and nuked, then turn a blind eye when she lets her hair down and embarrasses herself in the cab on the way home.

I've been known to leave her in the car all night – out in the cold, that'll teach her – when she hasn't quite performed up to scratch. Most of the time I just bring her home, hose her down and hang her up, ready for next time.

I say 'just'. Who am I kidding? There are the hair extensions to unpin, comb through, soft-bristle brush, spray with leave-in conditioner and plait to prevent tangling; the real-hair eyelashes to peel off – trickier than it looks; the eye make-up to melt – I usually have to do this twice, couldn't tell you why I'm still using waterproof pencils and mascara every day when I never swim except on holiday, and, of course, the Worst Lady never weeps, as *if*, but anyway; the Polyfilla and the face paintwork to remove; the serum, eye-cream, neck emulsion and moisturizer to apply; the heel salve, the elbow grease, the hand lotion, the nail oil. I'm a walking, talking branch of Space.NK.

Sometimes I even wear cotton socks and gloves in bed over this lot, sight for sore eyes, especially since James went. The dental regime is complete science: flossing, TePe-brushing, three minutes of all-out scrubbing and polishing, two different electric toothbrush heads, followed by a gargle of twelve-hour mouthwash, just in case kissing might be on the cards. The routine repeats each morning, with rotation of night and day unguents, as well as everything that goes on in the shower; you don't want to know.

On office days I detour via my uber-up-himself but indispensable hairdresser, Dicky in Mayfair, for the full-on camera-ready coiffure. I used to leave an hour earlier and fit in the gym, too, but these days my trainer comes to *me* three times a week. We work out for an hour, with balls, bars, dumb bells and the occasional bottle of fizz (come on, kids, there's got to be *some* fun in it).

I sometimes stand in front of the bathroom mirror, pinch the flab on my upper arms, the dead bits on the backs of my thighs and the Mars bars around the middle, and ask myself if all this exercise is really truly worth it. I generally conclude that I am better off doing it than not. No image-slippage, missus, not at any cost. Never, ever, ever, *ever* give up.

She serves her purpose, the Worst Lady, or 'WL', as I call her. There are times when I wonder what the hell I would have done without her. We're so chalk and cheese that we get on like the proverbial, most of the time. We have our moments. Entire days, of course, when we loathe each other's guts.

Potato, potahto.

It can get confusing. I admit there are times when it all overwhelms me, when I feel like one-woman conjoined twins, a beast with two heads. There are plenty of times when I forget which one I'm supposed to be, and trip myself up. I might be out shopping as 'me', mousy*hausfrau* 'Neen', as Rhett used to call me and as James still does, or at least *did*, until I showed him the door. I'll have lost track of myself, and I'll suddenly hear Nina Vincent, Worst Lady of Fleet Street, sounding off about something or other, and I'll *cringe,* coming out in sympathy with the woman embarrassing herself – before realising with shock/horror that the voice is coming from *me*. I then do a quick *volte-face,* mumble my excuses and beat it.

I'm trying to remember when I first came up with the idea of WL, but it's all a bit hazy now. The thousands of miles flown, millions of words typed, countless celebrities interviewed, and gallons of booze gulped must have taken their toll over the years. I don't remember ever making a conscious decision to create her, in that one moment I was just Nina, knocking about in jeans and a leather jacket and scrubbing up for the odd big occasion, and the next I'd created this exaggeration via which to channel my inner Boadicea.

I would say that, wouldn't I? I keep it vague in interviews, for the sake of the profile, but in fact I know exactly when it was.

The concept occurred to me not long after Charlie was born, while I was still on maternity leave, so we're talking 1991. I knew I wouldn't be going on the road with rock bands anymore – how could I, with a baby under one arm? – and if I wanted to carry on writing for papers, I was going to have to make my comeback as someone else.

Rhett was right, way back, when he pointed out that I'd always aspired to being one of those formidable female columnists my mother was so obsessed with.

The so-called 'Lennon connection' had been a ride and a half, as often cursed as blessed, and I was fed up with it following me around, with it defining me. Now was my chance to go for it, drop my showbiz-writer shoes in the bin, relaunch myself as an over-opinionated gob-job with something to say about anything and everything that was absolutely none of my business.

It's well known on Fleet Street that you don't go looking for columnists' gigs. They come to *you*. But they *weren't* coming, because nobody *saw* me as that. I had a reputation as a good-time girl gadding about the globe with the stars. Getting the exclusives, sure, but gadding nonetheless. Which of course one could do in those days, but which rendered me something of a lightweight.

How to get them to take me seriously in the mainstream, let me write about politics and sport and scandal and international affairs (which at times were all the same thing)? That was the question.

Then, one morning, coffee on, TV blaring, iron heating up to do James a shirt, Charlie wailing for his Farley's: a moment of epiphany. Scales fell from my eyes. I could recreate myself in the image of the legendary Glenda Slagg, but I'd go one better. I'd glam her to the nines, make her a caricatured composite of her predecessors, have her take the piss out of herself as well her readers, yet maintain an air of innocence, of butter-wouldn't melt. Plus, also, give her the most enormous balls.

What I couldn't tell you with any degree of certainty is when the line was crossed – when WL ceased to be merely a suit of armour, a convenient fiction, and came to life. If I knew that, perhaps I'd have the key to my existence. I might even be able to find the lock.

On the other hand, maybe that's the last thing I want. There's no denying the Frankensteinian arrogance in creating a persona and discovering that ordinary people – readers, folk who pay money for newspapers, listen to her on the radio and watch her on television – believe that she's real. And not only ordinary Joes, but the privileged great and good too. I mean Sir Bill Hollins and Tony Keen are hardly your window cleaner and your binman, are they?

At what point did WL step out from behind the mask? You'd have to ask *her*. Would men like Bill and Tony give a second glance to the old Nina, the *real* Nina, and want her on their arm as they boy it about town, the way they want WL? You'd have to ask me.

Thing is, you know the answer as well as I do. Not that I invented her with the intention of hiding behind her for evermore, if that's what you're thinking. My idea was only to build an extension of me, a beefed-up Nina, someone larger than life, who could handle the crazy job I'd opted to do. But at some point, something breathed life into her. I was forced to take notice of her, have conversations with her, respect her opinion, give her her due. Ask 'what would the Worst Lady do?'

~

The great unwashed defenders of the rock 'n' roll faith are up and at it early this morning, God love 'em.

The readers' comments below the online version of my feature seethe with indignation and bile. What does a vicious old has-been groupie like me know about the intrinsic value of rock music anyway? Not much. If I'd ever spent any time actually *listening* to live music, hanging out with real musicians and soaking up even a smudge of the genius they emanate – *emanate*! – I might find myself wanting to scoff a bit of humble pie. What gives me, sour old cow, the right to pontificate on a subject I know eff-all about? I clearly haven't a clue about the meaning of the term 'musical legacy'. Clearly. A curse on my children, my children's children, their cats, their guinea pigs, their salamanders, for the vastness of all eternity and then to come. They'd like to rip my ugly, inflated, filled-in mush to shreds, and feed it minced to next-door's Rottweiler. Thanks, I appreciate it.

Look, I can hear as well as the next punter that Elton's voice is shot to pieces, that Sting is stung, that Macca's songwriting has never amounted to much since Wings – and even *that* little outing didn't exactly ignite the world, did it? It was always and only ever about the Beatles. My point being that the genre has had its day and its purveyors are obsolete – rendered so by the way the young consume music these days. The 'rock superstar' era has passed; those dinos have had their day.

When we listen to our exalted rock elders, it's not the new stuff they're pumping out that tugs at the heartstrings. It's the memories they evoke in us: of times gone by, of all our personal little tragic loved and lost scenarios, all the will-he-won't-he-calls, all the did-she-didn't-she-really-love-mes, of a carefree youth not exactly misspent, but that perhaps should have been.

It's about the music that they *used to* make – not the music they're making now. We listen. We play 'Let's Pretend'.

Take Queen: bigger today than they ever were during Mercury's lifetime. The guy's been a gonner for, what, getting on for a quarter of a century. They are nothing without him. Would they have lasted this long, had Freddie not died? Hey, keep playing their songs and he lives, he breathes.

It's all it takes. We don't need to see Jagger jogging his way through his seventies, Bill Wyman zimmering into his ninth decade. It breaks all the rules. Pull out *Exile on Main St*: that's what the Stones are supposed to sound like. What they will *always* sound like.

Rock was never meant to be about decaying axemen with malignant prostates. Even Elvis expired way too late. He should have done a James Dean before he discovered Demerol and Dilaudid. Townshend hoped he die before he got old, poor sod. The Ox, Entwistle, dead at fifty-seven, just about made it under the wire. Couldn't have planned quite the exit he got – out of his attic on drink and drugs and under a broad in Vegas – but way to go, dear John. Rock 'n' roll.

Having said all that, there is consolation. Something new breaks through every now and then which stops my heart, which reminds me why I got into the game in the first place, but which is essentially an echo of rock as it was when it began.

I'm talking Roxy Rome, have you heard of her? The Californian singer-songwriter with the Bambi legs, camel lashes, buttercup curls and Seventies maxi dresses, not to mention a face like a Biba poster, who'd apparently taught herself guitar by the age of ten.

She's heading for multi-platinum, a couple of Grammys and a brace of BRITs within the year, or I'm Wilma Flintstone. And she's only just begun. More emotion, truth and pain in that voice than in Aretha's.

~

It's too early to be up. I'm in a taxi on the way to Broadcasting House for a live interview on BBC Radio 4, still smarting from last night's farewell supper with Charlie. Don't think about it, relax, he'll be back in a year. Only twelve months, you're bound to see him sooner, didn't we say we'd hook up for a bit of a holiday together somewhere? Focus. Job in hand. Call him later.

My BlackBerry buzzes on cue. Note, *not* iPhone, there's only so much technology I can take. Besides, I'm a writer: I need a keyboard.

It's Phil. 'You sitting down?'

'The options tend to be limited in the back of a cab. Especially at this hour. You?'

He ignores me.

'Eddie Laine's announced the dates for his comeback world tour?'He ignores that too.

'I give up.'

'You must have known Chas Channing, way back?'

'Is that an order? Wait, don't tell me he's jumped on the Eddie Laine bandwagon with a geriatric album about to launch. They're all at it. Who can cope.'

'Not exactly. Although I predict a rush-release 'Best Of' within the week.'

'He's *croaked*?'

My heart doesn't miss a beat, the way they tell you it does when you hear bad news. It's odds-on favourite in the coronary Grand National. And it's about to get worse.

'Details to be confirmed, but hard to see how it could be anything but murder. I'll spare you the gruesome. I don't know whether it's out there yet, the tip-off came our way about thirty minutes ago via Dan Bates in LA. It might break at the top of the hour. I didn't want you to hear the news through your headphones and be caught with your Ks down. They'll cut your interview and make you talk about this instead, if they do have it. Watch your mouth, I know you. Buzz me when you're out.'

~

It was worse than anything even I could have imagined. Worse than everything I've ever wished on him myself. Even if I thought he had it coming. Which of course I still did.

A harbour patrol boat found what was left of Chas in the early hours, facedown in his fifty-two foot yawl. The Rhapsody was moored off Venice Beach. Hearing its name again, seeing the images on screen, made me go cold.

The coastguard had been alerted by deafening music booming from her decks. On approach, getting no response to their megaphoned attempts at making contact, they climbed aboard and discovered the blood-sodden corpse. He'd been well and truly butchered: heart and larynx hacked out, eyes gouged, fingers and both thumbs severed.

The Rhapsody was towed in. A comprehensive search gave no clue as to the whereabouts of the murder weapon, nor indeed of the missing organs and digits, which were presumed to have been hurled overboard by the killer and consumed by marine life.

The post-mortem revealed fingers rammed deep into his rectum, as if in a nod to his time-honoured catchphrase: 'stick it up yer arse.'

The music industry claims to be 'in shock'. The media overflows with agonising interviews by pain-wracked peers. They're all muscling in on the act, even sub-Chas musos who never could stand the bastard. What a great guy Chazzy was, what a remarkable musician, what a truly special bloke, what a tragedy, blar blar blar. Privately, people reckon he had it coming. Not quite like this, perhaps, you'd have to say, but some kind of inglorious, wretched end was always on the cards.

That's rock 'n' roll. He'd led such an untidy life, they reason, behaving like a reckless teenager well into late middle age, that what else could he expect? The commentators are tutting for England, but *please*: show me a grown-up rock star.

Did he owe money, people are asking. I can't imagine it; he was filthy-loaded. The royalties must still be flooding in. It's a rare week when you don't hear two or three Dead Jameses records on the radio. Chas wrote most of their hits himself.

He'd give anyone anything, I'll say that for him. He was blissfully indifferent to material possessions all his life. He squandered his millions on good times and bad friends.

His five wives – 'no rock superstar ever stays married to his first wife,' he once told me, 'and after you've left one, you leave 'em all' – gave him six official children.

Half a dozen or so live-in mistresses provided more twilight offspring than he could count. He'd never even met half of them.

He once took in a dazzling eighteen-year-old blonde with eyes the same shade of seaweed as his. Refusing to believe her claims that she was his long-lost daughter, he began an affair with her instead. She didn't complain at the time. When he eventually kicked her out, she sold her story to the *Enquirer*, but later retracted it and claimed she'd made the whole thing up. Who was leaning on her? She also declined to submit to a DNA test that might have proved her to be Chas's child. Refusing to make a formal complaint to the LAPD, she retreated east and fell off the radar. No incest charge was ever brought.

Could he be forgiven for such abominable behaviour, this chronic alcoholic who was also helplessly addicted to nicotine and cocaine? His many women seemed to think so. An impressive number of them wept estuaries at his Inglewood Park funeral service, four days after he was found. Those same sirens wailed in knee-buckled unison as his ashes were scattered from The Rhapsody during the late afternoon, where they held his teetotal, vegetarian wake. I found that in poor taste, to be honest. There's no accounting for Americans.

~

Now, a week on, it gets better. Here's a Californian detox doc revealing on US breakfast television that Chas was only a couple of months ago in his care.

Terrified by the effects of the bucket of vodka and yards of coke he was dependent on daily, he'd sought help at this guy's clinic and paid up-front for a platinum-service twenty-eight-day programme.

The quick quack claims he had Chas on 100mg of Librium every two hours, to bring him down slowly and prep him for treatment.

But Chas checked himself out after only five days and resumed hell-raising. Someone else took it upon themselves to ensure that he got checked out for good.

We believe what we want to believe ...

Oyster sandwiches were Chas's favourite. At least they were when

I knew him. Smoked oysters on white, no butter, sluiced down with Krug. I find myself wondering when he'd last enjoyed that dainty repast. It'll have turned up in the autopsy report, of course, whatever he'd consumed just before he died. I'll have to get my hands on the path notes.

It won't last forever, but the memories will ...

He's still in me. However much I don't want him to be, however hard I try to visualise his sodden ashes disintegrating in the surf, Chas Channing is alive and kicking inside my head.

And still the question. Who would do this? Who on earth would want to kill the poor sod?

That would be me.

CHAPTER TWO

JAMES

James Kendal made the 17.30 out of JFK to LAX by the skin of his crowns, the last passenger to board. A good thing he was booked in Privilege and was carrying only hand luggage. Having flung his Fendi holdall into his dedicated overhead locker, he knocked his head on the bin door as he sank into the black leather aisle seat. *Every* time; when would he learn to be more careful. Probably never, get over it.

He buckled his seatbelt, smiled self-consciously at the pop-eyed stewardess hovering over him, and rubbed the side of his forehead.

The flight was full, and the seat beside him was fragrantly occupied. He couldn't help but notice the smooth, slender, flesh-stockinged legs stretched out to his left, the feet hidden by the seat in front.

He found himself immediately intrigued by invisible shoes. Heels? Pumps? Flats? Flip-flops? Nancy Sinatras? He'd see the tops of those, surely. Trainers? Definitely not trainers. She wouldn't be wearing running shoes with that neat little frock; Vivienne Westwood, he'd hazard a guess. Signature tartan. Voluminous folds.

Then again, she might be one of these throwback New York yuppies, the type who leap athletically around town in the latest Nikes, making sure everyone knows they're carrying their arm-and-a-leg Jimmy Choos or Pradas in that white-lettered black shopper from Barney's, the Bergdorf's lilac carrier or the brown-and-white striped swag bag from Henri Bendel, changing into them when they reach their destination.

He glanced again, discreetly. Nah. And definitely not flip-flops. She wouldn't get them on over a pair of tights. He presumed they were tights; more was the pity. For no reason at all, other than that he was a bloke – can't blame him for that, can you? – he really badly wanted there to be suspenders.

He wondered fleetingly whether he should acknowledge whoever she was with 'hello' or 'hi' or even just a nod, but then thought better of it. It would probably be taken the wrong way, he thought ruefully.

Ignoring the safety routine – heard it a thousand times, know it by heart, I know I should pay attention, can't be fagged – he folded his arms across his black cashmere chest and closed his eyes. It had been an exceptionally long day, and he was exhausted.

He opened them again a good quarter of an hour after take-off, when he heard the unmistakable clinks and rattles of the drinks trolley heading his way.

He told himself he'd more than earned a Boston Sour. Not that he was going to get a hand-mixed cocktail with fresh egg white back here. Who did he think he was? Get real. Gone and never to return were the days when the agency flew him First, when he could expect his share of luxuries at thirty-five thousand feet. At the hotel later, he promised himself; he could wait six hours for a real drink. He requested Scotch on the rocks when it was his turn.

It was the nuts that did it. He never could get the pesky packet open without some sort of drama; he didn't know why he bothered. He really shouldn't have. He twisted and yanked, trying to tear off the corner, but it wouldn't give. *So* annoying, these stupid little bags – the technology we have today and we're still fiddling with midget packets of peanuts, *honestly*.

Then the same thing happened as happened every time. The whole thing split, corner to corner, and cascaded its contents, most of them across the tray table and into the glass of white wine, yes, right inside the glass, of the woman sitting next to him. He wouldn't mind betting she'd think he'd done it deliberately. Groan. He probably ought to say something.

'God, I am sooo sorry, that so wasn't mean to happen. Let me call the stewardess, get you another …'

'Oh, please,' lilted his neighbour, 'don't even think about it!'

She was American, obviously. He turned his head and saw an indifferent beauty. Michelle Pfeiffer falling out of bed in last night's make-up. Round but square, if you can have both at the same time.

Her face murmured innocence, vulnerability, and seemed to beckon him. The black mascara'd eyelashes were tiny fingers. Loose blonde hair –

could be dyed, hoped it wasn't. Peachy lips – a little bit downy along the top; she could wax that, not that it bothered him. Not really. Moist-looking skin, maybe she sprayed it with one of those facial mists; Nina had a MAC one that he borrowed sometimes. Used to. Good word, moist. So natural-looking; nothing else on it as far as he could tell. Bloody good foundation if it *was* foundation – probably MAC or Charlotte Tilbury.

He might be a bloke but James knew about these things, he'd worked on more than a few cosmetics campaigns in his time. What were the words that always cropped up? *Flawless. Dewy. Glowing. Bright. Like real skin, only better*. Way, way better. This was skin straight out of slumber at the crack, a face beaming like a daisy at dawn.

Christ, get a grip; she'll read your mind and take you for a trainee copywriter.

Although he was trying to avoid it happening, their eyes met. Unexpectedly, hers were green. He'd kind of assumed they'd be blue, or might well have guessed so, had you asked him. They usually were. Blue or brown.

Did you know that only one to two per cent of the entire global population has green eyes? No, he didn't either. At least he hadn't known that fact until a week or so ago when he was skimming through background info on a new contact lens contract his agency had just landed, and came across it.

Green eyes are most evident today in central and northern Europe, but also found in southern Europe, and central, western and southern Asia. More common amongst women than men. Among European-Americans, most often seen in those of Germanic or Celtic descent. Green eyes are the rarest of all eye colours. Dominant over blue, but very few carry the gene for green. It can skip generations, and it'll depend on the type of melanin within the iris, as well as on lipochrome.

Will you listen to yourself! What the fuck are you on about, do you even know what lipochrome *is*? Some sort of yellow stuff. All Greek to him.

They were stunning, magnetic eyes, was the size of it. He fell right in.

'I think we should have another drink anyway. Just to make sure,' he announced, belling the stewardess.

'You're right,' she responded easily. 'Just to be sure.'

She smiled at him the way women always smiled at him, absorbing what he knew to be casual good looks. A man knows when he has this effect on women, he thought, and he goes one of two ways. Disdainful, dismissive and arrogant, or …

'I'm Daphne, by the way. Daphne Greene.'

His mouthful of Scotch doubled back on him as she said it. He coughed himself mauve.

Not just because she'd told him her surname was the same as her eye colour, but because he'd spotted, that same second, the face on the page of the magazine she was reading. She noticed him noticing.

'You're English.'

'Ten out of ten.'

'Ha. Do you know this woman here? She's a British newspaper columnist, Nina Vincent? I've just been reading about her in *Vanity Fair*. Piece of work or what. She sounds terrifying. I think if I ever met her I'd run a mile!'

'I'm sure you would,' phlegmed James, recovering his colour, wiping his mouth on the wristband of his sweater. 'She's pretty fierce.'

'You *do* know her!'

'Some might say,' James replied with a grimace. 'She's my wife.'

'You're *kidding* me. No way! Of all the …'

'… gin joints in all the towns. Indeed. I wish I were, and no, I'm not, and yes, what a coincidence.' He grinned at her.

'No such thing as coincidence.'

'You think?'

'I know.'

They sat in silence for several moments, which Daphne was the first to interrupt.

'Forgive me for saying so – we've only just met and all, I wouldn't want to intrude – but …'

'But what?'

'It's just that you don't sound too happy about it.'

'About what?'

'That she's your wife.'

James took another jawful of Scotch. Choked. Tipped again, draining the glass.

Looked at her.

'I'm not, as it happens,' he said at last, 'but I don't want to bore you.'

'It's not boring!'

'Believe me, it is. Why would I tell you, anyway?'

'Strangers always tell each other things on planes.'

'Why *is* that?'

'Something to do with the fact that you have stuff on your mind that you need to offload. Anything could happen up here above the clouds. It's quite liberating to be detached from terra firma; you want to get things of your chest, just in case. You're never going to see the person you're confiding in again …'

'Is that true?'

He could tell from her expression that she knew he was flirting with her. Not that he was certain that he was.

'Is *what* true?'

'That I'm never going to see you again?'

Daphne looked away, ignoring the question.

Jim, Jim, get your hoof out your gob, you great plank.

Silence again. Shit. He wished to God he hadn't said it.

Then she spoke.

'So tell me.'

'You really wanna know?'

'I really wanna.'

'Let's see how short I can make this. I am married to Nina Vincent, but she's not the woman I married. So to speak. She's changed.'

'People do.'

'I don't mean in the normal way.'

'Is there a normal way?'

'You know what I mean. My wife – Nina – reinvented herself for the purposes of what she does for a living. One minute she was a showbiz writer on a newspaper, a good one too, doing well, loving every minute of it. We'd met in the early eighties …'

'Where did you meet?'

'On a plane.'

'No way!'

'Way.'

'This is getting spooky.'

He ignored that. She let him.

'Where were you going, then?' she tried again.

'When?'

'When you guys met on that flight. Where were you heading?'

'New York. From London. She had an interview with David Bowie. July 1983, Serious Moonlight tour, he was playing Madison Square Garden. I'd just joined a new agency …'

'What is it you do?'

'Advertising. Trainee account exec back then; I'm a director now. I also have more of a hand in the creative side. Anyway. What about you?'

'Excuse me?'

'What do you do?'

'I'm a publicist. I work for Axel Koch.'

'The celebrity chef?'

'Him.'

'You live in New York or LA?'

'West Hollywood.' She paused, perhaps kicking herself for having given away too much. 'You were saying.'

'So Nina and I went out for a while, and then we broke up.'

'Who broke up?'

'Does it make a difference?'

'Always.'

'*She* did. As it happens. And then we bumped into each other again a few years on. I always want to say Paris but I know it was Rome. We had a pan-European deal with Pepsi at the time. They were sponsoring Michael Jackson's BAD tour; Nina was there to interview him. Complete coincidence.'

'There's no such –'

'Right. All very fancy-seeing-*you*-here. She dragged me along to the concert. Flaminio football stadium. And I suppose we must have been ready, second time round. Things fell into place, like I'd known her all my life. We went on to the after-show, incredible party, missed the coach back, couldn't find a cab, wound up having to walk all the way back to the hotel. I asked her to marry me with my key ring at about two o'clock in the morning, on the Spanish Steps, next to the Keats-Shelley house.'

'Romantic.'

'Set the bar a bit high, didn't I?' He grimaced. 'She cried Niagara.'

'Who wouldn't? Where did you get married?'

'London, the following spring. Low-key, register office, a few mates, no big church do or anything. Neither of us wanted all that.'

'You mean *you* didn't.'

'Maybe, Mrs Freud! Didn't give it much thought at the time, just wanted it done and dusted. We had lunch at Joe Allen's after, then went home. Never did get round to a honeymoon.'

'Telling. Why not?'

'Stuff kept cropping up.'

'But you were happy.'

'Very.' James nodded, maybe too enthusiastically. 'Our son was born the year after.'

'What's his name?'

'Charlie. We had him, a great house, a lot to live for. But he was a challenge. It was complicated; I think we didn't always know what we were dealing with.'

'In what way?'

'Don't go there. He's all grown up now, doing OK. We've moved on. I'll get to see him in LA this trip, as it happens. He's staying with friends for a bit before he goes on to Australia.'

'What's he going to do in Oz?'

'Look around, hang out, see what turns up. He's not sure yet what he wants to do with his life. He'll get there, in his own time. Charlie's not the kind of guy to work to anybody else's timetable. Anyway, the next thing, Nina comes home one day with this … 'creature' is the only way I can describe it. And the monster took over, and subsumed my wife, to the point that the two are now pretty much indivisible. Got to the point where I couldn't even be sure who to expect for dinner. Will it be her, or will it be *her.'*

'You're not serious.'

'What I wouldn't give. Newspaper columnist Nina Vincent lives in a house where dust doesn't exist, and which never runs out of toilet paper.

She actually writes about this kind of thing. But *Nina*-Nina turns a blind eye to domestic disarray and the normal running out of stuff. She'd say, which I happen to agree with, that there are more important things. She'd quote Quentin Crisp, that queer English writer-actor-bloke, remember him?'

'I don't think …'

'Anyway, he was famous. Dead now. Moved to New York, lived in a one-room apartment which he never cleaned, reckoned after four years you didn't see the dust. Nina loved that. She was always sacking cleaners who weren't any good, saying there's no point paying someone else to clean up after you when they don't do it as well as you do it yourself. And she'd say you can always find a corner shop open when you need a bog roll. We were on the same page. Mostly. But then things changed. What was it the Princess of Wales said? Three people in that marriage? I know millions of women were on Di's side, but I can't imagine many men were. I was one of the few. I was in that situation myself.'

'You're exaggerating, right?'

'I wish.' James sighed. He was on a roll, trying to shut it but couldn't help himself.

'It's like she believes the publicity. Like her millions of readers, she's gone and fallen for this fake she made up. Her biggest problem is that she actually believes she has the answers.'

'To what?'

'Who knows. You know. The human condition. The meaning of life, love and the universe. The pointlessness of our shallow, materialistic world. Which is rich, coming from her, because Nina Vincent is the most materialistic woman you could ever meet. *Stuff* really matters to her.

'The right stuff. Rich coming from me too, I suppose. I mean I make my living coming up with ways of getting people to buy things.'

He looked sheepishly at Daphne, who was listening intently. Where had her smile gone? Had she swallowed it?

'But you get my drift,' he continued. 'Everything would have been fine, I'm sure, if only she'd kept made-up Nina at arm's length. I should have seen it coming. I should have done something.'

'What could you have done?'

'Fuck knows – excuse my French. Then again, as I've so often asked myself, was this also some sort of escapism from our family life, from the problems we were going through with Charlie? Was the alter ego a necessary invention, Nina's way of switching her real self off? A way of staying sane? Anyway, it's all academic now.'

'How?'

'Because we're separated. We're getting divorced.'

'*Why?*'

'Because she wants to.'

'Because she has a split personality? She could get help with –'

'Because I slipped up one night. At a conference. Sank a barrelful, wound up in the sack with a secretary.'

'Ah. That'll do it.'

'*One shag*?'

'Don't you know anything at all about women?'

'I'm beginning to think I never, ever did.'

~

They ate. They dozed. They pretended to. He knew he must have about twenty years on her. He wondered whether she'd noticed his flecky hair and baggy eyes.

He also wondered whether she'd be up for it. Too pretty to be a pushover, she must have men hurling themselves at her. I bet she's sick of it, he thought. I'm not sure I can take the withering sneer if I suggest meeting up for a cocktail sometime.

Drink, better not say cocktail; now there's a word that's always misconstrued. You can't be too careful.

He wondered what her skin felt like. How it smelt. There was a soapy waft in the air, but that could be the plane toilet freshener or somebody's hand cream for all he knew. It didn't seem like the kind of scent that could be a smart bird's perfume.

He wanted to touch her hand.

Down, Jim.

Then the plane hit a pocket of turbulence and the move was made for him. The aircraft's lurch caused James's left arm to throw itself smack across her breasts.

'Fuck! God! I'm so sorry. The plane leapt, I …'

'Don't apologise.'

By the time the landing gear was down, they were swapping cards.

Not that James would ever call her; don't make him laugh, he was only being polite. He couldn't exactly refuse when she offered hers, could he. I mean. He then had to offer his own in exchange, it would've been rude not to. But take things further? *Sur ton bicyclette, Jean.* That would be asking for it.

He watched her rise from her seat, got an eyeful of neatly contained cleavage, couldn't help but notice her black suede pumps. Told you. Definitely not trainers. Not a designer department store carrier bag in sight. It was perfectly possible that she was wearing suspenders. No, he definitely would not be calling her.

The last thing he needed right now was more of the same.

CHAPTER THREE

CHARLIE

Charlie spent his first free morning in Los Angeles by himself, riding a hired bike from Santa Monica all the way down to Venice boardwalk.

The weather was beautiful for late September, with a sky too blue to be real. A Crayola blue that reminded him of brushed cotton pyjamas he'd worn as a child, when his mother still bathed him, warming the towel and the pyjamas on the radiator while she did so. He was thinking of a particular pair he'd had once, the ones with little red sailing boats on. The kind of boats he wished he could see now. But there was not a vessel of any kind on the untroubled ocean. He felt fleetingly sad about that.

A washing powder breeze rippled in off the waves and found its way through his hair. He liked the feel of it. It was not yet noon.

Dropping the bike at the depot and getting a stamp on his pass, he palmed the sweat from his arms, readjusted his backpack and stood with his hands on his hips, watching a crazy world go by.

Muscle Beach Venice. You don't have to be mad to hang here, but it helps. He watched street performers doing freak stuff, whackos smoking weed, drunken bums begging beer money, tourists filling their faces with ice cream. Muscle men pumping, dogs humping, every kind of nutter and rutter (he must remember to write that one down).

He wandered in and out of open-air kiosks, perused postcards he couldn't be bothered to buy, let alone write and send, and wolfed down a hot dog for the hell of it. Not that he was hungry, even though he'd missed breakfast.

Finally he flopped, exhausted, into a chair outside an OK-looking café on Ocean Front Walk, pulled out his book, and sank a couple of 7-Ups to wash the morning down.

He was reading *Bloodbath: A Geography of Sadism*. He'd ordered it from Amazon quite by accident, believing it to be a biography of

Swedish death metal supergroup Bloodbath, whom he followed, along with Britain's Venom and America's Cannibal Corpse, all in the same genre.

He got more than he bargained for. But he'd paid good money for it, so he might as well give it a go. Once he started reading, he couldn't stop. This was his second reading, in fact.

The book explored the life and perverted times of Hungary's 16th-century 'Blood Countess', the most notorious female serial killer in history. True story.

Brutal Elizabeth Bathory de Ecsed captured hundreds of adolescent girls, abused and mutilated them, chewed the cheeks from their faces and hacked the fingers from their hands, burned, starved and froze them to death, or tortured them horrifically with needles.

Charlie was fascinated by the idea of a woman who would bathe in the blood of virgins to preserve her skin. Like some female Dracula. Same part of the world, he supposed. Wasn't it?

Only Bathory's accomplices were eventually tried; this is where he was currently up to in the torrid tale. Not Bathory herself, the claim being that her noble status conferred immunity from prosecution. Dozens of witnesses testified, and all except one of her servants gave evidence against her. The girl who refused had her eyes gouged out and her breasts torn off, before being burned at the stake.

So far, so vile. Not that Charlie was squeamish or anything. If anything, the opposite.

He'd been surprised to discover that Venom had recorded a song called *Countess Bathory* on their 1982 album *Black Metal*, which he didn't love as much as their 1981 album *Welcome to Hell*, but he adored this particular song.

This in turn had led him to Seattle rock band Aiden's 2009 single *Elizabett*, also about the demon Countess. There were a variety of others, she'd inspired a heap of songwriting, but these were the two he liked the best. Coincidence or what.

His dad was supposed to have called him at around midday to give him the low-down on lunch. But at a quarter to one, Charlie still hadn't heard from him. He was about to make his way back to the bike booth and pick up a ride back to his friend's mother's place when his iPhone buzzed.

He checked the face on the screen, and thumbed green.

'Hey, Dad.'

'Son. You in shape? What's cooking?'

'Don't say what's cooking, Dad. Nobody says what's cooking.' Charlie's light, breathy voice rose with teenage resentment, the way it should have stopped doing years ago. He didn't even try to keep it down. He wanted to, but he couldn't bring himself to. It was as simple and as complicated as that.

'Whatever,' said his father, who could never win.

'Don't say whatever. It's uncool, Dad. You're being a dick.'

'Yup,' said James, not missing a beat.

'So. You still up for lunch today?'

'I was beginning to think you'd forgotten,' said Charlie, resentfully. He knew he was being childish, yet he couldn't hold back.

'Sorry, no, of course I didn't forget. How could I? I was tied up in that meeting; they got to us late. I've only just managed to get rid of them.'

'How'd it go? Did you get the contract?'

'Too soon to say, but quietly confident,' said James. 'The presentation went really well. We should know by the end of the week. So, where'd you like to meet? Somewhere near you? Back at my hotel?'

'I'm wearing shorts …'

'Welcome to LA. No one's looking at what you're wearing. Scruffier you come, the more money they think you have. We can get a bit of lunch on the pool terrace. There's a beautiful view from up there.'

'Sounds nice.'

'Half-past one work for you?'

'I'll be there.'

'How're you coming, Charlie? I don't mind doshing you up for a cab –'

‘I said I’ll be there, Dad. I’m *twenty-four*. Fat chance making it to Australia if I can’t even get from Venice to West Hollywood.’

‘Good thing you’re not Italian.’

‘Funny. Not.’

‘In a bit.’

~

Several palm-lined boulevards later, Charlie found himself soaring in a polished glass lift to the fifth floor of his father’s hotel.

Not that he’d want to give the impression that he was blown away or anything, but this could never be described as your average pool terrace. On the contrary. It was just awesome. A lushly landscaped tropical paradise with movie-star views over Beverly Hills and downtown Los Angeles, it could have been some extravagant Old Hollywood film set.

His mother would like it here, he thought, before remembering that she was bound to have stayed here already. Of course she had. Not with his father, either, he wouldn’t mind betting.

Not too many places she hadn’t been. Not too many types she hadn’t met, come to that. ‘Face’ people, he meant. ‘Name’ people. People whose names appear in newspapers and magazines in **bold**. People who ‘mattered’.

He felt his fingers making involuntary quote marks as the thought occurred to him. It freaked him out to think of the mother he longed for – the warm, cake-smelling woman from his childhood, from his dreams – being the sort of person who functioned naturally in this kind of world.

He recoiled from the idea of her hobnobbing, as she called it. Having dinner with and holding her own amongst the movers and the shakers. Among loaded creeps like …

No. He didn’t want to think about it. Not here. Not now. The thought actually frightened him. Now that he was old enough, he wanted to scoop his mother up, save her from herself, take her away somewhere. Somewhere nice. Somewhere far from her rotten world and all the self-serving, lying bastards she hung with.

He could never admit it to himself, he knew that much, but he really needed his mother to be who she used to be. Or at least, the woman he remembered. Before all this.

It occurred to him, as he sat at a corner table under a white canvas umbrella waiting for his father to arrive, that he had never watched his mother on television. Nor had he ever listened to her on the radio.

His excuse, the one he gave himself at least, was that he couldn't stand that voice she put on when she was 'being her'. He avoided her 'acclaimed weekly columns', and was frankly embarrassed by the kind of features she wrote, with their meaningless headlines and that hideous picture of her fake-smiling, the one the size of a bathroom tile.

This campaign she'd been on lately, about rock stars: it made him cringe so hard, there were times when he wanted to die. He could well imagine what his friends' parents were saying.

He knew they read everything she wrote. Especially the mothers. The Botoxed-tennis-playing-lunch-bunch, as she called them. They enquired about her nicely whenever he happened to be round their houses hanging out or anything, but he knew how much they bitched behind his back. It wasn't just the paper she worked for, which he knew people called a 'fascist rag'. Didn't stop them buying it, though, did it? If they despised his mother as much as he sensed they did, why the hell couldn't they just ignore her, maybe read a different paper?

Probably because she was precisely the kind of woman you couldn't ignore, he thought, his sap rising. And maybe because they were a bit jealous.

Not that she'd give a toss. He could hear her now. 'Never bother about what anyone else thinks of you,' she'd say. 'Haven't I brought you up to believe in yourself? It's what *you* think of you that matters, darling. Fuck everyone else!'

Even now, she was everywhere he looked. Even when he closed his eyes. Perhaps especially then. Thousands of miles and millions of thoughts away, there was no escaping her. Not even if he wanted to. Which, he thought, he probably did.

Suddenly a voice interrupted his thoughts.

'You've grown!'

His father slapped him on the back.

'You always say that. You only saw me last week.' Charlie made himself grin, stood up, and slapped his father's back a couple of times in return.

'As long ago as that. How time flies when you're enjoying yourself.'

'You always say that, too.'

James shrugged a 'what can you do'.

Charlie mirrored him.

They took their seats, a little awkwardly.

Charlie stole a glance at his father while he was ordering drinks, when he thought he wasn't looking. Took in the slightly sunken cheeks, the just-enough-tan, the squirrelly fuzz on his face. His dad looked quite cool, Charlie thought. Cool in that way you never want your dad to look. Cool in that 'please don't let my girlfriend fancy him' kind of way. Charlie cringed again.

He noticed that James's grey-blue linen suit was crinkled from the heat, but even that looked OK. The white shirt suited him, too. Accentuated the tan. He couldn't remember having seen his father in a white shirt before. Why was that weird? Why did he even notice it, and why did it matter?

It didn't, did it? It really didn't. Actually, it kind of did.

'What have you done since you got here?'

'Not much. Sleeping. Hanging with Ed. We played pool a few times. Went on a couple of long bike rides.'

'Planning on seeing any sights?'

'We're gonna go down Hollywood Boulevard tomorrow, see the Chinese theatre, the Walk of Fame, the Capitol building, all that stuff. Ed's mother wants to take us out to Disneyland. A bit babyish, but I've never been. So …'

'Go, go,' enthused James. 'You've got to see these places. We should have taken you ourselves, I suppose, but you seemed happy enough with Euro Disney when you were little. You grew out of that fast enough. I was sorry when you did, actually.'

'They call it Disneyland Paris now.'

'What else?'

'Oh. You know. I'm here for a couple more weeks,' Charlie lied. 'I might do Universal Studios. I quite fancy that. And catch some live music. Ed's brother Callum, he's a guitarist, he can get us into a couple of the clubs he plays at. He's taking us to a party he's playing on Friday, at the Chateau Marmont.'

'Cool.'

'Don't say cool, Dad.'

'Watch your step in that joint.'

'You been there?'

'A lifetime ago. Long before André Balazs got hold of the place and made it hip again. When I was young, and …'

'… all was frolic and fun,' groaned Charlie. 'Do you have to?'

'If you must get in trouble, do it at the Marmont, someone once said. You can check out any time you like …'

'… but you can never leave. Yep.'

They sat in silence as a cute waitress landed a well-done burger and fries and a medium rib-eye with salad, no onions. She paused to smile at James, who either didn't notice or pretended not to.

Charlie did.

'I'm not even hungry now,' he said, frowning at the girl.

'Eat. You never know where your next meal's coming from.'

'*Dad!*'

'So. Who else are you seeing on your travels, again? You did tell me …'

'A coupla mates,' said Charlie. 'Howie and Deisel from uni.'

'Uni one or uni two?'

'You always have to remind me I'm a student dropout, don't you? You can never let it go. Jeez. As it happens, uni two. Anyway, and Neesha –'

'Who's Neesha?'

'Venetia Bolton. Friend of a friend. I met her at a party about a month ago. It's all mapped out. A few of us are gonna hook up in Sydney just before Christmas.'

'Barbecued turkey on the beach?'

'Is that what they do? Sounds OK. Maybe. If we don't sink too much of the amber nectar beforehand.'

'You're going to have to watch yourself, Charlie. Keep an eye on your budget, protect yourself when you're off the beaten track, have back-up –'

'Be sensible, you mean? What, like you?'

They ate in silence, each half-willing the other to speak.

'I wish Mum was here,' muttered Charlie, after a while. He dropped his fork. The words fell out of his mouth before he could slurp them back.

He started picking petals off a white rose in the small glass bowl on the table. As he did so, he was reminded of that summer he spent catching butterflies in the back garden with a little green net, trapping them in jam jars, tearing off their wings. He must have been about nine. Once or twice he tried eating the wings. They didn't taste of anything. They just stuck to the roof of his mouth.

'I do too,' said James.

'Do you really?'

'You know I do.'

'Then why are you getting divorced?'

James parked his wine glass and leant back in his chair. He fiddled with a snagged thread on his shirtsleeve.

'You really want to do this?' he said quietly.

'I just want to know, Dad. I just want to know what happened. This is hard for me …'

'I know it is,' said James, 'It's hard for me too.'

'Then why did you go and shag someone else?'

James winced. He sat up slightly, and rearranged his face.

'Is that what she told you?'

'*She* didn't have to. I have ears. And eyes. Plus, I'm not stupid.'

'These things …'

'"Just happen"? You're giving me that old crap now? Like you think I'm still twelve? I'm not a kid, Dad. This is all bollocks. You worship the ground she walks on, anyone can see that, but you can't stop yourself from sticking it in someone else?'

'Charlie …'

'*What?* Wash my mouth out? Well, what else do you call it?'

'I hardly think it appropriate …'

'… to discuss your sex life with your son? Is that what you were going to say?'

'Well …'

'I'm not a baby. And anyway, you *love* Mum.'

'Yes, I do.'

'You went with another woman behind her back. At least I assume it was a woman …'

'Charlie, *please.* We happen to be in LA at the same time, we hook up for a nice lunch before you move on, and you have to start…'

'Don't say hook up.'

'You know what I mean.'

'You hurt her.'

'She's not the easiest. You know as well as I do.'

'Excuses. She's *Mum!* She's always been there. *You've* always been there. You and her.'

'Divorce is always hardest on the children.'

'*Child,'* said Charlie, bitterly, forgetting that he was no longer one, as he so often did. He snorted into the back of his hand and swiped it down his shorts.

'It's just that I'm finding it really, really difficult to understand why you would cheat on the woman you always said you wanted to grow old with, which means that you're going to lose everything you ever had. Everything that was worth anything. For the sake of one shag.'

'You think I don't know that?'

'It's not too late.'

'I told you I love your mother, and I always will. I meant that.'

'Tell *her,* then. Get her back, Dad. It's not too late.'

'I've a feeling it is for your mother.'

'Have you even tried?'

'She's seeing someone …'

'I'd call that an understatement!' In spite of himself, Charlie laughed out loud. James stood up, and excused himself. Charlie was still laughing, shaking the fingers of one hand, when his father returned from the bathroom.

James sat down, caught the waitress's eye and mimed the signing of a check.

'What did you mean by that?' James asked.

'By what?'

'Calling it an understatement.'

'Oh, come off it, Dad, everybody knows. They've even written it in the rags. They've got pictures of Mum with both those old gits. Tony Keen and that other old has-been. Bill Hollins. Sorry: *Sir* William Hollins, patron saint of clapped-out rock stars. That guy who's got the new show, it just opened, the one we wouldn't be seen dead at.'

'You know about all this?'

'Like I said. It's obvious to me that she's only tarting about with these losers just to make you jealous.'

'What makes you say that?'

'Come *on*! How old are you? Can you really see Mum ending up with either of them? They're both *married*, for a start! Mum's making a right idiot of herself, larking around town with that pair of tossers, getting herself talked about, and you're letting her.'

'It's what she does best.'

'Don't you think she's doing it to –'

'What? Make me jealous, as you say? That what you think? One thing you should know about your mother by now: she doesn't play games. At least, not that kind of game. When she does something, she means it. She never gives energy to anything she doesn't want. Anyway, the divorce is going through.'

'You can stop it,' urged Charlie.

'She'd never listen. Look how thick she is with that lawyer of hers. Neal what's-his-name. Can't be right, can it?'

'Goddard. Neal Goddard. What a weirdo *he* is, have you Googled him?'

'Not yet. But you read my mind.'

CHAPTER FOUR

JAMES

After slapping Charlie goodbye, insisting he take a cab outside the hotel, and pressing a couple of fifties into his hand, James made his way back to his room in pensive mood.

He called room service for a bottle of Gavi di Gavi, told the waiter who delivered it that he'd open it himself, and settled down with his iPad on the pristine, alpine expanse of bed. It was time he met his adversary. Well, one of them, at least.

Neal Goddard. Pictures? A couple of press shots, an official portrait on his chambers' website, nothing much else.

James enlarged and studied it with a practised eye. Was he really only thirty-two? He would have said he was younger. A bit keen looking, for a barrister. Weren't they supposed to be jaded and rheumy-eyed? Iffy teeth; he'd get those fixed. But he had to admit, an honest-looking smile. Hair receding already; he could do something about that, too.

Goddard was a member of Lybbarde Chambers … James had to look that one up. A lybbarde was a mythological beast, apparently. Like a leopard, born of a lioness and a panther. The heraldic symbol of boldness. Symbolic indeed. James quite liked it. Goddard's chambers were located in London's Temple, which James found oddly reassuring. At least she wasn't wasting their hard-earned on some quack.

'Family Law Set of the Year 2000,' he read, scrolling rapidly through the Lybbarde website. 'Specialists in all aspects of family law. Divorce, financial claims, arbitration, jurisdictional conflicts, pre-nups, inheritance, civil partnerships, property disputes, injunctions, child abduction …'

'Serious guns, this lot,' James mumbled.

'Must be costing a bundle. About half their members in the Legal 500. What does Goddard's profile say?'

He scanned the page. Ampleforth, Brasenose, all the right educational establishments. Velvet and steel. A smooth operator. Brilliant. Inclusive. Charming. Pragmatic, no-nonsense, client-focused, achieves the best possible outcome at the least possible emotional cost. Lots of celebrity divorces.

Then he noticed something odd. Goddard appeared to be trying to say he didn't believe in divorce. Cutting his nose off to spite his face?

'Nothing delights me more than the handful of cases I've known in which a couple reconciles, sometimes literally on the steps of the court. We simply rip up the file and off they go into the sunset. It's never too late.'

Charlie, Charlie. James drained the bottle, thought he might dial down for another, then thought better of it. On a whim, he fumbled in his pocket for his wallet, pulled out Daphne Greene's card and dialled her number. Straight to voicemail. He didn't want to leave a message, you never knew who might be listening. Email? Text? Leave it? Email.

'Long time, fellow passenger. Who are you doing for dinner tonight?'

He should have known she'd respond in a blink.

'You, apparently. Give me 'til seven. I'll meet you at your hotel.'

Funny. He couldn't remember having told her where he was staying.

He thought about having a shower. Could he be fagged? He probably should. He sniffed an armpit to confirm. Maybe a sundown swim instead? Then again, the pool was bound to be brimming with Camerons and Ashtons at this time of day, swilling *cocktails* and strutting their stuff. He couldn't face all that. Been there, done it. Not that you could swim anyway, in human minestrone; it would only be a bit of splashing about. He padded over to the window to think about what next, or maybe to take a breather from thinking. Couldn't decide which. Lunch with Charlie had unnerved him; he needed something to take his mind off it.

He took in the sunset. Spindly palm trees rose in front of him, their fern-like branches fanning at the top like feather dusters, silhouetted against a backdrop of slate-grey towers. The orange-peel sky was punctured by a gaping yellow furnace that seemed to suck him in. It seared his eyes.

In the foreground, the low-lying buildings directly below him had taken on the coolest purple hue.

Charlie, Charlie. Where did you go, little boy?

James remembered the time he and Nina had got up one morning – Charlie must have been about three – and realised he was missing.

He wasn't in his room … they couldn't find him anywhere in the house. They searched and searched, up, down, in, out, no joy, until Nina was beside-herself hysterical.

Their minds did nineteen to the dozen. James wanted to be sick; it was as much as he could do to keep himself calm.

Had someone broken in during the night and taken him? Had he managed to climb out of the window in his room, even though it was locked and barred? Been snatched by Peter Pan, or aliens? *What?*

She had him running up and down the street banging on neighbours' doors while she screamed down the phone for the police.

When the Bill rocked up, they took the place apart. Searched the garden, the shed, the cars, everything. Everything but nothing. Then the fire brigade.

Then finally the fireman who heard mewling like a newborn kitten's; how on earth had they not heard it first? Who traced the sound to the chimney breast in Charlie's room.

When they shone a light up inside, there was Charlie. Trapped in the chimney, he couldn't move up nor down. He said he'd gone to look for the blackbird that took the letters to Father Christmas.

They'd had to sledgehammer the brickwork away to get him out. He was blackened and bleeding, but he didn't cry.

Nina stuck him straight in a hot bath, warmed his favourite blue PJs with the little sailing boats on, and brushed his wet hair. The doctor came round to check him out, but there wasn't so much as a scratch on him.

James would never forget his little face that night, as they snuggled him in bed between them. That was the Charlie he still saw. Even as he stood there on the pool terrace earlier that day, two or three inches inches taller than him and with a world to go and find, he was still his little boy.

'Everything'll be fine when you get back,' James had said, slapping him.

'If I *come* back,' Charlie grinned.

Was he joking?

CHAPTER FIVE

NINA

Paul Judd is dead.

They found him in Dublin, a weekend too late in his room in a small hotel on the west side.

The maid was used to not being able to get into Mr Judd's room to clean, and didn't give it a thought for two whole days. On the third, she noticed black spots on the clover-coloured carpet. Blood, it looked like, coming from under the occupant's door.

She fell to the front desk. They thought better of going up there, and somebody called the police.

Eyes, heart and larynx torn out. Fingers and thumbs severed. No body parts found, at least not until the post-mortem.

Dear Paul. God help him. It's only a fortnight since Chas in LA – don't tell me there's not a connection.

They must think I was born yesterday.

How long has it been since Paul first took me to Dublin? Early 80s, after I met James the first time, and definitely before Live Aid in '85, so let's say '84. So what would I have been … twenty-three, twenty-four? All so long ago, it's so easy to lose count.

Paul was a huge solo star for about thirty years. Now he's gone. What do I think? What *do* I think? I'm beginning to think I don't even know my name.

We met in London, at the old Marquee Club. I went to see the band he was fronting then. The V-V-Vandals. I was down to interview him after the show, bit of an exclusive, feeling chuffed.

He didn't want to sit in some smoky bar, he said, and anyway he was starving – he never ate before a gig and he was always up for a blowout after one.

We shared roast pork, steamed scallops, sweet and sour chicken and stir-fried veg in a greasy Cantonese off China Town. Christ, I can even remember what we had.

By the time they brought the fortune cookies, I was in his hand. So young, and God, yes, I fell hard.

Larger than life on the streets of Soho, Paul was a legend in Dublin. I can see him now, giant, gushing, stalking the streets in search of the *craic*, clacking the spoons around the Temple Bar pubs, dragging himself out of prize-winning hangovers to the tune of room-serviced full Irish and Black Velvet.

We'd muster strength to face the day, and soon he'd be cramming it again. Davy Byrnes on Duke Street: that was his favourite. The one in *Ulysses*. Once or twice we stopped by for olives with a gorgonzola sandwich and a pint of the burgundy, because 'you just *have* to, Nina, it's really the *point*.'

'*Nice quiet bar*,' he'd quote as we stepped inside. '*Nice piece of wood in that counter. Nicely planed. Like the way it curves there …*'

And then: 'Joyce knew a thing or two, Missy, about the complexity of simplicity.'

Don't tell me.

I can hardly believe it. I close my eyes at the thought, but I know too much. I think I'm going to vomit. I really don't want to go back to the memories of *then*, but I just can't help myself …

~

The V-V-Vandals live are something else. Paul's the ultimate frontman – walking mayhem, he shoves Ozzy and the rest in the shade. Growling and gutting, summoning the gonners, wrenching off his clothes, collapsing to the floor and humping the boards, honking like a seal on heat.

This is the most exciting thing I've seen in years. The guitarists hurl themselves into the audience and tramp about, hacking at their instruments in people's faces, drumming up handclapping and dancing and necking and general wildness, while the drummer climbs on his stool and launches himself across the riser and on top of Paul.

That neither of them smashes his skull is a miracle. Any of this for my benefit? I don't believe so, not from what I've read and heard.

I get a wink, once or twice, but those could easily have been for someone behind me. I'm excited by the show, though; I haven't seen anything quite as mad as this since that early punk scene in New York, which I do still miss from time to time, I've got to admit.

He's not quite pissing in people's beers and having them drink it, but you can't help feeling he'd not only get away with it but have them rocking in the aisles in sheer delight if he did. Paul would get away with anything; he's that kind of guy.

'So, Missy Vincent, very nice to meet you at last,' he quavers, boring my skull with his eyes, reaching for my right hand with his left, twirling the silver ring on the third finger that I never take off, not even sure I could *get* it off. Not anymore.

Without looking, I sense the others in the restaurant draining away, waste water spiralling down a plughole. I feel a distant vibration as the walls fall away. The whole place recedes, until all that's left is the table we're at, with its salmon-pink tablecloth, mounted on a glass, revolving platform like the lazy Susans they bring you to spin your food.

It's as if we are centre-stage at a concert, in the round, a massive venue, all eyes on us. We have morphed into our own audience. We lap up the show, demand encore after encore, applauding ourselves in our minds.

'Your boyfriend give this to you?'

'What? No.'

'What, your boyfriend didn't give it to you, or you've got no boyfriend to give it to you?'

'I *had* a boyfriend,' I say. Why the hell am I blushing? 'But it wasn't him who gave me the ring.'

'You *had* a boyfriend?'

'We broke up.'

'Who chucked who?'

'Does it matter?'

'Always.'

'I think it was me.'

'You *know* it was you,' he retorts, pressing the ring into the thin white flesh above my knuckle.

'Oww!'

'Am I hurting you, baby? Oh, no!' He looks horrified. 'Sorry, sorry, I'd never hurt you. I *promise* I won't. You know, don't you, that I never, ever will. Not on purpose, I really swear.'

'Why?'

'Because *I'm* your boyfriend now. I'm assuming the role, Missy, and just in case you object, where I come from, irrational objection is not allowed.'

It's all Irish, everything about him. The beachy hair, the peaty eyes, that voice, sucky and bog-like – it's as if I'm sinking in it, being swallowed by it whole.

There's something bent and damaged and primeval about Paul. A terrifying urgency. Something raw about the way he shines his spotlight face into mine, trying to make me see inside his brain, or to see into mine.

I know the things he says to me – the things he does to me – are the merest tip. That there's a great volcano inside him, threatening to blow at any moment. He has a pot of gold for a heart, a rainbow for an aura; goodness radiates right out of him, like a fire.

But there's an air of doom about him too, and it makes me want to sob. How has he seen so much, understood so much, at such a young age?

He's not the first guy I've ever been with. I wish. I want so badly for him to be. I adore him with every nerve. Our fibres have knitted together so tightly; we could be wearing each other's souls.

Where does he go? On the road. What do I do? I go with him. Sometimes. Never enough times. The girls get to him in the end. The girls always get to them. That's boys. When you surprise your way into your rock star boyfriend's dressing room in Manchester and find a tweeny blonde on her knees with his Levi's clamped to her ears, you wise up pronto.

Actually, I knew. I was no stranger to it. Had I allowed myself to think about what happened down that tunnel in time, when things were blacker than they could get, I might have twigged that not even the past could have made me immune.

~

I can't think about Paul anymore. I won't. It's not going to bring him back.

I'm a bit in denial, I suppose, if I'm honest. I'm concentrating on something I *can* do something about, so I'm being mad at Bill for humiliating me. I'm refusing to take his calls.

The excuses Allegra's been coming up with are priceless; Phil should stick her on a contract on Features.

Dearest Bill will get the last laugh, as always. He knows I'll come round in the end. He's well aware that I won't refuse him forever. That I'll say no and I'll say no and I'll say no and I'll say no, and then I'll say yes. This is what guys like him are used to. Maybe money can't me buy love, but it'll cover the rest.

Why am I even bothering with him, then? I sometimes wonder. I seem to have become involved with him by mistake.

We met at a mutual friend's birthday, he twinkled at me over the torte, sidled up and slipped me his card on his way back from the gents, suggested 'a lunch sometime', and before I knew it I was into the twice-weekly romantic dinners, I'd emptied the Rigby & Peller opposite the Harrods entrance on Hans Road and was upping and weekending with him in the sticks.

Way too soon he was declaring undying love – maybe not in so many words but I could tell that he meant to, and had started asking me to move in and grow old with him.

I still can't fathom it. He's been married for a hundred years, to the mother of his two adult sons, both of whom are now hitched with kids of their own. He'll never divorce Lady Litsy (wouldn't you insist on 'Laetitia'?!) for 'tax reasons'. They got as far as the Nisi but never the Absolute. Insists they never will.

What, he says, would be the point of marrying again? He's had his kids, he's past retirement, he's got too many to count on his payroll, why pay more? He had an affair for a decade and a half with a dancer who hung around like a malodorous spaniel waiting for him to dump the wife and make an honest woman of her. About that. He was never going to, she couldn't be *that* short of a fry-up. Eventually it was she who did the dumping, after which she legged it to New York. Too old for Broadway, so she opened a dance school.

He then embarked on a very odd affair with a bony blonde athlete he met at an awards do and moved her into Bladington, but then that went tits up. The next thing some bird pitches up to ruler the place for the new kitchen his housekeeper decides she's got to have, and before you can say waste disposal unit, he and the cookie cutter are under the five-tog, taking somewhat more personal measurements. She saw him coming. Nine months later, out bursts baby Freesia, and he's moving them into Richmond Hill. Didn't last beyond the third birthday. Too panto to be real?

Reader, it happened.

It's flattering to be pursued all over town by a knight of the realm; I won't say it's not. Especially one who won't take no.

Our first date was lunch at one of his clubs, on St Valentine's Day.

He winked as we sat down. 'A very significant date, people say.' What was coming?

'Shall we have champagne to celebrate?'

Four glasses, and then a bottle – what the hell? He ordered for both: Dover sole off the bone, and steamed spinach. He had boiled potatoes and cauliflower cheese on the side. Why do I remember the details?

We melted onto West Street and fell into the Merc. His chauffeur dropped him in Pall Mall, then drove me home. Even though Bill was no longer beside me, I held his hand all the way. Late that night, he called me from the car.

'Tanner is now driving me home from a dinner with the Education Secretary.'

He woke me to tell me this?

'About free schools. Dinner in a private house, only sixteen or seventeen of us. I don't much like these political things, but this one was quite informal. He's a good chap, I enjoy and support him.' God bless the old school tie.

He kept texting me all the next day. How fabulous I'd looked at lunch, how much fun he'd had, what was I doing, what was I wearing, what underneath, when could he see me again. He wouldn't leave me alone. It was like teenagers.

It was always amusing to see his initials pop up on the screen: 'SBH.' Sir Bill Hollins. Not that he calls himself 'Bill'. It's always 'William,' and terribly formal, especially when he's been drinking, when he speaks even more slowly and enunciates every syllable, as if terrified of being caught slurring. As in, 'Hellooo, Ninaaaa. It's *Will*iam here. Trying again. You really are terribly hard to get hold of.'

There is something about him. I look at him in the half-light when we have just made love and he's already nodding off, snoring on his back with his mouth open, making that vaguely diarrhoea-ish smell from the depths of his throat that probably means he ought to have had his tonsils out, donkey's ago.

They couldn't do it now; it would kill him. My grandmother had that op in her forties. It was like prising trees out by the roots, my mother told me … she bled half to death. For a man his age it would be insane.

I know he turns seventy next year, because he bangs on *ad infinitum* about the bloody party, where can he have it, who should he invite, does he ask Rod or Macca or Mick to be the Turn. 'Wait and see which one's still alive when the time comes,' I suggest, to annoy him, because he doesn't find it funny. He's still attractive in his way. Incredibly tall for a start, and solid. I've always adored men who make me feel small, perhaps because, as James would say, I can be such a 'handful'.

'He fills a room with flesh,' wrote some hack or other recently, in a somewhat condescending profile. Bill found that outrageously rude.

His skin is papery, his hairless body pinker than dawn. His paunch droops over the jewels when unsupported, he has a scone of a face, and neck, hands and arms the colour of biscuit. He worries about his skin, rarely exposing it to the sun, of which I approve.

He loves to inhale my nakedness. He relishes the feel of my body, adores me most when I'm freshly bathed and 'all creamed'. He can't get enough of me then, bless him. His thin silver hair is a baby's brush. His eyes are Paul Newman-blue. Kissing him is like eating avocado. He has his good points.

What I wish is that he would quit equating every last celebrity death to his own. The morning he was getting ready for Lady Thatcher's funeral – I declined to go, for obvious reasons, such as, I'm not a bloody hypocrite – he said, 'that could be me in eighteen years.'

I howled.

When news broke of Lou Reed's not entirely unexpected demise, given the existence he'd led, Bill cried, '*See*? I might have only a year or two at the outside. What's Freesia going to do without me? She's only sixteen!'

'For God's sake,' I tell him, '*live*. Just *live*, while you still have the chance.'

The first time Bill and I had dinner together, he took me to The Stable, a nice enough nook close to his place on Richmond Hill. That was when he told me that he can never marry again, because everything's in Lady Litsy's name, and it would be far too costly and complicated to dismantle it all.

I thought, and I said, that it was a bit much to be talking marriage on the second date. He invited me to stay, of course. Men always do this: ask you over to their neck of the woods, tank you to the cap and then expect you to go home to bed with them. I didn't. I was several over the eight and scraped his Corvette with the Jag on the three-point turn. He never said a word and I didn't get arrested.

On we go.

That weekend, he invited me to Somerset. To Bladington, his country estate: a stunning Grade II-listed Georgian manor house in acres and acres, with chapel, stable block, croquet lawn, cricket pitch, orchards and *two* pools. When I arrived I found him ripping papers into a rusty incinerator at the top of the tea lawn behind the apple orchard.

'Burning old love letters from my first girlfriend,' he said. 'Monique, my PA, came across them in a box in the cellar when we were sorting junk. Hundreds of the bloody things, the woman could have re-written *War & Peace*. Thought I'd better get rid of them, before they get rid of me.'

'What do you mean?' I asked.

'Hate to think someone might go public with them after I've gone,' he said. 'Plenty of publishers would have a field day with this little lot. Best deal with it myself.'

He was wearing a lilac shirt with chinos and blue, suede loafers. No socks. As we retraced our steps through the orchard, I noticed for the first time that he was slightly hunched. The balding patch on the back of his head was dear. I reached up and smoothed it. We decided not to swim.

~

OK, I've given him the silent treatment for long enough, and I've given in and started taking his calls again. I didn't last long, only a fortnight. I must be losing my touch in my old age. He's hard to resist, I'm only human, and he clearly doesn't take no for an answer. I have to admit, there is something irresistible about that.

We've necked a couple of stiffeners at The Cricketers and are back at Bill's on Richmond Hill, drinking the view across the terraces. Twickenham Stadium is over there somewhere, he insists.

I take his word for it.

He gets lyrical: 'the turn of October, the resigned look of trees, the green to red and a nod to inevitable winter. The yellow, though draining from the sun, holds light enough to polish the river to a blinding sweep of steel …'

'Get you,' I say.

'The only view in all of England protected by an Act of Parliament,' he whispers in retort, easing off my black, suede, stiletto-heeled boot with one hand.

'Immortalised by Sir Walter Scott in *Heart of Midlothian,* the seventh of his Waverley novels, and by William Wordsworth in his sonnet, June 1820: "*for I have heard the quire of Richmond hill … Chanting, with indefatigable bill*" …'

'And are you?'

'What?'

'Indefatigable, Bill.'

'You're incorrigible.'

'But you like me.'

He peels the other boot. Then he kisses me softly, filling my mouth with wine.

'Reynolds and Turner painted it. Both lived up here. As did Bertrand Russell, as a boy. Glover's Island there, between the locks, that was once called Petersham Ait. Could be Cockney rhyming slang …'

I'm not listening. I mould into his clothedness. But then my mobile rings from my jacket pocket. He sighs, and retreats discreetly, on a mission for more wine.

I answer it.

'You sitting down?' It's Phil. 'You won't believe it …bad news.'

'Don't tell me there's –'

'Roger Blacker. Found by his cleaner in his house in Kent. The wife could be a suspect –she's not been traced – but for the fact that …'

'… that he's been similarly mutilated.' I finish the sentence for him.

'Nothing similar about it. Exact same attack. With the added attraction of the Little Richard. That's gone too. The boy's buggered. You knew him, of course. Commiserations.'

'I didn't say yes.'

'To what?'

'That I knew him.'

'I didn't ask because I know you knew him. It's *you* we're talking. So what are we going to say about it?'

'Let News cover it. It's too heavy for the column.'

'I'm not talking column. There's a feature in this.'

'Speculative. Waste of inches. We've got nothing to go on, Phil. What have the police said? Serial killer? Copycat?'

'You know we can't go there. I'm talking misspent pasts.

Drunkenness, druggery, debauchery. You ate, slept and breathed these people for twenty-odd years. You saw it first-hand.'

'Meaning?'

'You tell me.'

He hangs up before I can reply. I think about calling him back, but then I think better of it. What would I say to him? That I can't possibly write about people I've been so closely involved with? I know precisely what his response would be. That it's a sackable offence.

~

The death of a genius.

It takes you back.

Rock 'n' roll had got very complicated by the early 70s. Too many breakout genres, too inconsistent to last.

Pretty much anyone could master three chords and be gigging on the circuit within the week; it was as loose as that.

Thanks to the Beatles, every boy in the land was trying to be in a band. Musicianship – the talent to tame an instrument as if it were a wild animal, to command its respect, to get out of it sounds that no one else knew it could make – *that* became dominant.

As virtuoso guitarists go, there was none to touch Blacker. I didn't meet him until after Paul and I broke up, when D.I.Y. were still a struggling college group several years after Roger graduated.

They were thinking of jacking it in, so painfully two-steps-backwards had been their progress.

Then, an extraordinary breakthrough: out of the blue, a replacement lead singer bursting with creativity who muscled in and came on like a moonstruck clown, with an extraordinary five-octave range and a manner with an audience that took them up a notch, and made the mainstream notice them. Robbie was just what Roger and the boys needed. Success came as a relief, especially to him.

I was sent to interview Robbie and Roger – it was how we met, at their threadbare little offices on the wrong side of Wandsworth.

I was a 'rock and pop writer' on a bestselling tabloid shifting a couple of million a day, at a time when newspapers had just woken up to the mileage to be had from musicians. One or two of the red tops even hosted their own pop awards.

D.I.Y. were celebrating 'Hanging Gardens', their first Number One. It was an audio-obscurity the BBC didn't have a clue what to do with, but which commercial radio wet itself over and which the kids made a hit, simply by racing each other down to Woollie's with their pocket money and buying it. Don't look back.

We hit it off, they invited me on the road to a rockfest in Italy, Roger asked me out to dinner. Rebound, you're thinking? Look, it was the world I moved in. These were the people I met. Times were different. No AIDS yet. It doesn't mean I didn't love him.

It doesn't mean I didn't still love Paul.

~

'A penny?'

Bill wraps me in his liver-y leather jacket, helps me up, leads me gently from the drawing room.

I welcome the reassuring bulk of him beside me in the dimmed bedside light.

'Oh,' I say eventually, with a sigh. 'Horrible. Not you. We were talking about Chas and Paul. There's been another one.'

'Roger Blacker.'

'How did you know?'

'Overheard. Got a very loud voice, your editor.'

'Sorry.'

'Not at all. It's shocking. Awful. I feel as though I ought to be calling people. I knew them well too, you know. Roger played guitar with a rather good R & B outfit at my first wedding.'

'Your only wedding.'

'Indeed.'

~

Later I wonder how much he knows. I stare at him in the half-light as he fades to sleep. He can never stay awake on his back for long. I find myself wondering if he takes Viagra. How would you *know*? Do I know him well enough to share the past? To get the skeletons out? He tells me he loves me.

How could a man like him love a woman enough to accept all that?

It's not dignified. He dines with Her Majesty. He's old school. Even his 'rocktaculars' could be staged in St Paul's. So darling in his sinusy way.

If I write the reveal-all, the one Phil is about to demand, I'll be pilloried, and not just in *Private Eye.* It will embarrass Bill terminally.

They'll accuse me of jumping on the bandwagon, of betraying the families, of being another hideously confessional Fleet Street *grotesque*.

I'm halfway through a divorce, which I can hardly bring myself to think about. James's lawyer could probably use it against me. Accuse me of demeaning the marriage and corrupting our son, or something equally damaging.

I could talk it through with Neal, I suppose. But the bottom line is, I have to think of Charlie, who is heaven-knows-where on earth right now, doing God-knows-what with Lord-knows-who.

I need my son to come back to me. When he's ready. However long it takes. There's only one thing for it, in that case. I'm going to have to zip it.

CHAPTER SIX

NINA

I don't go to too many gigs these days. You can have too much of a good thing. Besides, I'm too bloody knackered most of the time. My days spent fighting my way through platoons of paying punters with plastic pint beakers of slopping beer and piss-warm wine in their hands to reach the VIP area but then having to queue with the drunks for the same shitty toilets are far behind me.

Do I sound up myself? Sorry. I don't mean to. Live gigs were my *job*. No one could accuse me of not having done my share.

What were the stand-outs? This is something I always get asked in interviews. You sit down with some child from somewhere like the NME – I did one recently with *High Voltage* magazine in LA … lovely girl, called me a 'legend', *yeah* baby – and they want you to name your 'all-time top-ten live shows'. Groan. So hard to say, too many to choose from; I probably can't remember half of them. All I can say about those is I bet they were fun.

Bowie at Madison Square Garden, the Serious Moonlight tour, 1983: that was a trip. I always used to say 'because I met my husband-to-be on the plane going over', but I don't say that anymore, for all the obvious. I still have the set list for the show. Gorgeous Carlos Alomar, we're still in touch, and Earl Slick, ex-New York Doll … didn't we have a ton to talk about.

I interviewed David in his dressing room, pre-show – he always preferred to do the chats early, get them over with – and we all had dinner together afterwards.

I was invited back out to the last gig on that tour, at the Hong Kong Coliseum in Hung Hom. The show coincided with the third anniversary of John Lennon's death.

David and Slick were thinking of playing 'Across the Universe' as a tribute, but then David said, if we're going to do it at all, we should probably do 'Imagine'.

They rehearsed the song in Bangkok and performed it in Kowloon. It was from heaven.

David was looking right through me as they sang it; I could feel his odd eyes drilling a fire exit through the back of my skull. I've always wondered. Did he know something?

'Listen to it,' he'd remarked, as he passed me in the corridor backstage, pre-soundcheck.

Listen to *what*? What did he know?

Could he tell that underneath my impassive exterior, I was a wormery of guilt?

What else? The Who revisiting 'Tommy' at the Universal Amphitheater LA, 1989, one of my last before I came off the road full-time. A charity gig, unforgettable.

'Have a little respect, it's a fuckin' *opera*!' Pete said Keith Moon would have told the crowd. Elton, Steve Winwood, Phil Collins, Billy Idol and the rest performed with Pete, Roger and John. They'd just parted company with Kenney Jones after a decade, sadly, so Simon Phillips was on drums. The after-show was a train wreck, I lost three days.

The Stones, 1982, for *Tattoo You*, an extension of their massive arena tour across America the previous year. The tour on which Keith whacked a fan.

Hampton Coliseum Virginia, December 1981. This guy leapt out of nowhere and came charging across the stage towards Mick during 'Satisfaction' – God knows where the hell security were.

Keith walloped him with his black Fender Telecaster and carried on playing as the guards woke up and manhandled the guy off. The guitar stayed in tune, too! He'd never get away with that now – there'd be aggro left and right, and Keith would probably wind up in clink.

Memorable for all kinds of other reasons, that tour, but this is a family show. Keith was off the smack, he'd cleaned up, he was singing and playing better than ever. Drowning out Jagger, at times, though better not say that, had I. Turned out to be their last road trip for about seven years. The European leg opened May '82 in Aberdeen, but I didn't get to

Scotland; I was up to no good elsewhere.

I caught up with them in Rotterdam that June, playing the Feyenoord, then hit the road with them for about a week: Hannover's Niedersachsenstadion, Berlin's Waldbühne, the Olympiastadion in Munich.

I did the interview with Keith and Mick in Paris, after their show at the Hippodrome d'Auteuil. Keith was animated, high on nothing but adrenalin. I don't remember Mick bleating two words. He was game for a dance, though.

Live Aid, of course. 1985. Queen stole it. Who remembers much else about that day? We remember Bowie, all cool in his powder-blue suit. The sound going down on The Who. Phil Collins catching the Concorde to perform at JFK Stadium in Philadelphia, right after Wembley.

Paul McCartney playing live for the first time since John died, and his piano mic going down at the start, and Geldof, Bowie, Pete Townshend and Alison Moyet singing back-up on 'Let it Be'. Madonna's gravity-defying antics, le Bon's bum note of all time, on 'A View To a Kill'.

But it was Queen and Freddie Mercury who owned Live Aid.

I saw Prince play an impromptu gig at the Kensington Roof Gardens, I can't remember what year, but is was unforgettable. Saw INXS the first time at the Montreux Rock Festival in 1986, and couldn't take my eyes off Michael Hutchence. Ten sex symbols for the price of one in a white jeans jacket and smudgy strides. So much of the Jagger about him even then; even the hands were hypnotic.

What about women? Tiny Pat Benatar. Tina. Whitney. Dolly. Debbie. My favourite Blondie show was Hammersmith Odeon, January 1980; all the girls fell for Debs that night. 'One Way or Another', remember that? Those guitar chords still thwang in my brain. So many shows, so little time. Moving on.

I couldn't do it now. You'd be lucky to get me down to the Indigo 02 to see Colin Blunstone and Rod Argent. Actually I *did* go to that one last year, for old times' sake – can't let the good old boys down. What about Colin's voice, then? Still got it. But still a hell of a schlep for an old bird, that venue, and the parking's a curse.

Having said all that, tonight I'm going to a gig that I could well do without. But it's only an early at Ronnie's, and I have to be in Soho later anyway. I know the promoter. Who doesn't? Gorgeous Sian and I go way back. I owe her a favour. A few, possibly. She's been raving on to me about this little girl for months.

I mentioned her before, didn't I? Roxy Rome. The Californian songstress with the Bambi legs, camel eyelashes, buttercup curls, Seventies maxis. Looking exactly how we all used to look, in our virginity. Still only twenty-something, she'll have won everything within the year, I'd put money on it. More emotion, truth and pain in that voice than in Aretha's. But how much of that is created in the studio? Can this bimbo deliver live? Not too many doing it for real nowadays. They all pray to Auto-Tune.

Ronnie Scott's is an odd choice for her first London showcase, it's got to be said. Better than it was, since Sally Greene's refurb a few years back. At least she got rid of that manky carpet, host to the ghost of Dizzy Gillespie's puke.

They've moved the bar and the food looks half-edible, I haven't tried it myself but the reviews weren't bad. They've retained the brothel-red lighting and the low ceiling, sensibly, to preserve the club's intimacy. They've respected the sound, too. I take it back; all in all, it's a good place to see a new sensation.

This kid could probably sell out the 02 Arena already, but there's a subtle art to a rock career. It's about pacing, timing, building the buzz. If she's to have longevity, it's going to have to be earned. What the fans don't know is that it's all a tease, a cynical seduction. Start small, get people talking, sell out the clubs, put it about that half the tickets will be available on the door on the night, then make sure most of the punters who turn up can't get in.

She's bound to make the front page of a couple of the red tops tomorrow, though it depends what happens tonight, which celebrities turn up. Plus all the music press. Radio will be all over this, too. So far, so according to plan.

~

Ronnie's is heaving when I arrive. I almost pass out pushing my way through the crowd.

The record industry and its mistress are out in force, which is always a good sign. Always a wonder the place can cram this many in.

They're doing all the right things, I'll say that for them. Developing demand, slowly but surely. Feed a steady flame and she could burn eternal. Fire it too fast and it'll flare and snuff. I should write lyrics. It's not an exact science – showbiz can't be, and it can so often backfire, heaven knows. But if anyone knows what she's doing, Sianie does. She's been at it long enough.

The first time I met her, she was still an in-house photographer at EMI. She reinvented herself as a record plugger and fell on her feet. With her Whitechapel wit and gift of the gab, not to mention the medieval hair and the gravity-defying boob job, she was in demand all over the place.

I'm late, I'm stressed, I'm wearing all the wrong clothes.

'Vinnie!'

Her nickname for me.

'Sianie!'

'Good to see ya, kid. Been effin ages. Lookin lovely, as always. You're late, you're stressed, you're dogged up in all the wrong gear, babe.'

'You read my mind.'

'When didn't I? Thought I'd get it in before you did. What you 'avin?'

'Pint of Ribena, darl, any colour.'

'Good of you to grace us with your presence.'

'That's what they all say.'

'I said it first.'

She slides her arm around my shoulders and zigzags me through the squeeze towards a table on the far left-hand side of the tiny stage. It's set up for drums, guitar, bass, keyboards and a couple of backing vocalists. Gonna be full, gonna be loaded. No sign of the main event.

'I thought I was late!'

'I delayed it specially for you, Vin.'

'You didn't!'

'I didn't!'

I thump her on the arm.

Someone gets up, sleazes an intro, and the crowd responds with uproarious applause. They're raring to go now. Her band take to the stage and the venue goes gorilla.

After about three minutes, Roxy inches on and she's *pint*-sized, knotted into ethereal emerald chiffon and wearing a little black raffia top hat. Stevie Nicks rides again.

When she parts her lips to sing, I half-expect Stevie's miraculous Orson-Wells-on-helium gurgle. But this is sleigh bells, compared. A little thin and wobbly to start with, she sparrows it a bit until she finds her groove. Maybe she should have warmed up more. Perhaps the pitch is a bit off, too. Could be nerves, the airways seizing.

Three songs in and you know you've heard better singers. Technically, I mean. But you also know this is the real deal. Her vulnerability's knocking them dead. There's an aura about her, something strange and off-the-wall. Something supernatural. I can't put my finger on it. Can I? It's deceptive, it's dangerous, and can I say this – anyway I'm going to – she reminds me of *me*. Not that I could sing for Callard & Bowser's. *All* these twenty-something songbirds remind us old birds of ourselves in our heyday. Is this the first sign of ageing?

Don't.

'I'll introduce you after,' Sian stage whispers.

'I won't have time, babe. I've got to make a publishing reception in Regents Park by eight, then back over Dean Street to the Groucho by nine. I'd say bring her in after you've finished with this lot, but I've got a dinner.'

'We could all have dinner?'

'Can't, darl, wish I could, truly. But Bill Hollins is hosting …'

'How *is* the old slapper?'

'Throbbing on.'

'You've seen this?'

'You don't wanna know.'

'I so do!'

'To be continued.'

'Pig. Snogs to Sir Billiam, can't remember the last time. Sure we can't kill two vultures with one boulder?'

'Don't think it'd be up your *strasse*, this one. I've only got to sit there for two hours with some bishop he picked up in the south of France.'

'Nooo! In the *Grouch*? Heard it all now. Real-life vicars 'n' tarts!'

'In one.'

'Stephen Fry and Keith Allen will be havin' heart failure.'

'No comment.'

'Look, don't worry, darlin' … do it another time, OK?'

'How long's she in for? She's perfect, by the way. This could be the icing on your cake, Sian.'

'Not before flamin' time.'

'Look, I'd love to interview her for the paper, but you wouldn't believe it, I'm on the first plane to New York in the morning. Got an exclusive with Bin Biddulph …'

'That muppet reckons he made a comeback from the Bermuda Triangle, wrote the bestseller with the Bazzer Manilow title?'

'"Try to See it From My Angle". Exactly. Him.'

'You get all the good jobs.'

'So they tell me.'

Sian opens her mouth, thinks better of it, closes it again. A gag too far. She refills my glass from her own, despite my protests, then announces:

'"Make every moment of your life count; you never know when you'll get sucked in." And I quote.'

'Don't, I'm having a job and a half taking this one seriously as it is.

Perhaps I could do something with Roxy when …'

'Leaving tomorrow, darlin'. Crack of dawn.'

'How *is* Dawn?'

'How did I know you were gonna say that? We've got showcases all over: Oslo, Stockholm, Paris, Munich, Barcelona, Rome. Only a ten-day meet-and-greet.'

'Cheapskates.'

'Not like the good old days, me old mucker. The budget won't stretch to it. Her manager's as tight as a mallard's crack.'

'Aren't they all.'

'It's on the plane and A to Zee before you hit B nowadays. Remember when we used to do Land's End to John O'Groats in the Bronze Records Learjet with Alice Cooper for three never-knowingly-sober weeks at a stretch?'

'How could I forget?'

'And the snake.'

'How could I forget the bloody snake?'

'Talking of reptiles. I didn't tell you who Roxy's manager is, did I?' Sian asks.

'I'm listening.'

'All very hush-hush, they haven't announced it yet. You won't believe it, either.'

'Suspense is killing me.'

'Clive Clifford.'

'I'll get my coat.'

~

I make the flight by the skin of my teeth, the morning after a laugh and a half with the Bish, who was a game old boy as it turned out, and an if-but night with Bill.

Don't go there. I've got a monumental hangover. I've been trying to flush it out in the Ladies. I'm the last one to board. At least I'm in Club and I've only got hand luggage.

I bung my bag in the empty locker above my seat. I can't help thinking of James as I do this, how he always used to smack his head on the door of the overhead. Christ, *every* time … when would he learn? Bound to be never … probably still doing it.

I wonder where he is. I don't even know where he's living. How is that possible?

I fasten my belt and it's as if he's here beside me. Rubbing his forehead sheepishly. Reaching for my hand.

I think of him every time I get on a plane. Hard not to when you met in the sky.

I re-live the 'eyes' moment, feel the fizz up my spine and the light go on in my head and his hand on my arm. I can *smell* him. It's not a scent I recognise. It doesn't seem very 'him'.

He jokes that it's a Ferrari car-deodoriser someone gave him for Christmas, 'for the man who has everything'.

I laugh out loud at the memory. I see his Disney face, the skewy smile, the unbleached-linen teeth, the too-symmetrical features.

The thing is, I knew. I knew the moment our eyes locked that he was the one for me, that I would marry this man. How ridiculous is that? I did, though.

Every hope and dream I'd ever had for my life made sense in that earth-splitting moment. I'm going to marry him. Maybe not now, maybe not for a few years, we're still young, there's still stuff to do.

We'll eat supper in some unpretentious place and he'll walk me back, but he won't kiss me goodnight; he'll go to shake hands and then realise that's stupid and look all awkward, and I'll laugh and he'll nip me on the cheek and leg it.

We'll meet up again the next day, or the day after, maybe have a wander over the park if the weather's still nice … no reason why it shouldn't be.

We'll stop off at the boathouse for a drink, use the loos, steal some crusts of bread left over from lunch off the tray on the side when the barman isn't looking, and feed the green turtles, and he won't let go of my hand.

He'll invite me out in a while, won't he? We'll go out again after that, maybe to the gig, if I can bag another ticket. Maybe a couple more times, but nothing will happen, we'll both hold back.

We'll be cool. Maybe I'll ask him to go back there with me. To West 72nd Street, to the Dakota. I haven't been up there in three years. Or maybe not yet. One of us will have to leave before the other.

We'll plan on hooking up back in London. It'll get a bit intense, it'll be amazing, neither of us could ever have imagined that it could *be* quite like that. I won't think about anything else, I'll want him all the time.

And then the tide will go out. That's the rhythm, isn't it? The way these things work? Why, when it couldn't be more perfect? Because we'll both know that it's too much. Too soon. Not ready. Not yet. But neither of us will want to be the one to end it. So one of us simply won't call back one day, and the other one won't wonder. We'll get it, we'll leave it, and then it'll simmer down. No argument, no tears, no stalking, no sleepless nights, no mad stuff. It'll be over, almost as soon as it began.

But he'll be back. Or I will. The ending is never the end.

There's still the fat lady.

CHAPTER SEVEN

MONTREUX

'Fuckin' Disneyland for fuckin' grown-ups.'

'Don't knock it.'

''Til you've tried it.'

'Moaning again, are we? There was a time you said you'd give anything to wake up to this every day. Finest view on the planet, for my money.'

'It's *my* money.'

'What's yours is mine.'

'And vice versa. Who made who?'

'Anyway.'

'Meaning?'

'Lot of smoke on that water.'

'Lot of ghosts in that lake.'

'Tell me about it.'

Eddie Laine is standing at the vast picture window of his apartment on Lake Geneva. With his back to his manager, the only other person in the room, he surveys the surreal scene. The morning mists have yawned to reveal a shimmering blur of water that stretches silently towards the Alps.

'Majestic', they always call them, don't they, he thinks. Sod that. From this distance, the mountains look like the worst kind of dental wreckage. What sort of nightmare would that be: a decade's-worth at least of bonding, crowns, veneers and root canals. He knows about this stuff. He's been there. Resisted the gob-work for years, didn't he, but had to give in to it in the end.

He'd been worried it might change his voice or even deprive him of it completely. It happens. He knows he's been lucky. Drifting off last night, moonlit snowcaps winking at him from the black of beyond, he dreamed randomly about a broken tooth.

What the fuck? He couldn't remember doing that before. It unnerved him. What did it all mean? He's been going for dream therapy in LA on and off; it was recommended to him during his last round of rehab. It quite appeals to him. No denying there's something in it, he reckons.

He's got this book, quite good it is. He looked up the tooth thing to find out what it all meant. Broken promises, it said. A lack of balance. Instability. A price to pay for ill-advised compromise.

Load of old tarot, he told himself, yet it still freaked him out. But why? He walks on water bigger than that duck-flea-infested piss-pond down there, doesn't he? Bloody *puces de* fuckin' *canard* – bloody wormy little parasites. Got a nasty rash from them once, years ago, when he was in to play the Golden Rose festival and wound up over the side after too many doubles on Phil Collins's paddle steamer. Swimmers' itch. Fuck that. The irritation drove him deranged for about three weeks. *Lac Le*-bloody-*man,* as they call it round here. Constipated fuckin' Swiss Rolls are fuckin' welcome to it.

Where was he? Sizing himself up. He's a global superstar, a legend in his lifetime; even the records he made in the late 60s still sell.

All they've got to do is keep repackaging him. Redesign the sleeves, stick a couple of bonus tracks on, a touch of the old Never Before Released, maybe a few 'rare out-takes' and a bit of old chat they pretend has surfaced on the end of some rehearsal tape from the 70s, previously believed lost – amazing what turns up in the skip when you're having a clear-out – and the mugs are rushing to buy the bloody albums in droves. Even though they've got everything he's ever recorded in other formats already.

It makes you a bit cynical, Eddie thinks, and he doesn't much like that about himself. But old Clive comes up with these ideas all the time, and not even Eddie can say no to Clive Clifford. Not after all these years. He does resent the fact that Clive controls his life, of course he does, but what's he gonna do?

He'd be Turpin without the Dick without the old bastard. He wouldn't know where to start. He couldn't be bothered, more to the point, and he could hardly cope on his own, could he? The empire would collapse. He's been dependent on Clive for, what, must be the best part of fifty years. How the fuck could he call it a day with him and begin again with someone else? Who *with*? Most persuasive bastard in the business, old Clive is, and that's an understatement. But you know what they say: better the devil you know.

It wasn't Eddie's idea to do this new album and tour. He'd been quite happy languishing in semi-retirement with his fourth wife and yet another set of kids, reappearing at locations around the globe to play the occasional benefit gig or a charity concert, having learned his lesson the hard way after telling Geldof to have a shit, shower and a shave in 1985.

Live Aid? Don't mention the fuckin' war. But he has to admit, Clive knows what he's doing.

This whole comeback caper has been inspired. They release this new studio album of original tracks after more than three decades. He even wrote a couple of them himself. OK, *co*-wrote them. It implies on the sticker on the front that the songs are all his own work, but who's to know?

It shot straight to Numero Uno regardless, didn't it?

He announces a comeback tour and every UK show is sold out within fifteen minutes. Faster than a fart, in the States. Australia and New Zealand, Europe, Far East, South America; the entire planet seems to be back under his spell. What's not to like?

So why the hell does he feel so insecure?

It's his fear of failing health that's doing it. Has he still got what it takes to go on the road for the best part of two years? He's doubtful. His ticker's been dodgy. Look what happened to Michael Jackson: no way was he ever gonna manage that punishing schedule at the 02, little wonder he was knocking back the smarties.

That, and the ageing thing. There's no denying it. It comes to us all, Eddie knows, even rock superstars.

He knows his money can't buy him eternal youth. He knows, but he can't come to terms with it. In his head he's still a shit-hot Jack the Lad.

Facing up to the diminution of what he once was is the door he's never going to open.

Now that he's back, the desire to recapture himself at his peak is what drives him.

Drives all us old rock 'n' roll cunts, he thinks. We're all the fuckin' same. Not that we'll ever admit it. But anyway, getting back to this tooth business.

A bit scary, innit? What else is a broken tooth but a symbol of loss?

Clive Clifford has barely changed position on Eddie's long, grey, leather sofa since he came up from his own apartment one floor down, more than an hour ago. Eddie's glad. Not that he's scared of Clive, not anymore, but he can kid himself he has the upper hand when his manager's sitting down.

He can't really explain it, he'd tell you until he's blue in the face that psychology's a load of old cobblers, while privately conceding there's probably something in it. It's just that Clive's such a *big* bastard. Got to be six foot four if he's an inch, and not exactly a bag of bones, is he? Could probably shoulder a brick shithouse down if you jumped the queue in front of him. Wouldn't put it past him.

Eddie knows not to even try.

He turns away from the lake to look at Clive, and sees what he always sees: someone much older than the Clive his mind's eye remembers. Someone much *less*.

Eddie clings to the long blonde hair and crispy tan of Clive's extended youth. The kaftans, the beads, the stinking sheepskin waistcoat, the hippy jeans with the little triangles of orange and brown curtain material sewn in the sides.

He sees deals spilling out of those dark, cauldron eyes, pink-rimmed and virtually lash-less. He hears a voice crackling with risk. Recalls a man incapable of keeping still, who's all over the room at once, more fizz than an FA Cup final. A quick, cantankerous, ruthless sod with flaring nostrils and a nose for blood, ready for the charge.

Eddie needs to see *that* Clive, not *this* Clive, for a reason he could never own up to. Clive as he was equals Eddie as he was. Who's kidding who?

Clive's still sat there, droning on in his stupid little yellow felt cap. It covers his big bald patch and what's left of his scrubby barnet. Look at his big flaky ears and his soppy dog lips. Imagine kissing the bastard. Second thoughts, after *you. He's* talking tour dates, destinations, promotion and security, which are more important than ever after what's been going on.

Who can believe it? Eddie can picture his old mate Chas as if it were yesterday. He can see him right here, as it happens.

Montreux was where they first met: in that manky truck Mick and Keith and the lads used to have. 'The mobile', they called it, parked up beside the casino with the all-guzzling, all-snorting recording studio inside. What didn't go on in there …

Maybe that, subconsciously, is why Eddie chooses to be here now. Touching base with his old partner-in-crime, if only on a spiritual level, as well as keeping his head down. He can hardly forget there's a killer out there, can he? A killer who's been chopping up his mates.

So what's that about? Some rank freakin' groupie with a grudge, he wouldn't mind betting. Some screw-loose slapper with a moth-eaten fanny and a whopping great axe to grind.

His eyes water as he runs the details past himself again. He imagines how much it must hurt to have your eyeballs gouged out, not to mention your Jolly Roger torn off. He winces.

Had she been on a bender down the local butcher's? Did she torture them before she did them in? He could be next, for fuck's sake.

He can't let it get to him; he's got to keep his head. They're in one of the safest havens on earth right now. He's never on his own; he's under closer observation than Her Majesty's best titfer. Rochelle and the kids are safely tucked up at home, and he's got armed bodyguards ferrying the boys to and from school. Never take their eyes off them. They're better off in LA than being dragged out of school and their routine and halfway round the world, he reasons. Clive's taken care of all that. Clive takes care of everything. Not that Eddie likes it, can't much change it. We are where we are.

Deep Purple put this beautiful little town on the map when they made *Machine Head* here in 1971, he remembers. One of the greatest albums of all time. Ian Gillan, what the hell's happened to the old sod? RIP

Lordy; what a gent Jon was.

So after *Machine Head* and *Smoke on the Water*, written after a fan fired a flare gun at a Frank Zappa gig in the Casino and the place went up like bonfire night, every rocker on earth wanted to record here. It just had a magic, the place. A different sound.

What was it, something in the water? Were there sirens in the lake? It's said to be as deep as the Alps are high. Or is it just the squeaky mountain air? Who knows? Can't put his finger on it. Nor can anyone else. But almost any artist could get a sound in this place in the good old days that was almost spookily, brilliantly, a cut above everything they'd done before.

He swoons at the memory of *Bonzo's Montreux*, John Bonham's drum solo, recorded at Mountain Studios in, what, must have been about '76. Off the album *Coda*. Jimmy put the electrics on after. Then Freddie and the boys bought the studios two years later, and a whole new era was born.

Freddie Mercury. It pains Eddie to wander down the Place du Marché and see the bronze statue that is all that's left of his old mate, where the fans all leave their little posies and coloured notes and diaries and flags and scarves and photographs and the bottles of wine they were drinking the night before.

Poor old Freddie, peering out into oblivion. From the place where he felt more at home than anywhere else in his life.

Local rumour has it that an urn containing his ashes was dropped in the lake from a rowing boat one night, by a woman who was the spitting image of that girlfriend of his. People say they can pick up Freddie's spirit here. Wishful thinking?

As much as he wants to believe it, Eddie's inclined to think that once you're done, you're gone.

Mind you, Queen aren't doing so badly for themselves all these years on, are they? Could that be the secret of immortality? Live fast, die young, leave a beautiful corpse, as James Dean probably never said – ? Just saying. Jesus.

None of the obituaries he'd read did justice to the genius with the gnashers. 'Bucky', they used to call him at school, Freddie once told him.

'Bucky'. Bloody hell. Eddie called him 'darling', which was what Freddie called *him*. He'd say they were good friends; yeah, course he would. Not that he'd ever been privy to the inner workings of his convoluted mind, understand. He has to wonder, though: had *anyone*?

Eddie shudders. He doesn't want to think about it. He doesn't want to think about anything right now. It's got to be time for a drink.

'I thought we might go for an amble,' says Eddie to Clive, bouncing on Nike'd heels and knitting his shoulder blades.

'A pleasant little stroll down the Blanc Gigi?' Clive grins, then rises to his feet.

'Why not? he asks. 'I could do with a pint and a sarnie. You wanna talk press?'

'I'm not doing any fuckin' press,' says Eddie.

'I thought …'

'Look, man, you know what it's gonna be. All they're interested in is Chas and Paul and Roger, how well I knew 'em, spill a bit of dirt, how fuckin' terrified I am that I might be next. Asking for it, innit. Come and get me, you murderous fuckin' slag, let me give you my address and phone number while I'm on. Oh, and my private email. Oh, and while we're down there, here's where you can find my wife and kids. An' all me previous wife-and-kids.'

'What makes you think the killer's a woman?'

'Ploughman's lunch. Hunch. I feel it in me water. It's gotta be. Who else would have the kind of unchallenged access this whore's getting? I can well imagine it; I've been there ten thousand times. Tart dolls herself up to the fuckin' nines, stalks you into a hotel bar or some strip joint, comes on all irresistible, promises the best blow you've ever had, worms her way back to yours. I can see it now. There she goes, onto his boat, into his hotel room, into his own fuckin' house while the wife's away, for Christ's sake. Pulls out the plums, shows him half a good time, then Bingo, they're down the carvery and he's the main course.'

'You could have written the script.'

'I *am* the fuckin' script.'

'Well, you don't have much to worry about. I've got it covered. We've got muscle and ammo all over the Riviera. Border guards and Swiss military at the airports, private security everywhere else, including on every floor of this building. I've even got snipers in two lake-view suites at the Montreux Palace.'

'Nice work if you can get it. All on a handsome bung, presumably.'

'What do *you* think? Nobody works for nothing.'

'Not even me.'

'*Especially* not you.'

'You think I'll be all right, Clive?'

'Look, you're not even going for a piss on your tod.'

'There is that. How very reassuring. Anyway, as I was saying. We don't need press. The album's through the roof, the promoters have flogged every venue, we're looking at putting on more dates, you *said*, right? All we've got to do now is approve a few T-shirts, yeah? Let the press make the fuckin' interviews up. It's what they do best.'

~

Clive sits grinning to himself. The response is exactly as he'd expected. He can more or less read Eddie's mind. They have known each other their entire adult lives; he's had him from day one. It is what it is.

It's symbiotic. Clive the drop-out politics student, a wizard self-taught accountant, the fiercest dealer in the business, a genius at working the money angle to his own best advantage, then his client's. They even call him 'the Mafia' in the trades. Eddie the sexagenarian playground rocker, the talent, the package, the biz. The voice: gravel-in-a-biscuit-tin, a knock-out blend of blues and rock. The look: post-coital hair, robust little frame, a casual, blokey style that dresses up or down as required. His passion for football and cricket: he'll always turn out for a charity match, which has been fantastic for profile and goodwill. His cheeky-chappy gobbiness that makes him a chat-show host's dream. Perhaps the secret of Eddie, Clive thinks, is that he appeals to men as much as to women. The girls want to bang him senseless, the guys want to pile out on the pull with him. It was never just a knicker-throwing exercise, this. The lads got him too. They still do.

What Clive will never admit to his charge – he can barely even admit it to himself – is just how much he envies his turn's global fame and sex appeal. The older Clive gets, the more it irritates him, annoyingly. He knows he should have his head round it after the best part of fifty years.

'Smile,' he says to Eddie, watching the apartment lift door drag open.

'What about?'

'You're on *Candid Camera*.'

'*What* … ?!'

'April Fool. You've got everything to laugh about, you should be splitting your sides. You're on the verge of becoming the biggest star in the history of rock. There'll be no one to touch you.'

'Not hard,' scoffs Eddie. 'Not if this bird keeps knockin' off the competition. The way things are going, there'll be no one left. Not even me.'

CHAPTER EIGHT

NINA

I'm missing Charlie. It's a physical ache, a pain in the guts, and it's hurting me. It has me waking in the night, the way I used to when he first started going out in the evenings with his friends.

I'd lie there glued to my phone, imagining all kinds. He'd be under a bus, crushed in a car, lying mashed all over a rail track having jumped the level crossing, been snatched off the streets by paedophiles or knife-brandishing gangsters or terrorists. He'd have killed himself diving off a bridge, just for the fun of it. He'd have vanished without trace with a bunch of circus gypsies, never to be seen nor heard of again.

I'd sit there worrying myself bald. James would pour us both a glass of wine, but neither of us could ever bring ourselves to drink it, just in case Charlie called and needed us to go and fetch him from somewhere. In case the police phoned, or the hospital, or one of his mates. Telling us the worst.

The old agonies are on a never-ending loop, they torment me constantly. Is this just motherhood?

I sometimes catch myself wondering whether James does this too. I try not to think about him most of the time, the cheating scumbag, but whenever I do, it's almost always concerning Charlie.

I know they've just seen each other in LA; I got a curt email from James, saying he seems fine – if a bit vague and non-committal.

Oh, Charlie, Charlie; I know you're angry and upset about the whole divorce thing, but you could *call* me. *Please*. I'm paying for your damned phone, but it's never switched on when I ring.

If only you knew the things that go through my mind. What the hell happens, that I can be dragged out of nowhere into a blind-panic re-run of random memories for no apparent reason? Why am I forced to relive old anxieties all the time when I've got so many other things to worry about?

For example, this one, that recurs like a nightmare and that I remember word for word, as if I learned the dialogue from a bloody script: the time I couldn't find him outside school all those years ago, when I thought I was meeting him at 4.30 p.m. after a piano lesson, and 4.30 p.m. came and went. As did 5 p.m. It was already dark and I was frantic.

I called the school.

'Hello, I'm sorry to bother you. I'm waiting on Parkside for Charlie Kendal: would he happen to be there in reception, by any chance? I'm his mother.'

'No, Mrs Kendal, I'm afraid he's not here. Does he have an after-school activity today?'

'Piano. He had a piano lesson. Any chance you could try the music school?'

'I'll give them a call. OK to hang on a moment?'

'Of course.' Precious moments, ticking.

'I'm sorry, they're not answering, they must have gone home. What year is he in again?'

'Year nine, it's …'

'Charlie Kendal, Year nine … just making a note of your number, so I've got it to hand. Just having a look on the screen here … Yes, he's definitely marked present at registration after lunch. Have you tried any of his friends at all?'

'I don't have their numbers, I'm afraid.'

'OK. Don't go worrying, Mrs Kendal, I'm sure there's a simple explanation. Might he have gone up to St Paul's for the choir rehearsal?'

'He's not in the choir.'

'OK. I'm trying the art room now, then I'll call the library, the sports centre, the …'

'We're going to have to call the police!'

'Please calm down, Mrs, erm, I'm sure there's a …'

'... simple explanation, yes, you said. I don't know what to do.'

I wasn't even trying to stop myself crying. By the time I'd moved the car into the overflow car park and rushed into reception, my face and shirt were a mascara-stained wreck. Not that you give a toss what you look like at times like this ...

Danny! There was Danny, Charlie's best friend, running red-faced from the orchestra rehearsal with his trombone case under his arm.

'Danny!'

'Hello, Mrs –'

'Charlie! Have you seen Charlie anywhere, Dan? We've been looking for him all over the place; nobody seems to know where he's gone. It's so not like him to go off without telling me. He always calls me to let me know if there's been a change of plan and he's got to stay late or anything, you know he does. Has he gone back with someone, do you think? Did he say anything to you?'

'No ... no, he ...'

'When did you last see him?'

'In the changing room ... at about four o'clock.'

'What was he changing for? Where was he going, Dan?'

'I don't know ... I don't think he ...'

'*Think*, sweetheart.'

'*Rock-climbing*! There's a rock-climbing thing, I think he said in Tunbridge Wells ... there was a coach leaving.'

'Tunbridge Wells! What the f– ... Sorry, sorry, I don't know anything about this ...'

'Charlie's not on the coach list for Tunbridge Wells,' butted in the receptionist.

'I wonder why ...'

'Is there a way of getting hold of the teacher who's gone with them? Find out if he's on board? When do I get him back?'

'They're due back here at eight.'

'EIGHT!'

~

They were the longest three hours of my life. When the coach finally appeared, I couldn't even be cross with him for not telling me where he'd gone. This was just Charlie being Charlie, complicated, strange, detached little boy that he was.

And people ask me why I never had more children. I used to think about it sometimes, especially at the end, just before the equipment packed up. Unfathomably sad, that made me; I've never quite got my head round it.

James had badly wanted a little girl, and I wouldn't have minded. I do sometimes catch myself wondering what it would have been like to have a daughter. Too late now.

But then I'd multiply the amount of stress and worry since Charlie was born by the so-called 'ideal' number of children you were supposed to want – they used to say four, didn't they? – and I'd have to go and lie down.

I never knew how other women coped. It couldn't all be about nannies and au pairs, could it, supposedly freeing you up to get out there and get on with your job? As if motherhood isn't a 'real' job, a view with which I've always disagreed. To a point.

Where they go wrong, these stay-at-home mums – *and* dads – is that they don't help themselves. They make parenting their *raison d'être.* They lose themselves in it.

When at last they find their way out of the maze – much earlier than they anticipate, because kids grow up so fast these days; by the time they hit fourteen they're pretty much out there, doing their own thing – they find they've lost their identity, if not the will to live.

They have no idea who they are anymore.

In my personal experience, the women most concerned with finding the right help were the ones who rarely ventured beyond the gym or the beauty salon. The employed among us mostly muddled our way through. We got there, didn't we?

Besides, I've never been very good at the whole live-in staff thing, and I'm useless at delegating. I've sacked an agency's worth of cleaners, ironers and gardeners in my time. What's the point in paying these people if they don't do the work as well as *you* do? I've never been afraid of swabbing a kitchen floor, bunging in a casserole, pressing a few shirts.

Margaret Thatcher once told me that whenever she had a problem, she'd stand and do a pile of ironing. By the time she hit the bottom of the basket, she'd have somehow come up with the solution. So, if it was good enough for her …

No, time has always been the issue, but I'm not exactly on my own there, am I? Not just *of* the essence, it *is* the bloody essence. Still. I never left Charlie more than I had to.

I probably never left him enough.

~

'That piece you wrote about the dead rockers.'

There's an editor standing in the door frame of my office, and it's not a pretty sight.

'Yes, boss.'

'Tip of the iceberg, right?'

'Depends what you mean by iceberg,' I say, shaping a smile that never reaches my eyes.

I lean my head on the back of my desk chair and fold my arms. It's an instinctive, very Worst Lady kind of move, this, but I suddenly realise it's defensive body language which he could take the wrong way. It's never a good idea to piss off an editor more than you have to.

I opt for damage limitation, pretending to examine my fingernails, and notice in passing that my gel French manicure is on the way out. Time for a polish, but *when*? This week is just chock.

'I mean,' says Phil, pulling up the spare chair and plonking himself down across from me. He helps himself to a sip from Allegra's holy offering, my foaming mug of cold coffee, knowing that I never touch the stuff, and grimaces.

'I mean,' he repeats, swallowing the liquid as if it were a throat infection, 'is that there is obviously a lot more to this than meets the eye. Three rock musicians die presumably unplanned, identical deaths in far-flung locations which may or may not be significant in themselves: Los Angeles, the leafy 'burbs of London town, and Dublin. What do they have in common? Who would have it in for them? Who did they upset, who did they owe money to, who would deem the world without them a better place?'

'You're asking *me*, Boss?' I reply. 'Like I'd know.'

The look he gives me is one of disbelief.

'Talk me through the possibilities,' he says, gnawing on a flap of skin on the knuckle of his left forefinger. He bites it off, and spits it onto my desk. I give him my 'blokes are disgusting' look, followed by the one that says 'do you *have* to?'

'It's your old stomping ground,' he goes on, 'the murky world you grew up in, inhabited by crooks and conmen, a cast of very sinister types indeed.'

'You writing the intro?'

'Just helping you out. Your starter for ten. Agents and promoters who dangle artists by their feet out of fifth-floor windows to force them to sign contracts. Unscrupulous managers doing deals with narcotic allocations thrown in that could supply the entire North American continent …'

'Imagination. Exaggeration. Hearsay, most of it.'

'*Some* of it. You remember Don Arden, I take it. No smoke without fire, Nina. There must be people we can get to, individuals with insider knowledge, even if we have to cough a couple of quid. Who's that old guy always sniffing around, been up here a coupla times trying to sell his story, knew the Beatles back in Hamburg, reckoned he was a roadie for Bob Dylan and the Stones. Derek someone?'

'One of any number,' I reply.

'You're not helping.'

'Phil, I don't know what you want me to say here. *Yes* it could be a big bossman or some hard done-by flunky out to settle a few scores and balance the scorecard a bit. I've wracked my brains on that, let me tell you, and I've been asking around: not that I'm a news reporter or anything, you've got a legion of those on the desk out there in case you've forgotten – or are they out chasing stories by any chance, as they bloody well ought to be? Just can't get the staff these days, can you? No one I've quizzed so far can come up with anyone those three would have had in common.'

'Who were their friends? Who did they hang out with? What about the women in their lives? Maybe *one* woman: a lone female they might have shared. It's not unlikely, is it, with the careers these guys have had, should I say *had,* and the amount of criss-crossing the planet they did in their time, that they might have all had flings with the same bird. I'm not suggesting by the way that such a woman would be the killer …'

'But then again she might be.'

'What about the super-groupies?'

'The Swedish band?'

'Very funny.'

'They really *were!* Not in the ABBA sense.'

'Anyway. What about so-called road wives? Do they still exist?'

'Your Nancy Spungens? Less so, I think. Been a long time since Frank Zappa and the GTOs.'

'GTOs?' Phil looks perplexed.

'Girls Together Outrageously. Kind of a band of Band-Aids, as such women used to be called.

Like the girls who hang around Formula 1 racetracks are called "screw drivers". Pamela Des Barres was a Band-Aid.'

'Yep, I've heard of her,' Phil says with a nod. 'Exactly the kind of woman I mean.'

'But that's all so long ago.'

'These old rockers were all so long ago! All well into their sixties, peaked in the seventies, early-mid eighties …'

'How long's a girl gonna bear a grudge?' I ask. This could just as easily be a deranged fan on a mission. Plenty of nutters out there. Those are the ones to be scared of … you never know what they're gonna do next. Remember that case in the States a few years ago? Some Texan couple brought a multi-million dollar product-liability lawsuit against Chas Channing. They sued the record company too, something like a million for pain and suffering, three million for wrongful death and five million in punitive damages, from memory, for the suicide of their fifteen year-old son.'

'Remind me?'

'Subliminal lyrics. They claimed to have found Satanic verses in songs on that very odd album of his, *Damnation*. Kid started knocking off cats around the neighbourhood, buggered them inside out, divvied up the corpses, fed some of the meat to his dogs. The next thing, he's hanged himself in the school bogs, using a couple of his own mother's semen-soaked bras knotted together as a noose.'

'Sick. Now you mention it, I do remember.'

'Subliminal messages unprotected by the First Amendment, of course.'

'Did they win?' Phil asks.

'Who?'

'The parents. Keep up. Did they win the case?'

'Kicked out of court. Judge ruled on no evidence. They could prove the boy had abused and killed the mogs; his DNA was everywhere. But did he take his own life as a direct result of having listened to a Chas Channing album? How does anyone prove that?'

'He had all his other albums, right?'

'Not the point, Phil. Chas was lucky, I reckon. There were several similar suicides in the ensuing months. Some of those kids left death notes, specifying precisely what they believed they'd heard in the songs, but those cases got nowhere. Chas walked free, but I know he was scared.'

'What are you suggesting? That these murders could be payback for the suicides that didn't pay?'

'Now who's sick?'

Phil sighs eventually, getting up. 'That aside, people want answers.'

'That's my problem?'

'You knew them all. You're probably the only living columnist who has – how shall I put this? – extensive insider knowledge of all three.'

'What are you implying?'

'Look, Nina, we're sitting on something huge here. If we manage to crack this and expose the killer before the police do, we'll sell it all over the world. We'll be looking at a nice little place in the sun each and a whacking great pension to drink.'

'Flog your soul and there's no way back,' I say under my breath.

'What's that?'

'Nothing. First sign of madness, must be. Just waiting for the devil to call.'

'What are you on about now?'

'A long time ago,' I say. 'Nothing can ever be forgotten, can it. Perhaps that's the beauty of it.'

'You've lost me.'

'You're not the only one.'

~

I file my column and leg it out of the place before Phil cuts me off at the pass. Harry will be pacing at the Royal Garden.

I dump the Jag on the forecourt for the hotel valet to park, make a detour to the ladies for a wash and brush-up, and race to the bar.

As I cross the thickly underlaid carpet, a fritz of static shoots up my left leg. I scan the room. No Harry.

I choose a table in the corner near the window and glance around for a waiter. No waiter. Looks like there's nobody in the bloody place at all apart from a cobwebbed old-timer tinkling the ivories over the back. Where *is* everyone?

I yank out my BlackBerry, start trawling my emails, and the next thing I know there's a heavy sleeved forearm across my throat, someone right behind me, *take* the fucking handbag, the phone, the lot, *don't* panic, Nina, *don't* freeze, *react*, *react*, counter-attack, ignore the pain, pain equals alive, duck your chin, tighten your neck muscles, grimace, hit, lash, bite, claw, *scream*, twist out from under him, get in front, he's bound to be bigger than you, *keep* reacting, *go* for it, if he's not hurting you you're dead, *elbow* to the solar plexus, *fist* to the chin, *knee* to the groin …

'What the – *Harry*?'

'If it isn't the Worst Lady.'

'What the fuck are you *doing*, you *idiot*? You could've fucking throttled me!'

'Just testing, making sure you still remember your training.'

'Oh, for fuck's *sake*, I'm not *that* late.'

I flop back in my chair, press my eyeballs into my head with my fingers, smooth my skirt, and try to look very cross. But it's Harry – love him.

'How long ago was all that?'

'1981.' My friend smiles fondly. 'There I was minding my own business, almost at the end of my stint at Hendon, looking forward to a nice few days off, and some wanker newspaper editor in his infinite wisdom decides to stick a *showbiz* hack on a police training course, for a poxy *feature*, and who does Yours Truly get lumbered with?'

'I didn't hear you complain.'

'Why would I? Drew the long straw, didn't I? Why did they send you on that again? That oil heir geezer, wasn't it?'

'John Paul Getty the Third. Destroyed by the family billions. Swallowed a lethal cocktail of drugs and booze, liver failed, left paralysed and as good as blind. He was only a few years older than us.

As if the poor sod hadn't been through enough, he was then condemned to three decades in a wheelchair, spoon-fed round the clock. Couldn't talk – all he could do was scream.'

'I know how he felt. He was kidnapped as a teenager, right?'

'Yeah, Italian bandits. Held him for five months in a cave in northern Italy, beat him and tortured him. 1973 … we were only kids.'

'I do remember it, though.'

'So do I. When the legendary miser and womaniser known as JPG1 refused to pay the ransom, the 'nappers cut the boy's right ear off and posted it to his grandad in America. Trouble was, there was a post strike, and it had half-rotted away by the time it was delivered. Imagine the stench. They said if he refused to cough up a second time, his grandson would be returned to him bit by bit.'

'Big girls' blouses. I suppose it's one way to an old codger's heart. I can't remember, did he pay in the end?'

'He did. Too late to save him though. The boy never got over it, toppled right off the rails, and eventually took an overdose. You would, wouldn't you? Very sad.'

'Money can't buy me love.'

'No amount could have kissed that one better.'

'What was your involvement again?'

'The usual. Editor sent me to interview JPG3, despite my protests he'd be off with the fairies, and wouldn't even know who I was. He made me go anyway.

'I had to write this big colour piece from Lough Derg in Ireland, where JPG3 was living with his mother on and off. The kidnap info was supposed to be a sidebar, a sort of How-To "Don't Let It Happen To You" typical sensationalist crap. As if your average mid-market tabloid reader risks kidnap every day.

'The Nordoff Robbins music therapy charity was getting quite high profile around then; we'd started going to these big fundraiser lunches. The idea was we'd get JPG3 involved in that year's bash, but it didn't happen.

'I'll never forget him rocking up at Tramp in his wheelchair. He got in, too. Anyway, RIP. You know the actor Balthazar Getty, the one who had the affair with Sienna Miller? That's his son.'

'You learn something every day,' exclaimed Harry with a yawn, scratching his scalp. 'What kept you, anyway?'

'A date with a toothbrush and a deodorant. It has been a very long day.'

I'm suddenly aware of what must be Harry's aftershave. A pungent stench of indeterminate origin that knocks me for six and clogs in my throat. I choke politely.

He's wearing the navy suit that I presume to be his only suit, since he has it on every time we meet, with an M&S-looking lilac cotton-poly shirt, single-cuffed and buttoned at the wrists. There is something heart-wrenching about his magenta fake-silk tie.

This is my mate Harry making an effort for me, bless him.

He's a little greyer and thinner in the thatch than when I last saw him, which has to be about four months ago now. How time flies. The over-belt bulge talks books about his lifestyle: single, middle-aged, far-from-home flat-dweller, living on takeaways, red wine and fags. Harry was caught out last year by his ex-wife in Just One Shag with a nameless hairdresser from Dudley. Michelle is so having the last laugh.

He hands me a flute of champagne. I gulp it in one. Without batting an eye, he refills the glass before the waiter can get there.

'You smell all right to me,' he says.

'Sorry?'

'You said you needed a wash. You smell lovely, in fact. It's good to see you. How have you been?' He studies me.

'I can't complain.' I grin at him.

'Well, you can …'

'I so can. But I don't want to bore you with it. The divorce is still going through, James is still an arsehole but we won't go there, Charlie's off on a jaunt around the world, don't go there either …'

'I read your piece.'

'Which one? I'm in the bloody paper three times a week, Harry.

"Bitchiest and Best-Loathed", you know me.'

'The rock stars,' he says, eyes crinkling. 'So you knew 'em, then? In the flesh, as it were? All three?'

'I knew 'em. What can I say?'

'What a girl.'

'All blood under the bridge, Harry. I haven't got the foggiest who killed them, if that's what you're asking. You're the cop. I was hoping you might tell me.'

'Ah.' Harry reaches for the bottle and refills our glasses, nodding to the barman for another.

'Not my remit, really, is it.' He shrugs.

'Typical detective.'

'Apart from the fact that only one of the crimes was committed in London, it's a long time since I was involved in a murder investigation. They put me out to grass, remember. The department don't get me to LA very often. Never, if I'm honest. Mostly Ghana and Nigeria nowadays. Romance scams, internet dating fraud, women done out of their two-up-two-downs and their life savings by conspiracies of West African shitbags posing as love gods.'

'Don't. Just the thought of it gives me a headache. But you know people who deal with the sort of people who might have insider knowledge of this kind of thing.'

'I don't, Nina,' he says, peering at me the way you study the Mona Lisa. Looking for the laugh.

'So you must have an inkling.'

'If I had a quid for the number of times? What exactly are you asking me?'

'I know you can't give me specifics,' I say. 'I'm just wondering whether you think it could be a serial.'

'I'm no expert, and I'm only guessing, but the evidence to date, such as it is, would suggest yes.'

I gaze at him.

'So talk me through the serial killer thing.' I say. 'I don't know much about this stuff, and I'm fascinated. Why do they do it?'

'Why is wood made of wood, you mean,' says Harry, frowning. He looks away, into the distance, and starts poking around inside his left ear.

'Any number of reasons.' He licks his finger. Gross. 'From what I can remember. Psychological gratification, mostly. They're obviously unstable. Not insane, usually, but there tends to be a sadistic bloodlust which is hard to explain. They might have been exposed to so much violence and perversion in their younger lives that it's turned their heads, made them immune to the depravity of it.

'Look at those boys who killed that little girl in the railway siding. They would have killed again, I bet, if they hadn't got rumbled. Or that school caretaker in Scotland … did five boys from the school he worked at before they got him, didn't he?

'Once they get a taste for it – and part of it must be a power thing – there's no stopping them until the law does. Or you get the type who had a physical affliction or some other specific difficulty in childhood, who was made fun of, became isolated, grew up hating everyone. There are signposts.'

'Such as?'

'They tend to be fantasists as kids. Or they set light to things. Other people's possessions, or even houses – sometimes with the people inside. They get a kick out of destroying stuff. Pyromania can be sexually stimulating, allegedly. Takes all sorts. Come on baby, light my fire.'

'Sick.'

'Just saying. Or, they might torture animals.'

'Charlie used to do that.'

'He painted his guinea pig.'

'*And* barbecued the school hamster, when we had it home for the Easter holidays. *And* cut the whiskers off next-door's cat …'

'I don't think it's quite the same thing, Nina.'

'What else would he have done, if I hadn't found him and stopped him?'

'He would have done much more than that by now, believe me. Quit worrying about Charlie, he's on his way now. As I was saying, these three factors are generally good indicators, but of course they tend to find out stuff about a killer's past only in hindsight. Hurting helpless animals; that's the clincher, for me. What else can that be but practice for the real thing?'

'So they're not coming at their victims as human beings, but as mere animals, or worse, as objects?'

'Either that, or they've got a monumental grudge.'

~

We resist the temptation to call for a third bottle. I do the right thing for once, and leave the car.

We dither about dinner, then decide we're not really hungry. But neither of us is ready to call it a night. For want of anything thrilling to do, who the fuck goes dancing at our age, we cab it up to Soho and wander into one of my clubs.

The night is in full swing, not one but two pianists hammering for all they are worth, and at least a hundred Technicolor punters hitting it large in the bar. Half of them look as though they've just stumbled off the stage of a dead West End musical. The other half just look dead. The lipsticked demi-monde in full-on sleaze mode, or is it just me, getting old.

I'm inclined to quit while we're ahead, but Harry's up for it. He doesn't get out much.

We hang around for a while, getting trampled on, spilled on, deafened to shreds, failing to get anywhere near the bar to yell for a drink.

We give up, not before time, find a corner seat in the much more civilised bar upstairs, progress to the hard stuff, and surrender to a brace of club sandwiches with a bowl of fries.

'So how about you, Harry,' I say, chewing a chip. 'You haven't said much about yourself this evening. Has the dust settled? Have you sorted it all with Michelle?'

He winces at the mention of his ex-wife's name, and thumbs a blob of mayonnaise from his lip.

'Nothing to sort.' He shrugs. 'I kept the house; she didn't want it. Couldn't bear to stay there, she said, knowing "where I'd been". *One shag*! I bought her out. Had to borrow on the place to do it, of course, but I was glad to keep it. My little security blanket, my gaff is. I've repainted it all and everything, done it myself, it's not blokey, but all her frilly shit has gone now. Quite tasteful. You'd like it, I think. Her daughters aren't talking to me, but that's par for the course. I miss my grandkids, of course.'

'Not really your grandkids, though, are they?' I reason. 'More like step-grandkids, since you took the girls on when you and Michelle got married.'

'It doesn't matter.' Harry half-smiles. He fingers the rim of skin under his eyelashes. 'They've been in my life since they were born. They're my grandchildren as far as I'm concerned. Anyway, it helps that I'm in London all week. Either that, or in Africa. Takes my mind off things. I'm just plodding along, minding my own business, trying to stay out of trouble. I've got twelve years to go until retirement.'

'Retirement.' I wheeze the word, over-enunciating, as if it derives from a foreign language I have no idea how to pronounce. 'So how do you feel about the divorce now that it's all over?'

Harry looks at me as though I've been decapitated. He hesitates, and then opens his mouth to speak. Nothing comes out.

I take his hand.

'Don't do it,' he says, at last. 'It's not exactly in my best interests to say this to you, is it?'

'Oh, Harry, you know it's not ...'

'"Like that" between us? Just good friends? Yeah, I know. I knew that a long time ago, I'm only kidding. You're the only proper friend I've got. But the grass isn't greener, Nina. See, told you I was a poet. Where you are, at this stage in the game, you are. We're old gits now.'

'Speak for yourself.'

'I'm not being offensive, don't get me wrong. What I mean is, we've got less to look forward to than we've already had. No marriage is perfect, and yes, I should have made more effort with Her Indoors, and, no, you're absolutely right, I can hear what you're thinking, I shouldn't have gone with someone else. I was away on a lead in the Midlands. It was a long and stressful night. We did get the bloke, so at least that. I went back and got smashed in the hotel bar. This *sort* happened to be hanging around with her mate, quite nice-looking. I picked one of 'em up, copper I was with had the other one. It just happened.'

'Dirty Harry.'

'Never heard that one before. I wouldn't mind betting there isn't a man alive of about our age who hasn't done the same on an away night. Doesn't make it right, I know. But it happens.'

'*Shit* happens.'

'I never even saw her again. If Michelle hadn't clocked that text on my phone, she'd probably never have been the wiser. I didn't give the woman my number; she must have got it off my mobile when I went for a slash. She wasn't there when I woke up next morning. I never replied to the text. One shag and I lose everything. I might as well have paid for it.'

'You *did* pay for it.'

'Didn't I just.'

Harry looks like he's about to break down. More vodka.

'The thing is,' I say, as the waitress serves the refills, 'if you could, would you turn the clock back?'

He sucks a long glug from his new drink, shudders as if someone's walked over his grave, puts the ice-packed tumbler down again. He leans back in the low leather seat, scratching his arm with chipolata fingers.

'It's a good question.'

'People always say that when they don't know the answer.'

'Oh, I know the answer all right,' Harry says. 'What it is, see, you can't go back, in life. Where you are, you are. The whole point of staying married to someone you've been with for decades, after the kids have grown, once your cock has shrivelled and her tits have receded into empty pitta breads …'

'Spaniels' ears ...'

'Teabags ... is only that you've been together all that time. That's the size of it. The hard-earned history. You can't go out and find someone new at this stage in the game and recreate all that with them instead, can you? For one, there isn't enough time left. But for two, you didn't have your kids with the new one, nor the grandkids with the new one. You're starting from scratch, and there's not much point.'

'Companionship? Sex?'

'You know as well as I do that you can feel lonelier living with the wrong person than you can all on your own. As for sex, how many married couples our age do you know who are doing it every night?'

'I wasn't even doing it every night in my twenties.'

'That I find hard to believe. Good-looking woman like you. But you get my drift.'

'I do, Harry, I do.' I hug him. He neglects to hug back. He's on a roll.

'As for these people who get re-married to their original partners after twenty-odd years apart or whatever,' he bangs on, 'you read about them all the time in the *Daily Mail*. And I get it. Some people say they must be fantasists. "Are they really in love?" "Is there such a thing as 'true love' anyway?" "Are they genuinely happy?"'

'*Are* they?'

'You're asking me. What do *I* know? What I *do* know is that most people can't bear the thought of growing old on their own. Who's gonna run you up the hospital when you've got to get your leg dressed? Who'll go over the road for your prescriptions and do your steak and kidney when your fingers have gone arthritic? Who's gonna change your pissy sheets?'

'You never hear a woman saying that kind of stuff,' I say. 'Look at the millions of widows and spinsters out there who are stoically getting on with it. It's men: as long as they've got a mummy changing their nappies at either end of their lives, they think they can do what they like in between.'

'So the one they thought wasn't right for them in the first place,' he continues, ignoring my two pence-worth, 'who's also never found a good enough replacement, often turns out to be better than no one at all.'

'This is all very profound and puzzling, Harry,' I say, or should I say slur.

I'm drunker than I ought to be, considering the plateful I have tomorrow. Bloody *Question Time*. Live from bloody Manchester.

'What I'm trying to say,' Harry continues, 'and not very well, obviously, is that your James is not a bad bloke. You married him; you must have loved him once. Or, if there isn't such a thing as love, and the jury's miles out on that one, you must have cared about him enough to think you could spend the rest of your life with him. Knowing the kind of woman you are. I mean, I bet you didn't settle lightly. I bet you played right hard to get when it came to it, and I'd put money on James being the kind of bloke who wouldn't take no for an answer. Am I right?'

'Getting warmer.'

'You had a child together. A child who, as anyone who knows you appreciates, has not exactly been a skip down the Serpentine. You've brought him up together, you've got him to a point at which he can actively be out there in the world, independent, travelling, exploring, making his own way.

'That's not nothing. You've done that together. You two. No, Nina, James is not a bad man. He's just another good guy who screwed up. He's only human. Like you. If you want my opinion.'

'Did I ask for it?'

'Shut up and listen for a moment. All I want to say is that the victim in this mess is *you*, because you're letting him go, and you shouldn't be. It's none of my business –'

'No, it *isn't* your business …'

'I'm gonna say it anyway: you're cutting off your nose to spite your face.'

'Christ, not you as well.'

'It's not too late to change your mind about the divorce, Nina. What you got to lose?'

'Face.'

'Who gives a sod about *that*!'

'My reputation's all I have.'

'Utter bollocks. Anyway, you could write about it.'

'I write about *everything* I do, that's not exactly a bonus ball.'

'All I'm saying is, give peace a chance.'

'Thank you, Yellow Peril. Harry, believe me. Until some nutter out there started rubbing out rock stars, I thought about little else.'

'A good time to be employed in personal security.' He chuckles, calling for the bill.

'Let me get this, you did the Royal Garden. You mean you think there's more to come?'

'Bound to be.' Ignoring my protests, he signs off his credit card and slips the waitress a twenty. 'They haven't got him yet.'

'What makes you think it's a he?'

'Why would a woman do it?'

'Insanity? Money? Revenge? Same reasons a bloke would do it, according to what you told me earlier. Let's not be sexist here.'

'There can't be a rock musician out there who isn't shitting Stonehenge.'

'Terrifying.'

We revolve our way out of the club onto the cold, glistening street, and peer for cabs.

'Question is,' says Harry, pecking my cheek, 'who's next?'

CHAPTER NINE

TOKYO

For a man who has traversed the globe more times than he can count, touched the lives of millions on six continents and made more money than almost anyone in the game – except perhaps the artist he owes it all to – Clive Clifford has some curiously small-town tastes.

He's never been when-in-Rome. He likes to hang by himself and do his own thing.

When dealing with promoters, attending conferences, giving interviews, negotiating licensing and performance deals for Eddie, walking the walk and talking the talk, he prefers to travel alone.

He always books his own flights and hotels, most unusual for a rock manager.

When a trip involves multiple others, he'll always choose a different hotel. At his own expense, but why not, he can afford it. He has his rituals – his 'little habituals', he calls them – set-piece routines in the cities he visits regularly, which help him to acclimatise and feel in control. It's not the kind of thing he shouts about, because he knows very well that it's not cool.

Rock 'n' roll is about spontaneity, about winging it, about taking risks. He'd feel a bit of a prick if people knew what a creature of habit he really is. He'd never hear the last of it from Eddie, for one thing. On the other hand, he thinks, stuff him. Clive can do whatever the fuck he likes.

Every time he lands in New York, for example, he'll stay at the Mark on the Upper East Side, eat a waffle and bacon breakfast at the Pershing Square Café in midtown, stop for a glass of champagne in the oyster bar in Grand Central, grab an early supper of Waldorf salad and maybe a bit of fish at the Waldorf Astoria Hotel.

If there happens, on a rare occasion, to be a two-hour window in his schedule, he'll jump in a cab down to South Street and take the Staten

Island Ferry to his other favourite view in all the world. New York Harbour still smiles on all who sail at her, he thinks. Even better than Montreux. Even without her front teeth.

The ferry is Clive's secret obsession. The ten-mile, fifty-minute round trip takes him back in time, to when his life was a simpler place. To when there was a girl he loved more than he imagined anyone could love anyone. Leonie. She had hair like her name, an ochre honeysuckle tangle. Her eyes were like midnight; he could still see them now.

He'd saved for more than a year to buy her the ring, its central stone the exact shade of her irises, and circled with diamond glints. The best he couldn't afford. He'd presented it to her on the Staten Island Ferry, and she'd laughed in his face.

'I can't *marry* you!'

It dented him like giant hailstones.

'Why not?'

'I can't marry anyone.'

'But why?'

'I can't tell you. I'm sorry, Clive, not now.'

'When, then?'

'I don't know.'

A year or so on, before he got his explanation, he heard third-hand that Leonie had passed away.

He's always assumed that's why she refused him. She must have known she didn't have long left.

It's what he tells himself. All these years later, he prides himself on the fact that he's never looked at another woman. A real woman. He doesn't count the trash he pays cash. He and Leonie had never more than held hands, exchanged kisses. She is thus preserved in his memory, perfect and chaste, the angel on the Christmas tree of his life. He has often imagined their wedding night, has sometimes wept at the thought. Deluded though it seems, and he knows how this looks, he has always thought of Leonie as his wife. What's it got to do with *you*?

She said no, that was all there was to it. They disembarked in silence at the St George Ferry Terminal, strode the ramp and queued for the turnstiles, then got back on the boat without daring to look at each other. They fixed their gaze on the Statue of Liberty and Ellis Island as they passed, and watched the waterfront loom.

To this day, the ferry fascinates him. Perhaps it's the numbers. It never ceases to amaze him that the yellow fleet carries some seventy thousand passengers on a hundred and nine trips a day, thirty-five thousand trips a year; that's about twenty-one million lonely people. Where *do* they all come from?

Astonishing. It doesn't cost a dime. One of the most iconic sights in New York, which could net a mint from tourists alone, and it's a free ride.

Perhaps the real reason he has to keep going back is that it was from the ferry that he dropped Leonie's ring, still sitting in its velvet-lined leather box. He tossed it over the side: one rash, irreversible flick of the wrist, because she said no to him.

Impetuous bastard, he thinks; you'll never learn. To this day, he beats himself up about it. How he wishes he had that ring now. Every time he boards the ferry, he peers into the waves, always wishing that the little blue box would reappear.

~

Right now he's in Tokyo, mid-ritual, waiting on a promoter with an offer for a dozen or more live shows.

It's been at least three decades since Eddie last played Japan, but his albums have never stopped selling here. The new one's a smash. Clive knows that he can more or less name his price, and he's bloody well going to.

For the past ten years or so, since it opened, he's stayed at the Four Seasons. 'Fifty-seven rooms, fifty-seven steps from Tokyo Station.' The hotel porters even meet you off the Narita Express.

It's an impressive landmark with a chic minimalist interior, not counting the over-the-top flower arrangements and swishy fabrics all over the place. Don't they have moths in Tokyo?

He always takes a one-bedroom suite on one of the hotel's four corners, with a massive bathroom and an oval tub. He's a shower man mostly, too much to do, too little time, and anyway it's more hygienic. But the occasional wallow in one's own filth can't hurt. It's what he tells himself.

The routine is precise. His first morning in town, he takes a stroll to the Tsukiji fish market for breakfast sushi, freshest in the world.

If he's free until lunch, he'll wander over to the Meiji Shrine, dedicated to the late 19th-century emperor who opened Japan's curtains to the West. The shrine is discreet, serene, and not much to write home about – not a patch on most Asian places of worship and barely a tourist trap at all because of it.

He'll stop at the cleansing station, dip a bamboo ladle in the communal water tank, and sluice his face and hands. You are supposed to offer a prayer at this point, after the act of purification, but Clive can never think of one. All around, people stand scribbling wishes on little slips of paper and tying them to the wall of prayer. Others toss yen into an offertory box, then engage in a little routine involving bowing twice, clapping their hands, then bowing once again. It fascinates him. When it comes to rituals, he's got nothing on the Japs, he thinks. He finds this reassuring to say the least.

The Yoyogi Park is a must; he hates to miss it. All human life and more. He comes for the hip-hop dancers, the horn players, the rockabilly gangs, the gaggles of Japanese Elvises, who congregate at the park's eastside entrance and croon themselves hoarse. He likes the crazy dog run – could spend hours watching the double-denimed, trainer-clad terriers, the cheerleading chihuahuas, the freaks who cart them here.

What else? He makes time to go and stand at the second-storey window of Starbucks in the Tsutaya building on the north side of Shibuya Crossing. For the price of a latte, you get organised chaos personified as nowhere else on earth. Around the famous junction outside Shibuya Station, commuters, couples, students and shoppers fickle about like coked-up ants. But when the lights flash red simultaneously in every direction, frantic traffic grinds to a halt and pedestrians flood the intersection, like thousands of tennis balls cascading off a truck. It's a sight for sore eyes. Clive likes it because it just about sums up his life.

His favourite lunch would have to be Ganso Kujiraya. Whale meat again; don't know where, don't know when … or a little place in the trendy Ebisu neighbourhood. He might call in at a couple of the izakaya: tiny taverns offering sashimi and other snacks with drinks, the food cooked in minute kitchens and served on doll-sized plates.

But his favourite destination of all is a karaoke bar called Smash Hits. Not your run-of-the-mill Tokyo karaoke experience, this, not by any stretch.

None of your secretive singing-behind-closed-doors, as if you've got a hooker in there, with the Geisha girlies knocking politely when they rock up with the next round.

This joint is gritty and downbeat. It smells rank, of cold sweat and warm beer. Its walls are plastered with dog-eared album covers and faded Polaroid snaps. It's laid out like a real music venue, and is as close as Clive's ever going to get in this lifetime to attracting a rock audience of his own.

Which is the rub. You choose your song, you leap on stage in front of a bunch of boozed-up revellers who could be anyone, and you belt it. Queen, Billy Joel and Guns N' Roses are the done thing here, but honestly, anything goes. Everyone cheers everyone else, even the pro singers who get paid to whip up the crowds.

Clive likes to rock up early, and get four or five numbers in. What would they say if they knew he's the real-life manager of one of the biggest rock acts on earth?

Actually, *two* of the biggest rock acts on earth, counting Roxy. Which he really must get around to telling Eddie about. He's managed to keep his involvement quiet until now, but the industry's starting to talk. It's bound to leak sooner or later, and it'll be headline-grabbing when it does. Eddie should probably hear it from the horse's mouth. He owes him that much.

So yeah, if these people in here knew who he was, he'd be a laughing stock. It's the reason he left his trademark yellow headgear back at the hotel, and is wearing an LA Dodgers baseball cap. He likes to be away before midnight, before shit-faced expats surge into the place like a mudslide.

Imagine if he were recognised, which he could easily be – he's on television and in the press all the time. Doesn't bear thinking about. The cap should help. Who's he trying to kid? Have another drink, Clive. Moving on.

Some nights, after a bellyful at Smash Hits, when he's neither drunk enough nor jet-lagged enough and still has envy to kill, he makes his way over to the Gigabar, where the rock 'n' roll-wannabe experience jerks up a notch.

Not only do you get to sing, you can get up and play – drums, bass, guitar, whatever you fancy – with a ready, willing and able – if somewhat bored – house band.

The Stones, Led Zeppelin, Clapton, Deep Purple … he's banged them all out in here in his time. It's the most fun you can have with your clothes on, as no one said once. It's better than orgasm.

If Eddie could see him now. Thank God he can't. In his element, Clive hangs about until almost closing time, well into the early hours. But there's always time for one for the road. Go on then, you've twisted my arm.

Silly not to. You know me so well.

~

Everyone in showbiz knows the Park Hyatt Tokyo. An unmissable tower near Yoyogi Park, it's the hotel in *Lost In Translation*, the film with Bill Murray in the bar, karaoke-ing away to Roxy Music's 'More Than This'.

For years, to the initiated, it was *the* Tokyo hotel. Vast rooms, ancient panelling, panoramas to stun the most been-there-seen-it jet-wanker. Incredible glass-roofed swimming pool on the forty-seventh floor: a haven in the clouds. You can flex your breaststroke while looking out over the maelstrom, or you can lunch from a Kozue bento box seven floors down and gorge on Mount Fuji.

The Park View Room boasts sensational vistas in two directions, its bathtub overlooking the metropolis. It was in the tub that they found Jerry Colbert submerged in his own cold blood, his fingers and thumbs severed, his eyes, heart and larynx ripped out.

Doomed with a view.

~

Clive reads the *International Herald Tribune* to catch-up on the latest:

There are variations on the rock star murder theme. For one, Colbert was American. The sex-god lead guitarist and vocalist of New Jersey band Brindisi had been born Geremia Colasanto to Puglian parents in Trenton, N.J. He formed the band with classmates in 1980, naming it after the city on the Adriatic where his paternal grandfather still lived, on sales of almond milk and limoncello, pecorino and ricotta from his dilapidated miniature seafront store. The name appealed to Colbert because it was also the name of a revvy Italian song encouraging the drinking of wine or other alcoholic curses – as in 'Brindisi: The Drinking Song' from the opera La Traviata. *He was mad about that opera, and was even planning a new rock variation on the theme of the hypnotic fallen woman of Verdi's masterpiece. He'd talked about it in exclusive interviews ahead of the tour.Brindisi hit the big time in 1983. With a line-up of guitar, bass, drums and keyboards, their third album* Luther *had proven to be their breakthrough: a concept album fusing rock, metal, country, blues and African beats to reflect the life and achievements of black activist Martin Luther King. His inspiration was the Trenton Riots of 1968, a mass civil upheaval in Colbert's home town that had flared in the wake of the civil rights leader's assassination in Memphis on April 4th that year. Colbert himself had been eight years old at the time, but his memories and the fear had never left him. With fifteen US Top Forty hits, five Number Ones, three thousand concerts in some sixty countries to fifty million fans, they've sold a hundred and fifty million albums worldwide to date.*

The latest offering from America's top touring act, How About No, *has just been released. Father of five Colbert, who was married to his childhood sweetheart Amy but was well-known for fooling around, was a publicist's dream. He'd turn out for every cause going, every fundraiser he could cram in. As for his image, what he lacked in height, he more than made up for in tumbling blond locks and blue-eyed cool. His leather-and-denim, chains-and-shades image made him accessible to fans of all genders. He'd made a clutch of well-received movies, had an Oscar, two Emmys, a handful of BRITS and a star on the Hollywood Walk of Fame. He was one of the world's highest-paid musicians and screen actors, yet he'd managed to stay one of the boys ...*

So who did this one piss off? Clive wonders. Who'd want him dead?

~

There are indeed, as the newspaper report stated, aspects to this murder that not only set it apart from the previous three, but which are confounding the investigation.

The lingerie strewn all over the bathroom floor of the suite appears not to have been worn. The handcuffs, ropes, black tape, paddles, ball gag, blindfolds and vibrators found around and under the bed and among the bed linen, all hinting at some torrid scene, are also in virgin condition.

There are traces of cocaine on a glass coffee table, a fold of new US dollar bills, a pair of crystal glasses and two bottles of Salon Blanc de Blancs 1999 champagne, one drained, one two thirds-drunk – but nothing to prove who'd imbibed them. If anyone.

Tokyo's forensic authorities are struggling. Touch DNA samples have as yet yielded no evidence of Colbert having had direct contact with any of these recreational items. There is no blood, no semen, no saliva on anything, not even on the wine glasses. Nor is there any consistent suspect DNA.

Fingerprints presumed to be those of the victim have been collected from his personal effects, but there are no fingers with which to match them.

It has not yet been established whether the missing digits have been concealed inside the corpse, a hallmark of the other three killings, nor whether Colbert consumed any of the alcohol and drugs during the hours preceding his death, because the post-mortem has been forcibly delayed.

Tokyo's US Embassy is working overtime thanks to the demands of Colbert's devastated wife, who is refusing to sign the compulsory 'Affidavit Of Surviving Spouse Or Next-Of-Kin' until she has seen the body for herself. She has as yet been unable to fly to Japan, however, because of the fragile condition of two of the Colberts' children.

Meanwhile, Amy's lawyers have consulted American funeral directors to determine the advisability of her viewing Colbert's remains. They have been told in no uncertain terms that their client should not plan on holding an open-casket funeral.

Further complications have arisen from the impossibility of obtaining a Japanese death certificate without both the deceased's hospital death record and his official identification. But Jerry Colbert's passport has not been found. Neither has any other form of ID.

The lawyers are now demanding that Colbert's remains be embalmed and freighted home as cargo, to be received by a licensed mortician at JFK. But they are up against the Tokyo Met, who are withholding permission to cremate or embalm 'for as long as necessary', the death having resulted from a crime in their city that they remain obliged to investigate.

So far, the frustrated police have drawn blanks. They have not even been able to establish who raised the alarm.

There is no clear evidence of the perpetrator or perpetrators' entrance and exit, nor even any reliable CCTV footage. Equipment may have been tampered with: the hazy figures captured on camera around the hotel, and in the corridors and lifts closest to the suite, could be anybody.

The entire hotel is sealed off until further notice, other guests are rehoused, and a statement is released by the police.

'We seek the public's assistance in tracing the victim's last steps and his final movements before he returned to the hotel, where he arrived only two days ago,' it says.

'We are interested in talking to anyone who may have seen him out around the city on the night in question. Anyone with even the most seemingly irrelevant information is asked to come forward immediately.'

~

'I met him loads of times, he was a good bloke,' a fetchingly made-up, yellow-capped Clive Clifford tells his Japanese television interviewer the next evening.

'Good family man, did his bit for charity. Him and Eddie worked on fundraisers together a few times. That was how we met. We'd hook up for dinner whenever we found ourselves in the same city. Mild-mannered sort, he was. Had what you might call Californian ways. For a Jerseyan, I mean. Laid back, cool dude, never threw his weight about. Went with the flow. The lad liked a beer and he liked a laugh. We played pool. I let him win! He's been round my house. He was always showing you pictures of his children on his phone. His wife and kids were everything to him.'

'What about the –'

'I can't talk about the crime itself, if that's what you're asking. That's a matter for the police. No comment, as they say. They're asking us not to speculate, but it's difficult to see how this and the previous three murders are not connected. Chas Channing, Paul Judd and Roger Blacker, I mean. Unless this is what they call a copycat killing. Some sick chancer getting in on the act.'

'What about a motive?' his voluptuous young female interrogator presses him.

'*Motive*? I haven't got a clue, love. I'm a rock 'n' roll manager, not the old Bill. But I'm warming to the theory that the killer is some old groupie with a grudge. A woman all four of them would have socialised with, shall we call it, who perhaps feels disgruntled about not being treated very nicely, or was left behind on the way or something, who's hell-bent on having her revenge. They say it's a dish best eaten cold, don't they. Whoever "they" are. Whoever she is, she's clearly got a few quid. She must have, she's getting herself about a bit. I mean, LA, Dublin, London, now here ...'

'Is this going to be good for business?'

'If you're asking me will Brindisi's record sales go through the roof, now that Jerry's shuffled off this mortal coil, I think it's a bit of a disrespectful question, to be honest,' sniffs Clive, pinching the bridge of his nose between thumb and forefinger, dabbing an invisible drip of snot. He smiles sorrowfully.

'We've gotta think of his wife and kids at a time like this,' he continues. 'My heart goes out to them. Having said that, what they won't be short of is a few bob. Call it the Elvis Effect, the Michael Jackson Effect. Not that they haven't done brilliantly up to now, we're talking one of the biggest bands in the world here, as you know, but their back catalogue will now go stratospheric. You live fast, you die young, you get cut off in your prime … pardon the pun, sorry, know what I mean, love? An early death preserves you at that age for eternity. What was it the Stones said? Not fade away. No one could accuse Jerry Colbert of that. It's an ill wind. What I do know is that rock 'n' roll heaven will be having a blinder of a jam tonight. RIP Jerry,' he says, kissing his bunched fingertips and flipping them at the sky.

'See ya, mate. Meanwhile, I only hope they get whoever did this soon. Not many of us getting a lot of sleep right now. Did they say this interview's being syndicated?'

CHAPTER TEN

NINA

Jerry Colbert. It can't be. Dear God, it bloody is. Jerry, Jerry, not you too. What year was it we were in Miami? With all those balloon-breasted female quartets in tinselled swimsuits in the pool, do you remember them, down for their annual convention? We were barbershopped out by the time we left. Jerry, Jerry. We met in the middle. It didn't last long, but I've never forgotten you. I can hardly bring myself to think about this. I need a drink.

And Clive Clifford, what the fuck's *he* doing on the news talking about it? Nothing to do with Brindisi, was he. Or *was* he? According to Sian the other night, he's now taken on this new girl Roxy Rome, and he's still got Eddie Laine, so I suppose it's perfectly possible he could have done some deal with Jerry on the quiet. They don't call him 'the Mafia' for nothing. It would make sense, listening to what he's saying on the telly. Couldn't they get anyone else? Not too many rock superstar managers available in Tokyo at no notice, I suppose. God, it's weird, how he still makes my skin crawl, even after all these years. Can't remember the last time I saw him, but it isn't long enough ago. There ought to be a law against people like Clive. Maybe there is.

I remember the first time I met him.

It was at the Hippodrome off Leicester Square. Eddie was shooting a video for a new single, and we were all in it: 80s London's rock 'n' pop fraternity … the hipsters, the hacksters and the hangers-on, whose legend shall have no end.

I remember nipping into a ballet shop in Covent Garden on my way over there and buying a transparent pink chiffon practice-dress thing to wear over my uniform of black leotard and tights, which I sported under cut-off Levi's and a pair of manked-up biker boots.

I diverted to the loos and caked my face in shimmer powder and lip gloss, backcombed my hip-length hair into a gull's nest, tied a ribbon on, *ta-dah*, instant rock-chick video-star outfit. Well, it was the 80s. Anything went. Everything did. We *all* did.

~

Clive was holding court in the upper gallery, being pandered to by a couple of camp midgets performing card tricks and having his shoulders massaged by a stark-naked girl whose entire skin was painted to look like she was wearing a bell-hop's uniform.

He was slurping milk and cramming bits of buttered scone into his cakehole. From under his stupid yellow flat cap, he stared down on proceedings on the disco-balled dance floor with the little stage at one end, plotting.

The club was a pretty dreadful disco in those days, but we loved it. It was our kind of place. I'd been there as a child, when it was still The Talk of the Town. We went to see Jack Jones.

All these decades later it's a twenty-four-hour people's casino with three floors of gambling. You can even get married there – presided over by an Elvis lookalike, no less – should the mood take. Las Vegas revisited, on a windswept burger-box corner of Charing Cross Road. Class.

I'd been summoned. Clive wanted to talk to me. He was into his second dynasty of management with Eddie Laine, sights set on global domination.

He'd been studying the methods of legendary rock managers of acts gone by, he told me. Immersed himself in the highs and lows, identified all the pitfalls. He knew where his predecessors had gone wrong, and he'd worked out the 'blueprint', as he called it. He'd fathomed how to make Eddie the biggest star on the planet. So far, so up-himself twat.

'Why you telling me?'

'I want you to write about it.'

'I'm not sure my editor would be interested.'

'How do you know he wouldn't be?'

'How do you know my editor is a he?'

He tossed me a look. I blushed like a twelve year old, instantly regretting the diaphanous pixie get-up, wishing I was wearing a pinstripe suit.

It was a pin-drop moment, the first time I remember being aware of the need for a sartorial overhaul. Of the fact that image and style were going to have to play a significant role in my reinvention. Eventually.

One thing at a time. I had to get back to filming, the director was doing his nut, wanted everyone on set at once. Extras were falling over each other, all wanting to be in shot. Clive said we'd 'talk more later'. I clopped down the staircase and immediately fell arse over tit, having neglected to notice that the dance floor was now covered in about a hundredweight of silver glitter, a dense layer about six inches thick, which little wind machines would soon be whipping into clouds of stardust that had us longing for painless puffs of smoke. The stuff was lethal, I'd be finding it in my hair and underwear and rubbing it out of my eyes for weeks.

It was midnight before Clive and I found ourselves sitting in the upstairs bar of one of his Soho haunts, I can never remember the name of it but the one with the blue glass floor. He evidently thrived on elevation, and enjoyed looking down on people.

'It's no accident,' he began, ordering a brace of Margaritas.

'What isn't?'

'Rock superstardom.'

I flashed him my bored face.

'It's not about the music, if that's what you're thinking.'

'Really,' I withered. 'Look, if you want me to remember any of this, just in case my editor does turn out to be interested in a piece – who for the record *is* a he, by the way – do you mind if I just stick my tape recorder on the table, and make a few notes?'

'Go for it.'

'I've probably got about half an hour, I don't mean to be rude, but …'

'Perfect.'

Tools of the trade installed, I was as good as all ears.

'Colonel Tom Parker,' announced Clive. 'Everyone thinks he was a bastard for not allowing Elvis to perform overseas. Put the King off with talk of security scares, terrified him with nightmare tales of touring away from home. The reality was, the Dutchman was an illegal alien. Leave America and he might not get back in.'

'How come Parker was in the US in the first place?' I said.

'Landed during the thirties, along with millions of other Europeans. Worked in a circus, where he took on board the two most important rules about getting bums on seats. Number one, always have a gimmick, something no one else is doing. Number two, pitch your act at the masses and you'll always have an audience. It doesn't do to be too highbrow and elite. Think hip-thrusting and piss-poor movies and you get my drift.'

'And the lesson you learned from him is?'

'Less-*ons*, plural,' smiled Clive. 'The man invented modern rock-star management. Get paid up front, take fifty per cent of everything, wield total media control, and always put the merchandising first.'

'Makes sense,' I said, 'but he wasn't a good guy, was he? Someone told me that on the day of Elvis's funeral, the Colonel went straight from Memphis to New York to commence negotiations for Elvis memorabilia. He was addicted to gambling, too. Squandered most of his hundred million dollar fortune.'

Clive shrugged. 'I never said he was perfect.'

'No one is.'

'Not even me.'

'Next?' I sucked the straws in my drink, I hoped provocatively. I couldn't stand this sleazebag; he was the kind you push the boat *in* for. Still, it was all about keeping your hand in. Like blagging your way backstage when you've got a pass.

'Tony Defries,' he said. 'Ring any?'

'Bowie.'

'Correctamundo. Magnificently ruthless. Modelled himself on Colonel T. Met David, signed him to Elvis's label RCA, set about working the magic. He'd pull stunts like flying in a planeload of US hacks for an exclusive gig at the Dorchester, then get them all up to his suite after, where David would hold court still dolled-up and give the interview as Ziggy.

'Defries had way more money than David in those days, although David was the guy grafting his arse off for it. Owned eight New York apartments, had personal bodyguards, a designer wardrobe, the works.'

'More of a rock star than his rock star, in other words,' I said. 'Is that what you want to be?'

'Don't be ridiculous,' said his face.

I could see where old Clive was going with this. He could talk my ear off about the primary role of the rock star manager being to put himself between the artist and the public, to keep the media at bay, to maintain an aura of mystery and to honour the talent at all costs. I wasn't fooled. Nor would you have been.

The back stories of these characters were legendary: Allen Klein, the so-called Robin Hood of Pop, who got the Beatles after Epstein died, though not for long. Don Arden, rock's Al Capone, who infamously set his Dobermans on his own daughter, causing her to miscarry. Sharon married Ozzy Osbourne and stole Black Sabbath from under his nose. Albert Grossman, the great bear, who minded Bob Dylan and could literally stare people into signing contracts. Big Peter Grant, who lived, loved and breathed Led Zeppelin, but who went to pieces after Bonham died.

There were good guys: Robert Stigwood, who adored his Bee Gees. Malcolm McLaren, who dared to declare that the music is not as important as the intent and the attitude, and who, in a masterstroke of publicity, staged a riot of a gig on the Thames opposite the House of Commons, thus immortalising the Sex Pistols. But they all fell out in the end. They always do.

'All very fascinating,' I said, going to get up, 'but I don't quite …'

'Hear me out,' said Clive, leaning across to hold me down.

'Was it something I said?'

He withdrew his paw.

'Forgive me. What I'm trying to say is, there's a science to this business. It's mathematical. Play their cards right and almost anyone can be a superstar.'

'You think? What, without talent? Without star quality? The all-important *je ne sais quoi*?'

'Don't be fooled.' His smarmy look annoyed me. 'I'm the first to admit that Eddie Laine is not the greatest singer in the world …'

'I bet he'd argue with that.'

'He could try. He's not much of a guitarist, either. Thank God he only picks at his acoustic on the odd chorus here and there. He's not the best songwriter, not by any stretch. Between us girls. But it's not exactly hard to buy help with that. Nonetheless, I can almost guarantee you: Eddie Laine will have retired from arena rock within five years. He'll be so fucking huge, there'll be nowhere left for him to go.'

'Where does that leave you?' I said, sarcastically.

'Rock managers never retire,' he stated quietly, staring right through me. 'They just carry on selling their Turn.'

'Down the river? Up shit creek?'

'You think you know it all,' he replied, snapping for the bill. 'You will one day, Miss Vincent, I'm beginning to see. I think you'll be sorry.'

CHAPTER ELEVEN

SYDNEY

Charlie squandered his entire morning in the Fortune of War on George Street, which was not exactly what he'd had planned. But Yoko Ono's 'War Is Over If You Want It' exhibition at the Museum of Contemporary Art proved a challenge too far with a hangover, and he'd needed to find a pub before he passed out.

He sat slumped at the bar of the Rocks hostelry, which dubbed itself 'Sydney's oldest', just a rubber's bounce from the MCA, quivering and sweating as though it were the height of summer.

The dawn shower that cleansed the cobbled streets had long evaporated, leaving a bright, sunny lunchtime in its wake. Everywhere he looked, ribboned garlands and wreaths dangled from lamp posts and door knockers.

In what felt like a blazing heatwave, the unexceptional Christmas trees failed miserably to evoke excitement and expectation the way they had when he was a child. They just made him feel worse. He felt like climbing up and tearing the lot of them down.

His scalp was still stinging from the bleach he'd applied the day before, turning his hair into a wheaty flop. His skin stank of Rich Tea biscuits dunked for too long, thanks to a cheap and pungent fake tan. He was wearing new clothes, bought locally: bottle-green shorts, an ill-advised white T-shirt growing carroty streaks by the hour, and a pair of red Havaianas a couple of sizes too large. The webs of skin between his big and second toes hurt like mad. The one on his right foot had even begun to bleed.

He stuffed a wedge of paper napkin against it to soak up the drips. At least the footwear was an appropriate colour, he smiled wryly to himself. He never could wear flip-flops, not since the time he'd tried to slice out the webs of skin himself with a penknife when he was on a Scout camping trip in Haywards Heath once, and ended up in hospital.

The two beers and steak and kidney pie were beginning to kick in now. He felt his eyes zoom back into focus, glanced about at the peculiar clientele. Half of them appeared to be downbeat locals, the kind you might expect to find in a working men's club. The other half were obviously tourists, the in-out crowd, the sort who'd read about this quaint old establishment in their guide books or online, and stopped by for a quick tipple just to say 'we was 'ere'.

A few of them entered, did a once around the room, clicked a few snaps – Charlie ducked several times – downed their drinks in two and promptly departed. He couldn't fathom it. Come lunchtime the place was heaving, thanks in part to some surprisingly good tunes by an ashen dude in knitted tank top and chains, strumming guitar and sucking harmonica, and singing – everything from T. Rex to Take That.

Charlie couldn't work out whether he had hours or days to kill. Howie and Deisel weren't due for about three more weeks, and he still hadn't heard from Neesha.

Did he want to see her? He couldn't say. Half of him did, the other half really didn't. The thought of her face, her hair, her currant-bun breasts, those funny white buttoned tap-dancey shoes she wore without socks or tights, that made her feet smell, that sagey-green musliny dress that clung to the backs of her cricket-bat thighs, made him hot and cold and everything in between.

He had checked into a not completely flea-pit of a small hotel behind Harrington Street, slept solidly for twenty hours, and then taken himself on a mini-bender – why not – with the intention of getting up early and doing the sights.

One hit. Get it over with.

He loathed sightseeing. He always had. His parents had made him do so much of it when he was a kid that he could never be bothered now. But you needed to get your bearings in a new place, and the easiest way to do it was by looking at landmarks.

It was enough to look, Charlie never wanted to go *in* things, nor *up* things, and definitely never *under* things – like in a submarine, say, or a dungeon, or catacombs. Except the odd museum, and maybe the smaller galleries. Not the big places, like the Met or the Uffizi or the Prado. He'd always preferred the quirkier little places, like the Guggenheim, the Courtauld, or the Frick. They had good places to hide in. Secret places where you could jerk off. Leave your mark. It always gave him a thrill to think of some of the unlikely places he'd done that in. There was almost a book in it.

Did this make him weird? Who cared. His childhood was hardly his fault, was it? While normal kids were having the old Viva España knees-up experience on the Costa d'Arsehole, he was getting dragged kicking and screaming by designer-clad parents on fancy city breaks around Florence, New York and Madrid.

Couldn't exactly say no, could he? He'd rather have been on a beach in the Med with his mates, but what choice? His mother would never hear of it. Loved her to death, course, but God, sometimes …

He interrupted himself.

Change the subject, Chas. The thought of a boat trip around the harbour clicking photos of the bridge and that ridiculous nuns'-hat, dish-rack, mating-turtles opera house with the great unwashed made him want to go out and kill things.

He paid up, left the packed bar to its own devices, and went walkabout.

This colonial corner of the city rather appealed to him. There was an edge to it, a feel about the place that reminded him of New Orleans or San Francisco.

Out of nowhere, he thought of his Geography teacher, who'd no doubt bang on learnedly about 'the striking juxtaposition of ancient and modern, of historic merchants' houses, banks, police stations and hospitals, restored workers' dwellings, elaborate architecture and wrought-iron balconies, set against modern restaurants, boutiques and souvenir shops, against soaring glass and steel.' Or some other bollocks.

He wandered the wharfs, looking for action, encountering little of much to interest him. Back among the aimless, nameless pleasure-seekers he just followed the flow, to an animated gathering around a group of Sgt Pepper dress-alikes.

Three of them were palming at a pile of steel drums, and the Paul McCartney one – at least he presumed it was the Paul McCartney – was grooving out of time on a bass.

A reggae Beatles tribute. God. 'Come Together'. 'Hey Jude'. 'With

A Little Help From My Friends'. 'Imagine'. But that one was just Lennon on his own, not the Beatles, wasn't it? Academic, he supposed.

Charlie half-closed his eyes and sponged up the sound, then opened them again, startled. Funny, that. It couldn't be, could it? The slightly podgy Paul one really reminded him of that freak from school he'd invited home that time, when things got a bit out of hand.

Who knew he was a shirtlifter?

All Charlie could think of to teach him a lesson was to tie him to a pipe in the basement and switch the light off. Left him down there in the dark for a couple of hours, mentioning in passing that they had rats. How else was he going to learn to leave him alone? Had it coming. Served him right.

Shame his mother got back from work, just as he was about to enjoy a little torment. Just playing hide-and-seek, Mum. Up in a minute. Yep, coming. No, he's fine, we're just having a laugh.

'First time?'

'Sorry?'

Charlie was startled out of his skin when the pigtailed girl in a short, yellow sundress beside him started talking to him. Her smile was in his face like a dentist's. He could see the veins in her gums, a thin lacing of plaque along her bottom front teeth, the brown spidery stains where braces had been. He default-winced, but then forced himself to decide he didn't mind.

'First time you been here. You been in Sydney before? I haven't. This place r*ocks*! Where are you from?'

'London,' he said, inhaling her ice-cream breath.

'London, England?'

'Of course England!'

'Cool! We have a London in Ohio! There are a lot of places in my country named for cities in yours. We did it in Geography class. Boston Massachusetts, Birmingham Alabama. There's an Exeter in California, and a Manchester. A Bath in Pennsylvania, a …'

'Stop! I get it. I need a beer. What's your name?'

'Chelsea.'

'You're shitting me, right?'

'What's yours?'

~

She was eighteen, and on holiday from the US with her parents. She'd just finished school, and was dithering about college. They'd come to Oz for the Christmas holidays, and were supposed to be visiting friends all over the place. Melbourne, Sydney, Brisbane, you name it. Her folks were into the great outdoors – surfing, sailing, spear-fishing with Aborigines, sleeping under the stars at cattle stations.

'It makes me want to lie down,' said Charlie.

'Tell me about it.'

'So where are the intrepid explorers now?' he asked, as she slid the key card into the slot beside her hotel room door.

'Uluru.'

'Who-a-loo?'

'Ayers Rock. Though whether they'll get to do this Mala Walk around the base of the rock, which is what they've gone out there for, is anybody's guess. Killer heat in the outback this time of year, though it's absolutely freezing first thing. They cut the walk right off if it goes over forty, did you know that?'

'I didn't.'

'Me neither. Who cares. Drink?'

She plundered the minibar, tossed him a can of beer, and opened a baby plastic bottle of Scotch with her tarnished teeth.

'Where are they staying out there?'

'Sunset Rock. Heard of it?'

'Nope. I've only been here two days.'

'It looks OK. They take you out to dinner in the desert at night.'

'Kangaroo soup and crocodile steaks, yuk. Bush tucker trials. After you.'

'What?'

'Nothing. Not my cup of tea.'

'Mine neither! Best stargazing in the world, though. Milky Way. Constellations. I'm sorry I'm missing that bit. And they have real didgeridoo players, you can buy their CDs. And Aboriginal dancers ...'

'Like *they're* gonna be genuine. I'd rather watch stuff like that on TV.'

'Me too!'

'So why haven't you gone with them?' asked Charlie from his tub-shaped armchair, willing his eyes to stay out of inappropriate territory.

'Oh, ya know. Bugs. Spiders. Lizards. Snakes. And flies. I'm allergic to flies. My sister and I decided we'd hang about in Sydney, do some bike tours. They've got a couple of really good four- and five-hour trips.'

'I'm into biking too,' Charlie told her, noticing the whites of her underwear; he couldn't not. Chelsea was sprawled diagonally across the bed, on her front, facing away from him. The little yellow minidress had ridden right up. Hadn't she realised? Should he tell her? What?

'Maybe we could all go together,' he said, trying to take his mind off it. 'What's your sister called?'

'Kari-Ann. She's twenty-one.'

'Where's she now?'

'It's kind of a secret.' Chelsea smiled, winking bizarrely with both eyes.

'She met a real cute guy in a bar, the night we got here. She promised Mom and Dad she'd take care of me while they were gone.'

'I guess I'll just have to do that for her, then. Being as I'm here.'

~

When he awoke some time in the small hours, the overhead lights were blazing, the television was blaring and the air-con was barking ice.

Chelsea must have woken ahead of him, got up for the bathroom or something and put everything on, then fallen back to sleep. She was curled in a tight ball halfway down the bed, with goosebumps all over her golden skin.

Charlie stared down at his own streaked flesh, and winced. He billowed the duvet with one foot, the one that wasn't scab-encrusted from the flip-flop, and kicked it over her. He broke wind without meaning to, and blushed to his roots.

But Chelsea didn't flinch. Was she really asleep? He hoped so. He reached for the remote, and killed the glottalized English assaulting his ears.

'… Not fade away. No one could accuse Jerry Colbert of that. It's an ill wind, I guess. What I do know is that rock 'n' roll heaven will be having a blinder of a jam tonight. RIP Jerry. See ya, mate. Meanwhile, I only hope they get whoever did this soon. Not many of us getting a lot of sleep right now....'

Who the hell was *this*? Clive Clifford, the woman said? Who was he when he was at home? Wanker. Look at his ears. Talk me through that stupid yellow cap. I bet my mother knows him, too; she knows all these losers.

Then some detective came on and started talking about all the other dead rock stars, something about a connection.

My mother, Charlie thought, in spite of himself. It's my mother they want to talk to. Mommy Dearest, the goody two-shoes whore.

He flipped channels, got MTV, and groaned when he realised they were playing Brindisi videos back to back. He flipped again, some Aussie jukebox channel, found much the same thing. Everywhere he looked, the news was dominated by the 'shock death of this much-loved rock superstar'. You could have fooled me, he thought. Anyone would think it was the Queen.

He'd never cared for Brindisi. A bit middle-aged blue-collar for his taste. Give him death metal any day. And Nile Rodgers. He had to admit to being a closet Chic freak, though nobody tell his mum.

You could keep Jerry Colbert and Brindisi. Stupid name, anyway. Guy should have been put out of his misery years ago. Charlie's sap was rising.

He flicked the TV off altogether, flopped back onto the bunched pillows, pulled a corner of the duvet up to his chin and snuffled into it, closing his eyes. He wanted his mother.

~

Charlie's dream was so vivid, he could smell mincemeat, as well as the faint gunpowder smell from crackers that comes just after the snap, if you get ones that actually work.

It was about two weeks before Christmas Eve, and he was sitting with his mother on the big grey couch in her bedroom, leafing through a fat red book. Her Christmas Book – a beautiful, old, scarlet velvet-covered thing with tiny brass bells stitched down the spine – that she kept in a tissue-lined box in one of the drawers under her bed.

At the front, the Twelve Days of Christmas, with gilded Victorian illustrations of partridges and colly birds, *not* 'calling' birds, as the other kids always said, of leaping lords and milk maids, and golden rings.

She sang him the song as they turned the shiny pages, to find the picture of the perfect Christmas drawing room.

There was an old brick fireplace with a marble mantel wreathed in ivy, Christmas cards pinned on red satin ribbons underneath. In the hearth, a pyramid of logs flamed brightly. He and his mother would stretch out their hands towards the photograph, rub them together to 'feel' the heat. The framed portraits on the walls had sprigs of holly tucked in the top. The armchairs were draped with tapestries. To the right of the fireplace stood an enormous Norwegian spruce hung with tinsel and garlands, tiny candles, glittered fir cones, glass angels and birds. The presents piled under the tree spilled onto the faded hearth rug, where an adorable white West Highland terrier lay sleeping, nestled among the gifts as if he were one too.

'What are you going to ask Father Christmas for this year, darling?' asked his mother.

Charlie pointed at the dog.

'I want him.'

There were endless pages of how-to-make robins, banners and snowflakes, of gingerbread-men paper chains, cellophane sweet parcels, lollipop trees, needlepoint stockings. And cookery chapters: hazelnut cookies and tangerine shortbread, spiced pigeon, glazed duck, and venison pies.

There were the recipes for the brown bread and cranberry sauces and chestnut stuffing his mother always made. The parsnip and carrot purée to go with the turkey and roast potatoes, the walnut tarts and the smoked salmon stars, the mince pies, the peppermint truffles and the chocolate log, and Charlie's favourite, the magnificent snow-dome cake. He was so overwhelmed by the picture of that cake, it made him cry.

The longer he slept, the further he drifted. He was five or six years old now, and woke in the night to see his father bending the legs of Thunderbirds dolls and sitting them in the little blue and white wicker chair by his bed. Why was Daddy doing this? Why couldn't Father Christmas do it himself, or get one of his elves to do it?

He knew, not that anyone had ever told him, that he must pretend to be asleep. He soon fell back into his dreams, and he flew, in his pyjamas like the boy in *The Snowman,* over frosted rooftops and naked branches and almost as high as the clouds and the aeroplanes until his nose dripped, and icicles came out, and he was looking everywhere for eight reindeer and a sleigh, and was back at the children's party they always went to in the big brick house on the Heath, that smelled of oranges and cloves and roasting chestnuts, where the pristine white tables stretched further than he could see. Where the giant, fairy-lit fir tree seemed to burst through the ceiling and shoot into the sky, like the beanstalk in Jack's pantomime. Where he was surrounded by sallow children in home-knit cardies and tartan trousers and party petticoats stitched from nets, like the ones his grandma hung at her windows. Where he looked and felt out of place all teatime in his blue velvet suit that he mustn't get dirty, and his girly patent shoes, his face scrubbed, his hair licked, his mother nowhere.

He remembered his grandparents. Four lovely parchment faces who were once upon a time at their table, who would snore away the day in front of films. *White Christmas. It's A Wonderful Life. Miracle on 34th Street. We're No Angels*. Titles he knew so well, but with imagery he could recall only vaguely, that had faded away to nothing like the parents of his parents, who one day weren't there any more.

He never really noticed who went first. But sometimes, when he focused, he could conjure the scent of his grandmother's powder and lipstick, the cigar breath and pipe tobacco of the grandpas, a whole childhood of unforgettable Christmas smells.

Charlie's nose twitched at the aroma of a snow-dome cake being baked in the kitchen.

His heart almost broke when he awoke, and remembered where he was.

CHAPTER TWELVE

HOLLAND PARK

They meet out of the way like illicit lovers, in the basement bar of a place they both frequent. From the outside it looks like every other whitewashed Victorian mansion on this millionaire square off the beaten drag.

There's neither banner nor neon to identify it. Only the out-crowd know where the action is.

This is the sort of establishment where everyone turns a blind eye, where most are up to something, where no one's counting, nobody recognises you and who the hell cares anyway. Where you can stay all night if things go your way. Dinner with benefits.

The half-dozen bijou suites on the second and third floors, with circular beds, curtained baths and sound-proofing, are equipped with every amenity unimaginable.

Neal Goddard arrives first, nabs a couple of stools, orders a chocolate Martini. He throws it back while paging the *Evening Standard*, and nods for another.

The barman smiles at the beautifully dressed boy-faced lawyer, raising his eyebrows at the harpist in the corner. On cue, she plucks a celestial take on the theme of 'Me & Mrs Jones'.

Nina arrives twenty minutes late, which is good, for her. Neal has given up complaining about her disregard for punctuality, having tried and failed to meet her as arranged. He has even tried tricking her into thinking they'd agreed to meet half an hour earlier than the appointed time, so that whenever she pitched up late, she would still be on time. It didn't work for long. She got wise to it. Nina Vincent gets wise to everything sooner or later, Neal thinks. Mainly sooner. He adores her for it.

'Vodka soda, freshly squeezed lime juice, ice and a straw, please. Absolutely gasping. And a glass of water on the side, no ice, no straw, no lemon, still, not fizzy.'

She kisses Neal on his freshly defuzzed cheek, and thinks he must be the only man in London who routinely shaves twice a day. She hoists one generous buttock onto the burgundy leather bar stool cushion, bunches the other upwards to join it before the seams in her skirt give way.

'Do myself a mischief on this thing! Nowhere more comfortable?'

'First things first,' he murmurs, drinking her in. 'You're looking fabulous, Nina. Divorce obviously agrees with you.'

'What the fuck … I could so do without it.' She sighs, rolling her eyes. 'Sooo much hassle. I sometimes think, whose smart idea *was* this.'

'Yours.'

'If I'd known then what I know now. Honestly, it couldn't be happening at a worse time as things have turned out, what with Charlie off on his travels and all the fuss over the murders.'

'The rock stars? Did you know any of them?'

'All of them.'

'Intimately?'

'Well enough.' She frowns.

A tic begins to flutter under Neal's left eye. It catches Nina's. She stares at him, wondering what brought that on.

'Are they any closer to solving the crimes?' Neal asks.

'Depends who you mean by "they". I don't think any of them knows where to start, to be honest,' she replies, fascinated by the vibrating eye bag.

Nina knows all about nervous tics; Charlie suffered with them for years. Nothing the specialist could do for him, said he'd grow out of them eventually. He did.

Girls hardly ever suffer from them, interestingly, which she couldn't help thinking said much about the male psyche. Big boys don't cry, they're taught to bottle their feelings and keep a stiff upper lip. Girls weep all over the place, wearing their hearts on their sleeves, and bleeding copiously. All food for thought.

She sucks greedily at her drink, and meets her companion's gaze full on.

'Problem is,' she continues, 'too many police forces involved. They're not even speaking the same language. They can't seem to agree on whether it really is a serial killer they're on the hunt for, let alone where or how to begin the search.'

'An international investigation with too many strands.' Neal nods. 'I can appreciate the problem. Meanwhile, we've got to get you out of *your* mess.'

~

Thirty minutes and two rounds on, they are fortified and ravenous. Their velvet-curtained booth in the lower dining room is to the left of a huge open fire, which crackles and spits as if in greeting as they approach. Garlands of fairy lights are strung around the alcove, which is decked, like some exotic mini antiques shop, with ornate mirrors, Kama Sutra carvings and tiny leaded stained-glass Biblical scenes.

Nina remembers – with a giggle, which she quells before Neal notices – the last time she had dinner in this booth.

It was with that stage-screen actor who'd made his name in the Nazi-hunter films, you know, the lanky dude who had that great cameo in one of the Harry Potters.

He was clearly on a mission in that interview, to reinvent himself as Sexiest Hunk On Earth. She wondered which smart-arse PR had come up with that bright idea.

It was so funny. There he sat, rubbing dribbles of Sauvignon Blanc into his lips with his forefinger as if it were Vaseline, ordering sole on the bone, deconstructing it manually and even eating it with his hands, the broth and lemon juice running down over his wrists and into his shirtsleeves. He licked it off as he went.

Far from finding the performance erotic, as she was clearly supposed to, the idea being that she would scuttle away and big him up in print, Nina wanted to puke.

To compound the farce, the photographer turned up mid-main course, demanding to prise the hapless thesp onto the terrace and get the pictures over and done with while the light was still good. He annoyed the guy so much that the actor refused to do any mug shots at all. Exit furious fish-faced Oscar-winner and apoplectic snapper without a snap. Hilarious interview, Nina had a book's-worth, but they had bugger-all to illustrate it with. You win some.

'Crab linguine and a lobster risotto, starter not main,' Nina tells the waiter.

'*Two* fish dishes?' says Neal.

'Is there a law against it? What are you having?'

'Deep-fried squid. Duck sausages. Virgin olive oil mash and steamed mixed veg.

A bottle of the Vaudesir 2010 as well, please, and a jug of tap, if you would. So, Nina, tell me.'

'I thought,' she says imperiously, 'that tonight was all about *you* telling *me*.'

Neal loosens his Lanvin tie, unbuttons his collar, shoulders his way out of his jacket. The maître d' materialises from nowhere to hang it up.

Do they have hidden cameras and mics in this booth, Nina wonders. They'd better be careful. Second thoughts, sod it. She remembers where they are.

'OK, let's get it out of the way and then we can let our hair down,' he says, undoing his cufflinks, a pair of tiny gold frogs with ruby eyes.

'I've been tied up in court on other cases for the past fortnight, but Jago managed to leave a lengthy message for James at the end of last week, asking him to deal with outstanding matters that need to be put in hand. We gave him until early next week, and also threatened him with an enforcement application.'

'And his response to that was?'

Neal pauses for effect, trying his damnedest not to look as though he's enjoying this.

'He's counter-suing you, Nina.'

'*What*? What on earth *for*?!'

'Same thing. Unreasonable behaviour.'

'The fucking bastard! He's having a laugh! How exactly can he sue me for that, when *he* was the one caught shagging away from home? What the fuck is he playing at?'

'Our job as divorce lawyers is to obtain the best possible financial settlement for our client, given all the various circumstances of the case –'

'Yes, yes, I *know* all that,' flares Nina.

'Look, I should remind you that we're petitioning for unreasonable behaviour, as you instructed, but that your petition doesn't contain sufficient allegations of …'

'One shag isn't enough?'

'One unproven implication of adultery won't necessarily suffice, no. We need to satisfy the court that you are legally entitled to a divorce on the basis of his unreasonable behaviour. Only going through the motions, of course, but five or six specific allegations will usually do it.'

'That's a relief.'

'Sarcasm doesn't suit you.'

'Grow up, Neal, I make my living out of it.'

'I suppose you do. Be that as it may. The first question to ask is, could you not forgive him?'

'I don't *want* to!'

'You're on thin ice, Nina, because James is not in agreement. Furthermore, he has now decided to counter your accusation with allegations of his own.'

'What *of*!'

'That you are maintaining, I quote, "*brazen* affairs" with not one but two individuals, one of them an international celebrity, and are therefore humiliating him publicly.'

'Rot! I didn't start seeing Bill or Tony until well after I'd kicked James out and filed for divorce!'

'It's not the point, Nina. You're still legally married.'

'In name. Not even in name, actually; I kept my maiden name, Vincent, as I've always been known professionally, and he's a Kendal. We didn't fancy the double-barrelled.'

'You're splitting hairs. In my experience, the Respondent would have accepted the allegation and allowed you to divorce him quietly, had he lost interest in you, the marriage and the family, provided you could come to a mutually beneficial financial agreement. The fact that he's prepared to fight it suggests extreme emotional attachment. He probably still loves you. I expect he's still hoping you'll back down, that misdemeanours on both sides will cancel each other out. Reconciliation would be my advice.'

'Who asked for your advice?'

'You did. You're paying me for it.'

'There is that.'

Nina drains her glass and accepts a refill.

'It's all very complicated,' she says eventually.

He nods. 'A classic case of unreasonable behaviour continuing after separation,' says the polished lawyer.

'In other words, you are both at fault.'

'What do we do now?'

'If you insist on proceeding as things stand, you are going to have to convince the court that you are the injured party. This will be difficult to say the least, given that your dalliances …'

'*Dalliances*!'

'Forgive me … given that your "relationships" with Sir William Hollins and with Tony Keen – both legally married men, remember – have been dissected and pored over by the media. There's plenty of evidence –'

'*Evidence!*'

'You haven't exactly raised formal objection to any published article or gossip item, have you? You've not threatened anyone with libel or slander, so by default you've as good as admitted guilt. In a normal case of adultery – if there is such a thing as "normal" – it is possible to allege an improper relationship with a third party as an act of unreasonable behaviour only where the offending spouse does not object. In that case, it is not usually necessary to name the third party. Indeed, they should *not* be named...'

'Oh, God,' groans Nina, 'I can't go dragging Bill and Tony into all this, can I? How's that going to look? What about the wives? Aren't they likely to initiate proceedings of their own, naming me? *Both* of them naming me?'

'You've got it.'

'Imagine the scandal.'

'Imagine.'

'Poor Charlie will never live it down.'

'Unlikely.'

'But why haven't their wives divorced them before now? Bill's had half a dozen affairs over the past twenty years, and those are only the ones we know about. He and Lady L haven't lived together as man and wife for about a century. As for Tony, he says he can't even be sure he remembers his wife's first name. He and Melanie are still under the same roof, granted, but hardly ever at the same time. So how on earth could I be perceived as being to blame if both decided to call it a day?'

'It's called discretion, Nina,' says Neal, leaning across the table to press the bulging blue vein on her hand.

'Men like Bill and Tony get away with whatever they like, provided they carry on footing the bill for everything, and everyone involved keeps *schtum*. Once such affairs are out there, the wives are perceived as pathetic doormats for turning a blind eye and putting up with it. They can't have that. It's undignified. Humiliating. Exposure forces their hand.'

Nina groans.

'I can see what you're saying.'

'Another bottle, shall we?'

~

He is fighting the urge to touch her, to take her in his arms. She's irresistible. She's got twenty years on him at least. She must be old enough to be his mother. He's got her date of birth on record somewhere, of course he has, but he's forgotten it. Anyway, it's all academic. The numbers mean nothing.

He only has to meet her gaze and he melts. It's not about looks. Not that she isn't attractive. Not that she doesn't make the best of herself, quite the opposite. She is striking, a tad brassy, but nothing he can't live with. That's her style. Could probably pass for a woman fifteen years younger.

Her glamour is knowing and earthy, which excites him, but is offset by an innocence that makes her seem vulnerable, that thrills him even more.

He doesn't want her to mother him, *God*, no. He wants to protect her. Not since his first, excruciating love has Neal felt this way.

He certainly didn't feel it when he married Gael. Why did he marry Gael? He's forgotten now. She was never his type, just a pretty enough little legal secretary from a council house in a Medway town.

To put it nicely, his girlfriends at Oxford had both been plain. What they lacked in beauty, they more than compensated for with grey matter. But they were ballbreakers. He couldn't handle it. Anything for a quiet life.

Gael was completely the opposite. As good as ignorant. When he once mentioned his college, Brasenose, she thought he meant a Jamie Oliver cooking technique. But she'd turned his head with her blonde hair, her tiny breasts, her nipped-in waist, her munchable top lip.

They'd been going out together for about six months when she started dropping hints about a ring. He got bored of listening to it in the end. Where they are, they are. Jesus, imagine what the press would make of him and Nina Vincent. They'd have a bloody field day.

'MAN-EATING COLUMNIST DIVORCES HUSBAND FOR ADULTERY, FALLS FOR HER OWN MARRIED LAWYER.'

You couldn't make it up.

He could be disbarred for misconduct, he supposes. For engaging in dishonest behaviour involving deceit and misrepresentation. A sticky one. The lawyer-client relationship is fragile at the best of times.

A sexual relationship with Nina would of course be unethical. How could he represent her adequately and impartially if they were making the old beast with two backs on the side? Conflict of intent, he must remain detached – or else give up the case.

She wouldn't like that. They've got to know each other. There's an understanding. She trusts him. He would even go so far as to call them friends. She has neither time nor inclination to begin the whole tedious, soul-destroying process with someone new. He's even telling her to consider reconciliation, for God's sake.

If he got involved with Nina, he could be accused of actively hindering attempts at repairing the marriage. He'd never live it down; he could be jeopardising his entire career. No, he thinks, he can't possibly. Not until this is all over, at least. Not until they're out the other side.

Maybe he'll try again next year, provided Hollins and Keen stick to the rules. Nina will soon get bored with being their bit on the side; she's the kind of woman who needs much more. Who *deserves* much more. Maybe he'll even be rid of Gael by then. Where there's a will.

And yet. Can he detach himself enough to remain at arm's length? This isn't just sex, he knows too well. He already feels part of her. She of him. There's never any awkwardness, no lull in conversation; he can't imagine feeling ill at ease with Nina.

It doesn't take much effort to picture them waking up together, perhaps in some chic hotel overlooking Lake Como, the light rising golden on tomb-still water, the waft of coffee curling in his nose, the morning sun in her face, exposing her age.

He has never seen an older woman this close. Not even his mother: it's been so long since he last saw her that her face was still young.

The idea of Nina's rawness without all the make-up fascinates him.

He can picture it clearly. Tiny vertical lines dent the top lip, one side tilted. Marshmallow jowls pull the edges of her mouth, the jawline puffing softly beneath the chin.

He's sure she's had work, and he wishes she hadn't. Tell-tale scars and knots behind the ears are what he doesn't want to see. Her panda-less eyes are creased and closed. The lashes are sparse, the sculpted eyebrows flecked with white. Silver whispers along her hairline match her parting, there's even grey in the pallor of her skin. All of this is revealed in the brutal light of day she now sleeps through.

The fortunes she must spend on maintenance! Why do all that, he wonders. Professional image, he supposes. The media expects. Got to keep up.

But the face behind the mask is a thing of beauty. To him, it is. Its nakedness speaks to him, it involves him, it puts him at ease. It reminds him how much he prefers bare brick, unvarnished wood and stripped-back paintwork to anything disguised and overwrought.

This face tells the truth. About ageing? Maybe. About how women have got it so wrong? Perhaps. Youth has nothing on lived-in and comfortable. Youth has so much to learn. Younger faces, even exquisitely pretty ones, can be so flat and impenetrable that they push you away.

This is a face you could sink into at the end of a knackering day. A deep-cushioned sofa of a face, one that time will honour and respect, drawing people into it, even in her seventies and eighties. Why doesn't she know that this is lovely? Why does she have to hide behind a mask?

His mind nuzzles down her broad, strong body, nosing into an ashen armpit, reminiscent of an old man's chin. Braless breasts with obsolete nipples lie like uncooked samosas on soft pink, blue-veined flesh. The belly lolls nonchalantly over the ridge of a glossy Caesarean scar, a full fringe lushing lightly into her thighs. She has heavier than average, round-kneed legs, he notices, which at least are perfectly waxed. The stub-toed feet are sanded, the toenails polished, the same sex-scarlet as her hands.

He'd asked her about the song once. Neal was the first to admit he didn't know a lot about rock music; he was more of a classical man himself. But he wanted to show willing.

'"Maggie May"? You like that? Rod at his finest. Number One for five weeks, October 1971, also topped the charts in the US and Australia. Said he wrote it about the first woman he ever had sex with – at the Beaulieu Jazz Festival, one of the first open-air fests, 1961. He was born in 1945, I think. He must have been, wasn't he? He's gone seventy now; can you believe that?

'Neither can I.

So he would have been about sixteen when he lost it. Maggie was obviously "the older woman" who taught him everything. Every young man's dream, so they say.'

'They do?'

'You've never been involved with an older woman?'

'I don't know. I've never asked. But it don't worry me none.'

'Ha.'

He wants, more than anything, to wipe away the cosmetic disguise, to immerse himself in the Nina she really is. If only she knew. He knows why he can't. What the hell.

He excuses himself to go to the gents, takes a detour via reception, and cancels the room.

CHAPTER THIRTEEN

NINA

I was doing really well until yesterday. Until we sat down in the office to write cards. Only the ones we absolutely have to send. I'm so over all this card business; it's so infuriatingly, time-wastingly last century. Then Allegra had to go and spoil it all by saying, 'What are you doing for Christmas?'

Of course she meant well, bless her; it was a perfectly innocent question. She always gets so excited this time of year, it reminds me so much of when I was young.

I love it. Usually. She didn't mean to upset me, but I really did think I was going to cry. Not that she hasn't seen me in tears before; there's not much Allegra and I haven't shared over the years. But still. It caught me unawares.

Never in my life have I had to spend Christmas alone, and I can't quite imagine what it's going to be like. No James, of course, and Charlie's still in Australia. My parents are long gone, God rest them, and I've no siblings that I know of, though I suppose anything's possible.

Bill will be with Lady L at Bladington. They've got this long, allegedly unbreakable tradition of Christmas with their children and grandchildren, the whole mistletoe-infested shebang. They're welcome to it.

Tony admitted a couple of days ago that he's off to Gstaad with Melanie, Christmas lunch at the Eagle Ski Club on Wasserngrat, darling.

So exclusive that even the police can't get in. '*Especially* the police can't get in', as Geoffrey Moore once told me, during Son of Double Oh-Seven's spell as a Mayfair restaurateur. *Le* jet set. International celebs and European royalty. Christ. Rather stay home pulling your toenails out? I'll be round in ten.

I'd never have said all that was Tony's mug of vin chaud, to be honest, but it's certainly Melanie's, from what I can make out. All very Rolex. Very Patek bloody Philippe. Perhaps she'll seek a replacement husband among the counts. I said counts.

What about Harry? What *about* Harry. He had asked. I'd said I was going away.

'Where to?' he had asked, taken aback.

'Stick a pin in the atlas,' I'd said. 'Anywhere that's as far away as possible from James will do.'

'What about Charlie?'

'Having a whale of a time in Sydney with his mates. I'm hardly going to embarrass him by crashing that, am I?'

'Lord Bill?'

'*Sir* Bill. With the fake wife and family.'

'Tony?'

'Skiing with Melanie.'

'*Me*?'

'Oh, Harry. I don't think I'd be the best company. It's family time, isn't it? We're not … Anyway, what are your lot doing?'

'Going to Michelle. The kids did say let's meet up and do presents in the morning, but where does that leave me for the rest of the day? Feet up in front of the box with a bottle of Scotch and a party bag of Cheesy Wotsits, watching *Only Fools & Horses* specials and sobbing me eyes out.'

'I don't know, Harry,' I'd said truthfully, 'I really don't. You know what Christmas is like. You can go with the flow all year, but then along comes Christmas and everything in your life gets crystallised by it. Which either makes you feel all smug and cat-that-got-the-clotted, or like a ripping great failure.'

'We'll have a tipple, though, yeah? Toast the season of goodwill?'

'We'll have a Christmas drink, Harry,' I'd lied. He could forget about New Year's bloody Eve, too.

All I wanted was January.

~

The dream never varies.

'I told you, I'm not telling you,' says James, 'it's a surprise.'

'What kind of surprise?'

'If I told you, it wouldn't be a surprise.'

'OK, *where*, then?'

'Patience, wench! Jesus, you get worse. You'll just have to wait and see.'

Our first Christmas Eve, and it's snowing. By the time we make it down the A303 as far as Stonehenge, the flakes on the windscreen are the size of Rich Teas. James flashes our fridge of a VW off to the right, skids in his eagerness to make the turn, recovers control at the last minute.

We race the ancient black shapes lumbering along on our left, great ogres in the twilight.

It's dark by the time we bump into the car park of the Red Lion in Avebury, its thatched roof blanched with piling snow. The night feels starched; my teeth are aching. I can hear everything I've ever thought. I'm half-starving, half-dying to melt into bed.

'We're staying *here*?'

'As if.'

'Why are we here, then?'

'A quick drink and a bite before church.'

'*Church*?'

'Midnight communion. In an 11th-century Saxon church with original windows, you'll love it. But first things first. I wanted you to see my favourite pub in the whole of England's green and pleasant land. We won't get near the door tomorrow; they flock here from all over. It's the only pub in the world enclosed by a prehistoric stone circle, and it's two thousand years older than Stonehenge.'

'What, the pub?'

'No, thou dunce, the stones. I call the big pair Mick and Keith. Pub's about four hundred.'

'I feel about four hundred myself right now.'

'It'll be all right once we get a bottle of wine and a bit of fish inside you. Er …'

'I see where you're going with this. Best quit while you're ahead.''Plus it's built over a well.'

'Well, that explains everything.'

We pull up at the cottage at nearly one in the morning. Finally.

I'm two-and-a-half sheets to the wind. I can remember nothing of the service beyond candles and carols. It's about the size of it. And we're staying in a dolls' house. I'm guessing eighteenth century, but what do I know?

Neatly white, shallow pitched roof, brick chimney. Dry-stone wall and cast-iron railings, interrupted by a painted wooden gate, couldn't tell you what colour, it's too dark out here.

A brick path paces us to a lamp-lit sage front door, a home-made wreath of holly knotted tightly to the brass knocker.

Someone's been in ahead of us; they've left the lights on. Woodsmoke pricks my nose as I flatten it against the window, feeling like a Victorian urchin on a Christmas card, the one on the outside. I can see bare wood floors, old rugs, a pair of ancient armchairs pulled scorch-close, snapping flames in a broken brick hearth. A clumsily bucketed spruce, glittering whitely. A shabby dresser, leaning with plates and fruit, a supermarket box of chocolates, a church-fete nativity of knitted dolls.

James pinches my arm as he slides the key in the front-door lock.

So *this* is Christmas.

'You've done all this?'

'I've done all this.'

'For me?'

'For *us*. Merry Christmas, wife,' he says, kissing me.

I awake for the loo in the early hours. I'm half-under a bunched duvet across a narrow four-poster.

I must have been pissed, I didn't even notice getting in. White linen, at least, and six pillows, a bargain, and a multi-coloured patchwork quilt. A stale, snoring husband. Mine? Christmas stockings, one on each post, misshapen with tiny parcels. A threadbare teddy in a scuffed Lloyd Loom chair.

'That's not for you,' he murmurs, yawning, as I climb back in. It really *is* a climb.

'What isn't?'

'The bear.'

'Who's it for, then?'

'Our baby.'

'What baby?'

'This one.'

~

I could do with a break. I told Phil I'd write the column from home today. He was OK with it.

He knows what I've been up against lately, what with the divorce and James's recent bombshell and Charlie being gone, and how knocked out of shape I feel about that.

The whole murder thing hasn't helped; in fact it's got to me more than I'm admitting. It doesn't matter that those guys were so long ago. People get under your skin. No love ever leaves you. There's a huge 'If Only' factor to every affair.

Time fills the cracks like Pollyfilla, until the memories are smooth and sound. But pain lingers. The rifts remain. Plus, it's always a shock when a lover dies, even if you hated their guts by the end, wanted to hang them by their ankles over the Ronda gorge for dumping you the way they did. Chas was the nightmare from the depths of hell.

It's all I'm saying. That's a time in my life I've had to learn to leave behind. For the sake of my sanity.

I used to drive myself crazy obsessing over what happened. I had professional help to forget – I saw a woman up in Highgate for years. I think I've got it in perspective now. At least, I thought I had. There are still things that I can't bring myself to think.

The upside? I have only positive memories of Paul, Roger and Jerry. Yes, we went our separate ways. Everything ends. There's never a *good* ending, is there? But they were the loves of my life while they lasted. *All* of them. A fact I've managed, so far, to keep from Phil.

I am safe in my nest – my nice warm office at home – surrounded by my books and pictures and mementoes, all the little models and cards and bits and pieces Charlie used to make for me at school. This is where I tuck myself away, amongst the security blankets.

My framed photos with the great and good are all here, the kind of pictures other people hang in their downstairs loos to impress the guests at their poncey dinner parties. Smother me if I ever contradict myself and invite you to one at mine; they are so not my scene.

I've got me with Liza Minnelli, Frank Sinatra and Sammy Davis Jr, taken at the Albert Hall in April 1989. 'For Once In my Life', 'I Get A Kick', 'Strangers In the Night', 'Mack the Knife'... God, the memories. That show will last forever.

I've got me standing next to Nelson Mandela in 2008, at his ninetieth birthday party in London for his HIV/AIDS charity. Amy Winehouse, Roger and Brian from Queen, Simple Minds, guys from the Soweto Gospel Choir – they're all in that one.

I've even got me with Her Majesty and Danny Boyle at the London 2012 opener.

And my favourite, with poor Paula Yates and Paul McCartney – the one dear Hogie took at Live Aid, in 1985. I can remember Paul turning back to me as he walked away with Linda after it was taken, in that funny little makeshift studio they had backstage.

'You're the girl John spoke to.'

Why deny it? Not that I wanted to. Did I want to? What would he say? Rabbits in headlights.

Linda frowned.

Did I miss something? Did he mean to say more, but couldn't bring himself to?

I've chosen to think of it over the years as a moment of recognition. Now and then, when crass self-importance gets the better of me, I'll dare to acknowledge the connection. Such as it is, and don't get me wrong.

It goes like this. Paul's had a career because of John. *I've* had a career because of John. The similarity ends there. While McCartney has no reason to be anything but insanely proud, I can't feel anything but secretly ashamed of myself. I sold my soul for all this, whatever *this* is, and I can never escape. I can't change it. I can't put it right. Never going back.

Whenever I look at that photo I see Paul's face behind the one in the picture, the face he couldn't have meant to show me that day. Would it even have been possible to photograph it? To get emotion so raw on film, the way Kirlian photography captures auras? I can't imagine it. There are things about our deepest selves that aren't meant to be recorded.

This reminds me of something Andy Peebles said to me years later, about Macca making contact with him shortly after John was killed. Paul knew that Andy had done the radio interview that turned out to be John's last. He wanted to ask him something. Lennon and McCartney were estranged at the time of John's death, and never got the chance to make up. Paul showed up unannounced at the Dakota once, hoping to make peace.

As the story goes, he got short shrift. John refused to see him. Andy knew what he wanted to ask him before Paul opened his mouth.

'Did John say anything about me?'

'That's between me and Paul.'

'Here Today' was the song Paul wrote about his love for John, on the 1982 album *Tug Of War*.

It was the conversation they never had. It was never a single. It didn't need to be.

~

The phone goes.

'Are you sitting down?'

'Very comfortably, Phil, thank you. I'm in my tracky bottoms and cashmere dressing gown,' I taunt him, savouring the moment. 'I've got Bowie's *Santa Monica '72* on vinyl in the background, a nice hot chocolate with marshmallows, pink *and* white, and a plate of –'

'There's been another one.'

'Oh, Christ, who the hell this time? Don't tell me it's ...'

'I don't think you'll have heard of this guy,' says Phil, 'which probably comes as a bit of relief. It's not someone you ... this one's different. Not even a musician, as far as we can tell, but of course I'm only guessing. For all I know he had a gig playing bass for some geriatric outfit down the local chip shop on a Friday night, not that he seems that kind ... but you never know with people, do you? Ever since I heard the one about our parish vicar, the closet naturist.'

'Isn't "closet naturist" an oxymoron?'

'As I was saying. Infertility specialist, British, living and practising in Toronto. Fifties, married, three teenagers. Quite a guy by all accounts. One of a team who perfected some groundbreaking technique for intra-uterine fertilisation …'

'… using lasers and robotics,' I said.

'Phil, I know this guy.'

'Christ, we're not paying you enough. Is there anyone you *don't* know? Don't tell me you and James …'

'Charlie's conception occurred entirely naturally,' said the Dalek in me. 'I've never been a patient of Joseph Llyn's.'

'Christ, you *do* know him.'

'I just told you I know him.'

'*Knew* him,' he corrects.

'What's happened?'

'The usual.'

'All the –'

'Exact same. Found him in the freezer cabinet at the back of his clinic, crammed in among the sperm samples. More than a mouthful's a waste …'

'You're a very sick man.'

'I'm joking. Bet that's scuppered a lot of people's plans for New Year. Family reported he'd gone on a stag weekend, fishing on Lake Simcoe with the boys. One of their wives died of cancer last autumn; he's getting hitched to the nurse who looked after her until she snuffed it or something. The prof's missus raised the alarm when he failed to return on Sunday night and she couldn't get hold of him on his mobile. It wasn't even ringing, though I'm not frigging surprised at minus two hundred degrees. His assistant found him next morning. What was left of him. A bit of a shock for her as well; it turns out they were doing the nasty in the lab of a night. Is there a bugger out there *not* knocking off someone they shouldn't be?'

'I hope that's not aimed at me.'

'If the cap fits.'

'Boss.' I hear my voice, as if I'm speaking under water. 'Sorry. I'm going to have to call you back.'

~

We were at the same school. He was a couple of years ahead of me. I don't think we'd exchanged so much as hello until that party at Anita's just before we broke up. We all took our own LPs. We'd scribbled our names on them, lugged them there on the 128 in Sainsbury's carrier bags.

My contribution was *Catch Bull at Four* and *Band on the Run.*

We had a good selection between us: *Don't Shoot Me I'm Only the Piano Player, Aladdin Sane, Venus and Mars, The Dark Side of the Moon.*

I can't remember who brought Carole King's *Tapestry*, which I fell in love with at first listen and have been mad about ever since.

Not Ben, he had Smokey Robinson's *A Quiet Storm*, and *Quadrophenia.*Every girl in the room had hair like curtains, split ends glued with Protein 21. I think most of us were dressed in velvet, even though it had just turned July.

I wore a plum-coloured midi I'd picked up in the sale for about seven quid, which was as much as I earned for an entire day at my Saturday job in the high street bookshop. It had a hole in the front, just beneath the square yolk, which I disguised with an embroidered butterfly I'd got in the market square haberdasher's.

Ben's thick dark-blond hair curled down over his blue-and-white round-tipped collar, which he wore with a navy velvet jacket and jeans. He came and stood in front of me on the off-white shag-pile carpet in Anita's mum and dad's front room – you could almost see light through him – and smiled.

'Hi.'

I think it was the first time I'd ever seen his teeth. The front two were long like a hamster's in need of a trim, and slightly crossed.

'I'm Joe,' he said.

'I thought your name was Ben.' They called him 'CM' at school. 'Cough Mixture.'

Ben Llyn. Benylin. I'd have changed it too.

'Ben is actually my middle name.' He grinned. 'My dad got the names they'd chosen the wrong way round when he went to register me. Family joke, they called me Ben when we were out or went on holiday or anything. Indoors it was always Joe. Still is. Joseph Benjamin Llyn. So I have a very good excuse for having a split personality. What's yours?'

'My middle name?'

'Your excuse.'

'I don't think I have one.'

'Joke!' He laughed. 'Just kidding. Wanna get a drink?'

We sat outside on the concrete steps that led from the kitchen into the garden, sipping home-made lemonade out of plastic cups and pretending to listen to the music from inside.

It was almost the summer holidays, and the evening was light and calm. Part of me wasn't there, but floating above, looking down on what we were doing. I liked the view.

He started telling me about his plans to go to Cambridge, to read Medicine. He'd always wanted to be a doctor, ever since his dog Toffee got run over and he couldn't do anything, and he died. He asked me what I wanted to do when I left school.

'I've still got two years to go,' I said. 'I haven't really thought about it. Something to do with music, I suppose.'

'What do you play?'

'Nothing.' I shrank.

'Don't you think it would…'

'My parents could never afford lessons,' I said. 'My mum told me they had a piano when she was little, but they used to chop them up for firewood in those days. People didn't have the room for them, she said. I'm going to get a guitar soon.'

'When?'

'Christmas,' I said. 'One Christmas. Don't know if I'll ever be able to learn how to play it, but it's my favourite instrument. Yours?'

'Scalpel.'

~

It's pitch-black outside. I'm sprawled on the bedroom floor. My mobile's clutched in my hand, flashing fifteen calls from Phil's desk number.

Christ, I must have missed the deadline. I haven't done that since Charlie was born, which wasn't a bad excuse. Three weeks prem, he couldn't wait. I had him in the ambulance on the way to St Mary's; the cord was round his neck. Feels like a hundred years ago.

Did I faint? I don't faint. I haven't ever fainted. What's the difference between that and blacking out? Same thing? I've never done that. Maybe I have.

There's a sore spot on my head, right where a baby's fontanel would be. Maybe I fell against something. The corner of the chest of drawers?

No blood as far as I can see, but I could have knocked myself out. The phone call. What Phil said.

Joe. Ben. It's coming back. I don't know what to do. Will it be on the news? I can't find the remote.

I need a friend.

'Harry, it's me.'

'Nina? You all right? I'm in Abuja.'

'A–w*ho*–ja?'

'Nigeria. Back Friday, can it wait?'

'I'm in trouble, Harry. They got Joe.'

'Who's Joe when he's at home?'

'I haven't told you about him, have I. Joseph Llyn. We used to call him Ben, he changed his name to his middle name, or was that really his first name, can't remember now, bugger it. Anyway, first boyfriend. First love. Nothing … we were just kids. Older than me. We had one summer; never saw him again. Went to Cambridge, made a name for himself, big-cheese medic in Canada. You must have heard of him, always in the papers, on telly …'

'What's happened to him?'

'Same as the others.'

'Who?'

'The *rock stars.* He's dead, Harry. Same story. Thing is, no one knows about us. I've never written about him …'

'Why not? You've written about everything else.'

'Even I have a private life. Anyway, it's so long ago, I can barely remember it. My parents are both dead. It's not like anyone could've gone sniffing around them for info about my past or anything. Harry, I'm scared.'

'You sure you're not being paranoid?'

I retch.

'Breathe, Nina.'

'You know what this is, Harry.'

'I do?'

'*Think*!'

'No need to be …'

'I'm *not* being. I'm scared shitless. Five men, five murders, same method – all people I know. *Knew*. One of them when we were barely out of nappies, that no one could know about. I never even told James. Didn't keep letters, postcards, anything. Doesn't take a fright-haired theoretical physicist.'

'It's all relative …'

'Harry, *listen* to me.'

'I *am* listening. It's me you're talking to. You forget, Nina. I twigged the second I took the call.'

'You think you're next.'

CHAPTER FOURTEEN

JAMES

James huddled down into his coat at a corner table in Searcys St Pancras Grand on the upper concourse, staring outwards, observing the revellers at the Champagne Bar. There were a dozen or so in buoyant mood, enjoying a drink before boarding the Eurostar.

He was feeling sorry for himself, and trying not to. But the sight of people having too good a time together made him acutely aware of being alone. For want of anything better to do, he sat chain-drinking, wondering where the past had gone. No point dwelling on it, he told himself. Snap out of it. The more you chased, the faster it ran; wasn't that the rule? Like happiness. Whatever it was, you could never find that either. You could only hope that one day it might find you. How did he know? Couldn't tell you. Couldn't tell you anything much at all.

Three days of meetings in Paris. *Ouais*. He couldn't stand the place. Parisians could be so arrogant. You did your best to speak to them in intelligible French, they dismissed you like something wet behind the ears and answered you in *Anglais parfait*. With *une odeur de merde* under their nose, to boot. *Ta gueule!*

The most interesting thing about Parisians as far as he was concerned was their appearance, which wasn't saying much. Which was a bit of a *compliment detourné*, to be honest. But at least everyone made an effort.

Even the office girl in a white-stitched black cotton jacket had a cheap bag and shoes to echo the detail. Even the *femme de chambre* wore lipstick; even the *bouquiniste* cocked his cap. And yet, he couldn't help thinking, Parisians had no taste. Not *real* taste. Not in his opinion.

What little they did have seemed to be pilfered from the Italians. You couldn't call a Dior handbag 'tasteful', could you? Not those huge blue sacks with giant initials in silver gilt, slung over a sabled shoulder. As for Chanel, what a joke. *Habits neufs de l'imperatrice!* Even second-hand, those jackets cost an arm and a leg, he knew. Literally thousands on eBay.

He'd looked. And yet. There was something about the way they wore hats and gloves, scarves and lipstick. That withering sneer. That curdled accent. So French, it wasn't true.

As for the architecture, the art, all that, who could be arsed? The cuisine he'd always found so-so. Too much meat. Murky sauces. Those stinking platters of *fruits de mer* served in bistros late at night always made him want to heave. Even the sight of other people tucking into them would do it.

Who the hell could sleep with rotten shellfish churning their insides out was what he'd like to know.

A slice or two of Brie or *chevre* and a reassuringly brittle baguette were usually all he fancied when he found himself Seine-side, which was getting a bit frequent for his liking. He never had much of an appetite in France. Especially not when he drank, which was most of the time since Nina kicked him out. Since he'd been living in a suite at the Shoreditch House, pretending to be young again, and cool.

He found his seat in Business Premier and slung his holdall and coat in the rack overhead. At least there was no bin to bang his head on. The doors hissed closed just as he'd settled down and was opening his iPad. Within minutes, used up by an announcement or two, the train was on the go.

By the time it had lurched a right past the gas cylinders, entered and exited its long, easterly tunnel and swivelled southwards, James was nodding off.

'James?'

'*Wha* ... sorry, half-asleep. What's ... *Daphne*?'

'Of all the gin joints in all the towns.'

'In all the world.'

'What are *you* doing here?'

'I could ask you the same thing!'

'Have a seat … oh, no, there's not one. Sorry, would you like to sit here? Where are you?'

'Back in Standard. Executive cars were all full; this was last-minute. Just on my way to get something from the buffet car when I saw you. Surprise, surprise, as they say! You want me to bring you anything?'

'No. No, thank you. I've just ...'

'Yeah. I saw you in the bar back there.'

'You were in there? Why didn't you come over?'

'Didn't like to. You know, after ...'

'When did you get to London? Didn't even know you were coming. Why didn't you call?'

'As I said ...'

James felt uneasy, he was aware of other passengers eavesdropping and pretending not to. They always did this; he'd done it himself, loads of times. You never knew who might be listening.

He interrupted her. 'Well, anyway. Nice seeing you again. How long you in France?'

'Four nights. I'm moving around a bit. We're out in the Bois de Vincennes tomorrow, actually; Axel's looking at real estate. You know where to find me.'

'I do?'

'At his hotel.'

Was that 'at his hotel' as in 'at his hotel *with* him', as in, sharing the same fuck-off suite, not to mention sharing a *bath*, as in, Axel 'n' Daff were now an item?

Or did she mean she just happened to be staying at the hotel he owned? Could be the former, but probably the latter, James reassured himself. She did work for the guy after all.

But was that all? She said she was his publicist. Did he really need a publicist to hold his hand while he was house-hunting? The sour Kraut had a lustful reputation, had allegedly chopped more hearts than cloves of garlic. Daphne hadn't seemed all that surprised to see him on the train, now that he thought about it, which was unsettling. He folded his arms and closed his eyes, beyond desperate for sleep.

But he was too restless. Things kept nagging at him. Why had he changed his mind and put Daphne off, that night in LA? He hadn't really allowed himself to think about this until now.

Perhaps it was the way she'd answered his email. Too quickly. Over-confidently. Done deal. Maybe the fact that she knew where he was staying, without him having said. He knew for a fact he hadn't told her, he would have remembered. What was she, stalking him now? He could be the Michael Douglas in a real-life *Fatal Attraction* for all he knew.

Oh, come on. Get a grip. I mean. She's about a hundred years younger than Glenn Close.

Was he missing the point? Ogling a gift nag in the muncher? Not a bad-looking filly, you'd have to say. Broad chest, gleaming coat, flaring nostrils, wide-awake eyes. She was up for it all right.

She'd jumped off relaxed, she was down to the start in a comfortable rhythm, obviously gagging for a canter, and we're off. A gorgeous, apparently unattached younger woman was flying over the hurdles at him, a welcome distraction from a painful and costly divorce. And he was *thinking* about it?

~

He spotted her in the queue for taxis at Gare du Nord and began an awkward dance to reach her, dodging dog shit trodden along the pavement by some wanker.

She looked bored and the other way as he approached. She was making him work for it. He touched her arm, ignoring silent voices yelling abuse, 'we were here *first*', 'wait in *line,* asshole', 'no, we don't queue in France, but we're doing it here: get to the *back*!'

'Where you heading, Daphne?'

'Place des Vosges.'

'Busy for dinner?'

'Depends.'

'On what?'

'On whether you're going to cancel me again, just as I'm walking through the door.'

She could kill with those eyes.

'Want to share a cab?'

~

If he'd ever been in a more eccentric venue than the Hotel Koch, James couldn't remember it. Salvador Dali masterpiece meets high street butcher's window. Completely out of place off the city's oldest square, a kick in the face of its arcaded redbrick mansions.

The uber-cool Koch was a glaring shop front, its facade and the flagstones in front sluiced oxblood. Was this supposed to be the last word, the *sine qua non*?

The white reception was tiled like a kitchen. It had *'abbatoir'* written all over it. Which perhaps was the point.

They took the strangest lift – he'd never been in one that doubled as an art gallery before – and rose in silence. At least, he assumed it was on the up. The thing could have been descending to the depths for all he knew, in which case who *knew* what lay ahead. He glanced at Daphne, but she avoided his gaze. Turned her back to him, in fact.

He was in her hair.

'Don't turn the light on.'

'Why not?'

'Just don't.'

He felt the dopamine rush like an electric shock. His heart detonated. No sooner had she touched his face than he was gorging on hers, plunging his hands into the neckline of her woollen dress, gripping and kneading her so hard, she must have seen stars. He lunged for a nipple and gnawed, tasting blood, they were on the floor now, violent rain lashing the windows or was he just imagining that bit, and why wasn't this love? Ripped at her stockings, thank God they weren't tights, his for the taking, he tore into her.

Tried to.

Tried again.

~

The steaming water flooded his ears and mouth and eyes, drowning her out, thank God. He was sure he could hear her screaming all the way from the Marais. Talk about woman scorned. Christ.

He yawned over for the soap, showered long and hard, towelled his skin until it felt hot and raw. He had to scrub himself clean of every trace of her. He stabbed at his hair with a comb, feeling foolish.

He couldn't remember *that* happening before. He'd legged it from the Koch, don't look back, keep on running, got to get away.

By the time he reached Saint Germain in the Sixième, she would have promised herself she'd never, ever, speak to him again. *Ever*. Wouldn't she have? Sure she would. She was better off out of it, she must know by now.

Divorce is tortuous, it fucks with your head, it does weird stuff to people. It makes you go mad, it's a warzone. There are no winners. Only lawyers. The last person you want to go getting involved with is a man going through a divorce. What on earth must she think? Don't. Fingers in ears. *La-la-la.* Can't. Don't. Won't think about it.

Why?

How about Nina?

This was about the woman he loved, right? Maybe. It must be. Who else? There's only her, there could only ever be her.

He knew it the first moment, on the plane, flying to New York, when they first looked at each other, how right was that, and he knew it that night, the first Christmas Eve, the one when it snowed, the night Charlie was conceived.

You don't forget stuff like that. Family. Together. Forever. No matter what. They'd said it so many times, those very words. He used to say them to his little boy when he went in his room to tuck him up and kiss him goodnight.

Charlie would make him promise that they'd always be together and that his daddy would never go away, not like some of his friends' daddies had gone away. Call him what you want – he couldn't give a rat's arse – this is what he promised, OK? What kind of father, husband, human, would go back on that?

He'd get them back. There was time. He wasn't dead yet.

CHAPTER FIFTEEN

NINA

I've talked to Phil and we've spoken to the police. There's not a lot we can do at the moment. Not until 'something happens'.

'You mean to tell me I'm supposed to sit around twiddling my thumbs waiting for someone to come round and kill me before Her Majesty's cavalry can step in and save me,' I said to the twelve year old who rocked up to take my statement.

'That's about the size of it,' he confirmed.

Phil gave me that look, the 'don't wind him up he's only trying to help' look. From a *journalist*? Do me a favour. Ninety per cent of this job is winding people up.

What 'proof' can I offer that some unidentified hitman is out to slaughter me? Well, of course, none. You say you knew all the deceased? Correct. Forgive me for saying so, Mrs Vincent. It's *Miss* Vincent, actually. My apologies. Given the celebrity status of the individuals concerned, it seems likely that they knew many hundreds if not thousands of people during the course of their lifetimes. It's life*time*, singular. Really? There's more than one of them. Indeed; forgive me for being pedantic, but they only had one lifetime *each*.

I can't be the only person alive who was intimately acquainted with the victims, can I? Suppose not. I get his drift, but he's not getting mine.

Work with me here, I said. When we have something to go on, he said. Keep an eye out for anything suspicious. You'll be the second to know. All you have to do is call. So you said. On your bike. When I need you I'll yell.

I need pictures. Not the way he looked at the time of his death, the papers are smothered in them, but how he was when we were kids. There was a time when I took photographs of everything I set eyes on, pretty much. I got a Polaroid, the Christmas I asked for a guitar. It went to camera heaven decades ago, but a few of the prints survived. Never took any of Joe, though. By the time I got the camera, he'd chucked me. Didn't need a virgin girlfriend in school uniform when he had willing undergrads crawling all over him, did he? You know what med students are like. The one picture I did have of him, a tiny head cut from a black and white contacts sheet, I put in the heart-shaped silver locket he gave me the week he went up. I know I've still got it somewhere.

I came across it not long ago when I was looking for a pair of diamond earrings to wear to a drinks do at St James's Palace. It's in the old walnut writing case I use as a jewellery box, which I keep tucked on a shelf at the back of the walk-in wardrobe. Now what have I done with the key?

Here it is. And here's the locket.

Hey, Joe. Haven't seen you in a while. Boyish face. Old-man mien. A look that says he took himself way too seriously. Not that he did; he was always larking about. Perhaps he was just camera-shy.

I wonder about his wife. Where had they met? What is she like? How is she coping? Bad enough hearing your husband's been killed, never mind the fracture-compounding detail that he was playing away. What comes first, anger or agony? How do you mourn? What do you tell the kids? Does the tart attend the funeral? Over my dead one. It's so long ago, and yet. This makes me so sad, I can't even cry. Emotional numbing? The deadness is paralysing.

It gets me thinking. What would happen if anything happened to James? We're still married. Legally. We're still each other's next of kin. I'd still be responsible for him, as he would be for me. Is this what they mean by 'where there's life, there's hope'?

I'm on tiptoe trying to put the writing case back when I notice it. From the corner of my eye.

The six-drawer filing cabinet underneath the rack where James's shirts used to be, the one where I keep the back-up laptop, the old hard drives, the dozens of notebooks accumulated over however many years. And the diaries. Thirty years' worth. Jesus. When and how could this have happened?

The padlock's lying on the floor, and the diaries are gone.

~

I spend a couple of hours at least trying to get hold of Charlie. No luck, and James is who knows where.

The number of the local mobile Charlie's supposed to be using in Oz won't go through; it's not even ringing. Have I got the code right? This is definitely the number he gave me, I double-checked.

In desperation, I drop them both an email. Not giving anything away. Anybody could be reading them. All three of my accounts are probably being hacked; nothing's private anymore.

You can't be too careful.

Charlie. Charlie. Oh my God. It's just dawned on me. It can't be. It could be. It is. What if it *is*? *Charlie's* the killer? It makes sense, it does. He knew I kept a padlocked filing cabinet in my wardrobe. James knew too – we shared the bloody wardrobe all those years – but James is …

And anyway, why would James …? What possible difference could it make? He's not crazy enough to something like that; at least I don't think he is. He never used to be, though God knows the stress of divorce can shove anyone over the edge. People do change, but I don't think he …

Charlie. What? It couldn't be, could it? Come to think of it, I can just see him, flicking through my old diaries, piecing it all together, making mountains out of molehills, taking every last dalliance from the distant past and making a sex-mad monster out of me.

I don't look good on paper, I never did. No woman can in these situations; the media is merciless, they head straight for the jugular. Look at what the rags did to Nigella. Made chopped liver of her for hooking up with another bloke before John was cold in his grave. Even in this age of so-called equality we're supposed to keep ourselves unto only one man as long as we both shall live. God help us once we've given birth. It's the whole 'men are studs, women are sluts' thing. Promiscuous? What does that word even mean?

Charlie, Jesus. It's not our fault, is it? Did Daddy and I do this to you? You've always seen the world your own way, taking everything at face value, taking everything and anything to heart. You can be crazy at times. You were often uncontrollable. You were still wetting the bed well into your teens. You were all over the place at college; that was never going to last. But you've made such fantastic progress these past few years,

I'm so proud of you. Would you really do this? But *why*?

I know how persuasive you can be. I've spent more time with you than anyone. You *are* me, in so many ways. You've always been more like me than your father; he glides over things, bigger picture, takes the overview, misses the detail. Misses the bloody point, half the time. You go over things again and again, you dissect and you memorise, you ponder and you ruminate, you scribble, you write, you lose sleep obsessing. It's as if we mirror each other. We know what the other one's thinking.

You've inherited the skills, such as they are. You're cunning, you get in places, you keep a level head, you can pretend to care, you can cry at will, people tell you things.

I can just imagine you, seeking them out, hanging around, getting to know them, making yourself indispensable, and then …

But what about money? Your allowance would never have run to all that. But you've got your own credit cards, of course you have. Flights from LA back to Ireland, UK, Japan, Canada, when we thought you were in Australia all this time, you could easily have charged all those.

You could *kill* people? You could do such a thing? My own child? They're haunting me now, those times you were cruel to animals. There was that cat next door, the class hamster, your guinea pig, all those insects in jars in the shed. The butterflies. I'll never forget them.

And I pretended not to see. I didn't *want* to see. I didn't want it to be you. Remember the time you had that boy from school down in the basement? You thought I didn't know what was going on. You told me you were playing hide-and-seek. You lied, and I knew, and I didn't say anything. Christ, you think I haven't agonised over that all these years? I hate myself for it. Can you understand that?

I should have had you both out of there like a shot, driven him home, confessed to his mother. But he had to tell his mother himself. And then she went and told the school, and the head called me in, and I defended you. I *lied* for you, Charlie, so that you wouldn't get expelled – said boys will be boys, it was just child's play, no harm done.

I knew the truth, but I didn't *want* to know. I let you hurt him. I was as bad as you. What does that make me? I've so often wondered how the parents of killers feel.

Are they tormented by fear that it's all their fault? Did they see signs they chose to ignore, not wanting to believe their own eyes? Like the mother of a child being abused by its own father, she can't know that, she can't allow herself to, she doesn't want to lose her husband, her lifestyle, everything she values, she blanks it out and closes her eyes and she puts herself first. She allows him to *continue to abuse*.

What mother would do that? *Would that be me*? Am I any better? Can we ever be free? Can we ever move on? How do we stop feeling hunted by our own conscience once we've done such a thing? Isn't punishment a life sentence for parents too? What about their other children, if they have any? What happens to *them*? You're doing me in, Charlie; you're killing me. I can't believe it, I won't.

James. I've got to get hold of him. He hasn't changed his number, surely, why would he do that, especially with Charlie away right now. He never picks up. What the hell am I going to do?

Christ, I've just remembered, I'm supposed to be meeting Tony at Ted's in half an hour. He doesn't know any of this. Nor do I want him to.

Phil said to lie low. He's put me on leave from the column for the foreseeable, but that can't last more than a fortnight, can it? 'Nina Vincent is away'. Yeah, right. Then I make the mistake of going out as her, on my way to something or other, and get accosted over the carrots in Waitrose by some reader who wants to know why you've not been in the paper lately.

The police are doing sod all. I should be getting on their case big-time about this. It's piss-poor if you ask me; I can't be expected to be a prisoner in my own home for the duration, can I?

Bodyguard, you say? Oh, sure. Maybe I should just get a driver, like Bill, and at least avoid the whole having to park the car and walk thing, just have someone drop me and pick me up wherever I need to go. That would help, wouldn't it?

I could get the shopping and the dry-cleaning and stuff delivered, couldn't I? Get my hairdresser and the nail girl to come to me. Like I'm made of money. No, I'm *not* brave, I'm the least courageous person I know. I'm not nearly as confrontational as I was when I was young, all *her* chat is pretend. The real Nina tends to run a mile from stuff these days. How many times. Yes, there's history. No, I won't go there. I've got to go and find Tony now.

~

He's not here. He's always first, no matter how early I arrive, which I'll admit isn't often. I sit at our usual table in the corner overlooking the river, and I sit here and sit here, willing the hands on my watch to stop.

He must have forgotten. Has he? Can they have got to him too? Anything's possible after three vodka tonics and a bowl of pistachios. My stomach's ballooning. It's really giving me gyp.

I call and call; he's not picking up. I send two emails on my BlackBerry and then wish to God I hadn't, I could be alerting the enemy. My own *son*? The paranoia's all-consuming; my mind will believe anything right now. I know what to do, suddenly.

I shouldn't drive, but what the hell. I'm going over to the O2 to find Bill. He said they'd be rehearsing a new cast for the show all afternoon, and having dinner later. He's bound to be there.

It's a slow old schlep to the arena. The traffic's backed up solid the other side of Blackfriar's Bridge. Southwark, Docklands, Tilbury, Lewisham, the outer reaches of civilisation. I duck off left before the Blackwall Tunnel, and swing my way round and onto the Greenwich Peninsular. It's early yet; the car park's almost empty. There's no sign of Tanner or Bill's Merc. They could be anywhere.

I dump the Jag as close to the venue as I can get it. It could be rain or snow, this menace in the air. It's going right through me.

The guy on the back door knows me; he's seen me here a dozen times with Bill.

He grins, dismisses my handbag with a wave when I offer it to be checked, and leads me along a back corridor to a flight of staff stairs. Up these, down another flight. An even narrower corridor and a pair of blacked-out double doors later, and I'm consumed by domed darkness.

On the extended stage, a couple of dozen semi-clad, scrape-haired dancers are being barked through their paces by a blonde. Suddenly I see him. Block A, far left, about ten rows back. Eye off the ball. His right arm is draped across a young woman's bare shoulders, and his mouth is glued to her neck. It's Bill.

She's not Freesia, that's for sure. I've never yet been allowed to meet his daughter, granted, but that's no father-daughter thing. That's sex.

A prelude to it.

It's so true, everything they tell you about times like this. You freeze in your tracks. Your heart seizes, your blood evaporates, your knees go separate ways. You move as if wading through syrup, all hope falling out of your head.

I do none of the things I've sometimes imagined myself doing in such situations. I can't rage or scream or hurl my handbag or march over and smack them both in the mouth with it or anything. I can't even feel sick. It's like I'm watching it happen to someone else.

I'm not here, I'm not her, that's not him, it's not Bill, just a guy who looks like him, I'm time-travelling now, I've been sieved to some remote dimension, my eyes are deceiving me. None of it's true. I'm still at home, tucked up in bed, asleep, my mind's doing overtime, I've invented this, it's the whole Charlie thing, I'm cracking up. Not as if I haven't been here before.

I retreat, slow motion; I don't want anyone to notice me, least of all Bill. Whisper to the guy on the door that I've got to go back to the car, just realised I've forgotten some papers I was supposed to get him to sign. I choke on the future, was there ever such a thing? Knock it back or spit it out?

Either way, I'm a loser.

I remember nothing of the journey home. All I know is I got here. Is this here? The street is hushed, chilled and accepting. It absorbs my footsteps, disguising them with drizzle in the dark. No moon.

The safety of houses. Other people's houses. There must be plenty of log fires on the go; the night is choked with smoke.

A vague oily smell conjures huge, ugly AGAs belching carbon dioxide. Very eco, not; I should be writing about this. Pissing the smugs off. It's what I do.

The neighbours' cars are home for the evening, some tucked away in garages, you can tell because the gates are closed. Others are parked on driveways. There's only my Jag, a 4x4 and an old Beemer out on the road.

Curtains are drawn on almost every window, apart from those framing perfect Christmas trees. Every front door but mine bears a ribboned designer wreath. Next door's nude magnolia blazes with blue and white lights. The least Christmassy colour, blue.

Plastic recycling bins, green and brown, not mine, are stacked neatly in front gardens, awaiting morning collection. All normal. What is normal? I imagine getting into one of them, snuggling down, decaying to nothing by dawn.

Somehow I'm in the house. My house? I couldn't tell you. Am I home? It doesn't smell like ours.

Am I upstairs? Down? Which room? I've got no idea. There's no sign that the place is mine. It has a family-home feel, but there's no one else here. The photos in the picture frames have no faces. Unfamiliar odours. Betrayal. Death. The lights are out. It's not warm, it's not cold … I can't tell what it is. Have I got my coat on? Did I leave it somewhere? Scarf? I'm sure I had one. I know I did. The scarf is gone.

It was a new one. Liberty. Bill gave it to me. I liked it, I think. What colour was it? Orange? And was it made of velvet? Maybe it was wool. And what about shoes? We always take our shoes off at the front door, to preserve the carpet. What carpet? Isn't this bare wood? Am I wearing shoes or boots? I can't feel my toes, my heart … was there ever a heart, or just a gaping hole where Bill used to be? Was he really, or was I kidding myself all along?

Wasn't James there once, and Charlie, our Charlie, filling the void left by Jerry and Paul, and Roger and Joe? Men I loved. Men I really believed I loved. They're nothing but names now. Names that chip like chisels and hack at my soul, claiming pieces that I can't afford to give.

Not Chas. Never him. He couldn't love. He never even loved himself.

I used to think he did. He took what he wanted. He never asked, couldn't listen, and wouldn't learn.

All these years I've quietly congratulated myself for escaping the nightmare, for pulling myself together and rebuilding my life. For setting myself free. I didn't need him to release me, not in the end. Yet something in the core of me wants that. Still yearns for it. Why? What's the point? He can't give it to me now.

I feel old and cracked, an ancient map of a place no one visits any more. A place that maybe no longer exists. There's more to forget than to remember. More to regret than to celebrate.

Why *would* Bill have wanted a hag like me, when he can have freshly squeezed bimbo every night of the week? Why did he bother, then? He never needed to pursue me. Was it only because I didn't seem to care either way? Because I didn't jump when he snapped? Because he's not used to 'no'?

Was I kidding myself? No fool like an old fool? Or could he just have been trying to talk himself into something he knew might be good for him for once? Because it was all, always, only ever about him. I see it now, I do. He never learned how to put others first. These people don't.

I knew that – I'd known it for years – so what the hell was I thinking? He never loved me. Everything he ever said to me was only words.

It's not as if I haven't been here before. Been here, done it, ate the cast. Romantic love, the great Shakespearian delusion. It's only for the young, only for people too stupid to know what it doesn't mean. We need it only when we've lost it.

I'm beginning to think there's a lot to be said for growing old alone. What was it Allegra said her mother said? *All* men. Something about *all men*. Every one I've ever loved, every one I've ever lost. Even the one I gave birth to. They all betray us in the end – all we've got to do is give them time.

I have to ask. Are any of our happy-couple friends actually happy: the Paul-and-Marcies, the David-and-Sophies, the Ron-and-Janes? Or is it all just a stupid facade? Are they going through the motions, having affairs on the side, sitting it out, biting their lips, waiting for the kids to leave home? Why do we do this to ourselves?

It's easier, I suppose. It costs a bloody fortune to dismantle a family and go separate ways. Anything for a quiet one. And yet. It's all anyone wants, isn't it? Someone there. Someone looking out for you. Someone waiting for you to come home. Who cares when your car won't start, when your plane's late, who worries when you don't call. Someone to visit you in hospital, bring you clean pants and puzzle books and chocolate oranges. Who doesn't count the cost. Who wants to know, how did it go, did you get it all done? Fancy a drink? A Ruby? A foot rub?

Look how many people manage to extricate themselves from one marriage, only to leap straight into another. Frying pan, fire; they'll never learn. The truth? Wait for it. Most of us would rather have someone to share nothing with, than the wealth of the world to spend alone.

Silence deafens. You climb the stairs to goneness, to another night in an empty bed. Trying to ignore the uncrumpledness of 'his' side. Knowing you'll be just as tired in the morning. With no one there to wake up to. *Nessun dorma.*

It doesn't matter now. It's over. I've run out of words. I can't even talk to myself. I haven't heard my voice for so long, I can't remember what I sound like. Not that I care. It's so dark, I can't see a thing. My heart's in my mouth, I can feel it slamming, like a carpet being beaten behind my gums.

But it's the doorbell.

It rings and rings and rings and rings and …

CHAPTER SIXTEEN

MONTREUX

'All I'm sayin' is, you could've *told* me.'

'I *did* tell you, Eddie.'

'Only after I'd heard it on the news.'

'Since when do *you* listen to the news?'

'I find that offensive.'

'You find everything offensive.'

'You didn't deny it.'

'I didn't deny it because it's bloody well *true*.'

'S'what I'm sayin', Clive.' Eddie sighs. 'It *is* true, you *are* managin' that little bint with the squint. I just think I should have heard it from the 'orse's mouth, thass all. I do 'ave rights, you know.'

Clive flares at him. 'Don't call Roxy a bint. She hasn't got a squint, either. It's just a lazy eye. Heterotropia.'

'Hetero-whatie-ya?' Eddie laughs out loud; he can't help himself.

'I think it's cute,' replies Clive, defensively. 'It makes her look even more vulnerable, and that's dangerous, that is.'

'Eh?'

'It scares people. When your eyes don't quite focus together.'

'You know what causes that, doncha.'

'For fuck's *sake,* Eddie!'

'Touchy! Got a bit of a thing for our Rox, have we?'

'Don't be ridiculous. She's young enough to be my kid.'

' And? When did that ever stop you? Come to think of it, when did it ever stop *me?'*

'You can keep your mitts off this one, an' all,' snaps Clive.

'Calm down, Grandad, you've made your point.'

'Sorry. I'm sorry. It's just … I wasn't keeping it from you, Eddie. Promise. We've never kept secrets from each other, have we?' Eddie feigns hurt. 'I'm beginnin' to wonder.'

'You *know* we haven't. Look, you've had a lot on your mind lately. Four dead Turns, Rochelle and the kids six thousand miles away, the forthcoming tour, whether we even go ahead with it given what's going on out there, plus all the rest. You don't need an itemised flamin' bill, do you. Talk about plateful. Timing, ya know? I just wanted to do it right.'

'To my ugly mush?'

'To your ugly mush.'

'Thanks a bunch.'

'You know what I'm saying.'

'I sometimes wonder, me old mate. I really do.'

Clive Clifford and Eddie Laine are walking side by side along the slushed-up end of the Lac Leman promenade, towards the ghost of Château de Chillon. Switzerland's best-loved monument shows barely a turret today.

They can hardly see each other in this weather. If not for Clive's pathetic yellow cap, Eddie thinks, he'd be invisible. Fat snowflakes fall steadily, cascading in veils between them and a pair of armed bodyguards. One behind, one in front, eyes everywhere.

Eddie can't see them, but he can feel them all right. He's so cold that he's starting to feel warm.

The distant Chablais Alps, also known as 'Les Dents du Midi', are little more than a rumour through the swathes of silver mist, suspended like muslin cloisters across the blur. The lake's many swans, ducks and gulls, like the sun, are less than a memory.

'I'm not sure I can handle much more of this.' Eddie coughs. 'Me plates are killin' me, plus it's not gonna do me chords much good, is it?'

'True. Just to that big tree and back then, yeah? Pull your scarf up. I'm fed-up with being cooped up indoors for days on end, I had to get out for a little walk.'

'Do you think it might clear by the weekend?'

'So they're saying. Hell of a dump.'

'I thought you liked it here.'

'The *snow*, you berk.'

'Race you back for a hot chocolate?'

'Get out, you pussy. Nice bottle of Remy Louis Treize warmin' back in the flat, that'll put hairs on yer chest.'

'Louis Treize? Two and a half grand a bottle, that stuff!'

'I can afford it, can't I? Anyway, I didn't pay for it.'

'Who the hell did?!'

'Not you, keep yer rug on. It's the one Freddie got me when the *Helicopter* album went double platinum. I've been saving it. 'A century in a glass,' he said, when he gave it to me.

'Woss it taste like?' I asked him. 'Jasmine, saffron and cigar box, darling,' he said, 'with a whiff of muff. Never touch the stuff myself, as I'm sure you'll understand, but it does have its uses.'

'The mind boggles.'

'Even yours?'

'What's that supposed to mean?'

'*Jokin'*, Clive,' says Eddie wearily, stamping his snow-crusted boots on the path as they reach the rear gate of their lakeside apartment block.

'It's usually you accusing *me* of leavin' me sense of humour in a bog somewhere.'

'Sorry, sorry. Got a lot on my mind.'

~

Eddie has his damp-socked feet up on the glass coffee table when Clive returns from the toilet.

The bottle is open, and two tiny glasses have been poured.

'Savour it,' says Eddie, as they take one each.

'Take yer time. Just a little lick to begin with. They say you get a couple of hundred flavours exploding in your gob with the first taste. Once you've got your filters round that lot, you can knock it back like a good'un.'

'Here's to our eyes.'

'Here's to our thighs.'

'Our thighs have met …'

'Our eyes not yet …'

'Here's hoping.' They pronounce the final phrase together, raise their thimbles with grand gestures, then sip like girls.

'Phwoar.'

'Phwooaarr.'

'Phwwwoooaaarrr.'

'Phwoar with knobs on.'

'Phwoar's *knobs* with knobs on.'

'*Claude* Nobs with knobs on.'

'Aw, don't speak ill of the dead. Without poor old Claude, there wouldn't *be* a Montreux. So tell me, I'm all lugholes. Where did you find her, then?'

'Rox? She kind of fell in my lap, really.'

'Where? How?'

'LA. I knew her mother.'

'What, like that?'

'Not exactly.'

'Spit it out, Clive, yer clear as mud.'

'It's complicated,' his manager says with a shrug, blood pooling in the back of his neck. He rubs at it defensively.

'I met her when she was little, and then she turned up again, years later. I knew just what to do with her.'

'Saying nothing.'

'Best not.'

'And the plan is?'

Eddie stares at him.

Clive eyeballs him back.

'What?'

'*What*?'

'What are you asking me?'

'All this time you're gonna be spending on Miss When-In-Rome with the cute eye thing. That mean you're gonna be spending less time on me?'

'Is that what this is about! You daft apeth! You won't believe it –'

'I probably won't …'

'– but what I actually had in mind was to put you two in the studio and on the road together.'

'Shut yer bib!'

'Hear me out. Tried and tested, ain't it? Aretha and George …'

'"I Knew You Were Waiting" …'

'Elton and George …'

'"Don't Let the Sun go Down on Me" …'

'Aretha and Annie Lennox …'

'"Sisters Are Doin' It for Themselves". Is this a quiz?'

'No. Johnny Cash and Will Oldham. Gene Pitney and Marc Almond. Diana Ross and Michael Jackson …'

'Paul McCartney and Michael Jackson …'

'Quite. Bono and Pavarotti …'

'*Eh*?'

'You remember, that fuckin' weird "Miss Sarajevo" thing they did way back, with Eno.'

'Oh yeah, that bit after Bono's never-ending "is there a time", then in bungs the fat one with the note from scrote. And your point is?'

'Vintage recording artist, young pretender. You bring your die-hard audience, she brings the teenybop pop-pickers, the thousands of kids her own age who've just discovered her and are eating out of her mitts. That way you get to double your fanbase, and open up a massive new market. Record sales go through the slates, immortality assured.'

'I like it. I think I like it.'

'I thought you might.'

'So. Are we talking a one-off single? An album? A coupla singles and an album? Singles, album and tour? *World* tour?'

'We can do whatever we want. The planet's our bivalve ocean mollusk.'

'Woss the catch?'

'No catch.'

'You mentioned I've gotta keep me paws off.'

'Keep your distance to go the distance, Eddie boy. You know it makes sense.'

~

Half a bottle down and Clive's out for the count, or at least he's pretending to be, exhausted by this think-on-your-feet exchange. Talk about fly by the seat of your thong.

Eddie's mind, meanwhile, is doing overtime. About a thousand to the dozen. The implications of Clive's master plan are unbelievable. He's a dark old nag, innee? Who'da thought he'd have that little caper up his pet peeve. Could be bloody good an' all.

Bit of a shame he's got to keep his wooden leg in the cupboard, but mustn't shit on your own doorstep, not at a time like this. Clive must have his reasons for wanting him to keep his fingers out of Roxy's pork pie.

Probably time to hang up his crutchless, anyway. Didn't he say he was done with all that when he married Rochelle? You don't go out for a Big Mac and a milkshake when you've got Beluga and Krug indoors, do ya? Not on your nelly. Not if you've got half a brain.

She's a bit of a looker, though, old Roxy. Young Roxy. Whatever she is when she's at home. Just the thought of her's got him going; plenty of life in the old dog yet. A bit of a vampire thing, wouldn't it be? Like if he could get into her, *really* get into her, and have a little nibble on her talent and youth. That'd put lead in his pencil, wouldn't it? That'd give him a whole new lease of life.

Imagine if him and the squint-bint did end up together.

Anything's possible.

Imagine old Clive's ugly mush.

CHAPTER SEVENTEEN

LADY MUSGRAVE ISLAND

What day did Howie, Deisel and Neesha finally rock up in Sydney? Who the hell knew? What year was it, even? Was he still alive? Charlie had been squiffed out of his skull for four days now, topping up each morning before breakfast, lurching through lunch, collapsing again by teatime.

The extender-bender began when Neesha and Chelsea first clapped eyes on each other. It showed no sign of letting up.

What was he supposed to do? For all he knew, his friends weren't even coming to Oz after all – he hadn't heard a note from them for weeks.

Plus, they'd left him on his own for Christmas, the bastards. So much for the whole 'barbecued turkey and "Jingle Bells" and rounds of Dambusters on the beach' number he'd been so looking forward to.

Did Neesha really expect him to sit around bopping the bologna on the off-chance that she might one day tap-dance into view in her strange white shoes and geeky green frock, and all would be right again?

As for Chelsea, did she really expect him to just dump his girlfriend, just because he'd been boning *her* for a week?

Well, he and Neesha had been out together four or five times now, so he supposed that did make her his official girlfriend.

Women. He'd never get the hang of them. In fact, he'd made up his mind not to. Never in his life, OK? The bleeding bitches really were from the dark side of Venus, so what was the point in even trying? Let them slug it out among themselves. New Year's fireworks? *What* New Year's fireworks? He must have slept right through those, too.

'You can't understand why Chelsea's mad at you? You're having me on, bro.' Howie chuckled, tossing his black flip-flop repeatedly at the garish yellow cooler box a few feet in front of them on the scorched sand until Charlie had to plead with him to stop. The blurred image was like being assaulted by a giant plastic bee.

'That's what I said.'

'Mate. You're having a laugh. Not only does your girlfriend pitch up to find you mattress-dancing with another chick, and a Yank at that, but you've only gone and porked her nympho sister.'

'I never even touched Kari-Ann!' flared Charlie, pulling himself up on his elbows, surveying the sparsely populated morning beach, seeing dismally few bikinis, diving into the cooler for another beer, regretting immediately the sudden movement.

'It's *me* you're talking to!' Howie laughed. 'We *saw* you. Left you and Kari-Ann comatose in their room after the party, when we all went off for the midnight swim but you two were too skunked to join us. We decided you'd be all right and probably wouldn't choke on your own barf. At least there were two of you – you could look after each other if worst came to worst. We got back less than an hour later to find you buzzin' the brillo on the bathroom floor, thought Chelsea was gonna murder you or her sis or the pair of you. We had to tear her off.'

'You're winding me up.'

'Wish I was, mate. I truly wish I was.'

'So what happened next in your Oscar-worthy little thrillerette?'

'Neesha broke down, finally. It was the last bloody straw for her. She'd been keeping it together quite well 'til then, considering.'

'Considering what?'

'That she'd landed in Sydney to find the love of her life boffing another bird.'

'I am *not* the love of her life. She's only nineteen! She's still at college, for fuck's sake!'

'*She* thinks you are, which is the point. It's what girls do.'

'What is?'

'Oh, boy, when are you gonna grow up? Convince themselves that the bloke they're dropping their drawers for is the absolute love of their life, of course. It's the only way they can justify it to themselves.'

'Justify what?'

'The fact they're having sex. They find it all a bit sordid and indecent if they're not actually in passionate romantic love with the guy. It's the whole guilt thing, so they persuade themselves they are, just so that they can get on with it and have a good time. It has to have this great big dramatic, sweeping, world-without-end dimension to it, emotion coming out of their ears, otherwise they can't possibly live with themselves.'

'Since when were you the world expert on the sexual psychology of the lesser spotted teenage female?'

'Common sense, mate. I worked it out as I went along. Plus Ralphie gave me a few pointers.'

'Ah, the wisdom of the esteemed elder brother.'

'An advantage you will never enjoy in this life, my friend.'

'Thank you for pointing that out, arsehole. So if what you're telling me is true, what happened to Neesha in the end? I haven't seen or heard from her since.'

'Not fucking surprised. Deisel had to haul her away to persuade her to put a sock in it before she split her difference howling the place down.'

'I bet he did.'

'Not like that. He's a decent bloke as it happens. Not like …'

'*Me*, you mean? Not like me, is that what you're saying?'

'That's not what –'

'Course it wasn't,' Charlie snarled. 'Look, whatever did or didn't happen that night, this is all a right sewerful and I just want the hell out. They can all get stuffed.'

'I think they all did.'

'*Shut* it! Maybe if you lot had shown up when you were supposed to, when you actually promised you would, perhaps things would have worked out a bit nicer for all concerned. As it is, what's done is done, although I'm still not convinced by your version of events by the way, and there's not a lot I can do to change things, is there? Three nutters falling over themselves to chew my balls off and I haven't got the strength to fight them off. I'm outta here.'

'I get it. Take the cowardly way out.'

'Can you blame me?' asked Charlie.

'Not really,' Howie replied, scratching his head. 'I'd probably do the same in your shoes. So what you gonna do now, then?'

'You know we said we might fancy a bit of desert island somewhere up on the barrier reef for a few days?' said Charlie. 'I've been checking out a coupla places, and Lady Musgrave Island looks cool. Why don't you and Deisel follow me up there with Neesha, end of the week? She might have calmed down and forgiven me by then.'

'On the other hand she might be coming at your knob with a meat cleaver, but I'm with you, we should look on the bright side. Could do, couldn't we? How you getting up there?'

'Booked myself on a DH8 to Bundaberg. Really cheap, check it out.'

'Right-oh, Biggles.'

'Quit taking the piss. Gonna rent some gear in 1770, hang around in Agnes Water for a couple, boat it over to Lady Musgrave after that.'

'You booked?' asked Howie.

'Booked what?'

'The camping. You know you have to book it online in advance. We looked at all this before we came out. You know you have to take absolutely everything with you, even your *agua*. Five litres a day per head, they reckon. You can't get refills for a week until the boat comes in. You can have a fishy, on a little dishy …'

'Yeah, yeah, it's cool. I can get everything up there. Won't need much, that's the whole point.'

'At least you won't have to lug a portaloo.'

'What?'

'Not a totally uncivilised back of beyond; they've got toilets, haven't they? Just don't forget your bog roll.'

~

The transfer from 1770 took ninety minutes. It was so choppy, Charlie nearly lost his lunch. Most of his fellow passengers had gone green and were honking over the side before they were halfway.

He ignored all of them and sat very still, slowly gulping back saliva as it welled in his mouth and wiping his half-closed eyes.

I am heading for the most awesome coral cay on earth, he kept telling himself. The agony's gotta be worth it.

He wished he didn't have a titanic hangover. Perhaps the pristine sea air would help. Then again, yeah right. He tried to summon some enthusiasm, but kept wishing someone would put him out of his misery. The promise of unspoilt paradise failed to move him. For now, at least.

When they finally arrived, Charlie humped his kit down the beach in a battered wheelbarrow, pitched his tent amongst Noddy Tern-killing pisonia trees, set out his boxes and his tiny gas stove and spent the next couple of days silently forcing himself out of his sleeping bag and going through the motions.

He snorkelled the shallows, dived the coral, stalked turtles and birds, went fish-feeding and reef fishing and island-walking as if his life depended on it, which possibly it did.

In filling his head with new experiences, perhaps there'd no longer be room for the old. Who was he trying to kid? He spoke to no one unless he could help it, and nobody bothered him. He wanted his mother.

Yet what of his father? Charlie tried not to think about James. It hurt too much. They hadn't spoken in ages. He still felt angry beyond words that his dad had given in so easily, that his parents really were splitting up. What was it with adults? Why go to all the effort of falling in love, making plans, getting married, choosing a house, having kids … why build all that so painstakingly and expensively, put so much energy into it, only to fuck it up, chuck it away and bugger off without a backward glance, to the point that you'd lose everything and be looking at starting again in middle age? It made no sense. And the victims are always the kids.

Not that they'd ever understand, he thought. They'd never get what they'd done to him. Perhaps they didn't want to; they'd never be able to live with themselves. Perhaps they'd only stayed together because of him.

He started again, in his head, to ask the questions he'd never get answers to.

He re-lived the night his mother confessed what was going on. Remembered how stunned he felt, as if she'd slapped him round the face with a shark. He'd fled to his room and cried all night, feeling furious, wanting to kill them, someone. Wanting to make them pay for what they'd done.

They'd been lying to him for years; they must have been. Endless lies, terrible secrets. He wanted to know everything, and yet didn't. He longed for the truth, but he knew he couldn't handle it. He wanted someone, anyone, to pay for what he'd been through. He needed to get to the bottom of what had caused the split, but was scared of what else he might find.

The children always blame themselves, don't they? He'd read this. They can never accept the finality. Not even years later.

Like when a pet dies. Sitting there staring at the lifeless little creature that was once your best friend, putting your face really close to his until your noses touch, sharing your breath with him, rubbing the poor thing's chilly body like a genie's lamp, trying desperately to bring him back to life. This was what it was supposed to feel like with a pet, wasn't it?

Charlie knew he was supposed to be a man. To the outside world he was doing a decent job of it, he hoped.

I mean, such a complicated love life already. Must mean something.

But inside, he was still just a small, lonely boy who just wanted to go to sleep at night knowing that his mother and father were in bed together across the landing, with the lamp on, and that all was right in his world. Family. Together. Forever. No matter what.

~

'No fires.'

'Sorry?'

'It's in the rules. Can't you read? There are signs up everywhere. You're not allowed to make fires here.'

'All right, sorry, I'll …'

'People like you make me sick,' added his hefty half-naked neighbour. He'd seen her around the place, wearing a moth-eaten dressing gown, with a similarly pachydermous partner. Man? Woman? Both?

'Always gotta do things your own way, you young'ns. You think you own the darn planet. Think you don't have to bide by the same rules as the rest of us. These things are in place for a reason, pal.'

'Look, I've said I'm sorry,' said Charlie, reasonably. 'I did know, to be honest. I just forgot. I'll put it out now. Here, water bottle, flames, finished. Gone. Bury the ashes in the sand, no harm done. It's only a little fire. I haven't caught the reef alight or anything. Not that I can see the difference. I mean, they let us cook on a Primus.'

'Rules is rules. You think you're better than everyone else? Not so much as a squeak out of you on the way over, and look at you now, tucked up on your lonesome with your pree-tend friends.'

'Actually, my friends are coming out at the weekend.'

'They all say that.'

'You'll see for yourself.'

'We'll be gone tomorrow.'

'Not before time,' Charlie muttered under his breath.

'What did you say?'

'I said I hope you've had a good time.'

'Well, you too, Master Crusoe. Me, I'd live here all the time if I could. Does your mother know you're out here?' she added, softening now.

'I don't suppose she does,' admitted Charlie. 'But I *am* twenty-four.'

'You could have fooled me. Well, you take care anyhow.'

~

He sat cleaning a fish on a rock at sundown. It was a snapper he'd stalked and caught himself, with a spear he'd carved from a thin pisonia branch.

He was all Boy Scout again with his Buck hunting knife, and it felt good.

Charlie was methodical in his approach and more capable than he thought, taking the making of a spear in his stride, splitting the heavier end of the branch carefully down the middle, wiggling a small wedge-shaped piece of wood in between to keep the prongs open, lashing the wedge in place very tightly with twine, which he twirled and looped and stretched and overlapped, knotting it for all he was worth, knowing that it would work loose once it got wet.

He huffed and puffed as he went. He was quite breathless with excitement at what he could do when he put his mind to it. He carved the inner edges of the prongs into tapered points, then hardened them in the flame of his little stove. It seemed primeval, simple, a way of leaving the world behind.

He felt human and carefree and strong. Not a trace of the streaked fake tan now. His skin was burnished by the sun and soothed with oil. His wheaty hair gleamed golden. Five days without shaving had left his face bristled and burred. Not that he could see what he looked like; he hadn't bothered to bring a mirror … had merely a toothbrush and toothpaste, a little blue soap on a rope and a few plasters. He rinsed the fish with a splash of water from his bottle, arranged it carefully on a strip of foil and fired up the Primus. He had wine, too: some of the gullet-searing juice the locals called 'goon'. A four-litre box of it that had cost him about ten dollars.

Doom with a view.

~

The next evening, ahead of an amber sunset, the busybody land-blubbers despatched back to the mainland, he scraped twigs and dead leaves into the small hollow he'd scooped out and ringed with stones and shells, and kindled a camp fire away from prying eyes.

He had planned to try lighting one using the base of a can of Coke and a couple of squares of chocolate, a novel method he'd seen demonstrated on a wilderness survival show in LA a few weeks back, but his chocolate ration had melted in the heat before he got a chance to deploy it as aluminium polish. He resorted to his one box of cooking matches;

what the hell. Darting back into his tent, he returned with a heavy black rucksack, squatted down, crossed his bare legs, and began to pull out the notebooks, one by one.

How many years had his mother been keeping diaries? It was hard to tell. These were probably only the latest in a weighty stash. Where on earth could she have hidden all the rest? Destroyed them, maybe?

He could hardly imagine his mother doing that. She was a hoarder of the most annoying kind, she could never throw anything out. Not even used wrapping paper, which she'd been known to iron and use again, embarrassingly. Nor the shiny, tinselly, twirling bows that came stuck on Christmas presents; she always saved those for next year. Nor any bit of satin ribbon that arrived wrapped around bouquets of flowers. Nor even used stamps; she collected those in a cracked teapot and sent them off to a charity a couple of times a year when it got full. Nor even obsolete coins from deceased currencies; there was still a giant moneybox of Greek drachmas, Cypriot shillings, Italian lira and French francs on the radiator shelf in the hall.

For a woman of her income and reputation, his mother could be infuriatingly frugal.

Considering that their house was so stuffed full of junk, finding the spare key to the filing cabinet in her walk-in wardrobe had been a doddle. He'd had a hunch that her hiding place would have something to do with books.

Tracing his fingers along the heavily laden shelves in her study, one particular volume jutted out slightly, and had clearly been taken down recently. *The Tomb of Tutankhamen, Volume Two*, by Howard Carter, published by Cassell, he noted in passing.

It was a real book, all right. An actual book – an old one too – the pages of which had been carved into like a block, then glued together … an awful thing to do to a precious old book, really, to leave a small, yellowing, box-like cavity large enough to hide a key in. Sure enough, there it was.

He hadn't known what to expect of the filing cabinet. He just knew it was there, and that it had a padlock on it, which was locked, and that the fact that the cabinet was locked in this way meant that it must contain stuff he wasn't meant to see.

Maybe his father hid things in there too, though Charlie doubted it.

Nothing at all secretive about James; his life was an open book. Or was it? Charlie had always assumed so; how wrong can you be?

Anyway, there was an old laptop, a couple of dead hard drives, endless dog-eared, scribbled-in notebooks, and, tucked away right at the back of the bottom drawer, all these.

Without thinking, he'd gone into his mother's bathroom, pulled out a vanity bin liner from the drawer under the sink, lavender-scented and talc-y – a bit old-lady for his mother he always thought, how he loathed those little white plastic bags but what the hell, needs must – and crammed every last diary into it. He'd have plenty of time to read them on the plane.

Just one more thing he had to take care of. He didn't want his mother to know that he was the one who'd taken the diaries. Because she'd guess that he'd found the key. He had to cover his tracks, needed to make it look like an intruder had broken in.

He slid the filing cabinet drawers home, slotted the hook of the padlock through its corresponding loop on the cabinet, locked it carefully again, then went and replaced the key in its Boy-King tomb on the bookshelf.

He then crept downstairs and rummaged for the old plastic toolbox in the basement. Finding the pair of heavy-duty red-handled pliers, he ran back up to his mother's wardrobe and wrenched the loop right off the filing cabinet, leaving the still-locked padlock lying on the carpeted floor.

~

The diaries dated back to the early 80s. They were all here. The lives and loves of his own personal she-devil. How she'd met Paul Judd when she was little more than a kid, how they'd painted Dublin every shade of fruit. The reckless affair with Roger Blacker, what they hadn't got up to. All of it here in blood-curdling detail, spelled out in terms he'd rather she hadn't known.

Eddie Laine too, but he wasn't dead yet. What she'd written about him wasn't clear. There was a hint at something odd, but the handwriting was tiny and erratic and smudged, in black biro, as opposed to her usual blue fountain pen ink, and perhaps even tear-stained.

There were coffee-cup rings pressed into the pages, and even little swipes of dried blood. What did she do, peel her nails off while she was writing it? He couldn't make it all out; it was like trying to read hieroglyphics. And Jerry Colbert, that dead dude all over the television while Chelsea was asleep in Sydney. The man was an animal.

He knew it.

There was another notebook, a scuffed old thing covered in faded purple suedette. The kind with a magnet in the front cover flap keeping it closed when not in use.

Black text, the margins filled in with doodles of tiny houses and sunbursts, of front doors and tree-lined garden paths, of waterfalls and rabbit faces, cartoon crucifixes, even bones and skulls. The handwriting was even tinier than in the previous notebook, almost completely illegible in the half-light. Only when he held it closer to the fire did Charlie realise that the entries were written in French. Could he remember enough? Were his eyes good enough? He put his mind to it and got stuck in.

Three paragraphs along, the name 'Chas Channing' leapt out at him. It appeared more than five times over two pages.

He remembered this guy, didn't he? That old-time rocker whose body was found on a boat in LA. Chopped to bits. The one that started it all. From what he could make out here, she was writing about the killing of John Lennon. The shooting in New York, years before he was born.

She was outside the Dakota building, John and Yoko's place. Was she really? Like, on the spot, the night it happened?

Wow. She'd never said anything. Why not?

8th December 1980. Some dude called Andy Peebles. Charlie knew that name. He'd been round their house with his wife for dinner, hadn't he? Famous DJ, right? A phone conversation. Someone called Rhett. She was telling this Rhett about the murder. She actually *saw* that guy shoot him; she even knew how many bullets. Jesus. Then this guy seemed to be trying to talk her into … she had to write something. She was supposed to write about what happened. Then another bit, seemed to go off at a tangent. Nightmares. Sleepless in … *La nuit la musique est mort* ... the night the music died. *Je suis enfermé dans ma chambre putain, ma cherie ... ne veux pas etre une autre John Lennon ...*

What was he supposed to do but fear the worst? If you play with fire, you get burned. What else didn't he know about? He couldn't take it any longer. Ripping violently at the pages, blinded by tears, he sat crumpling them into the flames until all was ash.

CHAPTER EIGHTEEN

NINA

I do not cower. For the avoidance of doubt, I'm not one of these idiot housewives who sit there freaking out, paralysed by the sound of their own front door bell, terrified to twitch, let alone get up and see who it is.

I'm the type who chases rogue window-cleaners, tree-loppers, God-squadders, bogus charity collectors, door-to-door double-glazing con-artists and roof salesmen off my doorstep, fifty lashings of my tongue and don't come back. I'm not the kind of flimsy female who lurks in hallways, calling for The Husband to come quick, tip-toeing up under the spyhole to try and cadge a look, hoping and praying it's not some drug-crazed chancer about to kick the door in, rape me and hack me to bits with a bread knife. Even after everything else that's been going on, I do not and never will think like this.

The closest I've ever come to a real-life murder, so to speak, was a few years back when the bloke in the corner house got stabbed in the stomach with a kitchen knife by the Turkish waiter boyfriend of his soon-to-be-ex-missis, for nothing more provocative than returning to the Former Matrimonial Home one Sunday afternoon to drop their kids back after a weekend visit, and rocking up twenty minutes too soon.

He caught them at it, there was a hell of a ding-dong, and we had police here for weeks. I do have a vivid imagination, I'll grant you, but not much scares me.

My mother was the sort of woman who visualised life-threatening scenarios in every shadow, and saw accidents about to happen at every turn. You never wanted to be in a car with that one. I'm not like her; I never have been. I'm no victim.

Having said all that, here I am, cowering for England. It's not on. I am not this person, who the hell is she? And what the hell's she doing in my house?

'It's me, Nina, I know you're in there. Open this door for crying out loud, I'm freezing me nuts off out here.'

'Harry? What the fuck are you …?'

'Don't sound so disappointed, like you were expecting somebody more interesting.'

'Don't be daft, give me a mo. I can't find my keys.'

'Hurry up, brass bleedin' monkeys. I'm dying for a widdle.'

~

When he emerges from the downstairs cloakroom still zipping, I can tell what I must look like by his face.

'Don't ask,' I warn him. 'Today's not my best day.'

'Bill, is it?'

'Bill who?'

'That bad, huh.'

'You wouldn't believe me. In fact, you'd probably run right round there to knock his block off. Let's just say I won't be returning his calls. That's if he ever phones me again, which I doubt he will, not after … Anyway. Moving on.'

'You win some. There's always Tony.'

'Blink and you'll miss him. Things with dear Melanie – "Cheeks", as he calls her – are clearly not as over as he claims. I'm done, Harry, if you want to know. Too much else on my mind.'

'Like what? Rock 'n' roll bogeymen beating a path to your door?'

'Don't joke. Do *not* joke about this. It's all getting a bit close to home, what with Joe in Canada …'

'Canada's a seven-hour flight away. Bits of it.'

'You know what I mean. Not to mention my filing cabinet in the wardrobe being broken into, my old diaries being nicked but nothing else as far as I can see, so someone obviously knew what they were after. Don't know when and how it happened because I've only just noticed it …'

'Told the police?'

'I just have.'

'I don't mean me, you idiot. The local constabulary. You should've filed a formal complaint, got them round to dab the place, take a statement. There's a process. Come on, Nina, you know all this. You'll have contaminated the evidence by now.'

'Oh, so *what*.'

I flop into the sofa opposite the one he's perched on, put my feet up on the leather stool and close my eyes. Harry's got his shoes on. I decide not to say anything. He's *here*, isn't he? The place is warming up a bit now there's conversation in it.

'I can't get hold of Charlie, Harry. Haven't heard from him for weeks. He could be anywhere.'

'Everywhere and nowhere, baby. That's where he's at.'

I hesitate. Can I say this?

'What if he's the killer, Harry?'

'*What*? Oh, no. You really *have* lost it. ET phone home. Give us your GP's number.'

'Oh, har har. Take me seriously for once, can't you?'

'I always do, Nina. That's my problem.'

'Harry, please, *I'm not joking.* I honestly think Charlie might be involved.'

'*Don't* be so ridiculous. You've been watching too many films or reading too many thrillers or something. I need a drink is what I think. I'll leave the car and get a cab. That's if you're not inviting me to stay the night – only jokin', I know my place. Give us a drink, babe.

'Look, your head's doing overtime, your mind's playing tricks. You've been under a lot of stress lately. Charlie's off travelling, you haven't heard from him because he's having a whale of a time, hanging with his mates. He hasn't got time to keep checking in with his mum. No news is good news.

'He must be over the moon to be on the road without you and James breathing down his neck. Don't you remember what that felt like, to be rid of the 'rents? He'll be doing the five-day hangovers, feeling his way, finding his feet. He'll have a couple of birds on the go by now; it's all part of the process at that age. He won't know whether he's coming or going until he's been.'

'*What*?'

'Figuratively speaking. You've got to calm down, Nina. This'll put you over the edge.'

'It already has. Tell you the truth, Harry, I'm thinking of quitting the column, getting the hell out. Doing something else. It's time. I've been at it for far too long, and I'm bloody knackered. The murders. James. Bill and Tony. Charlie. I think it's all catching up with me.'

Pause.

'Was that your door again?'

'Can't be, you're already here.'

'There it is again! That was definitely your front-door bell. Want me to get it?'

Pause.

'Allow me,' says Harry, decisively.

I can hear him talking to someone on the doorstep.

Who the hell could it that be? I can't be arsed to go and look. I just sit here. Have another drink, Nina.

The next thing, they're standing there together in front of me. Harry and Neal Goddard.

'Hi, Nina,' beams Neal.

'*Neal*?'

'You know him?' says Harry.

'Harry,' I sigh, guessing where this is about to go, 'this is Neal Goddard, my divorce lawyer. Neal, this is Detective Inspector Harry

Hinton, my old friend. Formerly of SOCA, currently with the National Crime Agency.'

'Ah, *yesss,'* hisses Neal, sarcastically, '*very* front-line. Very British FBI. Do we really *need* a British FBI? Not exactly *British*, is it? Anyway, a mere re-branding, as far as your average tax-payer can perceive. A shiny new name for an unwinnable board-game of cyber warfare and fearless foreign gangs.'

'Harry …' I start.

'Sorry?' says Harry, ignoring me completely.

'Well, look,' sneers Neal, 'we've got MI5, MI6, GCHQ, Customs and Excise, the Special Branch, the Serious Fraud Office, Immigration, the Inland Revenue, Interpol, Europol, Eurojust, Cepol, Olaf, and now *this*? All a bit turf wars, isn't it? I mean, what on earth are you people tackling that isn't already covered?'

'Nothing much,' mutters Harry. 'Only organised crime, drugs, human trafficking, illegal immigration, cyber-crime, as you mentioned, oh, and the child sex trade. A poor excuse for a board-game, all told.'

'That's all very well,' scoffs Neal, unruffled. 'But you're going to have to try a bit harder, aren't you? SOCA spent £15 for every one pound seized; didn't I read in the *Telegraph* recently? And you forgot to mention counter-terrorism.'

'Still with the Met.'

'Of course.' Neal dismisses Harry with a curl of his lip, and turns to me.

'Drink?'

'Not for me, thanks, I'd best be off,' brisks Harry, kissing me on the cheek and making for the door.

'I've come armed.' Neal smiles, ignoring Harry, and proffering a boxed bottle of 2004 Louis Roederer Cristal.

'It *is* chilled, I had them put it back in the box. A more elegant offering.'

'You're an arse,' I hiss, before following Harry into the hall.

'I'm so sorry, he's being an arse. Thanks for coming round.' I pull a face, leaning towards him to tug up his collar, which he always hates, and moving in for a hug. But he pulls back.

'Are you sleeping with him?'

'*What*?'

'You heard.'

'As if it's any of your business. *No*, as it happens, but how dare you ask.'

'He who dares,' snaps Harry.

'Oh, Harry …'

'If you're sure you'll be safe in the hands of a wanker, I'll see you soon.'

~

'Was there any need for that?' I flare at Neal, irritated by the fact that he's shed his coat and shoes uninvited and is now sprawled across one of my sofas, loosening his tie.

'Nice place,' he muses, appraising the room with a glimpse. 'Now, where can I find a couple of glasses?'

'Don't you think this is …'

'Come on, Nina, I've made a special effort. All this way.'

'What did you want, anyway? I was just about to …'

'I thought it was time we had a proper heart-to-heart. In private. Away from prying eyes.'

'So you just rock up uninvited? How did you know I'd even be home?'

'I do my research.'

'What's that supposed to mean?'

'My little joke.'

‘Well, Harry didn’t find you very funny. A bit cheap, wasn’t it, insulting him like that? He’s my best mate.’

‘You surprise me.’

‘Excuse me?’

‘A bit NOCD.’

‘You fucking snob.’

‘Don’t mention it. Glasses?’

I’m too exhausted to fight. I neck the first glass in one; it barely touches the sides. The second goes down faster, it could be Lucozade. I feel my eyes droop, and when I open them he’s kneeling in front of me. *What?* He reaches his hand behind my neck and bends me towards him.

‘What the fuck are you... ‘

‘A little kiss,’ he murmurs, his dry lips on my throat and then behind my ear. I’m suddenly paralysed.

‘*Neal …*’

‘Come on, Nina. You always knew this was going to happen. You knew it the first moment.’

‘I didn’t think … I’m old enough to be …’

The awful thing is, the half of me that’s trying to fight this is easily overpowered by the half that wants him, desperately.

What am I now, a ‘typical woman’, showing unwilling, pretending I don’t want it when I do, I *do*, saying no and *no* when I mean yes and *yes*, *yes* again, like *that*, don’t we *all* do this, so the chauvinist pigs in them say.

I feel so detached, it’s like an out-of-body experience, the mouth on my mouth, the hand holding my head, the fingers inside my shirt: they’re nothing to do with Neal, they’re not even part of him. Something freakish, disembodied, something cold and phantom, is moving down my body, unpeeling me, murmuring in tongues, getting into my skin. Biting my hip bones.

I have *hip bones*.

He thinks I do.

It's all it takes.

CHAPTER NINETEEN

NINA

I crunch the Jag into the public car park at Pembroke Lodge, yank on my Barbour, tie the laces of my walking boots, and take off in the direction of Ham Gate. Though my mind marches me briskly through Richmond Park as if trying to catch up with someone, my legs are dragging like a dead guy's. I feel myself wading through the swamps of all the scandal to come. I'm up to my neck in filth and trying not to drown. And it's not even out there yet.

I head left at the Hamcross Plantation and approach the woods, my ankles at odds with my knees.

It's like I've borrowed someone else's legs and feet. *Breathe*, Nina, *breathe*. I can barely bring myself to.

I exhale in cold clouds, feel the gasps, shallow and silent. I must sound like a hacking dog. Trees. I need trees, I need ancient oaks, but why? I think I might be cracking up. What else do you get in here? Oh, yeah. Deer. Rabbits. Foxes.

Can't stand foxes, bastard things, ever since one ate Charlie's rabbit. That's what Charlie said, but they don't eat them, do they? They decapitate and make off, plus I don't need that on my shoes, thanks very much.

What's with the searing need for nature, to lose myself in a wooded park? Anyone would think I was running away from something.

The sky is a threadbare blanket, bearing down in billowing greys. A canvas canopy, sagging with rain and woebegoneness, the morning after a wedding the night before.

The wind is vicious, ripping through bare branches, worrying the daylights out of the grass. It snatches my hair, lashes my eyes, I feel my skin cracking underneath my clothes. I won't cry, I'm not pathetic. I have no inclination to walk, as I would usually, to King Henry VIII's Mound, and stand staring like a tourist, all the way to St Paul's. I've never thought about it before – this has only just occurred to me – a view like that is a reality check on what's left of your life. Like seeing where it ends.

Neal. Oh, God, we did it, didn't we?

On the one hand, you only live once. On the other, I must be old enough to be his mother. How embarrassing. I recall our many meetings, the drinks, the dinners, the teasing, the gags, the little tête-à-têtes.

Were there *signs*? Did I see them, but choose to ignore them? Was I playing that stupid game?

Was I ridiculous, was it a dare, was he only making fun of me? I have to tell myself not. Now that I think about it, I feel like I've known him all my life, but at arm's length, barely at all.

Nothing adds up. Is it that I can't believe what happened, or that I don't want to believe that it did? Is there a difference?

I can't think about it too deeply, but this could be a kind of mourning, couldn't it. For the woman I once was, the one young enough to match him, to rise to his occasion, to become indivisible from him. The woman he would promise to hold for a lifetime, the woman James wanted and won.

What will happen now, with the divorce, I mean? Who will handle it? Not Neal, surely. Apart from anything else, I can hardly bear the thought of facing him again. Not now that he's seen the stretch marks.

I reach a tear-shaped knoll among crumbling oaks, and I see it. I think I see it. A circular, marble, starburst mirage, thirty feet or more across, tiled in black and white. It is etched with a single, arresting word.

'IMAGINE'

A Central Park peace garden in the middle of a clearing in Richmond? Impossible. And yet, anything's possible. In which case, is anything real?

The air is suffused with exotic scents, an Eden of shrubs from every outpost. The only sounds are weeping regrets, the unflutterings of hope. The earth underfoot feels bogged with blood. Is this *here*, John? That guy back there, outside the Dakota, December 1980 – was that really *you*?

I suddenly remember the numbers, 1-8-8-1, above the Dakota entrance. *What if*? One plus eight is nine, and there are two of those. John's birthday was 9th October, he used to say nine was his lucky number, that it was the number of spirituality and change. He first met Yoko on a nine, 9th November, at London's Indica Gallery. Nine, and nine. Ninety nine. Add 99 to 1881, and what do you get? 1980. It was nothing if not the beginning of the end.

My memory brims with golden summers, with mellotron flutes and strawberry fields. With moss-cheeked, butterfly-netted childhood, snag-smiles and don't-be-lates. All four Beatles come cavorting across a meadow towards me, running forwards, backwards, hopping, leaping, clowning, changing clothes and expressions and places. John's teak eyes are all over me, I daren't move in case I lose sight of him.

Through the trees blasts a trumpet, a hum of cellos, a cacophony of cymbals; don't tell me you're not hearing all this too. Don't look back, don't look away, never break the spell. My memory rewinds him jaunty-red in coat and cap, jump-cut, dawn-dusk, plinking an upright, sloshing paint on it, re-stringing it impossibly from a tree. I can tell the moustache is irritating him, his face crumples and twitches, the eyes pucker like sweet-tin cellophane. Through pre-cracked specs, John looks diffident, spent. He's coming at me from all angles, tongue-tied and truth-ensnared. His tears are as silent as time.

And I remember, although I can't possibly, the first thing Yoko ever gave him, that day at the Indica Gallery. A tiny card bearing a single arresting word.

'BREATHE'

Breathe, Nina, *breathe*. Look for apples, not for acorns; they are falling, Chicken Licken, run with the sky, it's falling too. Climb the ladder, hammer the no-nails, climb, *climb*, as high as her hair will reach. Ringo's wearing a white tie, not George. Not Paul. Paul is dead, and therefore lives.

There's no one in John's tree.

Knole Park, Sevenoaks. We used to play there as kids. At least ten years after they made the promo films there, *Strawberry Fields* and *Penny Lane*. They could have been shot here in Richmond, for all the difference it makes. Identical landscape, similar odours, duplicate deer, same aching oaks.

A surreal scenario or a dulcet dream? A double fantasy?

~

About last night. I just want to say this. I crossed a line. I know I shouldn't have. I should have known better.

I should have known thirty-odd years ago, too, and don't think for a moment that hasn't haunted me ever since. Stepping over lines you ought to stay behind is always asking for it. Doing what you have no right to do. Doing what you know is wrong. Why did I do it, then?

Why sell out? For money, fame and freedom, so-called. To have everything I'd ever wanted.

All the things I'd never need.

'La guerra è finita.'

It was obvious. Once Rhett said it was Italian, and said what it meant. It echoed John's and Yoko's peace mission. It was in passing, a murmur, a blur. John Lennon didn't even know I was there; of course he didn't. I was no one to him. I was nothing to do with anything. Nothing that happened that night was about me.

But the thing is, I *made* it about me. This is what a hack's ego does to a situation. Insists on making its mark, staking a claim. You were *there*, you can't just leave it, it's your – inverted commas with crooked fingers – '*duty*' to be the reader's eyes and ears. You can't witness something like that and just walk away. I wanted to. Rhett wouldn't let me get away with it.

Egged on by that creep – how he basked in the glory – I looked again and I re-imagined what happened, that night in New York City. Re-invented, embellished, wrote, honed and polished it. I gave it legs. I bigged up my part, kept thanking my lucky stars, and I made that fiction sing – of John's struggle with abandonment by his mother, the solace in songwriting, the frustration of fame, the damage it did him, the relief he 'must have felt' when his war was done. He could fling down his guitar and he could rest in peace. He was ready. I knew all that, did I? Because he was dead, I had carte blanche to put made-up words in his mouth? Who the hell did I think I was?

'Alma, Mater.'

Ignoring the comma. Did he mean the Liverpool college where he'd studied art? I knew so little about the Beatles in their heyday. I only caught up with their music towards the end. As for their life stories, that all came much later. Who could I call? Frank Allen, The Searchers' bass player; he'd known and hung with them on the Reeperbahn. He'd moved in their circles, he was their friend.

'He must have meant Alma Cogan,' insisted Frank without hesitation, when I explained.

'It couldn't be anything else. "The girl with the laugh in her voice", they used to call her. She was the highest-paid woman entertainer in the fifties. The first female pop star. She was very big indeed at one time; she had a ton of hits.

'When television kicked off, she became a household name. She was your typical East End Jewish glamour girl, with a heart of gold and amazing frocks. She was always having big parties in her Kensington flat, where she lived with her mother Fay. Everyone who was anyone was there. Princess Margaret, Noel Coward, Audrey Hepburn, Michael Caine, Cary Grant, the Beatles – they'd all show up, her parties were incredible who's-who affairs. I never went to one myself, I wish I had now.

'We did have a fascinating "Ugandan discussion" in the back of a Mini once, but that's a whole other story. I've heard people say that John and Alma were having a thing, and that his wife Cynthia knew all about it.'

'You're kidding!'

'I'm telling you. John and Paul were spending a lot of time round Alma's at one point. John's nickname for her mother was "Ma McCogie". It was on Alma's piano, with her sister Sandra sitting beside him, that Paul composed "Yesterday". The working title was "Scrambled Eggs", because that was what Fay had just cooked them for tea. "*Scrambled eggs, oh my baby how I love your legs*".'

'Yesterday'. The ultimate Beatles song, for all the reasons, not least the fact that so many artists have covered it. Brilliant in its simplicity, universal in its appeal. It never got better.

'John and Alma really were an item, then?' I pressed him.

'So they say. I can see the attraction. She was about eight years older than John, and very much the materteral figure.'

'What does that mean?!'

'Aunt-like. Aunt-*istic*, like.'

'Get you, FA, very good! The feminine of avuncular.'

'Exactly. Don't forget that John was brought up by his mother Julia's sister, Mimi Smith, after his mum and dad broke up and Julia went to live with another bloke.'

'What happened to his father?'

'From what I've been told, Fred was away at sea, working as a ship's steward. Then out of the blue he came back, pitched up at Aunt Mimi's one day, and carted John off to Blackpool. Julia had to go looking for them. The story goes, although Beatles historian Mark Lewisohn disputes this, that Fred said he wanted to take John to New Zealand and start a new life. She said no way, and they made John choose. Can you imagine what something like that would do to a five year old?'

'What happened then?'

'Apparently, although of course this may all just be hearsay, he chose Fred. Julia left, John panicked, and rushed outside to chase his mother down the street. If it happened, what a terrible thing to do to a little boy. But even then she didn't keep him; she only dropped him off back at Mimi's.

'So yeah, I get his fascination for the older bird. Interestingly, Yoko was also older than John. Seven years, I think their age gap was.

'Like Yoko, in lots of ways, Alma was a very compelling woman. They were both driven by self-worth. You couldn't really say that either of them was beautiful, not in the conventional sense, but it was as if they truly believed that they were special. If you can convince yourself of that, other people tend to think you are too. They were very alike in that sense. No, the thought of John and Alma doesn't surprise me in the least.

'When Alma's star began to fade, she resorted to recording Beatles songs, such as 'Help' and 'Eight Days A Week'. She was desperate to hang onto her audience, to keep riding with the times.

'When she died from ovarian cancer in 1966, aged only thirty-four, John was apparently inconsolable. The woman perhaps earmarked to replace his beloved Aunt Mimi in his affections was now lost to him.

'He met Yoko when he needed to, only a fortnight or so into his grief. None of us got the attraction, she was just this strange little Japanese artist who had arrived on the scene out of nowhere. But she had a hold on John for the rest of his life. Yoko's secret was that she re-invented herself as "the new Aunt Mimi". She worked out what John needed in a woman, and she gave it to him. At least, that's what we all thought.'

Yet what if Alma Cogan was John's true love?

As for 'Mater'. I had a couple of thoughts about this one myself. Perhaps it's far-fetched, but who knows? I was particularly intrigued by a line in the lyrics of a song on the *Band on the Run* album by McCartney and Wings.

'*Ah, Mater, want Jet to always love me.*'

Was this Macca having another pop at John? It wouldn't surprise me; there were plenty of examples of the pair using their post-Beatles music to humiliate each other.

On Paul's solo album *Ram*, there was the track *3 Legs*, recorded while the Beatles were disbanding through the courts. From the same album, on *Too Many People*, Paul rips into John for both his political activity and his relationship with Yoko.

Lennon's *God*, from *John Lennon/Plastic Ono Band*, trashes the Beatle myth.

'Dear Friend', on Paul's *Wild Life*, festers with thinly disguised digs about their fractured friendship.

And in the deepest cut of all – *How Do You Sleep?* from *Imagine* – John goes for the jugular.

If this *Band on the Run* track was another one of those, then who was 'Jet'? Some dismissed it as Paul's musings about a much-loved Labrador retriever. Paul himself later shrugged off the song as an ode to a beloved pet pony. Many of us found that disingenuous. Those lyrics are so obviously not about a horse.

It was Andy Peebles who told me that John always referred to Yoko as 'Mother'. '*Mater*', Latin for 'mother'.

'*Ah, Mater.*' Could this have been John's subliminal message to Yoko, that 'Jet' (Alma), not she, Yoko, was the true love of his life? '*Alma,*

Mater.' As in, 'I'm going to be with Alma now, Mother'?

I speculated about all this in print. I actually dared to. To fair acclaim, it must be said, as well as to ridicule and vilification. Half the world still loathed Yoko; they blamed her for the Beatles' demise. Some folk seemed desperate for even his death to be her fault.

The rest blamed me. For breaking a perceived confidence, for spilling John's beans, for defiling his wife's grief, the lot. Guilty as charged. But it was water off a duck's back at the time. You don't care when you're young, ruthless and invincible. I was too busy being flown around the world, getting feted and fawned over as 'the Last Woman Lennon Ever Spoke To'.

What's the worst job you've ever had? I wrote to Cynthia and Yoko, my pen-and-ink guilt trip, seeking to justify what I'd done. I asked them both about Alma.

Neither replied.

Always something there to remind me. Morrissey, 1997, his track *Alma Matters*, on the album *Maladjusted.* The song was widely assumed to have been written about Cogan. I should have kept my mouth shut. What goes around.

~

My BlackBerry buzzes in my pocket. I resist the urge, but then remember it could be James or even Charlie. I hope against hope. But it's Phil.

'You sitting down?'

'Oh, no. Who this time?'

'What are you doing, Nina?'

'Walking … in my favourite park …'

'What are you doing in Richmond? Playing hunt the venison sausage with Bill?'

'Bill who?'

'Ah.'

'I'm just having a little walk, Phil. Keeping my head down. It's been one thing after another, lately.'

'Tell me about it. Did you think any more about what I said?'

'Which bit?'

'Are you going to write something for me about Interpol's photofit groupie, the loco with a motive to slaughter rock stars?'

'How long did it take you to think that one up?'

'Lifted. Allegra's.'

'Nice. I keep saying you should put her on Features. If not News. Tell her I said hi, by the way, I'm missing her. Tell her I'll be back in soon.'

'It's not the same without you.'

'I didn't know you cared.'

'I don't.'

'I knew that. I can't see how I could write anything personal without doing us a legal mischief, ahead of the fuzz arresting someone.'

'Good point. But you'll think about it, yes? You have a unique perspective, Nina. What is it with you?'

'I swallowed a bad-boy magnet when I was a kid.'

'You'll do it, then?'

'Talk to the lawyers, Phil. We need to be careful about what we're getting into.'

'That's not like you.'

'You sound surprised.'

'So what'll you do now?'

'I'm not thinking about that until after Joe Llyn's funeral.'

'Are you going to that?'

'Of course I'm bloody going. I can't not, can I? I grew up with the guy. I'll go out of respect to the family.'

'You never know, though – the mistress might pitch up, and then we've got a blinder.'

'The media will be there in force.'

'Yes, but you won't be playing "In and Out the Dusty Gravestones" with the riff-raff, will you. You'll be inside, in a pew with a view. What about your dead rock stars?'

'None of them can make it.'

'Everyone's a comic. Even you. What I mean is, there's some suggestion that your man was involved. Related items have been found …'

'Conjecture. Come on, Phil. Nothing's confirmed, nothing's official. For my money, there's no way on this planet that Joe could have been involved with any rock star.'

'Why not? He was an IVF specialist. The best. They could have consulted him, their wives could have had fertility issues, he might have fucked up, they might not have paid his bill …'

'It's possible, I suppose, but I'd have to say doubtful.'

'What makes you so sure?'

'I know Joe. I mean, I knew him.'

'You can prove something?'

'Of course not. I just know.'

'People will talk.'

'People *are* talking. About me and everyone else. It's what "people" do. They can say what the fuck they like.'

'I've got to ask, Nina.'

'What is it this time?'

Here it comes.

'There's more to this Joseph Llyn character than meets the eye, isn't there?'

'I'm not even going to dignify that with an answer, boss.'

'That's what I'm worried about.'

CHAPTER TWENTY

LADY MUSGRAVE ISLAND

He regretted it the next morning. He'd known even as he was doing it that he would. The sight of the shallow crucible devoid of ashes, scattered by the overnight breeze, made Charlie feel again like the little boy in *The Snowman* film, the bit where he wakes up on Christmas morning to see the snow's all gone, to find nothing but the hat and the scarf.

He knew he was being irrational. What good would a pile of ashes have been to him? He could have just kept them, he thought. He could have buried them, had a ritual, some kind of symbolic ceremony.

He could have saved some of the remains of his mother's diaries as a reminder of what he'd destroyed, as evidence that he'd taken charge and eradicated her past, once and for all. They could have served as proof. Of what? That he could get her back now. The mother he knew, the one he still wanted. The mother she had always been to him.

He was dreading the others coming, and wished he hadn't suggested it now. There was no way of getting word to them that he'd changed his mind, that this wasn't a good idea after all. That he didn't like it here much, he was bored, there was nothing to do, the other people were arseholes. That he was thinking of coming back to Sydney, where they'd be better off, where they could decide among themselves what to do next.

But they'd be here today or tomorrow, if all went according to plan.

He was guessing that Chelsea and Kari-Ann's parents had returned by now, and whisked them off somewhere else. Good riddance. With a bit of luck he'd seen the last of them. Too complicated.

As for Neesha, chances were she'd have got with Howie or Deisel by now. He'd be off the hook. He really hoped so. He wasn't ready for all this romance shit.

Sex was one thing, and believe him, he wasn't cutting off his nose to spite his face. Not that he was about to go the other way. He liked girls, he knew that much.

It was the stuff that went with it. The obligation.

As far as he could see, it was quite a nice thing to do with a girl sometimes, like getting drunk, or porking on chocolate cake and walnut whips or a bucket of salted caramel ice cream. Something that felt great at the time, but that made you feel a bit sick afterwards, so you wouldn't want to do it again for a while.

The trouble with girls, sex made them think they owned you. It only took a couple of goes and she was going round describing you as 'hers'. Seemed to think she could push you about, call the shots, tell you what to do, where to go, what to wear, eat, drink, who to hang out with. When you could and couldn't see your friends.

Sod that. Two women fighting over you because you happened to have had sex with both of them: that was the pits, the worst nightmare. If this was what relationships were about, you could keep them.

The sun was directly overhead. He could see it through the gap in the zip of his tent, the bit of seam that had come unstitched. He felt the heat; you couldn't not feel the heat.

He heard voices: chattering and laughter, people calling to each other. Splashing through waves, they must be after a ray or a turtle or something. For the first time since he'd landed on the island, he was in no mood to crawl out of his sleeping bag, kick-start his body with a pre-breakfast swim and get on with his day.

He just lay there.

Whether he closed his eyes or stared upwards at the roof of the tent, the view was the same.

He only half-wanted to know what was going on back home. Only a bit of him wondered about his mother and father. He couldn't care less how their Christmases had gone; he was so over all that now. Sure he was.

As for New Year, he still couldn't quite work out what it was supposed to be about. One minute it was this year, the next it was next year.

But time is man-made, he pondered, not for the first time. It didn't really exist before humans thought of it. Did it? So why does it count? It's not like it's some great cosmic invention that we have to pay homage to, right?

How does the space and time theory work again? Is time a scientific concept, or only a philosophical one? And if man really did invent time, what was the Big Bang all about? He'd never got this.

Time has always existed and has always been measured in one way or another, was what he remembered from school. Otherwise how would animals know when to hibernate, or plants to die, or trees to drop their leaves, or babies to be born, that sort of thing, unless the right amount of time had elapsed? Man got the idea for time by observing nature's cycles, he knew that much. The sun, the moon, the stars. The implication of time passing.

But why celebrate its coming and going on New Year's Eve? Other than to reflect on the good and bad of the twelve months just spent, and to make half-hearted decisions and promises to get fit, lose weight, save money, quit drugs, booze, spending, having sex with mad women in the year to come?

Not much to celebrate, was it? Just an excuse. All bollocks. Everything was.

Everyone knew you broke your resolutions on New Year's Day anyway, so what was the point in making them in the first place.

It did his head in, this kind of thing. At least he wouldn't have to think about it for another year. If he was going to get another year. That was the bit you could never count on.

Whether you'd still be here. Alive one minute, a gonner the next. Just like that. It can happen to anyone.

Charlie knew he should get up and drink something. He knew he should take a leak, his bladder felt fit to burst. In, out, shake it all about. You do the hokey-cokey and you turn around. Five more minutes.

There it was, time again. Even as good as stranded on a desert island, everything you did was ruled by time. Didn't seem right, you should be able to get away from it once in a while. He'd half-expected time to stand still when he got here, but it hadn't stalled for a second, it just kept rolling along. It was disheartening.

He forced himself to get up and do the necessary. He felt a bit hungry, but couldn't be bothered to eat. Instead, he pulled his sleeping bag off the camp bed and out of the tent into the shade of his pisonia tree, thinking that he might as well watch the world go by for a while. Some world.

Before he knew it, he'd drifted off to sleep again.

He was somewhere back in his first decade. About eight or nine, he would have been. It was October half-term, the last break before Christmas.

His mother had insisted on them going down to Devon. She'd wanted him to see some moors. There were wild ponies, she'd told him, and mythical beasts. Yeah, right. She'd bought him *The Hound of the Baskervilles*, said he couldn't go to Dartmoor without reading a bit of Sherlock Holmes. He'd only managed a few pages; he couldn't understand it. Besides, it had scared the shit out of him.

They'd stayed in a pub, sort of a mill, run by this couple with funny eyes. It had bedrooms upstairs, maybe half a dozen or so. Theirs was at the top of the main stairs and then up a narrow staircase. It was sort of in the attic, with a door on the slant. Pink walls, green carpet. He had a small fold-up bed against one wall; his parents had the big bed in the middle.

In the morning they'd shared a bath because the notice on the wall said hot water was limited and to use it sparingly. One after the other – he'd had it first – and then they'd gone down to breakfast, to a dining room with nasty maroon carpet, and pine tables and chairs, set out like in a restaurant.

They'd helped themselves to cereals and juice from a big table, and coffee for the mums and dads that came out of a machine, and a woman had brought the cooked stuff. Bacon, fried eggs, his mother had had scrambled, sausage, tomato, mushroom, baked beans, toast. He'd eaten everything. He'd been stuffed.

They'd better go for a long hike across the moor to walk it off, his father had suggested.

The moor had looked nice and dry but was spongy and wet; he'd felt himself getting sucked into it the moment he'd stepped on it, the strange-smelling mud was up higher than his knees within seconds and his mother was yelling at him to *come back*!

He'd been scared. He'd tried to run to her, but had sunk deeper. He'd tried to jump, willing his feet to spring, but it was like treading in fresh tarmac; he was stuck.

One giant leap, that's all it would take. He'd tried to launch himself, thought he could maybe bound, like an astronaut, and bounce, but he'd instead squelched, straight into the path of an oncoming truck – an artic doing fifty plus, must have been, his father had said afterwards.

The screaming. He could still hear the screaming. It curdled his blood. He could still see his mother taking off from the other side of the road to reach him, his father tearing at her, clawing her back.

He remembers tripping, falling backwards, downwards, over and over in a ditch, his heel catching on a jagged edge of rock that sliced clean through his shoe. He saw the huge black wheel of the truck flash past his head, could see right inside the treads, smell the rubber and dirt and oil.

The driver hadn't even seen him. It could so easily have been the end.

The three of them had sat afterwards in the dog-scented bar of a peat-brown pub. The pint of bitter, the dirty wine glass, the Coke in its dusty bottle with a straw: all untouched.

His mother had been bleached and yelping, making a really strange noise, like some zoo animal eating something it shouldn't. She'd sounded as though she was choking to death. He'd been able to tell she was crying but her face was dry; maybe her tears were falling on the inside.

His father had been like stone, a scowling statue. He'd barely moved for half an hour.

Charlie had timed it. He'd sat scratching his head – oh, no, don't tell me I've got nits again, she'll kill me.

He'd fished a bit of sausage skin from the back of his mouth, rolled it between his fingers into a sort of grey, motionless maggot, and flicked it at the bottle in front of him. No one else had moved. No one had uttered a syllable.

What Charlie had known was that his mother would have hurled herself in front of the truck, that she would have thrown her life away without a second's hesitation in order to try and save him.

But his father had stopped her. He'd held her back. His dad would sooner have seen his son wiped out than lose his wife.

From the age of eight or nine, it was what Charlie knew.

And yet. Were you to ask him now, why do you care so much about your parents getting divorced, he could have told you straight. A truck nearly killed him when he was little, and his mother tried to save him. His father saved his mother. It's all it takes. Love is greater than the sum of its parts. Two losers fall for each other, and they suddenly feel worth something.

Three people make a family, and can make things right. It's how it works.

CHAPTER TWENTY-ONE

NINA

I'm at the office today. It feels like only five minutes since I was last in the place. Only like I've been away on assignment or on holiday or something. But in another way it feels like years, like coming round after deep anaesthesia.

Not that I could say very much has changed. The doormen haven't got any friendlier. The receptionists aren't any uglier. No one's looking at me differently, wondering whether they should say anything or go all-out to avoid catching my eye. This lot are none the wiser, I suppose.

Allegra meets me at the lift with coffee in a white china cup, not mug. I texted her as I was handing over my car keys to the guy who parks the Jag, and by the time I've zapped through security and reached the fifth floor, she's right there with it.

I gave up coffee more than a year ago after an excruciating week in rehab, did I mention? But the last thing I want to do is hurt her feelings. She means well. What follows is such a ritual, it could be from a script.

'Coffee, Mrs V. How you like it.'

'You're an angel.'

'You too!' She giggles lightly. A sound like sprinkling talc.

'Keep telling me.'

'I will,' she says. 'It's so nice to see you again.'

'It's nice to see *you*. Phil tells me he sent you to Manchester to interview dear Johnnie Hamp and you made a bloody good job it. It's in next week, yes?'

'Oh, he was lovely. What a legend. Such great stories about Frank Sinatra and Cliff Richard and the Beatles and everyone.'

'Johnnie's an amazing man. A one-off. One of those classic old-timers who should have his time again.'

'Thanks Mrs V.'

'For what?'

'Putting a word in.'

'I didn't have to. I always knew you were wasted on the coffee machine.' I'm not being ironic.

'I've got a long way to go yet, Mrs V.'

'We all have.'

'Anyway, what are you doing here? I thought you were going to that funeral today.'

'I am. Phil wants me to file a piece for the edition. News will be covering the service and who turns up at the church and all that, but he wants me to do the human interest, the first-person, the overview. It's probably a good thing. High time I faced my demons.'

'Not worried are you, Mrs V?'

'What about?'

'That's what I'm worried about.'

'What is?'

'The fact that you don't know what you're worried about.'

'You're not making any sense, Allegra, but I can't be arsed. Sorry, I don't mean to be rude. Be a love, see if Phil's in.'

'He's in. Been here all night, he says. I don't know why. He's waiting for you.'

~

It's like Alice in bloody Wonderland in the office today. I have a weird feeling, a sense of having dropped down some hole with no idea of what's coming next.

There's an air of foreboding, of displacement, of time running out, as if it's my last day here and I'm about to meet them all downstairs for my farewell before crossing the street for more money, as they say.

I am drinking and shrinking, inhaling cake and tea. Here comes croquet with the Queen of Hearts. Metaphorically speaking. Yes, that would *so* be my leaving party. A deck of cards. I pass someone's desk and there's a pack of cards lying there. Random. Is there such a thing as coincidence? News. Features. Sport. Foreign. Back bench.

I can't think for the life of me how they get any work done out here, in the open-plan. It was never for me, I'm terribly old school. The day I got a corner office with windows on two sides was the day I thought I'd arrived.

Having said that, this is all so much nicer since the revamp. There's much more daylight, for a start. They got rid of the stale cubicles and all that manky furniture we lugged over from the old place off Fleet Street, and brought in padded, canvas-covered dividers, adjustable desks and ergonomic chairs.

There was a competition last year to come up with something to 'lift team spirit'. That was how we wound up with the botanical garden in the corner by the lift. I kid you not. I'm sure that whoever suggested it did so tongue-in-cheek, but they were laughing on the other side of their faces when it won.

You can barely move now for plants in what they've dubbed 'the Norwegian Wood'. We're a bloody laughing stock in *Private Eye*, but that's not the worst of it. They have to maintain a rota to water and re-pot the damned things. Roof Gardens meets rainforest; Morten Harket would be in heaven.

We've got wicker sofas and little coffee tables in there, plus a few pool-style recliners, not that there's a pool. And a parrot. People talk to it. Yep. And a library. Staff bring in their old paperbacks and swap them. Surprisingly few of us consume fiction on iPads or Kindles. There's still something about turning the pages of a book.

~

'You're in, then.'

Phil has his back to me. He is staring out of the window at the eternally fudge-coloured Thames.

'Looks like it.'

He turns round. His face is barely there.

'Dressed for the occasion, I see.'

'Black, you mean? It can't have escaped your attention that I wear black more often than not.'

'I've always wondered.'

'What about?'

'Black. What does the wearing of it say about a woman?' He flops down in his chair and grabs his mouse, wiggles it on the leather mat on his desk until he gets the cursor up, then types like a maniac, using only two fingers. As fast as hell.

'The black, you mean?'

'What are you, a bloody parrot now? You'll be talking to that giant budgie out there in the corner next. Bloody *ex*-parrot if I had my way, crapping disease all over the shop.'

'Maybe it's pining for the fjords.'

'Pining, my arsehole.'

'Beautiful plumage.'

'Thank you, John Cleese. When I want your opinion I'll ask for it. So what *is* it with the black?'

'Don't ask me. I've always preferred it. It's easier.'

'Because it doesn't show the dirt?'

'I don't think it's that. If anything, it probably marks more visibly than white.'

'So what does it say here?' Phil reads from whatever amateur website he's accessed. 'Black: the colour of dominance and command. In fashion it's slimming, timeless and stylish, a colour for all seasons. Paradoxically, it also suggests submission. Priests wear black to show their devotion to the Almighty. The woman in black can be seen as submissive to men. Hmm. The most sinister colour, implying villains and evil.'

'What *is* this, my horoscope?'

'Kaleidoscope. There's a piece for you in this.'

'For fuck's sake, leave it out. Hardly my bag, boss. Give it to Fashion.'

'Got it!' He beams. 'We'll get a handful of celebrities, pull in pictures of them in a rainbow of colours, get some fashion designer type to translate what it says about their personalities.'

'"Fashion expert"? Oxymoron. Maybe leave off the "oxy". You might as well get Gordon Ramsay to do it.'

'Come on,' says Phil, 'it's a really good idea, this. Look, there's loads here. White indicates purity and sterility, and is reflective of light. Red is the colour of love. Pink is for romance and calm. Blue evokes the sea, sky, and peace, but is also businesslike. It says here that you should always wear blue to a job interview.'

'Am I going to one?'

'If you play your cards wrong.'

Cards, again.

'Green is nature. The easiest colour on the eye. Refreshing, relaxing …'

'Bollocks.'

'Is it? You sit in a green room before you go on telly, don't you?'

'A lot of people think that green's bad luck.'

'Four-leaf clover?'

'When was the last time you fell over one of those?'

'Anyway. Yellow is cheerful, the hardest colour on the eye, and is said to aid concentration. Is that why legal pads are yellow, do you think? Purple suggests royalty, luxury, wealth and sophistication.'

'I've got a friend who rarely wears anything else.'

'She has taste, the woman. I presume it's a woman. What else? Brown: earth.'

'Also, excrement. I told you it's a load of old crap.'

'But this all makes sense. Nina, please, humour me here. It's also on about blue being the least appetising colour. See? You don't get too many blue foods, do you?'

'Blueberries?'

He snorts. 'So there's an exception to every rule. Green, red and brown are the most popular foods colours. Look how many restaurants have red walls, curtains, tablecloths and chair coverings.'

'I rest your case.'

'Sit down, Nina.'

Phil leans across the desk at me. Are his eyes bulging, or am I imagining this?

'What now?'

'You're not reading me, are you? You don't get it. I'm taking the piss.'

'That makes a change.'

'You *still* don't get it.'

'Get what?'

'Since when do I ask you to write poxy fashion spreads? It was, how you say, a send-up. Every spread-worthy piece I've asked you to do for me these past couple of months, you've refused. Any other editor worth his expense account would have fired you by now.'

It's like being zocked in the kisser with a Volvo.

'Meaning what, exactly?'

'I've got to spell it out?' says Phil. 'Really? Every one of those rock stars – whose murders police on three continents are no closer to solving, by the way – you not only knew professionally, you'd had personal relationships with them. You knew first-hand what made those men tick. Apart from one feeble feature any stringer could have cut-and-pasted in less time than it takes to nip down the canteen for a bacon butty, did you write it? No. That quack sushi'd into a spunk fridge in Toronto by his killer – possibly the same killer but we're still none the wiser – happened to be your first boyfriend. We couldn't make it up, girls and boys, could we? Did you write it? How about no.'

'Boss, I'm sure you …'

'See the funny side? The thing is, I'm really struggling with that.'

'That's not what I was going to say.'

'No? What, then? *What*, Nina? I've just about had enough. You're making me look like an idiot. What is it with you? Saving it for your memoirs? Your Graham-Norton-sneer-alike agent's done some megabucks book deal and you've been holed up bashing it out as fast as your five-star manicure will let you?'

'No! That's not true! I don't think you realise how –'

'– *hard* all this has been for you? My heart bleeds, Nina, it really does.'

Phil's in such a rage, he's spitting at me. I should go and wipe my shirt down. I get up.

'Can I go now?'

'Where?'

'Nothing pressing, only a funeral.'

'Oh, Christ, yes, I forgot. Remember, I'm not taking no for an answer on this one. I want two thou by five. How are you getting there?'

'Driving. I can make a quick getaway when I want, I'm sure an hour will be more than enough.'

'You can't leave until the end!'

'I might have somewhere better to go. I'll see how it goes, right? Look, I'd better get off, I don't want to be late and miss all the fun, do I?

Brief?'

'Hardly necessary, is it. You know what I want.'

'Yes. Jam on it.'

'No. Blood.'

~

The Sat-Nag – I do mean Nag – gives me thirty-three miles to the church. I hadn't come across this particular village before, but it looks rinky-dink. Typical Home Counties toy-town; you can bet they all wear Marks & Spencer's pants. A neat high street lined with tight, whitewashed cottages, some of which double as shops.

Where are all the brassed Shire horses supping at the trough?

There's a tiny post office, a general store and the half-timbered White Hart, which looks promising. It'll have alcohol in it, at least.

Also a railway station a mile away, according to a sign on the left going through.

The Saxon church of St Mary lies beyond the filling station on the way out, which seems appropriate. I can see its tower from here.

I'm a good hour early. It doesn't take much to talk myself into a gin and tonic. It's cosy and welcoming in the pub. Low ceilings, inglenook fireplace, a huge fire blazing.

There's barely anyone in here. A chap on his own in the corner with a dog that looks dripping wet, despite the fact that it's not raining outside. Perhaps he's rolled in something unpleasant, needed an emergency hose-down. Can't smell anything, thank God for small mercies.

A quartet of snappers – one in a fishing vest, the rest in Barbours – are gathered around a clutch of pint jugs and empty sandwich plates on the bar. Their camera bags are jumbled at their feet.

I ignore them, and cross to the other side. A fed-up-looking couple are seated at a small table near the fire, glaring at each other through their drinks.

'You down for the funeral an' all, then?' asks a barmaid with fright-wig hair. She indicates the photographers with a nod, handing me change warmed in her palm.

'I am, yes.' I pull up a bar stool.

We exchange thin smiles. She is polishing a wine glass.

'Awful business,' she says, after a while.

'You knew him, then?'

'I knew the family.'

'I didn't realise there was any family left.'

'Not to speak of, there isn't. The mother died a few years back, didn't she? The father's long gone, of course. Half-dead for years before he passed, rest his soul. And of course Joseph had been working abroad. Canada. I can't think why they've bothered to fly his body all the way back here, to be honest with you. People are funny, aren't they? There's a family plot in the churchyard, so I suppose that's why. The sister's organised all this.'

'All what?'

'The wake's upstairs here, didn't you know?'

'Of course. Sorry, my mind's not …'

'Only egg and ham sandwiches and vol-au-vents and a few sausages on sticks and that, nothing fancy. Belinda Llyn, that's his sister. Spinster, no kids, keeps herself to herself. She came to choir practice once, but didn't show her face again after that. She couldn't read music, she said, she could only carry a tune in her head and of course that's no good, is it, you've got to be able to sing from a sheet from scratch. Follow the parts.'

'She lives round here, then?'

'She does now. In the parents' old place. You're not family, then?'

'I'm not, no.'

'Funny, you look familiar. I don't know you from somewhere else, do I? Oh, *I* know. The Worst Lady! I've seen you on *Newsnight*, haven't I? Very good. You gave that Dimbleby and that Boris a run for their money, didn't you, last time? Good on you, my Jim was made up. Well, I'm blowed. Heard you on the wireless too, a few times. You're …'

'Nina Vincent, it's very nice to meet you.'

'Sarah.'

'Your place, this?'

'Don't be daft! I just work here. Man and girl. Skivvies-R-Us. Can I get you anything to eat?'

~

I leave the Jag on a sloping grass verge on the far side of the duck-less pond and walk the rest of the way, keeping my head down, winding my silk scarf several times until it obliterates most of my face.

I'm glad I wore boots. I can't imagine what I'm expecting. I tell myself over and over, *this isn't about you, this isn't about you*.

I enter by the north porch through a pair of yews. The tall, small church is chilly, and as yet fairly empty. There's the familiar dank smell of ancient stone and mildewed hymn books. A brace of disapproving stone angels with ornate wings and waterfall robes. A barely visible mural on the wall opposite, harking back, I'm just guessing, to when the place was first built.

There are a number of baggy women milling about with Orders of Service. I accept one of two offered.

The monochrome image in the middle of the front cover looks nothing like the Joe I knew. The hair's darker, for one thing. It doesn't even look like his face. Is he sitting on a beach? Leaning against a wooden breakwater, is that? He's wearing a jacket and shirt and slacks. Boring garb, none of it *him*-looking. Holding a guitar. I didn't even know he could play. He never said. This might not even be the same Joseph Llyn, then. It's as I keep saying, anything's possible. They might be wrong, they could easily be wrong, they could've made a mistake. There's still time. Always time. There is to me. Then again, those photographers, in the pub.

The mourners, do they call them? In they drift, in twos and threes. Needless to say, I don't recognise anyone. That lot coming through the door now, looking a bit out of place, they're probably the maple leaf contingent. Colleagues. Odd suits and macs.

There's one girl who looks a bit like Joe. She could be a daughter, or maybe the mistress, although she wouldn't dare show her face at this, surely? She's already crying, poor kid.

There's no sign of the wife as yet. Wait, is *that* her? It probably is, I think I recognise her from her picture in the paper. She doesn't look unduly distressed. I wonder who that is she's with. I'm sure I know the one on the right. He looks familiar. Not another old school friend, is he? I must get a talk with her after. Best make it after. That woman in the blue is the sister? She could be. She seems a bit agitated.

And that guy: the one who's just ducked through the curtains at the back, I could have sworn … it's *not*, is it? For a moment there, I thought it was Harry. It can't possibly have been; he's back in Ghana this week, I'm sure he said. I must be seeing things.

I take a pew two-thirds back on the far left, and get my BlackBerry out. Oh, look, wonders'll never cease. An email from Bill.

'Blame no one. Expect nothing. Do something,' it says in the Subject box. Typical Bill.

I smile, in spite of myself. I picture him in his lilac shirt and chinos, those beaten-up blue suede loafers he loves. It must be about time he bought himself a new pair, it's not as if he can't afford it. No socks. Walking slightly hunched. The bald patch on his grey head is dear. I smooth it with my hand. We decide not to swim.

'Nina, dear Nina, you are on my conscience,' he writes.

Men like you don't have a conscience.

'I'd love to know how you are, and I'd like to explain myself.'

We thank you for your interest, but this is an arsehole-free zone.

'We are all, ultimately, selfish losers.'

Speak for yourself.

'We're all guilty of putting ourselves first, of going with the flow, of doing what feels right at the time.'

Excuses, excuses.

'It's had me tossing ever since.'

No change there, then.

'I've behaved incredibly badly.'

Ya think.

'I didn't cherish what I had while I had it. I can't explain it, any more than I can explain the tides of the ocean, the phases of the moon. Now that I look back, at "us", I see myself as your Henry Weinberg …'

Who the fuck is *he*? Oh, God, not that flying Dutchman who had the fling with Liz Taylor just before she got old.

'Who was it said that, at the height of a woman's yearning for passion before she turns time's corner, the right man will appear?'

What? The bastard! Fuck *me*! He's telling me I'm past it and that he was my fairy godfather, treating me to one last round of hokey-pokey before I hung up my fishnets and dropped comatose onto the sofa with a packet of Jaffa cakes to watch re-runs of *Brideshead Revisited* and *Downton Abbey.* How fucking *dare* he, he's got *twenty years* on me! If anybody's past it, it's *him*!

If this were an actual letter I'd rip it to shreds, stamp it in the nearest available dog poo and post it straight back. I might even order a couple of hundredweight of horse manure to be dumped on his driveway to be going on with. I resist the urge to hurl the BlackBerry at that smug brace of angels sizing me up over there. I refuse to read the rest of this drivel. But I can't not. I'm pathetic. I blame him.

'… doomed from the start …'

So it seems.

' … and at *my* age …'

He truly doesn't listen, does he? I've told him over and over that after thirty-five, we're all *the same age.* That the difference is pennies. Maybe this is what did it. Perhaps this is what made him go out and nab himself a Twinkie.

'You are wrong, Nina, if you think the numbers are what I'm afraid of. What terrifies me is not the dying, but the going too soon. Not having achieved enough. And by the way, what really scares me is prostate cancer, I get checked every year.'

Good to know.

'Don't be a mummy,' I suddenly remember him saying to me once.

'*Mummies.* They plump up cushions. Fold things. Put mugs in sinks. Please don't. Please leave it. I have people to do all that.'

Significant?

I think I hate myself. There was I, thinking I was doing it right, for once. The weekly bikini waxes, the pedicures, the full-body tans. Every item of clothing bought with him in mind. What would Bill think of it? Am I too old for the racy lingerie, should I stick to functional black cotton Ks, or should I go for it, flinging caution to the wind? What about the lumps and bumps, the cellulite, the hideous awfulness that are my thighs? The upper arms, the poochy belly, don't mention the bum. Nothing's as firm as it once was. Whose is? Not his. He said he didn't mind.

Maybe he did after all. I think, out of nowhere, of Freesia's photograph on his piano, all fresh and girlie and peachy-pink. The paintings of her horse, I mean *proper* paintings, the kind one purchases at auction. In their downstairs loo. There was something immovable, something gaspingly 50s, about Bill's lifestyle and habits. If anything, *he* was the mumsy one. By criticising me, he was making fun of himself. Funny, the random things that re-run through your mind at the end.

The light goes, I'm struggling to see the BlackBerry screen. Looking up, I notice a vast black cloud dragging past, draining colour from the Victorian-looking stained glass.

It makes me think of that massive spaceship that dropped in over London in the episode of *Doctor Who* when the aliens zapped the Whitehall lot to skeletons. Not for real, of course. But anything feels possible today. As if I'm getting some sort of advance warning of the thing I fear the most, only I don't know what it is. As if life, somehow, will never be the same again.

Lofty altar candles flicker. A chill drops in, along with descending and ascending violins over a PA somewhere, probably behind us on the balcony. I *hate* recorded music at funerals, why can't they just have a choir? Even a bad one? A soloist, at least. Or a cellist, I've always fancied that, or even better, a nice soothing harp. It's probably the most appropriate instrument, given where you're heading. Where you hope you'll be heading, at least. If you played your cards right. The bulky tones of Pavarotti singing Puccini. 'Nessun Dorma'. None shall sleep: my theme tune, of late. If only it were live, I'd be sobbing my eyes out by now. It's an odd choice, in many ways. I didn't know Joe went for this kind of thing; not having seen him for several decades. Probably, he didn't. He was probably a closet metal-head on the quiet. It must be her.

It's a plain oak coffin, adorned with a single red rose. She loved him. Yeah, yeah, yeah.

It's unshakeable, isn't it, the belief that the one we marry – he to whom we pledge our heart on that scented, white-frocked, zonked-out-of-our-bodices day – remains magical for all time.

Only he will always be the real deal. Despite the daily grind, the unpalatable little personal habits, the tooth-loosening boredom, the desperate loneliness we sometimes feel within marriage.

There will always be something special about the one with whom we waltzed down the aisle. Even if the marriage turns out to have been a fake forged in hell and we've come to loathe each other's guts. Even if we do a Liz Taylor or a Joan Collins, and marry far too many times to be taken seriously. It's still *him*, the first one we said yes to. It will always be him.

Births, deaths, marriages. This whole business is so loaded, I sometimes wonder why we bother.

I was scornful of marriage for many years. I dismissed it as a facade, just a show-house, with little furniture or point within.

But then, along came James. I thought we were different. In what way? We could converse. We could communicate without words. We could share. I had a real man about the house who would deal with the crap without moaning.

He not only supported my advancement, but he never resented it. And he let me take part in his. He wasn't fazed by the Charlie scenario; he always cared very much about our son's development and growth.

He taught me things I should know without ridiculing me for not knowing them. I could laugh myself senseless with him. He could handle it when stuff went wrong, and was always a calming influence over me, as I do tend to panic.

James was, in all, a gentle and nurturing man. He really cared. The sex was real. He loved me. What more could I want? So what went wrong, and when did it happen? You're asking me. How come I didn't notice? Was it the same for Joe and his fish-lipped wife? Is it for everyone?

It's a woman vicar. Rector. Reverend. *What*? I've lost track of the whole Women in the Church thing. Can they be bishops yet? Finally. She's had a hairdo; I can smell the Elnett. She's giving a welcoming speech, and the place is packed now; they are spilling out of doors on both sides.

Funny, I wouldn't have imagined Joe having so many friends and contacts left, given that he lived so far from home. He was always quite insular and self-contained. They could all be people like me, I suppose. People who knew him for a long time, but only vaguely. Unable, as yet, to process his loss. Willing the unthinkable to be untrue.

Psalm 23. Everyone has this, don't they? I'm astonished to find that I know it by heart; I don't need to look at the words. It must be years since I've sung this. The collective sound is quite melodious, considering what a motley crew we are.

Towards the end of it someone stands and heads for the lectern; he might be a medical colleague.

He reads a Louis MacNeice poem. I like the line '*a mirror of wet sand*'. Then it's the tribute. 'Read by Belinda', it says on the sheet. His sister is composed as she reaches the front. She sets off in a loud, stable voice. Perhaps *too* stable. Perhaps reality kicks in as she fingers her way down her page. She suddenly strays, stumbles, loses her place, and the plot. She repeats a couple of lines. Her face changes colour; is that pink or green?

The audience starts to mutter and fidget.

She trails off, speechless, and looks dazed. The coiffed lady vicar comes to the rescue, asking us to join in silence to reflect and remember 'Joseph' in our personal ways.

Boyzone's 'No Matter What' kicks in from over the back there. *Really*? Prayers. The Lord's Prayer. I feel old.

~

We emerge, blinking in the daylight. The barging clouds have moved on, revealing a weak, water-logged sky.

The ground underfoot is not too wet, but it's a fair walk over uncut grass and molehills and a bit of a dance in and out of lichened gravestones to the far end of the churchyard. We're all in the wrong shoes, even the men. A bonfire burns nearby; God knows what they're burning.

The smoke drifts over us in acrid clouds as we wend our way, flecking our dark coats with ash. I can see the grave from here, gaping to receive him. It stops me in my tracks. For the first time all day, I feel like crying. I hang back for a moment, fumbling in my bag for a packet of tissues. The mourners go ahead of the coffin, which is carried by anonymous pallbearers from the undertaker's.

What if they drop it? What if they stumble and slip in the mud, keeling over and losing their balance and letting go of the box? What if what's left of Joe falls out, right in front of us? What if it's not even him? Anything's possible. They gather. I wait. Regain my composure. I make it to the graveside but hang right back, tucking myself into a corner behind the strangers.

It dawns on me. I'm not burying Joe. Part of me is *refusing* to bury him. Refusing to accept that he's gone. What's happening here is a much bigger farewell.

To mad Chas and all the pain he caused me, I'm daring to hope so, at least.

To irresistible Paul, his kisses, the gallons of Black Velvet we sank in Dublin. Were we ever sober? There's a thought. Who the hell would have wanted to be?

To sweet Roger, who played me like a guitar, the one he'd carved from one of the doors of his grandmother's old wardrobe. He was the lion; she was the witch. Imagine.

To forever-young Jerry, his too many faces, what a nice bunch of guys he turned out to be.

To our thwarted American Dreams, at last. At least we had them.

Could I be saying goodbye to my career? Phil hinted as much. He reckons I don't get it, but he's the one. There's only so much you can take. When your entire past comes back to haunt you at once, anyone would lose the plot. We're only human. Even Phil.

You can't write about anything cold-bloodedly, with detachment, if the subject matters to you. If it's got nothing to do with you and never did have, or if it did once but now it's dead and gone, you can just about get away with it.

But I'm not over it. I've *never* been over it. I can't air my past for the delectation and titillation of a couple of million anonymous readers when I haven't come to terms with it myself.

Cathartic exercise, Phil would call it. Cathartic my arse. It's what scumbag red top hacks bleat to their victims when they're trying to squeeze something personal or painful or life-changingly incriminating out of them. Coming on like their best pal, telling them whatever they think they want to hear, assuring them of friendship, of total confidence, your secret's safe with me – when in reality they'll have forgotten the poor sod's name by the time they get back to the office to write it up.

We'll only write what you want us to write. Yeah, right. You can approve the copy before it goes to print. Believe that and you'll believe anything. You've got their assurance in writing? Good luck with that. How many times have those words been said or penned? How many times have they not been honoured?

Don't tell me you're surprised. I wish I had a quid for the number of times. Tell them whatever it takes to get what you want, kiss them goodbye, then forget they have a mother. We're supposed to be better than that, at our place. But really, is anybody?

It's so cold, I can feel every bone. I'm starting to hear every note of every song I've ever listened to. Is this an omen?

I freeze, but not because of the fall in temperature out here. Not because they're dropping a box into a hole right in front of me, a coffin that contains a man I once loved.

It's because the feeling in my back couldn't be anything else.

It's the point of a knife.

CHAPTER TWENTY-TWO

NINA

'Walk' is all I can make out. The voice is deep, male and muffled; he must be wearing a hood or a scarf.

If I scream, that'll be it; the weapon's already through my clothes. I can't tell whether it has pierced my skin, but something's trickling down my spine that might not be sweat. I can hardly breathe. I do as I'm told.

Walking slowly, as normally as possible, stumbling in the grass in my heels, it seems an eternity before we reach their car.

Newshound instinct. Who-what-when-where-why. All I've got is the when and the where. What about the getaway vehicle. Make? Model? Colour? Reg? This I can do. Range Rover Sport SDV6. Black. Personalised plate, ARACH 24.

A song title leaps into my head. 'Spiders and Snakes' … Jim Stafford? God, that takes me back.

Breathe, Nina, *breathe*.

Their car's across the duck pond very close to my Jag. They'd better not have scratched it. The engine's running. Someone in the driver's seat. Also hooded. Assailant Two. Bestow identity on captors, note differences, keep track of their movements.

Remain calm, silent, keep still, cooperate where possible. The old hostage training is kicking in; it's all coming back to me. Everything always does.

The car exhaust coughs, and makes a tripping sound. Assailant One yanks open the rear nearside passenger door, shoves me in and holds me down, tossing my handbag to someone behind me.

My BlackBerry's in my coat pocket, I thank God for that, stupidly, but only for a second.

The moment they find it's not in the bag, Assailant One assaults my pockets for it. Finds it. Tosses it over my head to Assailant Three. I'm blindfolded and gagged from behind. The blindfold's so tight, it's forcing my contacts through my eyeballs. Only one nostril's left clear to breathe.

Then the first guy forces me to the floor of the car, ties my hands behind my back, binds them separately and then together, feels like some kind of plastic twine he's using, maybe washing line. It's tight. It hurts. The left side of the vehicle dips as he gets in and slams the door, resting his feet on my bum and back.

'Go, go, *go*!'

Accent? Can't detect one. Not much to go on. The others say nothing.

If I could, I'd kick myself. All that time I was obsessing over my stupid career and pointless relationships, I could have been thinking about the value of my life.

Breathe, Nina, *breathe*.

I barely can. I panic. I need to vomit. Tastes rise in my throat. Lemon. Gin. Bile. Fear.

Passive cooperation is the best defence. The best opportunity to escape is right at the beginning, during the confusion, while you're still in a public place. I've blown that one already. Scream, shout, create a distraction?

I didn't, did I? Probably couldn't bring myself to make a big fuss at such a solemn moment. How could you? Besides, I had a knife in my back. That might have been it. The more time passes, the better your chances of remaining alive.

Do not resist, do *not* resist, I tell myself, Steve Harley in reverse. Come up and see me. Fight it and they'll beat you unconscious, or worse. Don't struggle. Stay calm. Concentrate. Try to visualise the route, note turns, speed, sounds, smells. Try to keep track of time. Assess opportunities to escape. You're kidding, right.

We drive for what feels like hours. We must now be on a motorway or at least an A road; the route is smooth and straight. It's neither warm nor cold in the car. My neck and back are so stiff, I can't even feel them, which might be a blessing.

Even though I can barely breathe, I daren't inhale.

The carpet is thick with dirt and grit; I'd choke to death on it.

Half an hour or so on, I realise food is being passed around. Wrappers rustle; I can smell tuna and banana. I hear rumpling and tearing, the crunching of crisps. A bottle of fizzy drink is opened; I hear it hiss. One of them's biting into an apple. A whiff of food would normally get the saliva going, but the thought of it's making me heave.

I can tell by the shifting of his feet that Assailant One is taking a drag on the bottle of pop. I hear the glug of his gullet, followed by a deep, lubricated belch.

I feel more pressure on my spine as he leans forward, probably passing the bottle to the guy in front.

I'm offered nothing. I wouldn't take it anyway. Who could eat while gagged and bound and face down in filth?

The driver – I think it must be the driver – turns the radio on.

'*Idiot*!' yells the guy using me as a footstool. 'It'll pick up, we can be tracked from that!'

The sound flicks off instantly, only to be replaced moments later by recorded music. CD? iPod?

I know the voice, I know this guy; the voice is unmistakeable. It's Billy Nicholls. Clever musician. Not only a wonderful singer, but a terrific songwriter. He wrote 'I Can't Stop Loving You' for Leo Sayer, which Phil Collins also had a hit with in the States.

All those great songs for *McVicar* too.

Dear Billy, I haven't seen him in ages. Still Entwined.

Against my will, I doze off, tune out. After an hour, could be two, we seem to have arrived somewhere.

Assailant One, the guy holding me down with his feet, lifts away from me. The door opens, the car rocks a little, I feel him getting out.

A sudden blast of air tells me the boot has been opened. The load lightens further from the rear, alerting me to the fact that Assailant Three has also got out. The other passenger door is thrown wide .I'm yanked out roughly by the shoulders. I bash my left knee on the door frame. I feel four hands, four arms digging into me. They are holding me up.

Through the blindfold I can just see it's still light outside, not that I can see anything. But I hear birds. A blackbird, mellow and fluted. A robin's inhaled chirp. Since when did I recognise birdsong? I probably don't.

No traffic sounds, we must be remote.

Who are these guys? Why have they brought me here? What are they going to do to me?

There's a strong odour of dung. Countryside. A farm. The bulky pair stagger me into what must be a barn. I sense the light dim as we enter, can smell coldness, mouldy straw.

I need the toilet, how do I ask them? I don't. Dignity at all costs. Patience. Keep trying to keep track of time.

But they won't leave me here. This'll be a holding place, the first stop, where they'll keep me until they decide what to do with me. Until they get instructions. Don't think dead; think living and kicking.

I'm only worth something to whoever it is if I'm alive. Passive cooperation is the best defence. The more time passes, the better my chances of survival.

At least they haven't drugged me or clobbered me half to death. Yet.

It's cold but I'm sweating; my whole body feels damp. I turn my face into the straw, trying to ignore my bursting bladder. A leathered hand grabs me by the hair, more roughly than it needs to, and holds a wet, pungent rag to my nose and mouth.

~

It could be hours later, for all I know.

I feel myself coming to, notice the sound has changed, and the temperature.

I hear echoes.

The light appears to have altered again, as much as I can tell through the blindfold.

There must be electric light overhead: I feel warmth from above, and I hear a faint buzzing.

We're indoors, then. Walking not on carpet, but on hard stone. It could be flagstones. I say 'walk', but they must have dragged me until I regained consciousness. Did they use chloroform? A chemical smell lingers, and I feel sick. They've untied my arms, at least.

My tights, skirt and underwear are soaking. My shoes squelch as I scrunch and release my toes, trying to regain enough sensation in them to walk. I must have peed myself. Christ. Retain a sense of pride, but act cooperatively.

Is this actually possible when you've just pissed yourself in front of three strange men? What else have they done to me? They didn't. I'd know. I can't believe I wouldn't feel something if they had.

'Step up,' says a different voice from the one who first grabbed me.

'Staircase. Up, up, *up!* Hold onto the rail here, put your hand here.'

I vaguely feel a gloved hand on my bare one. I try to grasp, and I climb. I feel myself guided across a wooden floor, I can tell by the sound of it. Our footsteps are louder here. Concentrate, Nina. Focus on survival. Do nothing to antagonise them. Divulge only information that can't be used against you. Like what? They haven't asked me anything yet. Perhaps they already know all there is to know.

Remain observant. Memorise details of the room, the layout, sounds of activity elsewhere. Maybe if they'd remove this bloody blindfold.

I feel anger rising. I am ominously unafraid. Not wise, keep a lid on it, comply, do as you're told, say nothing, one word out of place could mean a knife in the heart. Note accents, physical features, names. Know your captors. Try to establish rapport, ask about their families, hobbies, sport, anything, try to get them to regard you as a real person rather than just an object. Listen attentively, don't praise, never complain. Ask for what you need in a reasonable manner. Do so quietly. Yeah, OK. All in good time. Let's get the gags off first.

A door groans. I presume I'm led through it. Bright light pierces the blindfold. This room is warm and aromatic; I can smell essential oils. It's a spa-type smell, the kind you get in the better beauty salons. One of the men shoves me in the back, urging me forward.

'Sit. Sit down here.'

A plump, cushioned surface, maybe a fabric-covered armchair. Wider. A sofa? Through my sodden clothes, I can't really tell.

'In one moment I take blindfold rag,' I'm told. 'You to not look round, to not look my face, to not shout. Nobody to hear you, no one to hear. Understand? Make noise this kind, this dangerous to you. I repeat, not to look to me. We leave. Door to be locked outside. You to use toilet, wash. You to find clean clothes, cleaning things. For face. For hair. To dress please for dinner. Understand? We to come back one hour.'

'How do I know how long –'

'You have still your watch.'

~

I'm still holding my breath, squeezing my eyes closed, not daring to move, when I hear the click, the key turning in the lock.

I wait as long as I can, maybe seconds. I look. I'm in a white marble bathroom. Sitting on a small Louis XV-style sofa, gilded and carved, padded with patterned golden silk. Staring at a vast sunken bathtub, a swimming pool for one. Gold taps. Luxurious piles of white towels. A pair of huge, gleaming basins, side by side, the glass shelves above them filled with Chanel cosmetics.

I try to stand. I look around for the toilet, and I stumble. My legs are weak. I haven't eaten since whenever it was. Yesterday? Before the funeral. Did anyone there notice what happened to me? Would someone have raised the alarm? I hope against hope.

Surely Phil will have smelled a rat. Maybe he just thinks I couldn't bring myself to file and went AWOL. He's probably written me off by now, my severance papers will be in the post.

Charlie won't be missing me, I don't even know where he is.

Nor James. What made me think of him?

Bill. Oh, Bill, he'll be in or out with his little tart.

Harry? Otherwise occupied.

Allegra might be panicking, she usually does; she'll have left me a dozen messages by now.

There's no one else.

~

The toilet and bidet are behind a separate door. I sit for what seems like hours, re-living it all, remembering suddenly that I'm supposed to be dressing for dinner. In what?

There's an ornate silk screen in one corner, behind which I find an exquisite Armani gown. Full-length. Black. Someone who knows me. The strappy heels are Louboutins, I don't even have to check. The La Perla lingerie is my size.

Well, if I'm to be held captive here for the duration, I could probably get used to this.

There's bound to be a bed somewhere. I'll do isometrics and flexing, keep the old muscles toned.

It's about establishing a daily routine. Eat whatever you're given; keep your strength up. Use techniques for reducing stress. I can keep my temper, I can be polite, I can do it. Maintain personal dignity. Do not compromise integrity. Be patient. I can do whatever they want if I know they're not going to kill me. There might even be a book in it. Look on the bright side, Nina.

I look at my watch, surprised it's still there, although I suppose someone who can supply Armani and Chanel would have little interest in nicking a Cartier, no matter how many diamonds it has.

I have less than forty minutes. Not long enough. Although I'm dying to run a deep bath and lie in scented oily water for hours, soaking away hideousness, I settle for a quick hot spritz and get to work on my face.

~

'Turn please, face to wall.' The instruction is shouted through the closed bathroom door.

The click of the key in the lock. Without looking, I can tell there are three of them.

'Very nice.' A different voice. One of them whistles. Low.

'Beautiful.'

'He to be pleased.'

'He?'

'Speak nothing. We take you now. To close your eyes, please, or we put blindfold again?'

That accent. Hungarian? Polish? Balkan?

'No need for the blindfold, thanks. I can barely see a thing anyway. Blind as a bat. My glasses and spare contacts are in my handbag …'

I hope I'm sounding cheerful and polite. And patient. Not demanding. Reasonable. Sticking to the rules.

'Your bag to be returned to you in room.'

'What room?'

'Down. Dinner. He waits.'

'And my mobile?'

'He has also the phone.'

One black-clad heavy descends the ornately carved staircase in front of me. Presumably in case I try to escape.

I'm guided from behind, a hand on each elbow. Flanked on both sides. I can now see that we're in a huge converted barn, its pitched roof soaring high above our heads, glittering chandeliers suspended from different heights. They don't really match style of the barn, but whatever.

At the bottom of the staircase, I'm led across a wide stone-flagged hallway, through a pair of huge doors, into a magnificent dining room with a massive medieval-looking stone fireplace. Giant pewter candlesticks, suits of armour, magenta velvet drapes.

It's like a film set; everything's too big to be real.

Maybe I've shrunk. Maybe that Alice in Wonderland moment back in the office was a premonition. My mind's doing overtime again. I'm not bloody surprised.

But then I see him.

At the other end of the longest refectory table I've ever seen – there must be thirty chairs – is a guy I recognise. Dead spit, the likeness is uncanny. It must be. It can't be. Of course it bloody can't be. I must be seeing things again. My host rises.

'Good evening, Mrs Vincent.'

'It's *Miss* …'

'Yes, of course. Forgive me. You won't mind if I call you Nina, will you. You look very beautiful, Nina, if I may say. For an old bird. I know you've had a very challenging day. But you've gone pale, is something wrong?'

I'd know that voice anywhere.

Clive Clifford.

CHAPTER TWENTY-THREE

NINA

I am sitting in a gorgeous Rubens wingback armchair beside the blazing fire.

He fills my glass, a Bohemian crystal flute, with '98 Krug Clos du Mesnil. This stuff's about five hundred quid a bottle. Delicious, but Christ.

'The signature bouquet,' comments Clive, nosing deeply. 'Toasty. Citrussy. Can you taste the vanilla notes?'

'Somebody's doing very well for himself,' I respond, 'if he can afford this every night.'

'Not every night – only on special occasions. I owe it all, as you know, to Eddie Laine.'

'Doesn't he owe it all to you?'

'He might argue with that.'

'No doubt. But you made him, didn't you? You set your yellow cap at being the new Colonel Tom, Tony Defries, Peter Grant, all them, and you made it. Bloody good for you. You told me you were going to, that night of the video shoot at the Hippodrome, remember? All that glitter.'

'Was not gold.'

'Tell me about it. Had it coming out of my eyes for about two months. You were trying to get me to write a piece about it.'

'What, the glitter?'

'Don't be daft. Your big ambition.'

He smiles.

'And you refused. How flattering that you'd remember a

conversation from a lifetime ago with a nobody like me.'

'I never said you were a nobody.'

'You didn't have to. You thought it. That was enough.'

'What makes you say that?'

'I could feel your scorn. I can still feel it. Sometimes. Coming at me out of your picture in the paper.'

'What, you let a stupid black and white photo get to you? Don't make me laugh. Look, I was young, full of myself, full of shit, just like you. People like us thought we knew it all. Ignorant gits, the lot of us. We weren't the only ones. I wasn't interested in behind-the-scenes back then; it was all about the artists.'

'It always was.'

'Of course. You wouldn't have got into it otherwise. So what's all this, then: punishment for an age-old snub by a two-bit hack you couldn't give a chimpanzee's about?'

'You call this punishment? Dolled to the nines, one of the rarest champagnes in the world in your hand, about to eat dinner with the manager of the most successful living rock star …'

'Abducted at the funeral of a friend. Dragged here against my will. If you wanted to have dinner with me, you only had to ring me up and ask. I'm not exactly low-profile.'

'You wouldn't have come.'

'Says who? How would you know, unless you asked me?'

'I don't deal in possibilities, Nina. Dead certs or nothing.'

'Emphasis on dead?'

'Dinner is served. Allow me. By the way, this is yours.'

He bends down and reaches for something. My handbag.

'What about my BlackBerry?'

He laughs like a drain.

Clive takes my glass and escorts me to the table. Pulls out my chair, unfolds my napkin, lays it gently across my lap. Only now do I notice there's no music. It seems ironic.

The meal is served silently by one of his heavies, a guy who could be George Harrison. I've seen him before somewhere, haven't I? Doesn't he play in a tribute band, The Trembling Wilburys?

It's all gourmet and a half, I'll give Clive that much. The starter is watermelon and goats' cheese – tiny cubes of pink fruit with the cheese shredded over it, garnished with olive oil and candied wasabi. Scallops on roasted swordfish for main: a small pyramid of fish on a hot vegetable salad, beetroot, haricots verts and creamed sweetcorn.

I wade in ravenously, which seems to amuse him.

Dessert, which I barely touch because I've eaten too fast, is a flat chocolate cupcake topped with raspberries and mint, floating on a smear of coulis and custard cream. I do half a bottle of Puligny Montrachet with this lot. Down the *Beaumes-de-Venise* in one hit, what the hell? I'm pissed now. Lay on, Macduff, and damned be him who first cries hold.

'Brandy?'

'I couldn't. I'm stuffed.'

Without another word, he moves me by the elbow from the table to a sitting-room arrangement at the far end of the room. There's a gigantic screen on the wall in front of us. He doesn't speak; he just fires up a laptop.

Showtime?

First up, five or six minutes of a Chas Channing and The Dead Jameses gig in Los Angeles, I'm guessing 1985. *What*? Why are we watching this? What does he know?

I'm getting into it, in spite of myself. Must be the booze. They really did have it, Chas and the boys; this footage is a thrill to see again.

I've been lulled into a sense of false security, I realise, when he hits me with the stills. Performance images of Chas, Paul Judd, Roger Blacker, Jerry Colbert. Mounted in chronological order of their death.

'What's this?'

'Keep watching.'

'Why are you showing me …'

'I said watch.'

The screen is black. Open bar chords. A spotlight, searing outwards at a broad sweep of audience. The camera zooms in on the back of a girlish figure with ridiculously long legs, standing solo at a mic on an otherwise empty stage.

She's strumming the acoustic we can hear. She starts to sing, a piercing flutter. I know that voice. Frail. Heartbreaking. Magical. The kind of voice you hear once in a blue moon and know that music will never sound the same again. Like when poor Amy Winehouse appeared on the scene. And then Adele. The camera focuses. The girl turns round.

She's staring, and strange. Head like a huge lollipop, with about five women's worth of hair cascading off it. Stick-thin body, a sort of cartoon hillbilly supermodel meets gauche Girl Guide.

Roxy Rome: the Californian songstress who caught the music business with its pants down. Even the cynics are raving about her. There's a quality to her songs and voice that remind me of the young Kate Bush, before the industry scared the shit out her, and sent her scuttling for the hills. Made a good comeback though, didn't she. Never too late.

David Stark's been organising Roxy Rome songwriting classes in schools all over London. Everybody's in on this act. She's captured the imagination of millions of young girls. Apart from that voice – which has been described as 'baby milk blended with battery acid, unlike anything you've ever heard', and 'six octaves of whale song and fox cries layered over trad folk, blues and country, it cuts like wire and almost draws blood' – she is still one of them.

'Champagne?'

'I'd better not.'

'Why not? It's not as if you've got to drive home.'

'Planning on keeping me here indefinitely, are you, or are there alternatives?'

'All in good time.'

He hands me a fresh glass.

'Neal Goddard,' he says.

'What about him? I've got to ask, by the way, who are your goons? A bit heavy-handed, aren't they?'

'They were under strict instructions not to hurt you.'

'I'm not saying they did, but it wasn't exactly Virgin Upper Class. Especially when they didn't share their crisps.'

'Sorry?'

'You had to be there. So what's it all about, Alfie? You're starting to scare me. Do you always go to such lengths to schedule a meeting?'

'I just like doing things in style.'

'Pull the other one. And Neal Goddard, since you ask: what's he got to do with anything? What about the guys you've just flashed there on the wall? You know very well they're all dead. So what's the connection, Clive? What the hell's going on?'

He moves me again, back to the fireplace, where the fire has been stoked. New logs. The flames appear to spiral upwards, leaping and dancing, looking more like fan-driven yellow and red paper strips in a stage-set grate than real fire. Must be the booze. How would I know, why would I care?

'I was married,' he says, easing his left Chelsea boot off with his other heel. He places it carefully under the chair, and pulls off the right.

'I didn't know that.'

'Callie.'

'What?'

'Callie was my wife's name. I didn't love her. I lost my heart to someone else, a very long time ago.'

'Who?'

'This girl called Leonie.'

'What happened to her?'

'She died. Not long after I proposed to her with a ring on the Staten Island Ferry. She turned me down, I lost my rag, and threw the ring over the side. I still can't believe I did that. I never saw her again. Every time I go back there, I still look for it. Stupid arse. Why am I telling you this?'

'People tell me things,' I tell him. 'They always have. I have that kind of face.'

'She grew on me.'

'Which one?'

'Callie. She was perfect for me. I could do no wrong. I walked on water as far as she was concerned. She worked in our office. She wasn't beautiful like Leonie. Callie was fluffy; she was like a little cat. She had this thing about her that made you want to look after her. You wanted to hold her tight. Not that she was helpless, far from it; she was a capable kid actually. She fell for me, big time. I ignored it as long as I could. Then I chased her and chased her until she caught me.'

'She knew there'd been someone else?'

'Oh, yeah. That there was still was someone else. Never dies, that kind of thing, does it? You just carry it around with you like a long-term illness your entire life. Even blokes do. You ever felt like that?'

'We all have.'

'No getting away from it. Wherever you go, it's there ahead of you. Waiting for you. Always something there to…'

'Sandie.'

'What?'

'Shaw.'

'Yes.'

'Anyway. What's it got to do with me?' I ask. 'And I'll say it again 'til I'm blue in the face: why the fuck did you have to abduct me from a funeral to tell me?'

'Goddard,' he says, reaching for the bottle, pressing a switch to one side of the mantelpiece, presumably to call for more.

'What about him?'

'Callie and I broke up. She wanted a baby, typical woman. Kept wanting one. Banged on about it. They do this, don't they? You got kids?'

'A son. Grown-up.'

He either doesn't hear this, or he ignores it.

'I was more than happy with what we had,' he says. 'She gave up work; we went everywhere together. More like brother and sister than husband and wife, if you read me.'

'Which could explain why you never had children.'

'I've often wondered.' He rakes his hand through hair that isn't there, sniffs his fingertips, examines his nails.

'Where does Neal fit in? Did he fit in? Had an affair with her?'

'Worse.'

'What happened?'

'She told me she'd had enough, that she wanted a divorce. Said she knew I'd never loved her, that it was doomed from the start, that I wasn't "being honest" in the relationship.'

'She was right.'

'Yeah. But then she fucked it all, big time. She went to Goddard.'

'He was her divorce lawyer.'

'As well as her lover.'

'For fuck's sake.'

'He got to you too?'

'No, it wasn't like that. He was just my lawyer …'

'You're lying. Did you know he only ever took on wives, Nina? Never husbands?'

'I didn't know that when I instructed him, no. Found out later. But Neal and I weren't lovers.' I feel my face changing colour and shape.

We sit in silence. Another bottle appears; I don't even see the goon.

Clive opens it deftly, refills both glasses, plunges the bottle into a fresh ice bucket that's been left on the floor.

'What happened?' I say, eventually.

'They took me for everything, the pair of them. She started taunting me with how good the sex was with him. That was a kick in the guts. How can that be right, divorce lawyer and client?'

'It isn't.'

'How can it be allowed, then?'

'You're asking the wrong person.'

'You sure?'

'I think so.'

I'm sweating like a pig inside the Armani.

'What do you mean, you think so?'

'You know how it is. Neal and I got pissed together. Quite often. It's the kind of thing that happens, in our lines of work. We're probably all incurable alcoholics when it boils down. I always mean to address my drinking, I try stopping altogether sometimes, but when everybody else is doing it, it's so tedious being the sober one. It makes everyone else seem like the boring gits they are. Suffice it to say I always went home alone.'

He gives me the look that says he knows otherwise. How long has he been having me tailed?

'I wanted her back, Nina.'

'But you've said yourself, it would never have worked. You didn't love her. Not really. You didn't *romantically* love her. It's the killer, for women; there are no two ways. You wouldn't give her a baby …'

'It might have happened of its own accord. It usually does.'

'But it didn't.'

'What happened was *him,'* Clive slurs, refilling again. Taking a swig straight from the bottle as if to say what the hell, and wiping his mouth on his dark sleeve.

'I could have got her back, if it wasn't for him.'

'The marriage was over.'

'I can't stand rejection.'

'No one can. Is that what did it?'

'She was all I had.'

'What happened to her?'

'This is the thing. No one knows. I got a letter from her solicitors saying she was terminating proceedings. Then she vanished.'

'Where did she go?'

'If I knew that, we wouldn't be sitting here.'

'Wait, that means you're still married.'

'So it would seem.'

'Join the club,' I say. 'Clive, can I ask you something?'

'What?'

'Am I getting out of here alive?'

'I don't think so,' he replies, matter-of-fact. 'I don't think anyone is.'

~

I can hear music, a drum beat at least, coming from somewhere in the house. The assailants grooving the night away?

I'm busting for the loo again, I'm going to have to go. If I just get up and wander off, someone might think I'm making a run for it and have a pop at me. I've no idea what the agenda is here. Clive has clearly lost the plot.

I try to wake him up, but he seems out for the count. I hop about the place, trying not to wet myself. I'm just about to press the buzzer beside the mantelpiece when he comes to.

'*Whaaa*?' He seems panicked. I put my hand on his arm to settle him.

'You're OK. It's Nina. You nodded off.'

'What are you up to?'

'Nothing, Clive,' I reassure him. 'Just dying for a wee, that's all.'

'We should probably go to bed.'

'You're not …'

'Separately. I'll call Jacek, he'll see you back …'

'I just did.'

'What?'

'Call him.'

'Oh. I hated him. With every hair I used to have on my head.'

'Jacek?'

'Don't be stupid. Goddard.'

Things are making less and less sense.

'You would see him dead at any cost,' I say. Tiptoeing on glass.

'I would,' Clive agrees, rubbing his eyes, staring madly. 'Give me time.'

~

'Jacek. Interesting name.'

'Not to speak. To walk.'

'Don't worry, I'm busting and knackered.'

'What?'

'Never mind.'

'Your room. To lock from outside. To return morning.'

'Sleep tight to you too.'

I'm often glad to see a toilet. The old bladder is not what it was. I sit, and contemplate. I throw the dress in the bath, and wonder in passing what tomorrow's wardrobe will bring. No sign of any other clothes anywhere. Maybe tomorrow's not even on the cards. I think I'm past caring.

The small, perfect bedroom is through a door I hadn't noticed before. Blanched everything; this'll be like sleeping in a branch of the White Company. Even the velvet curtains drape like fresh snow. I sink deeply into more pillows than I can count. Remembering.

I should have known that it would hit me sooner or later. I hear his voice, clearly and close, as if he were lying here beside me. I see his twisted face looming over me, his lumpen body crushing mine.

'*Don't wanna be another fuckin' John Lennon*,' he says.

'*Be me next*.'

'*They'll get me*.'

'*You've gotta help me, Nina*.'

'*I've got more whacko fans than Jesus*.'

And then the calls start.

'*Baby, it's Chas*.'

CHAPTER TWENTY-FOUR

NINA

I'll try to tell it the way it was, without emotion.

I can see him now, sitting on one of those quaint white cast-iron chairs on the terrace of his place out beyond Bath. Spilling over the side, pretending to fall off it or asleep, all the time acting the clown, it was as if he couldn't not.

The kids – twins, tiny, round-faced – are scooting up and down on a red plastic tractor and a yellow trike. The primary colours are blinding in the sun. Their childish screams are piercing; I could do with wine to numb the pain.

There's a small blue, shell-shaped paddling pool with about an inch of water in it that they keep getting in and out of. The nappy on the little boy is saturated, it's drooping down to his chubby knees. He doesn't seem bothered. She hovers, his wife, fetching biscuits and tea, smoothing his hair out of his eyes, thrusting a bottle of sunblock at him. 'Here, put this on, hon, you know you'll burn if you sit here too long.' She glares at me. Remembers to smile. She goes back inside. Amazing house, Cotswolds stone, a huge glass conservatory on the side with a flowering creeper growing through it. Wisteria? Returns in moments, bringing a hat, an old straw thing with a crack along the top. Asks if I want one too.

I'm OK, thanks.

My first major celebrity interview. It felt funny to be doing it at their house. Intrusive. Made me feel guilty, like I was crossing a line. Like catching them in their underwear, or peeping through a hole in the fence at a dimension of their life I shouldn't see.

Chas Channing, rock superstar, off-duty. Being a normal bloke, just a family man. Being like any other dad with his little kids. Being nothing like *him*. There was something almost indecent about it. I was used to hanging around after gigs for musicians, propping up bars, lurking late into the night in stinking kebab joints and rank curry houses and going home reeking of beer and onions and despair. Always pestering, muscling in, sticking at it, telling them whatever they needed to hear. Staying up all night if it meant getting one over the competition. After John, it all changed.

Rhett was right. In some ways. I felt like crap, even as I was writing it. I pretended not to. I managed to convince myself that I had no choice.

In a way it was what he said: a historical record. I had a 'duty', he insisted. You must *know* you do, Nina, to write what you know, tell the world what you saw.

But I could have said no. Only I could tell the story, perhaps, but I didn't have to tell it the way I did.

Rhett would have sacked me for refusing, and rightly so. I could see it from his point of view. If I'd been an editor with a hack out in New York on my ticket who'd witnessed the wipe-out of a Beatle but wouldn't give him a line, I'd have fired me too.

Look, I'd have got another job. Would I still be writing gig reviews and interviewing unsigned wannabes and would that be such a bad thing? At my age, are you joking? No, I'd have grown up, got out, gone and done something else, like all the other hustler hacks I used to hang with. Who got proper jobs and better clothes and left rock 'n' roll behind. It's what I should have done.

But it was the 80s. There was something in the air. Not that I was remotely interested in politics or the economy at the time, I was too young to care. However, even I could tell that things were on the turn.

Thatcher and the Conservatives tottered into Downing Street in May 1979 and suddenly the papers and the news channels were effervescing for England about 'a new era'.

The loss of confidence and pride that seemed to infect everything in the late 70s while I was still at school – the apparently collective fear that the country faced a precarious future, reduced circumstances and diminution on the world stage – seemed to be giving way to a revival of can-do spirit, a whiff of freedom and progress.

Yes, unemployment went through the roof, and the pay gap between men and women widened. That was hard to swallow, with a woman at the helm. But there was so much to write about. Yuppies, the Falklands, Charles and Di. New Romantics. Blondie. Culture Club. Adam Ant. Madonna. Jacko. Compact discs. Camcorders. Channel 4. Live Aid.

Rock and pop started having another 60s, it felt like. The great irony was that the death of a Beatle seemed to herald a rebirth for popular music. As if in homage to him. It was the way I chose to see it, letting myself right off the hook. That was the way the wheel turned for me.

I interviewed Chas several times for features over the next couple of years, all relatively civilised: in the kitchen playing Celebrity Chef, in the wings waiting to go on stage, in his garden, down the pub, posing as Doting Dad with the kids and the whatever number wife she was.

Hazel had to be seen to be believed. Hefty, mumsy, un-rock-wife. She wore sailor dresses with cardigans and pearls. What on earth did rock's ultimate wild man, who arguably invented Metal and who was lean, mean and relentlessly keen, even see in her? It must have been love. Really?

It was when John died that things took a turn for the sinister. How did Chas find out which hotel I was staying in? Who was watching me, or who told him, and how did he come to be calling me over and over that night? I must have told him myself, I suppose, and of course there were no mobiles back then. Things had been stacking up against him for some time. There was all that trouble with the lawsuits in America, the so-called subliminal lyrics cases, those teenagers apparently driven to take their own lives by words in his songs. He was desperate. He'd convinced himself that the nutters were coming for him.

I had a whole year of his moaning, and then the Reagan shooting.

~

March 1981, the Washington DC Hilton. John Hinckley Jr shot the president, hitting him in the forearm and chest, puncturing his lung and causing near-fatal internal bleeding. The would-be killer was obsessed with Jodie Foster after seeing her play a child hooker in *Taxi Driver.* Robert De Niro co-starred.

Hinckley, found not guilty by reason of insanity, had stalked Jodie all over America: signed up for a writing course at Yale in 1980, after finding out she was a student there, bombarded her with letters and love notes, but got nowhere. He decided he had to gain notoriety, make himself worthy of her, make her take notice of him. He started by stalking Jimmy

Carter, wound up half-killing Ronald Reagan. Chas seemed to know every last detail. He was obsessed with the case.

It got worse. Pope John Paul II worse. A couple of months later that year, a Turkish attacker, Mehmet Ali Agca, shot His Holiness in St Peter's Square, Rome. Again, Chas was obsessed with it.

'They're coming for me, darlin',' he'd wail, 'I know I'm next. You've gotta help me. What the fuck are we gonna do?'

There were whole life stories that Chas wanted kept out of the headlines. I don't need to spell them out. Many were the times we had leads that could have buried him and his career, if not get him banged up for a stretch, not to mention get him shredded alive by his Rottweiler wife.

He was more useful to us alive, the copy he gave was so great. It always fell to me to make the call, and tell him what we had.

He'd run it past his management and we'd have a summit, eventually coming up with some other, tamer revelation to offset whatever sensational titbit we'd been sold. No, I never felt guilty about it. If he wanted secrets kept off the front pages, then he had to compromise by offering alternatives. There aren't many of those to the pound these days, in a gone-wrong age of agents and middlemen on stratospheric percentages, calling the shots and rendering editors as well as managers as good as impotent.

I remember he was due to perform in Philadelphia for Live Aid. July 1985. I was covering the gig at Wembley, so I wasn't aware of what happened until afterwards. I think everyone knows he didn't turn up; it has become part of Live Aid lore. Like Bono's leap of faith. But this was negative. Massively, career-killingly negative.

Chas went missing. I knew how deeply he'd been affected by the whole American lawsuit thing. He was also fighting a losing battle against addictions to drink and drugs. This wasn't the first time he'd crashed spectacularly off the rails. Little did I know how bad it was this time, nor what it was going to do to me.

Countless 'friends' talked to the papers. They always do, especially where money's involved.

Plenty of papers invented 'friends' to talk to; there was a lot of that about in those days. There still is.

He'd vanished on Hazel and the kids, and left no clue as to his whereabouts. All his 'friends' began to fear for his life.

Then Chas sent her his hair, fingernail and toenail clippings, along with a plastic-lidded beaker containing his urine, with a note saying 'This is all that's left of me worth having. Take good care of my DNA. Love, C.'

The parcel had been mailed in New York. Hazel rushed to Manhattan with children and nannies in tow, deposited them in a hotel, and set off in search of her husband. Her quest led her to a rehab clinic in Tucson. Some months later, the family were reunited in their eccentric other home in Beverly Hills.

What Hazel never knew about were the desperate phone calls Chas made to me from the clinic before she tracked him down. Semi-coherent, confused, frantic, in his unmistakable drawl, which came during the early afternoon – the small hours for him. He told me that he couldn't sleep, that he was terrified someone might break into the place and shoot him.

He was so afraid this would happen, he cried non-stop. He'd ramble on, sometimes for an hour or more. Much of the time about John.

'*It's fashionable to blow people in the public eye away, darlin'*.'

'*Be me next. Bound to be. You watch.*'

He had a point – if only himself to blame. His demented bi-polar musical genius attracted the most extreme kinds of fans. The crazed on-stage antics didn't help. Neither did the drugs and drink, his wild admissions that he'd shot dead every pet his kids had ever owned, including two Alsatians and a horse, and had more than few times tried to kill his wife.

He'd even been arrested on a charge of attempted murder after chaining her to the front of a Land Rover and crashing it into a tree. Chas had sold his soul for rock 'n' roll. He was suffering the consequences. He saw killers in every shadow. He gave them names.

I wrote a series of articles for the paper about celebrities being stalked and threatened, including Madonna, Bjork and Donna Mills, the *Knots Landing* soap star who'd been tormented with death threats. Donna told me herself she slept with a loaded gun on her pillow.

Chas read the piece, as I might have known he would. He was getting hold, in LA, of all my articles in London. Seeing himself between the lines, even when he wasn't there. He called to say he'd got a gun, and was doing the same.

Then, a curious twist. I started to feel like the DJ in the 1971 Clint Eastwood film *Play Misty for Me,* the one with the radio jock getting pestered by a jealous and homicidal female fan. Coincidence, is there such a thing? Mills also starred in the movie.

In my disturbing personal take on the theme, Chas was the one calling me. He said he had no one else to talk to. He sobbed and sobbed for help. I would talk to him, and try to reassure him, but I don't think he listened. Most of the time he seemed out of control. He usually gave the impression of having been drinking, or worse, and seemed beside himself with fear.

'*I'm locked in me fuckin' bedroom, darlin'*,' he'd say.

'*I daren't even go out for a piss. I'm homesick and I miss my kids, and I don't know what Hazel's gonna do to me, but I can't come back, I'm finished back home, I've got no choice but to stay here. Don't know what's gonna happen to me. Scared I'm gonna be dead soon. You've gotta help me, babe.*'

The editor overheard us talking one day.

'Was that Chas Channing on the phone?'

I could hardly deny it.

'Yes, it was.'

'What did he want?'

'Just a friend in need,' I said feebly. I didn't get away with it. The editor had heard more than he was letting on. I was duly despatched to LA. Told not to return with less than a world exclusive.

~

We arranged to meet for dinner.

'I'm bringing a mate,' he announced over the phone, but refused to say who it was. I guessed it would be a woman, but I couldn't have been more wrong. When I turned up at the chic Beverly Hills restaurant he'd chosen, Mezzaluna, I think it was called, Chas was already at our table.

With Eddie Laine.

Unexpectedly upbeat and buoyant – I suspect he'd ingested Peru before he came out that night – Chas was in a fantastic mood, the absolute life and soul.

After three double Scotches, he asked for the wine list. I forget now which red he chose, but I remember the three of us had five bottles.

Eddie – who'd taken off his red-and-white striped shirt, crumpled it into a ball and commanded me to sit on it, because he was going on to do a late-night chat show and didn't want to 'look as though I got dressed straight from the packet' – then suggested a game, in which we had to calculate how many garments we were wearing and pay $20 dollars per item. If that didn't put enough money on the table to cover the bill, whoever was wearing the most had to cough the shortfall.

Needless to say, neither of them had any cash. Chas was way too out of it to have remembered his credit cards, and Eddie was world-famous for his parsimony. He still is.

The only non-millionaire at the table, it fell to me to pick up the tab.

After so much booze, the game deteriorated rapidly into a strip session that left Eddie and Chas starkers under the table with a rose in each mouth. It was then, having become extremely agitated during a discussion about the behaviour of Her Britannic Majesty's press corps, that they decided to take a hostage.

The hostage was me.

CHAPTER TWENTY-FIVE

NINA

My watch has stopped. It's been due for a service for a while now, I just haven't got round to asking Allegra to organise it.

I've no idea what the time is. It's broad daylight outside, but there's no sign of anyone. Not a goon has come to my door to escort me to breakfast. They haven't even brought me a mug of tea.

I've had an oily bath, I've got my face on, I'm back in the crumpled, sweaty Armani dress that I'd dumped in the bath, for want of anything else to wear. The clothes I arrived in last night are still in a heap. I wash them with shampoo and hang them on the towel airer. I rinse my boots under the tap, spray some Number 5 in them and stuff them with loo paper. It's the Girl Guide in me. Be prepared. Anything could happen in the next half-hour. Or not.

I'm ready to go, but there's nowhere to get to. I'd make notes about what's happened, get a timeline down before I forget, but my notebook's missing from my bag. There's not a thing in the room to write with.

At least I've got something to read: Simon Napier-Bell's book *Ta-Ra-Ra-Boom-De-Ay*, which'll take my mind off things for a while. I've got an eyebrow pencil, I can scribble in the margins.

I settle on the bed to read. With a glass of water. At least there's a tap.

The sound of silence. I should feel hungry. There's still no sign of anyone. Not a murmur from anywhere, inside or out. This doesn't feel good. I'm beginning to wonder whether they've deserted the house and left me to my fate. They're not going to torch the place, are they? In which case they'd leave it until dark before doing so, to make it more difficult for the fire service to tackle a blaze. I'm not feeling great, which could be a hangover. The slightest move I make deafens me.

The bile is rising. I'm aware of every millimetre of my skin.

Charlie. He won't know about this. Not unless Phil and Allegra have worked out that I'm missing, have alerted the police and managed to get hold of anyone. Maybe James? After all, he's still my next of kin.

I start to panic at the thought, feeling a desperate need to escape. I check the windows for the hundredth time. All three are still locked and barred.

I am dozing when I hear the key in the lock. No one speaks. I don't bother turning my face to the wall, I'm angry now. The heavies are not quite what I was expecting. They could be identical twins.

Thick-set, black-clad, both wearing glasses. No other distinguishing features. Ethnic origin unclear. Would I recognise them in a line-up? Would I even recognise myself?

'So what kept you?' I say, sarcastically.

No response.

I assume they're waiting for me to go with them. I get up.

'To please come.'

'Where now?'

'Down.'

~

Clive is sitting at the far end of the dining table. Like me, he's wearing the same clothes he had on last night, with the addition of his trademark yellow cap. He's unshaven and looks stale and dishevelled, as if he's been sitting there all night. All day. Contemplating. *What*? I dread to think.

'Apologies,' he says, glancing up at me as I enter. He nods to the goons and they reverse their way out, pulling the doors closed.

'What for?'

'Leaving you alone like that. I should've at least sent you up some breakfast, and something suitable to wear. I had a lot on my mind.'

'Like what?' I say. 'How best to dispose of a body without leaving clues?'

'That's the least of my problems, I can assure you. You're certainly not the first.'

My heart stalls.

He rises and paces slowly around the room. He's wearing the boots he had on yesterday, and there's grass on them. He's been outside. There's no fire, and the grate has been swept. They haven't laid a new one.

'You look nice in that frock I got you, by the way. Fetching. Not the first time you've been held against your will, is it?'

'I don't know what you're on about.'

'I think you'll find you do. That dinner in LA with Eddie and Chas Channing. What was that, twenty-eight years ago? I'm guessing. Although I suppose I could look it up. There's a record of everything. Drink?' He smiles. Like a great white.

'No, thank you. Bloody lifetime ago. How do you even know about that?'

He chuckles.

'Funny. I don't think there's a single thing Eddie's ever done, or thought, that I don't know about. Not since the day I first met him.'

'You stalk him?'

'I prefer to call it protection. I can't afford to take chances, can I? I couldn't risk the loss of my Turn. Where he goes, I go. If anything happens to him, it's all over for me. It's in my best interests to ensure at all times that nothing comes between us and that no harm comes to him. It puts me in a very difficult position at times, of course. I'm sure you understand.'

'Especially now that you're also managing Roxy Rome.'

'You know about that?' He smiles. 'I see things I could do without seeing, if you get my drift. Once you've seen stuff, you can't *un*-see it, you know what I'm saying? It's always going to be there. Behind your eyes. Quite a night, that, too, wasn't it? I hope you enjoyed it. At least some of it. That night and all the other nights. How long was it they had you, again? I lost track in the end.'

It's coming back to me. Can I die now?

'If you know so much about it, why are you asking me?'

'You didn't quite know where to put yourself when they got naked under the table, did you?' He chuckles.

'Your face was a picture. It said it all. You didn't know those two enjoyed each other's company, as they say in France, did you? I never understand why people are so surprised. Look at the fuss that was made at the notion of Jagger and Bowie together. I could never fathom it myself. There isn't a man alive who doesn't prefer his own, and that's a fact. Women are obsolete. Good for one thing.'

'Misogynist.'

'Sweet of you.'

I ignore that. But I still want to know what he's on about.

'You were there, or you were having it filmed?' I ask.

He studies me, as if learning lines.

'I don't need to have anything filmed.' He beams, as if he's just finished a good meal. 'Imagine! I never have, and I never will. Every wall has eyes. Every door has ears. There's always someone up for a bung, always something there to remind me.' He draws closer, and leans in. His bulging blackheads are like frogspawn.

'Did you think you were going to die when they locked you in the den round at Eddie's that night?'

I open my mouth to speak, but nothing comes out.

A buttery grin spreads across Clive's pocked face. I can smell his uncleaned teeth. What a sleaze.

I want to hit him.

'Oh, that's *right*! He drawls the word, gives it a couple of extra syllables. 'You didn't know you were at Eddie's, did you? You could've been anywhere, for all you knew. You had no idea what they had planned for you, either. Poor Nina. Still, I can't imagine it was an entirely negative experience. Two of the world's greatest rock stars, giving you what you want. Yours for the taking. No need to ask twice. For no more than the price of a good dinner. I'd call that a win-win.'

Keep calm, Nina. Count. Breathe. Bide your time. Don't let him get to you.

'Lobster,' he whispers, his vile face so close to mine that he's almost kissing me.

'What?'

'Boiled lobster. Your favourite. You had it no less than seven times during your stay.'

'Fewer.'

'What?'

'It's "no fewer than", not "no less than".'

'Is that so. Well, there you go. Didn't you hear them scream as he dropped them in the pot? Up in the kitchen? The only reason for eating lobster, isn't it? The screaming? Knowing how they suffer before they get to be food. Eddie brought them in by the armful. Kicking. Soon to be screaming. He got you to choose which one. He also cooked it himself; did he tell you? All the garnishes and everything. Lobster with sweet ginger; that was your favourite. He had a few lessons with Axel Koch. I bet he didn't tell you that bit. Didn't he do well?

'Chas's job was to teach you to play pool. He did a pretty good job of that, too, as far as I could tell. Not that I know much about pool. Then they took it in turns. You didn't put up too much of a fight, did you? Not that you could, once they'd chained you to the wall. You didn't suffer too much, I take it. You're not scarred for life, but still. You got what was coming to you, didn't you? It was time.'

'What do you mean by that?'

'Nina. Nina. Do I have to spell it out? It's time you were taught a lesson. There were a lot of people gunning for you back then. Perhaps you didn't realise. Perhaps there still are. Think of it as taking one for the team. He could hardly get his own back himself, could he?'

'Who?'

'John Lennon, who else? Eddie knew. Chas knew. You knew it yourself, only you never came clean. You just took the money and ran.'

'From *what*?'

'From what you did to John.'

'What did I *do*?'

'I have to spell it out? You sold him down the river. You used his murder to make a name for yourself. He hadn't even gone cold. It seemed to us cats in the business a pretty low thing to do. You gotta pay for a thing like that, there's no way round it. Debt cancelled by time? In your dreams. It's still outstanding. You settle today.'

But it's not just about John Lennon, this, is it. It can't be. There's more to it, there has to be. Then in spite of myself, I lose it. I fly from the chair, going for Clive's face with my hands. I'm immediately restrained from behind by four black-clad arms. I didn't even hear them enter the room. Perhaps they were there all the time. I'm going mad, truly, finally. I must be. Is this the end?

'Steady. You'll do yourself a mischief, as they say in Ho Chi Minh City.'

Clive sits, composed, resting his face in one palm. He stares at me, unamused.

'Didn't you ever wonder what happened to her?' he says.

'*Who*?' I snarl. 'You bastard. You'll pay for this. You wait 'til my husband finds out.'

'Your *husband*, now.' Clive sneers. 'The one you've been trying to get rid of all this time while you've been off shagging for England behind his back. So draining, isn't it, this divorce business? More stressful than bereavement or moving house, they tell me. It's a wonder more divorcees don't drop down dead in the process. Perhaps you should thank me for putting you out of your misery, saving you the trouble. Anyway, as I was saying. Haven't you ever wondered what happened to her?'

'I don't know who you mean.'

'You *don't*?' he says, incredulous. 'Let me jog your memory a little.'

He produces a photo album. The kind a woman keeps. One of those big, old-fashioned, screw-spined affairs with thick plastic leaves that peel back to reveal sticky pages beneath. You place the snaps on the adhesive side, then drop the cellophane over them and smooth it down. We all had them, back in the day. I had quite a library of them, once upon a time. Who knows what happened to them all.

This one has page after page of pictures of a pink baby, a cute toddler, a contrary Terrible Two. A little girl in a uniform, who is clearly on her way to her first day at school.

'You thought you managed to escape from Eddie's,' says Clive, lifting a bottle from the bucket and pouring two glasses. He hands me one. I knock it back, nothing to lose. It's the same stuff as last night. It tastes like shit.

'Didn't you ever wonder why it was so easy to get away that day?'

'They got bored, I guess. Got careless, left the door open when they went out. I took a chance. No one came after me. I just ran for it.'

'You never wondered why they didn't come looking for you? You had quite a story to tell, didn't you?'

'Who would have believed it? I didn't want to believe it myself. I thought I could put it out of my mind and it would go way.'

'Only it hasn't, has it, poor Nina? It has never gone away. What happened all those years ago has haunted you every day of your life since.'

He refills, and continues.

'You went to West Hollywood. To your friend Marco Macaluso.'

'How do you know all this?'

'I paid him.'

'You paid *Marco*?'

'They all have their price. You discovered you were pregnant.'

'How do you know *that*?'

'The gynaecologist you consulted at Cedars-Sinai was on my payroll.'

'Of course he was.'

'You booked an abortion, but you couldn't go through with it. You quit your job, had the baby. Dear old Marco helped you make arrangements for private adoption. What a *friend*.'

'You did your homework.'

'I did better than that. I adopted your baby myself.'

'You're lying!'

I seize the bottle, and fill my own glass. The tears cascade like rain.

'There is proof, of course,' Clive assures me, matter-of-fact. 'Where would we be in life without proof? Everything's documented. I paid a Mexican couple to bring her up, I brought them in as housekeeper and gardener at my house in Topanga Canyon. Who's the daddy, you ask. Eddie or Chas? That is the question. That will always be the question. But there'll never be an answer. There must *never* be an answer, as far as the girl is concerned. Let it be.'

He smiles.

'You mean ...'

'Of *course* they never knew. Eddie *still* doesn't know! It's of no consequence to poor old Chas Channing, of course. Not where he's hanging nowadays. Anyway, why *tell* them? The project was mine!'

'*What* 'project'?'

'Come on.'

~

We move, again, to the sitting room arrangement at the far end of the room. Clive flicks on the laptop. There she is, the girlish figure, standing solo at a mic on an otherwise empty stage. Strumming an acoustic as she sings, a piercing flutter. I know that voice. The kind of voice you hear and know that music won't ever sound the same again.

The camera focuses. The girl turns round. She seems staring, strange, and familiar ...

'Here she is.' Clive laughs. A tea tray clattered on a kitchen floor.

'My greatest achievement. Living proof of my genius. Of the fact that rock stardom has nothing to do with God-given talent. Whatever *that* means. Ask Simon Cowell; he reckons he has all the answers. He knows fuck-all.

'Here she is, the endorsement of my personal legend as the greatest rock manager of all time. Forget Parker, Defries, McClaren, Grant. Amateurs. They all had talent to work with. I invented this one from scratch, I even taught her how to sing. I, Svengali. She, Trilby. You know the novel, I take it?

'Ladies and gentlemen, please put your hands together and give a warm welcome to one of a kind, to a superstar in the making. What a shame you'll never meet Roxy, Nina. She's fabulous. She's my girl. And she *is* your daughter, after all. You always wanted a little girl, didn't you, Nina? All women want a baby girl, a nice little dolly to dress up in cutesie clothes. Gorgeous, aren't they?

'A bit sad for her, isn't it, losing you – before she's ever even met you. A bummer, that is. Never having known your real father, too. That's a shame as well. I know how it feels, as it happens. Still. It can't be helped. I made up my mind a long time ago. There's no way your little girl Roxy's ever gonna know the truth.'

'Why not? Why shouldn't she know I'm her mother? What on earth is it to you? What are you going to do to me, and what for?'

'All in good time. Why are you in such a hurry?'

'What about the others?'

'*What* others?'

'Chas. Paul. Roger. Jerry. Joe, even. *You* killed them all, didn't you?'

'Ah, at last! The pennies have all just dropped, have they? For an intelligent bird, you bloody well took your time! Who *else* did you think would've killed them?'

'But w*hy*? What did any of them ever do to you?'

'They got in the way of my Turn: my Eddie. It winds me up, that does. I never did like competition, did I? It gets on my nerves. But it was *more* than that. They'd all had *you*. My Roxy's mum. I'd think about that and I'd get a little bit cross, ya know? I'd see blood, even. They were all part of your past. And therefore of my Roxy's past. I couldn't risk saddling her with a shady background that some old has-been like you might go digging up and holding against her; and more to the point, maybe even *writing about,* when she turned global superstar – could I? It's like the palace rooting out Di for Charles, making sure he had a bride with no skeletons in her knickers. Same thing, really. Roxy had to come with a pristine slate. What's more, she could never, ever find out the truth about how she was conceived. What does that do to someone, discovering you were only born because your mother was *raped*? Which is what it amounts to, Nina, let's not beat about the bush here. Pardon the, er, *pun*. Worse than that, you've got two possible dads, who both shagged your mum at the same time. Not a nice thought, is it? A bit unsavoury, that. I wonder how you've lived with it, all these years. My heart bleeds for you, Nina, it really does. No, I couldn't have my Roxy worrying herself sick over all that, could I. It would follow her about for life. Might make her lose her voice. Her *mind*, even. Gotta protect my assets, haven't I. I'm sure you can understand that. What choice do I have but to kill the goose that laid me the golden egg?'

'But how did you …'

'Get in there? To do 'em all, you mean? That was the easy bit. I knew them already, didn't I? We'd known each other for years. We'd hung out. You know how it is, you run into people out and about … fancy seeing *you* here, wanna hook up for a pie and a pint? Pitch up unannounced for a swift half with a good old boy from the bad old days and they're hardly gonna slam the door in your mush, are they?'

'But why mutilate them?'

'Just my little joke.'

'*Sick* joke.'

'Too kind.'

'And Joe?'

'The mock doc? Got on my tits, that one did. Pompous twat. Had to do him so you'd know I meant business. So you'd realise it was all about *you*.'

'Nothing was ever about me.'

'You say that now. Pity you didn't twig it in the first place.'

'How did you even know about him?'

'You wrote about him, remember? Obviously you don't. In your *column,* whatever they call it.

'I kept every one. They'll be just about all that's left of you, come tomorrow.'

CHAPTER TWENTY-SIX

LACUNA

The Specialist Crime and Operations Firearms Command steal in out of nowhere, a tidal wave of body-armour rolling silently through the trees.

Some sixty officers, perhaps more, a good half of whom are ex-military, balaclava-clad and menacing, armed with Glock SLP 9mm pistols, Heckler and Koch G36 assault rifles, and lugging what feels like their bodyweight in ammunition.

On orders via digital encrypted radio attached to headsets and microphones, the police move in towards the barn and its outhouses in a painstakingly mapped configuration. Taking their pre-assigned positions, they flatten themselves into to the ground, as good as invisible. Snipers lurk on the roofs of neighbouring barns. The bomb disposal unit has arrived, as well as the dog squad.

All are on standby, awaiting instructions, along with the crews of three fire trucks parked back all the way back at the junction gate. The night air ripples with anticipation, the only sound a lone owl's hoot.

Despite his decades of training, Harry is amazed. How slick is all this; he's never seen anything like it. Not first-hand. It's so good, it's so *modern*; it's almost sinister. It's like being in a film.

He's quite envious, if he's honest. He's trying not to be. He should have been allowed to do his time out here, on the ground, working the frontline, orchestrating hostage and siege operations, dynamic entry techniques, distraction devices, dangerous hostage negotiations. All that.

Not put out to grass, poured through a pipe and banged down the blunt end, going through the motions and playing abstract police games the force hasn't got a hope in hell of winning. This is where the action is, he thinks. This is what being a policeman is all about. If only he could have his time again.

Thank God he went to the funeral, at least. He'd had a feeling in his water; he'd sensed something or other was up. He knew he had to follow her down there, keep an eye on her. Well he was right, wasn't he, look what happened right under his nose. Grabbed at the graveside and bundled away before he even knew what was happening.

It just shows you. He doesn't know *what*, quite, but it just shows you. These things happen so fast. One minute they were standing there, shrugging in the cold, leaning from foot to foot, minding their own business, waiting for the coffin to drop. The next, red alert.

Harry had hidden behind a tree trunk. He was ducking and diving, breaking his neck to make sure Nina didn't spot him. He thought she saw him there at one point. Earlier, in the church. He lurched to one side of a pillar, and managed to tuck in behind some curtains. He didn't want to alarm her; he'd already told her he was in Ghana. He couldn't let her go to Llyn's funeral on her own, though, could he? He'd had a hunch something would happen. A policeman's instinct? Possibly. If it *is* that, it's good to know it still works. There's life in the old mutt yet, even after all these years.

He remembers glancing down as he pulled a handkerchief from his pocket; he only took his eyes off her for a second. When he looked up again, she was gone. *Where*?

He was frantic. He scanned the graveside, peered into the hole, even. What the hell happened *there*? Did she give up and leave, too upset or overcome or bored to stay? Had she gone to find the ladies? Spotted someone she recognised? *What*? He knew Nina. The least predictable woman ever born.

His eye was caught by two men in black, nothing unusual about that at a funeral, but they were walking *away* from the churchyard. He couldn't see another funeral party waiting in the wings, so why were they walking away when the committal wasn't even over yet? Harry smelled a rat. There was something odd about the way they were walking. It looked too synchronised, as if their inside legs were tied together. Like Jake the Peg with the extra leg, although for Christ's sake, don't mention Rolf Harris.

He kept watching, he had to screw up his eyes to see. The men stopped when they reached a black Range Rover parked some distance beyond the pond, next to what looked like Nina's Jag. They stopped, then turned. It was then that he saw her, a fleeting glimpse, being wrangled into the back seat of the car.

By the time Harry reached his Ford, all the way back down the high street in the pub car park, he hadn't clocked that he could have parked nearer, *bugger it*, the Range Rover was long gone. No way was he going to catch the bastards now.

He pulled out his mobile, and could have screamed when he saw he was out of range. Zero signal. *Fuck fuck fuck.* He tore into the pub and almost threw himself at the firght-haired barmaid, who was moving from table to table collecting empties.

'Bit early for the wake, love. They're all still up at the church. I expect it'll all be over soon. Then we've got our work cut out for the rest of the afternoon. I'll be dead myself, come tonight.'

'It's where I've just come from! Something's happened!'

'A bit shocked, aren't you darling? Sorry for you. Awful business. Calm down, they'll be digging yours next. Take a seat, my lovely, I'll bring you a drink over. What you having?'

'I need your phone!'

'There's a payphone out the back by the gents there, love.'

'I mean the *pub* phone!'

'Not for public use, sorry.'

'Police!'

Harry flashed his ID. He wasn't joking. The barmaid fell aside to let him behind the bar, blinking wildly. It could be some sort of *Candid Camera* thing, though, couldn't it? You never know these days, there's more reality TV than actual reality. Within seconds, dialling a hotline, Harry was through to HQ.

'Six foot plus, stocky, dressed in black suits. Two of them. Nothing on eyes, hair, ethnic origin, too far away to see, but I don't think they were black. I'm guessing European or American but, as I say, I'm only guessing. Black Range Rover Sport SDV6, I think. Some sort of short personal reg, couldn't see exactly what it was from that distance. Third suspect driving. They went east …

'Nina Vincent.' He spelled it. 'Also known as Mrs James Kendal. Couldn't tell you her age, maybe early fifties but don't tell her I said that, for Christ's sake. Eyes dark green, hair … brown *and* blonde. *Highlights*, thass it. Black cashmere coat, large black handbag, black leather shoes, elegant, well turned-out, she's … *that* Nina Vincent, exactly. She's all over the Internet, website, everything, a … one child, adult, male, travelling abroad. Presume next of kin is still her husband. Separated. Advertising exec. I can't remember which agency. Google it. No, no other family I can think of …

'*Why?* Because I also happen to be a friend of the family. *Yes*, honestly. Look, she didn't go willingly, no *question* this is a kidnapping. *Yes*, I can think of a motive, not the time or place to go into that now. Here's my mobile, but I've got no signal down here at the moment. I'm calling her editor now; he might know something. I'll come back to you.'

~

Harry sits, cold and fidgeting, walkie-talkie glued to his palm. He flips it a few times, and catches it. He keeps checking to make sure it's still on.

He's nervous. *Too* nervous. It's taken too long, in his opinion, to close in on where Nina's being held. *If* she's being held. If she's even here, after all this time. She could be long gone from this place. He's not convinced. They could have dumped her somewhere en route. They could have done anything. He's seen it all before, and more.

The heat-seekers drew a blank. The police still had no idea of her whereabouts after almost twenty-four hours.

Then, a stroke of luck. A random woman happened to walk into her local cop shop to make a complaint about a black Range Rover that had cut her up and nearly thrown her off her bike on the lane up by the farm, the one they say that rock star owns, Eddie Laine. Not that anyone's ever seen him around the neighbourhood; he lives in America most of the time, doesn't he?

Bingo. How can they be sure he hasn't killed her already, thinks Harry. Your guess is as good as his.

Suddenly there is movement, up behind the house. Action! Countless men move like ants, covering all exits. Counting down, standing by. Something's not right, though. What have they done with the negotiator? Someone said she was here already, where the bloody hell has she got to?

Who's got Nina? No idea. Harry's got an idea. He doesn't want to think about it. Too emotionally involved in the case to be effective? It's about the size of it.

'Let *me* go in,' he pleads, 'let me handle it. I'm trained in hostage negotiation. I know what I'm doing. I can talk a mutt off a meat wagon any day of the week. I go in unarmed, obviously.

'Of course I've got bloody flak on. I hope I won't need it. Standing by.'

If the hostage-taker is disturbed, muses Harry, thinking on his feet, there's a chance he could be looking for 'suicide by cop', or by civilian. It's called passing the buck. You've got to be firm, no-nonsense, and you've really got to be direct, stay on target, a person's life is at stake. Not a person's. *Nina's*.

First goal, no one gets hurt, either in there or out here. Life and safety of hostage are paramount.

Second goal, resolve situation without assault. Attack only as a last resort, once it's clear the perpetrator/perpetrators is/are about to kill or has/have killed the victim.

Under no circumstances allow the perpetrator to leave with the victim. If no physical harm has been done, convince the hostage-taker to give up.

If all else fails, fucking murder the bastard.

~

The heavies are oblivious. They're having a beer or four in the kitchen. Playing cards. The Bon Jovi blaring from the beatbox out in the laundry is so loud, it's little wonder they've no idea what's been going on.

Given the nod, Harry marches in, bold as you like, keeping his hair on, through the front door, and strides confidently across the flagstones as if about to step onto a podium and give a speech. He shoulders open the closed double dining-room doors, just in time to see Nina, flat on her back, *tied down* on the refectory table, a long black dress yanked up around her hips.

Looming over her is not the person Harry was expecting to see.

This isn't Eddie Laine! It's his *manager!* Clive someone. *Clifford.* I've seen him on the box, right dodgy bit of work. He's got that Roxy bird everybody's raving on about, you can't miss her, the American kid who's absolutely everywhere you look.

Harry knee-jerks. He yells; he can't help himself. It's all gone wrong. He's down at the first fence. The plan falls apart before it even kicks off. Where the hell's the fucking cavalry? What in God's name is keeping *them?*

As for Clive, he's horrified. He panics, half-zips himself, makes like a bull, and charges right at him. Harry lashes at Clive's cheek. Clive's too quick for him, he kicks back, catching Harry between the legs, thankfully a little too low to incapacitate. Harry recovers fast, pulling himself up to his full average, his eyes practically giving birth. He rages at Clive and forearms him, smacking him full in the mouth.

'You *cunt*! What have you done to her? Why have you got her here?'

'What's an ugly little prick like you got to do with anything?'

Clive staggers forwards, wiping the bloodburst from his mouth with the back of his hand, and takes a hefty swing. Harry grabs his arm and they fall about like two drunks doing a Gay Gordon, ricocheting between chair backs.

'Stop, *stop* it, he'll *kill* you!' screams Nina.

SMASH.

Harry sees masked faces all around him, a whole armoury of weapons raised. About bleeding time, what kept you, you bleeding slackers?

He feels his molars departing from his jaw, sees a huge pewter candlestick leave Clive's left hand, watches it hurtle through the air in slow motion. The fallen, flaming candle lands unseen in the folds of a velvet drape, where it catches. The thick fabric appears to recede as it succumbs to fire, scorching orange tongues spiralling upwards. The flames draw breath, they suck along the walls, lick and leap and lash with abandon across the ceiling. Solids, melting, liquids, dripping, timber beams beginning to blacken.

One moment the room feels like it's fighting back, the next it's exhausted, it's giving in, it's all too much for it.

In the choking blackness, everything curling away, not least his eyesight, Harry fights for both breath and life, distracted for a second by sparks drifting down, floating ash, disintegrating elegance, a scene of deadly and unbearable beauty.

The heat is insane. Harry's throat is thick, with liquid leather, molten plastic, burning hair. What's left of his breath vibrates inside him like coins in a bucket. He is deafened by the sound.

He hears hissing, creaking, a cave-deep resignation, a great groan as mighty timbers begin to shrink. Glass explodes and windows shatter. Metal pipes leak, draining all hope.

Is that a siren? That could be wishful. Another time, another place, another memory.

'*Harry*?'

'Come *ON*!'

He rips Nina from her moorings not a second too soon, as a massive beam comes crashing towards the table. He clings to her. They run for it.

The room is a vacuum, sucking itself inwards, the whole structure of the roof is caving fast. The heftiest cross-beam finally cracks, and the vaulted roof gives in, letting it fall – imprisoning Clive within the terrible inferno.

Pinning him mercilessly to his own stone-flagged floor.

CHAPTER TWENTY-SEVEN

NINA

What is it, a month ago now? Time flies when you're enjoying yourself. I have so lost track.

I only got out of hospital yesterday. Barely a scratch, thank you for asking. It was more shock than anything. They kept me in for observation. I was on some pretty nuclear medication.

I'm off all that now, thank God. They told me I collapsed, that I was carted off in an ambulance. I have zero recollection of any of that. That's the self-preservation thing kicking in again, it must be.

I've been told not to be surprised if I never remember at all.

My hair got quite burned; I keep forgetting that, too. Quite a lot of it gone off one side. What the hell, I'll get it cut short. Time to lose these stupid extensions anyway. When I can be arsed. There are more important things to take care of first.

I've been told to avoid stress, to try not to think about it all. But that's impossible, or is it just me? It's like telling someone not to think of a panda. The second you say to yourself '*not* panda', it's all you can think about all day.

So I can't *not*, is what I'm saying. Badly. They've let me go home, I'm back in the house. Home, alone. It feels quiet and weird, but it's not forever.

I had to tell an entire streetful of reporters, photographers and news crews to sling their hooks when I got back. Who do they think they are! Talk about dog eat dog! I'm one of *them*!

I had to wade through the buggers to get near my own front door. You'd think they'd have some bloody respect. Second thoughts.

The offers are hilarious. Two hundred grand from the *Mail on*

Sunday for exclusive serial.

More book deals than I can count. *New York Times*, *Vogue*, *Vanity Fair* … they're all falling out of their prams to get a look-in.

I've hit the big-time, Liza Minnelli. Start spreading the news. I'm beginning to feel like Nigella or Rebekah. Now *there's* a double act. Feature films on the lives of those two, is Hollywood kidding me? Is *Cannes*? So the rumours go. I know, it's astonishing. Then again, nothing should surprise me anymore.

Let's face it, hostage flicks are mega bucks. They tend to be. Remember Patty Hearst? Natasha Richardson played her, didn't she? I loved that woman. RIP. What a terrible way to go, that skiing accident. Poor, poor woman. I wonder who'd play me. How up yourself can you get?! Only joking. Over my dead one. Probably would be, too. Sorry, my mind tends to wander at the minute. It must be the medication.

~

'What the fuck are *you* doing here?' I said to Harry as he tore me off the dining table in that room on fire, and then him telling me he was in church, at the funeral. I *knew* I wasn't seeing things; I knew it was him, the cheeky bugger.

He'd seen everything; he raised the alarm. It was Operation Nina out there. I couldn't run. He forced me to. Pulled me for miles, it felt like, but was probably only fifty yards or so, outside always seems so huge in the dark. The whole thing was chaos, a terrorist bomb site, police and dogs and fire engines everywhere.

'I couldn't let you go to that funeral on your own, could I?' said Harry. 'Anything could have happened, after everything that had been going on.'

Anything could, and everything did. He held my hand as if he'd never let me go.

Then suddenly I was standing there, screaming after him. *Now* what was he doing? What felt like ten but was probably only two huge guys grabbed me, held me back, wouldn't let me move an inch. And there went Harry, running the other way. What the hell was he doing? Had he lost the plot? It must have got to him, the nightmare full circle, the wading through treacle, the lung collapse, the loss of balance, I couldn't see, I couldn't hear, I couldn't *breathe*. I couldn't reach him. I needed to touch him. I didn't know, how could I know at that moment, that I'd never touch Harry again.

'I love you,' he called back, 'I always have. I always will. I mean that, you cantankerous old bitch.'

And he was gone.

It was the last time I ever saw him. Harry bolted like Usain, all the way back to the blazing barn.

He tried to save Clive. *Why*? Can you imagine? That was his instinct, his *training*, in the police force he so loved. He *must* have loved. How the hell he thought he was going to lift that huge beam off Clive is beyond me. It must have weighed a couple of tons. Well, he tried. He *died* trying. That was Harry.

'Every life is worth something,' I remember him telling me once.

'What, even the lives of evil scumbag psychopaths with no thought for anyone but themselves?'

'Especially them,' he replied. 'Life is life. You can't put a price on it, and you certainly can't pick and choose who's entitled to it. It's not for us to judge.'

They found his body on top of Clive's. They knew it was him, but … I don't really want to think about this bit. They identify them from dental records, don't they? The police said Clive would have been a gonner before Harry got anywhere near him. So Harry gave his life to save a man who could not have been saved. If I could turn back time.

~

And here they all are, surprise surprise. Here come the losers. Bill's been ringing me for England, and bombarding me with bouquets as big as my bed in the Princess Grace Hospital. He says he's desperate to see me. He's just got back from Mumbai. He wants to come round. He wants me to have Tanner and the car for the duration. He can't bear the thought of me having to deal with all this alone. You should have thought of all that before, petal. I'm over it. Get back to your pre-pubescent floozies, to where you once belonged.

I've even had Tony on, can you believe? Things didn't quite work out with dear Mel in Switzerland over Christmas. Well, I never, and they've been living like siblings ever since. Sorry, but it's hard to feel sorry for him.

Wrong number, as they say.

As for Phil.

Don't even go there.

It's not as if he was ever going to apologise, sorry being an admission of guilt. Phil doesn't do guilt.

Not if he knows what's good for him. He also knows that he pushed too hard; he can see that now. He claims he didn't really appreciate what I was up against. We've exchanged emails. It's all cool. People drop dead over less, I keep telling myself. The problem is, there's no genuine emotion in the man.

This does tend to be the case with newspaper editors. I've known more than my share in my time. I can think of one or two exceptions. Closet sweethearts. Have a guess. But as a rule, they're usually reptiles. The cruellest creatures on earth. I used to wonder what they thought about when they lay in bed at night with the lights out. I came to the conclusion that they don't do more of that than they absolutely have to. The lying around in bed, I mean.

As for thinking, they never stop. There's one vision, and it's tunnel. The edition at all costs. Beyond that, everything else is irrelevant. They get the big bonuses, the fat expenses, they live the life of bloody Riley, but they're sub-human. Emotion-free zones.

Some of them wind up in the House of Lords. They're having a laugh! They retire out of newspapers and get the whacking great corporate contracts, or go doing a Tony Blair, lecturing and 'advising' around the world. Then they die, like everyone else, and rest in pieces. See what I mean.

I haven't told Phil yet, but I'm so outta there. The memoir beckons. I could put my feet up for life on the contract. Wouldn't *you*?

~

Anyway, enough of all that. Charlie called tonight. He sounds great. He's having a fantastic time, a couple of them went over to New Zealand and they've regrouped in Perth, trying to figure out what they want to do next.

I'm glad his little gang has stuck together. He really needed this trip.

I'm meeting him in LA, as it happens, at the end of the month. We're thinking about a short Hawaiian cruise. I know, I know, I've always said I'd rather stick pins in my eyes than go on a cruise. I'd be the one who gets cornea'd – see what I did there – on the first sodding *day,* by the most unbearable people on board, then spends the rest of the week trying to hide from them, knowing that the only way out is over the side. Still, a boat's a good place to escape the glare of the media. Isn't it? Did I mention that James is thinking about coming too?

~

There's another reason I need to be in Los Angeles. Not to see Eddie Laine, though he too is bombarding me with dinner invites. This tickles me. He's probably terrified of what I'm going to say about him. He doesn't know the half of it.

Neither do I, yet. But give it time.

Graham King hasn't come bidding for the film rights yet.

I'm in no rush.

I have a world-exclusive interview to take care of first. A mother-daughter thing.

With Roxy Rome.

END

AUTHOR'S NOTE

Why did I write *Imagine* as a novel?

Armed with a brief of 'Shock And Amaze On Every Page', we were dubious stars on the most outrageous rag the UK had ever known.

Rupert Murdoch appointed Kelvin MacKenzie as the brash new editor of Britain's biggest-selling daily, the soar-away *Sun*, in 1981. Not long afterwards, MacKenzie hired me. He was the first newspaper editor to perceive that rock and pop stars were looting the limelight hitherto dominated by dull old Hollywood movie broads, and I was his brainwave: a fresh-meat girl-about-town columnist to augment the breathtaking celebrity gossip dished daily by jumpin' John Blake on his crackerjack spread 'Bizarre'. Too many adjectives for you? Never enough on the Currant Bun.

I was Kelvin's 'Cheeky Telly Girl'. A front-page headline proclaimed it, so it must be true. I'd got there via an internship (not that we had the word then) at Capital Radio, a stint writing sleeve notes in the art department at Chrysalis Records, and a Warholian stab at TV stardom as presenter of rock and pop magazine show *Ear Say* for the new Channel 4.

I soon found myself further down the Street, poached by the *Daily Mail* to interview rock stars. I spent the next decade on the road with the biggest bands in history, from Paul McCartney and Elton John to David Bowie and the Rolling Stones.

Those were the days, my friend. On the road, anything went. We rock hacks toed the line and kept their secrets, and got everything we wanted in return. Unrestrained by the managers, promoters, agents, PRs, record company reps and every other hanger-on hell-bent on scoffing their slice nowadays, journalists and musicians could and did forge close friendships. I was despatched to the New York bureau, where I shared rooms, briefly, with La Toya Jackson – making me perhaps the only correspondent alive who could contradict the rumour, having spent time with them together, that Michael and his sister were the same person.

Relocating to Los Angeles for the *Mail on Sunday*, I interviewed them all, in every imaginable circumstance: Grace Jones on a massage table; U2 in a swimming pool; Cyndi Lauper on a Vegas-bound aircraft;

Stevie Nicks inside the Betty Ford.

Graduating, after the birth of my first child, to the *Mail on Sunday*'s colour supplement, *YOU Magazine* – in those days more award-winning world features than beauty and couture – I broke my share of cover stories: hitting the road with Cher in a tour bus that also contained George Best's ex-wife Angie, the singer's personal trainer; getting nicked for speeding with Rod Stewart; cruising the blue Danube with Freddie Mercury and Queen in the Gorbachevs' private hydrofoil; painting Amsterdam pink with the second-hand car dealer who taught Liz Taylor to like sex. It's what he said.

Piers Morgan airlifted me to the *News of the World* in the mid-90s. I wrote the 'Lesley-Ann Jones Big Interview' for the title until Piers moved to the *Daily Mirror*.

By then, Fleet Street was a memory, technology had taken hold, and the unions were buried. Our beloved industry was dissipated and in the early stages of decline. I paused to marry and have another baby. I published a biography of supermodel Naomi Campbell, my first book on Freddie Mercury, and then came baby number three.

A night's a long time in rock 'n' roll. A year or two out of newspapers is a life sentence. I was in love with the job and took little luring back – post-divorce, cancer surgery and all the usual old heartache – to a world so changed that I barely recognised it.

I wrote freelance features for the *Mail* before taking a column on the *Sunday Express*. My editor there was Martin Townsend, one of the merry band of music-loving mischief-makers with whom I'd crashed around the globe on autopilot during the 80s.

A commission to rewrite my biography of Freddie Mercury, and then another to chronicle the lives and times of T. Rex frontman Marc Bolan, yanked me into another dimension. It was time to turn my training and showbiz experience into something new.

But how to park such a backstory and move on? I was never allowed to. It occurred to me how often I was invited to dinner parties and country-house weekends because I was a fount of filthy gossip and farcical yarns.

I'd meet people at functions here and in the States who'd perhaps seen me on *E! Entertainment* or some other celebrity show, and who would remark, 'You should write a book!'

'I have!' I'd reply. 'Look, and here's where you can buy them.'

'Not *that* kind of book,' they'd say, 'a book about *you*.' I'd laugh them off. 'Nobody would believe it.'

Eventually, it dawned.

I've had a life. Like my father Ken Jones, the *Sunday Mirror*'s 'Voice of Sport' and acclaimed *Independent* columnist, I have ink in my veins. I've worked on the staff of five national newspapers and have freelanced for many more – here, in the United States and as far afield as Japan and Australia, over a period of more than three decades.

I have wassailed with world-famous celebrities across five continents, got into mischief in countless countries, got away with it more than most would consider fair.

I've known my share of glory and ignominy, and have been party to the triumphs and despair of innumerable household names.

I knew I could write a book exploring the seething, faded, moth-eaten tapestry of my own life and times; about the hidden magic and dirt and marvelousness of the music industry and Fleet Street. I also knew that I had no choice but to fictionalise it. ***Imagine*** is the culmination of everything I've seen and done, and everyone I've ever known, loved and loathed in music, showbiz and newspapers, over an unusual and privileged career. It's the story so far.

Wherever real people have been named in this novel, the circumstances around them are entirely made up. All original characters are fictitious. Any resemblance to actual persons, living or dead, is completely coincidental.

Lesley-Ann Jones

www.lesleyannjones.com

IT'S ONLY ROCK 'N' ROLL ...

Roccain, the title of the music magazine referred to in the prologue, is an Old English word for 'rock', derived from the Old Nordic 'rykkja': 'to pull, tear or move'. Its earliest known use in music was in the ballad 'Rock-a-bye Baby' (Benjamin Tabart's *Songs for the Nursery*, London, 1805).

'Roll' derives from the Latin 'rotula': 'small wheel'. 'Rocking and rolling' was a term commonly used by 17th-century sailors, to denote the motion of a ship. By the early 1920s, the phrase had become synonymous with both dancing and sex. African-American Vaudeville entertainer Trixie Smith's suggestive 1922 blues number 'My Daddy (Man) Rocks Me (With One Steady Roll)' is believed to be the first recorded song to deploy it.

Also in the US, legendary DJ Alan 'Moondog' Freed, the so-called 'Father of Rock 'n' Roll', used the title 'The Rock and Roll Session' on his 1950s Cleveland, Ohio radio show to present a race barrier-bending blend of musical styles. The abbreviation of 'and' to 'n' in 'rock 'n' roll' is a variation on the theme of 'apocopation': the omission of a word's ultimate sound.

In the 1956 film *Rock, Rock, Rock*, Freed, playing himself, explains the term:

'Rock and roll is a river of music that has absorbed many streams: rhythm and blues, jazz, rag time, cowboy songs, country songs, folk songs. All have contributed to the big beat.'

ACKNOWLEDGMENTS

With grateful thanks to dear Ivan Mulcahy, Katie Green, Sallyanne Sweeney and Zaria Rich, who went above and beyond.

Thanks also to my children, who haven't seen much of me lately. And to Berni and Leo, for plying me with Friulano every time I came close to giving up.

ABOUT THE AUTHOR

LESLEY-ANN JONES is a British biographer, novelist, broadcaster and keynote speaker.

She honed her craft on Fleet Street, as a newspaper journalist.

Recent works include RIDE A WHITE SWAN: THE LIVES & DEATH OF MARC BOLAN, and FREDDIE MERCURY: THE DEFINITIVE BIOGRAPHY, published by Hodder & Stoughton in hardback, paperback, Kindle and audiobook. The latter appears in the USA as MERCURY by Touchstone/Simon & Schuster, and exists in many translations, including Spanish, Italian, Dutch, Polish, Swedish, Norwegian, Portuguese, Japanese & Lithuanian.

She is the mother of three children, with whom she lives in London.

Printed in Great Britain
by Amazon.co.uk, Ltd.,
Marston Gate.